D0160624

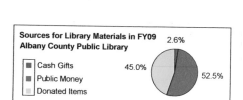

Sources for Library Materials in FY09
Albany County Public Library

2.6%

■ Cash Gifts
■ Public Money
▨ Donated Items

45.0%

52.5%

Watchlist

BASED ON AN IDEA BY

JEFFERY DEAVER

Watchlist

A SERIAL THRILLER

LINDA BARNES

BRETT BATTLES

LEE CHILD

DAVID CORBETT

JEFFERY DEAVER

JOSEPH FINDER

JIM FUSILLI

JOHN GILSTRAP

JAMES GRADY

DAVID HEWSON

JON LAND

DAVID LISS

GAYLE LYNDS

JOHN RAMSEY MILLER

P. J. PARRISH

RALPH PEZZULLO

JAMES PHELAN

S. J. ROZAN

LISA SCOTTOLINE

JENNY SILER

PETER SPIEGELMAN

ERICA SPINDLER

Vanguard Press
A Member of the Perseus Books Group
New York

Copyright © 2009 by International Thriller Writers, Inc.

Published by Vanguard Press
A Member of the Perseus Books Group

Designed by Trish Wilkinson
Set in 11 point Adobe Garamond

Library of Congress Cataloging-in-Publication Data

Watchlist : a serial thriller / based on an idea by Jeffery Deaver.
   p.   cm.
   "Linda Barnes, Brett Battles, Lee Child, David Corbett, Jeffery Deaver, Joseph Finder, Jim Fusilli, John Gilstrap, James Grady, David Hewson, Jon Land, David Liss, Gayle Lynds, John Ramsey Miller, P. J. Parrish, Ralph Pezzullo, James Phelan, S. J. Rozan, Lisa Scottoline, Jenny Siler, Peter Spiegelman, Erica Spindler."
   ISBN 978-1-59315-559-9 (alk. paper)
   I. Deaver, Jeffery.
PS3600.A1W37 2010
813'.6—dc22   2009038746

10 9 8 7 6 5 4 3 2 1

Contents

CONTENTS

PART II

The Copper Bracelet

Introduction

Your mission, if you choose to accept it, is to come up with an innovative idea to help put a brand new writers' organization on the map and then convince top thriller writers to donate their ideas and their time to make it work.

That was my main job when International Thriller Writers (ITW) was formed in October 2004 and I joined the founding board of directors.

As a thriller writer myself and owner of a marketing company for authors and publishers, the part of ITW's mission statement that was closest to my heart was: "To bestow recognition and promote the thriller genre at an innovative and superior level."

We came up with lists of ideas. Some fizzled right away. Others took a while to crash and burn. A few had some game and looked like they might actually come to fruition.

Of all possible projects, the idea of a serialized novel written by some of the genre's best writers—to be released first in audio—chapter by chapter over 8 weeks—was one of the most unusual and the one I was the most involved in coming up with and excited about.

Steve Feldberg, director of content at Audible.com, and I hashed out the idea over the phone first and then over coffee in person. A few months later Audible gave the idea the green light and the ITW board announced it was on board.

That's when the impossible mission really started. How could I convince dozens of writers to donate their ideas and their time to a collaborative project that was different than anything done before?

Take a look at the cover of this book. We weren't just talking about writers . . . but wonderful writers, successful writers, writers who are used to actually getting paid (a lot of money) for their ideas, whose books are on national and international best-seller lists. Writers who are household names, who have sold millions of books. Writers who are all on deadline with their own books and who have commitments to their fans, publishers, and families.

How do you get Lee Child to abandon Jack Reacher? Get Jeff Deaver to write about someone other than Lincoln Rhyme? To get Lisa Scottoline to leave her beloved Philly? To get Jim Fusilli not only to write a chapter but take on the Herculean task of herding these big cats and running the show? And on and on with everyone one of the eleven other authors.

Turns out you pick up the phone and just ask.

Amazingly every author I asked to be part of this ground-breaking project said yes. Amazingly. Eagerly. In fact so many said yes, I actually lost my own place in the book because I couldn't possibly take a spot that one of these luminaries was willing to fill.

The Chopin Manuscript—part one of *The Watchlist*—was the first ever audio serial thriller. It won the Audiobook of the Year and was an unqualified best-seller.

It was a unique collaboration among fifteen distinguished international thriller writers who came together with a single goal. To help establish ITW as a viable, valuable, important organization for its authors.

Jeffery Deaver conceived the characters and the setting and put the plot in motion with the first chapter. From there the story was turned over to fourteen authors who each wrote a chapter that propelled the story along. Along the way the plot took twists and turns as each author lent his or her own imprint on the tale. Characters were added as the action moved around the world—and the stakes got higher and higher. The book wrapped with Deaver writing the final two chapters, bringing The Chopin Manuscript to its explosive conclusion.

And then two years later everyone did it again (with a few new authors coming on board and a few who had prior commitments stepping out) with The Copper Bracelet.

Once again Deaver started it, a host of brilliant writers kept the story spinning and twisting and turning, and then Deaver finished it.

What you're holding in your hands is above all proof of how generous and talented the writers are who make up ITW. All of whom I want to thank for being part of a marvelous project that I hope you, dear reader, find as entertaining, breathtaking, thrilling, and un-put-down-able as I do.

M. J. Rose
July 2009

PART I

The Chopin Manuscript

1

JEFFERY DEAVER

The piano tuner ran through ascending chords, enjoying the resistance of the heavy ivory keys. His balding head was bent forward, his eyes closed as he listened. The notes rose to the darkened ceiling of the recital hall near Warsaw's Old Market Square, then dissipated like smoke.

Satisfied with his work, the tuner replaced the temperament strips and his well-worn extension-tuning lever in their velvet case and indulged himself by playing a few minutes of Mozart, A Little Night Music, an ebullient piece that was one of his favorites.

Just as he concluded, the crisp sound of clapping palms echoed behind him and he spun around. Twenty feet away stood a man nodding and smiling. Stocky, with a flop of brown hair, broad of face. Southern Slavic, the tuner thought. He'd traveled in Yugoslavia many years ago.

"Lovely. Ah, my. So beautiful. Do you speak English?" the man asked with a thick accent.

"I do."

"Are you a performer here? You must be. You are so talented."

"Me? No, I simply tune pianos. But a tuner must know his way about the keyboard too . . . Can I help you, sir? The recital hall is closed."

"Still, such a passion for music. I could hear it. Have you never desired to perform?"

The piano tuner didn't particularly care to talk about himself, but he

3

could discuss music all night long. He was, in addition to being perhaps the best piano tuner in Warsaw if not all of central Poland, an avid collector of recordings and original music manuscripts. If he'd had the means, he would collect instruments too. He had once played a Chopin polonaise at the very keyboard the composer had used; he considered it one of the highpoints of his life.

"I used to. But only in my youth." He told the man of his sweep through Eastern Europe with the Warsaw Youth Orchestra, with which he'd been second-chair cello.

He stared at the man, who in turn was examining the piano. "As I say, the hall is closed. But perhaps you're looking for someone?"

"I am, yes." The Slav walked closer and looked down. "Ah, a Bosendorfer. One of Germany's great contributions to culture."

"Oh, yes," the slight man said, caressing the black lacquer and gothic type of the company's name. "It's perfection. It truly is. Would you like to try it? Do you play?"

"Not like you. I wouldn't presume to even touch a single key after hearing your performance."

"You're too kind. You say you're looking for someone. You mean Anna? The French horn student? She was here earlier but I believe she's left. There's no one else, except the cleaning woman. But I can get a message to anyone in the orchestra or the administration, if you like."

The visitor stepped closer yet and gently brushed a key—true ivory, the piano having been made before the ban. "You, sir," he said, "are the one I came to see."

"Me? Do I know you?"

"I saw you earlier today."

"You did? Where? I don't recall."

"You were having lunch at a café overlooking that huge building. The fancy one, the biggest one in Warsaw. What is it?"

The piano tuner gave a laugh. "The biggest one in the country. The Palace of Culture and Science. A gift from the Soviets, which, the joke goes, they gave us in place of our freedom. Yes, I did have lunch there. But . . . Do I know you?"

The stranger stopped smiling. He looked from the piano into the narrow man's eyes.

Like the assault of the sudden vehement chord in Haydn's Surprise Symphony, fear struck the piano tuner. He picked up his tool kit and rose quickly. Then stopped. "Oh," he gasped. Behind the stranger he could see two bodies lying on the tile near the front door: Anna, the horn player; and beyond her, the cleaning woman. Two shadows on the floor surrounded their limp figures, one from the entranceway light, one from their blood.

The Slav, not much taller than the piano tuner but far stronger, took him by the shoulders. "Sit," he whispered gently, pushing the man down on the bench then turning him to face the piano.

"What do you want?" A quaking voice, tears in his eyes.

"Shhh."

Shaking with fear, the piano tuner thought madly, What a fool I am! I should have fled the moment the man commented on the Bosendorfer's German ancestry. Anyone with a true understanding of the keyboard knew the instruments are made in Austria.

When he was stopped at Krakow's John Paul II airport, he was certain his offense had to do with what he carried in his briefcase.

The hour was early and he'd wakened much earlier at the Pod Roza, "Under the Rose," which was his favorite hotel in Poland, owing both to its quirky mix of scrolly ancient and starkly modern, and to the fact that Franz Liszt had stayed there. Still half asleep, without his morning coffee or tea, he was startled from his stupor by the two uniformed men who appeared over him.

"Mr. Harold Middleton?"

He looked up. "Yes, that's me." And suddenly realized what had happened. When airport security had looked through his attaché case, they'd seen it and grown concerned. But out of prudence the young guards there had chosen not to say anything. They let him pass, then called for reinforcements: these two large, unsmiling men.

Of the twenty or so passengers in the lounge awaiting the bus to take them to the Lufthansa flight to Paris, some people looked his way—the younger ones. The older, tempered by the Soviet regime, dared not. The man closest to Middleton, two chairs away, glanced up involuntarily with a flash of ambiguous concern on his face, as if he might be mistaken as his companion. Then, realizing he wasn't going to be questioned, he turned back to his newspaper, obviously relieved.

"You will please to come with us. This way. Yes. Please." Infinitely polite, the massive guard nodded back toward the security line.

"Look, I know what this is about. It's simply a misunderstanding." He larded his voice with patience, respect and good nature. It was the tone you had to take with local police, the tone you used talking your way through border crossings. Middleton nodded at the briefcase. "I can show you some documentation that—"

The second, silent guard picked up the case.

The other: "Please. You will come." Polite but inflexible. This young, square-jawed man who seemed incapable of smiling held his eye firmly and there was no debate. The Poles, Middleton knew, had been the most willful resisters of the Nazis.

Together they walked back through the tiny, largely deserted airport, the taller guards flanking the shorter, nondescript American. At 56, Harold Middleton carried a few more pounds than he had last year, which itself had seen a weight gain of few pounds over the prior. But curiously his weight—conspiring with his thick black hair—made him appear younger than he was. Only five years ago, at his daughter's college graduation, the girl had introduced him to several of her classmates as her brother. Everyone in the group had bought the deception. Father and daughter had laughed about that many times since.

He thought of her now and hoped fervently he wouldn't miss his flight and the connection to Washington, D.C. He was going to have dinner with Charlotte and her husband that night at Tyson's Corner. It was the first time he'd see her since she announced her pregnancy.

But as he looked past security at the awaiting cluster of men—also unsmiling—he had a despairing feeling that dinner might be postponed. He wondered for how long.

They walked through the exit line and joined the group: two more uniformed officers and a middle-aged man in a rumpled brown suit under a rumpled brown raincoat.

"Mr. Middleton, I am Deputy Inspector Stanieski, with the Polish National Police, Krakow region." No ID was forthcoming.

The guards hemmed him in, as if the 5-foot, 10-inch American was going to karate kick his way to freedom.

"I will see your passport please."

He handed over the battered, swollen blue booklet. Stanieski looked it over and glanced at the picture, then at the man in front of him twice. People often had trouble seeing Harold Middleton, couldn't remember what he looked like. A friend of his daughter said he would make a good spy; the best ones, the young man explained, are invisible. Middleton knew this was true; he wondered how Charlotte's friend did.

"I don't have much time until that flight."

"You will not make the flight, Mr. Middleton. No. We will be returning to Warsaw."

Warsaw? Two hours away.

"That's crazy. Why?"

No answer.

He tried once more. "This is about the manuscript, isn't it?" He nodded to the attaché case. "I can explain. The name Chopin is on it, yes, but I'm convinced it's a forgery. It's not valuable. It's not a national treasure. I've been asked to take it to the United States to finish my analysis. You can call Doctor—"

The inspector shook his head. "Manuscript? No, Mr. Middleton. This is not about a manuscript. It's about a murder."

"Murder?"

The man hesitated. "I use the word to impress on you the gravity of the situation. Now it is best that I say nothing more, and I would strongly suggest you do the same, isn't it?"

"My luggage—"

"Your luggage is already in the car. Now." A nod of his head toward the front door. "We will go."

"Please, come in, Mr. Middleton. Sit. Yes there is good . . . I am Jozef Padlo, first deputy inspector with the Polish National Police." This time an ID was exhibited, but Middleton got the impression the gaunt man, about his own age and much taller, was flashing the card only because Middleton expected it and that the formality was alien in Polish law enforcement.

"What's this all about, Inspector? Your man says murder and tells me nothing more."

"Oh, he mentioned that?" Padlo grimaced. "Krakow. They don't listen to us there. Slightly better than Posnan, but not much."

They were in an off-white office, beside a window that looked out on the gray spring sky. There were many books, computer printouts, a few maps and no decorations other than official citations, an incongruous ceramic cactus wearing a cowboy hat and pictures of the man's wife and children and grandchildren. Many pictures. They seemed like a happy family. Middleton thought again of his daughter.

"Am I being charged with anything?"

"Not at this point." His English was excellent and Middleton wasn't surprised to notice that there was a certificate on the wall testifying to Padlo's completion of a course in Quantico and one at the Law Enforcement Management Institute of Texas.

Oh, and the cactus.

"Then I can leave."

"You know, we have anti-smoking laws here. I think that's your doing, your country's. You give us Burger King and take away our cigarettes." The inspector shrugged and lit a Sobieski. "No, you can't leave. Now, please, you had lunch yesterday with a Henryk Jedynak, a piano tuner."

"Yes. Henry . . . Oh no. Was he the one murdered?"

Padlo watched Middleton carefully. "I'm afraid he was, yes. Last night. In the recital hall near Old Market Square."

"No, no . . . " Middleton didn't know the man well—they'd met only on this trip—but they'd hit it off immediately and had enjoyed each other's company. He was shocked by the news of Jedynak's death.

"And two other people were killed, as well. A musician and a cleaning woman. Stabbed to death. For no reason, apparently, other than they had the misfortune to be there at the same time as the killer."

"This is terrible. But why?"

"Have you known Mr. Jedynak long?"

"No. We met in person for the first time yesterday. We'd emailed several times. He was a collector of manuscripts."

"Manuscripts? Books?"

"No. Musical manuscripts—the handwritten scores. And he was involved with the Chopin Museum."

"At Ostrogski Castle." The inspector said this as if he'd heard of the place but never been there.

"Yes. I had a meeting yesterday afternoon with the director of the Czartoryski Museum in Krakow, and I asked Henry to brief me about him and their collection. It was about a questionable Chopin score."

Padlo showed no interest in this. "Tell me, please, about your meeting. In Warsaw."

"Well, I met Henry for coffee in the late morning at the museum, he showed me the new acquisitions in the collection. Then we returned downtown and had lunch at a café. I can't remember where."

"The Frederick Restaurant."

That's how Padlo found him, he supposed—an entry in Jedynak's PDA or diary. "Yes, that was it. And then we went our separate ways. I took the train to Krakow."

"Did you see anyone following you or watching you at lunch?"

"Why would someone follow us?"

Padlo inhaled long on his cigarette. When he wasn't puffing he lowered his hand below his desk. "Did you see anyone?" he repeated.

"No."

He nodded. "Mr. Middleton, I must tell you . . . I regret I have to but it is important. Your friend was tortured before he died. I won't go into the details, but the killer used some piano string in very unpleasant ways. He was gagged so the screams could not be heard but his right hand was uninjured, presumably so that he could write whatever this killer demanded of him. He wanted information."

"My God . . ." Middleton closed his eyes briefly, recalling Henry's showing pictures of his wife and two sons.

"I wonder what that might be," Padlo said. "This piano tuner was well known and well liked. He was also a very transparent man. Musician, tradesman, husband and father. There seemed to be nothing dark about his life . . ." A careful examination of Middleton's face. "But perhaps the killer thought that was not the case. Perhaps the killer thought he had a second life involving more than music . . ." With a nod, he added, "Somewhat like you."

"What're you getting at?"

"Tell me about your other career, please."

"I don't have another career. I teach music and authenticate music manuscripts."

"But you had another career recently."

"Yes, I did. But what's that got to do with anything?"

Padlo considered this for a moment, and said, "Because certain facts have come into alignment."

A cold laugh. "And what exactly does that mean?" This was the most emotional Harold Middleton usually got. He believed that you gave up your advantage when you lost control. That's what he told himself, though he doubted that he was even capable of losing control.

"Tell me about that career, Colonel. Do some people still call you that, 'Colonel'?"

"Not anymore. But why are you asking me questions you already seem to know the answers to?"

"I know a few things. I'm curious to know more. For instance, I only know that you were connected with the ICTY and the ICCt, but not many details."

The UN-sanctioned International Criminal Tribunal for the Former Yugoslavia investigated and tried individuals for war crimes committed during the complicated and tragic fighting among the Serbs, Bosnians, Croatians and Albanian ethnic groups in the 1990s. The ICCt was the International Criminal Court, established in 2002 to try war criminals for crimes in any area of the world. Both were located in The Hague in Holland, and had been created because nations tended to quickly forget about the atrocities committed within their borders and were reluctant to find and try those who'd committed them.

"How did you end up working for them? It seems a curious leap from your country's army to an international tribunal."

"I was planning to retire anyway. I'd been in the service for more than two decades."

"But still. Please."

Middleton decided that cooperation was the only way that would let him leave anytime soon. With the time difference he still had a chance to get into D.C. in time for a late supper at the Ritz Carlton with his daughter and son-in-law.

He explained to the inspector briefly that he had been a military intelligence officer with the 7,000 U.S. troops sent to Kosovo in the summer of 1999 as part of the peacekeeping force when the country was engaged in the last of the Yugoslavian wars. Middleton was based at Camp Broadsteel in the southeast of the country, the sector America oversaw. The largely rural area, dominated by Mount Duke which rose like Fuji over the rugged hills, was an ethnically Albanian area, as was most of Kosovo, and had been the site of many incursions by Serbs—both from other parts of Kosovo and from Milosevic's Serbia, which Kosovo had been part of. The fighting was largely over—the tens of thousands of ironically dubbed "humanitarian" bombing strikes had had their desired effect—but the peacekeepers on the ground were still on high alert to stop clashes between the infamous Serb guerillas and the equally ruthless Albanian Kosovo Liberation Army forces.

Padlo took this information in, nodding as he lit another cigarette.

"Not long after I was deployed there, the base commander got a call from a general in the British sector, near Pristina, the capital. He'd found something interesting and had been calling all the international peacekeepers to see if anyone had a background in art collecting."

"And why was that?" Padlo stared at the Sobieski hidden below eye-level.

The smell was not as terrible as Middleton had expected, but the office was filling with smoke. His eyes stung. "Let me give you some background. It goes back to World War Two."

"Please, tell me."

"Well, many Albanians from Kosovo fought with an SS unit—the Twenty-First Waffen Mountain Division. Their main goal was eliminating partisan guerillas, but it also gave them the chance to ethnically cleanse the Serbs, who had been their enemies for years."

A grimace appeared on the inspector's heavily lined face. "Ah, it's always the same story wherever you look. Poles versus the Russians. Arabs versus the Jews. Americans versus"—a smile—"everyone."

Middleton ignored him. "The Twenty-First supposedly had another job too. With the fall of Italy and an Allied invasion a sure thing, Himmler and Goering and other Nazis who'd been looting art from Eastern Europe wanted secure places to hide it—so that even if Germany fell, the Allies couldn't find it. The Twenty-First reportedly brought truckloads to Kosovo. Made sense. A small, little populated, out-of-the-mainstream country. Who'd think to look there for a missing Cezanne or Manet?

"What the British general had found was an old Eastern Orthodox church. It was abandoned years ago and being used as a dormitory for displaced Serbs by a U.N. relief organization. In the basement his soldiers unearthed 50 or 60 boxes of rare books, paintings and music folios."

"My, that many?"

"Oh, yes. A lot was damaged, some beyond repair, but other items were virtually untouched. I didn't know much about the paintings or the books, but I'd studied music history in college and I've collected recordings and manuscripts for years. I got the okay to fly up and take a look."

"And what did you find?"

"Oh, it was astonishing. Original pieces by Bach and his sons, Mozart, Handel, sketches by Wagner—some of them had never been seen before. I was speechless."

"Valuable?"

"Well, you can't really put a dollar value on a find like that. It's the cultural benefit, not the financial."

"But still, worth millions?"

"I suppose."

"What happened then?"

"I reported what I'd found to the British and to my general, and he cleared it with Washington for me to stay there for a few days and catalog what I could. Good press, you know."

"True in police work too." The cigarette got crushed out forcefully under a yellow thumb, as if Padlo were quitting forever.

Middleton explained that that night he took all the manuscripts and folios that he could carry back to British quarters in Pristina and worked for hours cataloging and examining what he'd found.

"The next morning I was very excited, wondering what else I'd find. I got up early to return . . . "

The American stared at a limp yellow file folder on the inspector's desktop, the one with three faded checkmarks on it. He looked up and heard Padlo say, "The church was St. Sophia."

"You know about it?" Middleton was surprised. The incident had made the news but by then—with the world focusing on the millennium and the Y2K crisis, the Balkans had become simply a footnote to fading history.

"Yes, I do. I didn't realize you were involved."

Middleton remembered walking to the church and thinking, I must've gotten up pretty damn early if none of the refugees were awake yet, especially with all the youngsters living there. Then he paused, wondering where the British guards were. Two had been stationed outside the church the day before. Just at that moment he saw a window open on the second floor and a teenage girl look out, her long hair obscuring half her face. She was calling, "Green shirt, green shirt . . . Please . . . Green shirt."

He hadn't understood. But then it came to him. She was referring to his fatigues and was calling for his help.

"What was it like?" Padlo asked softly.

Middleton merely shook his head.

The inspector didn't press him for details. He asked, "And Rugova was the man responsible?"

He was even more surprised that the inspector knew about the former Kosovo Liberation Army commander Agim Rugova. That fact was not learned until later, long after Rugova and his men had fled from Pristina, and the story of St. Sophia had grown stone cold.

"Your change in career is making sense now, Mr. Middleton. After the war you became an investigator to track him down."

"That's it in a nutshell." He smiled as if that could flick away the cached memories, clear as computer jpegs, of that morning.

Middleton had returned to Camp Broadsteel and served out his rotation, spending most of his free time running intelligence reports on Rugova and the many other war criminals the torn region had spawned. Back at the Pentagon, he'd done the same. But it wasn't the U.S. military's job to catch them and bring them to trial, and he made no headway.

So when he retired, he set up an operation in a small Northern Virginia office park. He called it "War Criminal Watch" and spent his days on the phone and computer, tracking Rugova and others. He made contacts at the ICTY and worked with them regularly but they and the UN's tactical operation were busy with bigger fish—like Ratko Mladic, Naser Oric and others involved in the Srebrenica massacre, the worst atrocity in Europe since World War II, and Milosevic himself. Middleton would come up with a lead and it would founder. Still he couldn't get St. Sophia out of his mind.

Green shirt, green shirt . . . Please . . .

He decided that he couldn't be effective working from America nor working alone. So after some months of searching he found people who'd help: two American soldiers who'd been in Kosovo and helped him in the investigation at St. Sophia and a woman humanitarian worker from Belgrade he'd met in Pristina.

The overworked ICTY was glad to accept them as independent contractors, working with the Prosecutor's Office. They became known in the ICTY as "The Volunteers."

Lespasse and Brocco, the soldiers, younger, driven by their passion for the hunt;

Leonora Tesla, by her passion to rid the world of sorrow, a passion that made the otherwise-common woman beautiful;

And the elder, Harold Middleton, a stranger to passion and driven by . . . well, even he couldn't say what. The intelligence officer who never seemed to be able to process the HUMINT on himself.

Unarmed—at least as far as the ICTY and local law enforcement knew—they managed to track down several of Rugova's henchmen and, through them, finally the man himself, who was living in a shockingly opulent townhouse in Nice, France, under a false identity. The arrangement was that, for ethical reasons, the Volunteers' job was solely to provide the tribunal with intelligence and contacts; the SFOR, the UN's Stabilization Force—the military operation in charge of apprehending former Yugoslav war criminals—and local police, to the extent they were cooperative, would be the arresting agents.

In 2002, working on pristine data provided by Middleton and his crew, UN and French troops raided the townhouse and arrested Rugova.

Tribunal trials are interminable, but three years later he was convicted for crimes that occurred at St. Sophia. He was appealing his conviction

while living in what was, in Middleton's opinion, a far-too-pleasant detention center in The Hague.

Middleton could still picture the swarthy man at trial, ruggedly handsome, confident and indignant, swearing that he'd never committed geno-
cide or ethnic cleansing. He admitted he was a soldier but said that what
happened at St. Sophia was merely an "isolated incident" in an unfortunate war. Middleton told this to the inspector.

"Isolated incident," Padlo whispered.

"It makes the horror far worse, don't you think? Phrasing it so
antiseptically."

"I do, yes." Another draw on the cigarette.

Middleton wished that he had a candy bar, his secret passion.

Padlo then asked, "I'm curious about one thing—was Rugova acting on
anyone else's orders, do you think? Was there someone he reported to?"

Middleton's attention coalesced instantly at this question. "Why do you
ask that?" he asked sharply.

"Was he?"

The American debated and decided to continue to cooperate. For the
moment. "When we were hunting for him we heard rumors that he was
backed by someone. It made sense. His KLA outfit had the best weapons
of any unit in the country, even better than some of the regular Serbian
troops. They were the best trained, and they could hire pilots for helicopter
extractions. That was unheard of in Kosovo. There were rumors of large
amounts of cash. And he didn't seem to take orders from any of the known
KLA senior commanders. But we had only one clue that there was somebody behind him. A message had been left for him about a bank deposit. It
was hidden in a copy of Goethe's Faust we found in an apartment in Eze."

"Any leads?"

"We thought possibly British or American. Maybe Canadian. Some of
the phrasing in the note suggested it."

"No idea of his name?"

"No. We gave him a nickname, after the book—Faust."

"A deal with the devil. Are you still searching for this man?"

"Me? No. My group disbanded. The Tribunal's still in force and the prosecutors and EUFOR might be looking for him but I doubt it. Rugova's in

jail, some of his associates too. There are bigger fish to fry. You know that expression?"

"No, but I understand." Padlo crushed out another cigarette. "You're young. Why did you quit this job? The work seems important."

"Young?" Middleton smiled. Then it faded. He said only, "Events intervened."

"Another dispassionate phrase, that one. 'Events intervened.'"

Middleton looked down.

"An unnecessary comment on my part. Forgive me. I owe you answers and you'll now understand why I asked what I did." He hit a button on his phone and spoke in Polish. Middleton knew enough to understand he was asking for some photographs.

Padlo disconnected and said, "In investigating the murder of the piano tuner I learned that you were probably the last person—well, second last— to see him alive. Your name and hotel phone number were in his address book for that day. I ran your name through Interpol and our other data-bases and found about your involvement with the tribunals. There was a brief reference to Agim Rugova, but a cross-reference in Interpol as well, which had been added only late yesterday."

"Yesterday?"

"Yes. Rugova died yesterday. The apparent cause of death was poisoning."

Middleton felt his heart pound. Why hadn't anyone called? Then he realized that he was no longer connected with the ICTY and that it had been years since St. Sophia was on anyone's radar screen.

An isolated incident . . .

"This morning I called the prison and learned that Rugova had approached a guard several weeks ago about bribing his way out of prison. He offered a huge amount of money. 'Where would he, an impoverished war criminal, get such funds?' the guard asked. He said his wife could get the amount he named—one hundred thousand euros. The guard reported the matter and there it rested. But then, four days ago, Rugova had a visitor—a man with a fake name and fake ID, as it turned out. After he leaves Rugova falls ill and yesterday dies of poison. The police go to the wife's house to inform her and find she's been dead for several days. She was stabbed."

Dead . . . Middleton felt a fierce urge to call Leonora and tell her.

"When I learned of your connection with the piano tuner and the death on the same day of the war criminal you'd had arrested, I had sent to me a prison security camera picture of the probable murderer. I showed the picture to a witness we located who saw the likely suspect leaving the Old Market Square recital hall last night."

"It's the same man?"

"She said with certainty that it was." Padlo indulged again and lit a Sobieski. "You seem to be the hub of this strange wheel, Mr. Middleton. A man kills Rugova and his wife and then tortures and kills a man you've just met with. So, now, you and I are entwined in this matter."

It was then that a young uniformed officer arrived carrying an envelope. He placed it on the inspector's desk.

"Dzenkuje," Padlo said.

The aide nodded and, after glancing at the American, vanished.

The inspector handed the photos to Middleton, who looked down at them. "Oh, my God." He sucked cigarette-smoke-tainted air deep into his lungs.

"What?" Padlo asked, seeing his reaction. "Was he someone you know from your investigation of Rugova?"

The American looked up. "This man . . . He was sitting next to me at Krakow airport. He was taking my flight to Paris." The man in the ugly checked jacket.

"No! Are you certain?"

"Yes. He must've killed Henryk to find out where I was going."

And in a shocking instant it was clear. Someone—this man or Faust, or perhaps he was Faust—was after Middleton and the other Volunteers.

Why? For revenge? Did he fear something? Was there some other reason? And why would he kill Rugova?

The American jabbed his finger at the phone. "Did he get on the flight to Paris? Has it landed? Find out now."

Padlo's tongue touched the corner of his mouth. He lifted the receiver and spoke in such rapid Polish that Middleton couldn't follow the conversation.

Finally the inspector hung up. "Yes, it's landed and everyone has disembarked. Other than you, everyone with a boarding pass was on the flight. But after that? They don't know. They'll check the flight manifest against passport control at De Gaulle—if he left the airport. And outgoing flight manifests in case he continued in transit."

Middleton shook his head. "He's changed identity by now. He saw me detained and he's using a new passport."

The inspector said, "He could be on his way to anywhere in the world."

But he wasn't, Middleton knew. The only question was this: Was he en route to Africa to find Tesla at her relief agency? Or to the States, where Lespasse ran a very successful computer company and Brocco edited the Human Rights Observer newsletter?

Or was he on a different flight headed to D.C., where Middleton himself lived?

Then his legs went weak.

As he recalled that, showing off proud pictures, he'd told the piano tuner that his daughter lived in the D.C. area.

What a lovely young woman, and her husband, so handsome. . . . They seem so happy.

Middleton leapt to his feet. "I have to get home. And if you try to stop me, I'll call the embassy." He strode toward the door.

"Wait," Padlo said sharply.

Middleton spun around. "I'm warning you. Do not try to stop me. If you do—"

"No, no, I only mean. . . . Here." He stepped forward and handed the American his passport. Then he touched Middleton's arm. "Please. I want this man too. He killed three of my citizens. I want him badly. Remember that."

He believed the inspector said something else but by then Middleton was jogging hard down the endless hall, as gray as the offices, as gray as the sky, digging into his pocket for his cell phone.

2

DAVID HEWSON

Felicia Kaminski first noticed the tramp outside the Pantheon when she was playing gypsy folk tunes, old Roman favorites, anything that could put a few coins in the battered gray violin case she had inherited from her mother, along with the century-old, sweet-toned Italian instrument that lived inside. The man listened for more than 10 minutes, watching her all the time. Then he walked up close, so close she could smell the cloud of sweat and humanity that hung around people of the street, not that they ever seemed to notice.

"I wanna hear 'Volarè,'" he grumbled in English, his voice rough and carrying an accent she couldn't quite place. He held a crumpled and dirt-stained 10-euro note. He was perhaps 35, though it was difficult to be precise. He stood at least six feet tall, muscular, almost athletic, though the thought seemed ridiculous.

"'Volarè' is a song, sir, not a piece of violin music," she responded, with more teenage ungraciousness than was, perhaps, wise.

His face, as much as she could see behind the black unkempt beard, seemed sharp and observant. More so, it occurred to her, than most street people who were either elderly Italians thrown out of their homes by harsh times, or foreign clandestini, Iraqis, Africans and all manner of nationalities from the Balkans, each keeping their own counsel, each trying to pursue their own particular course through the dark, half-secret hidden economy for those trying to survive without papers.

There were other more pressing reasons that made hers a bold and un-wise response. The money her uncle had given her had not been much to begin with, though more generous than his meager living as a Warsaw pi-ano tuner ought to have allowed. Two months before, on the day she turned 19, he had abruptly announced that his role as her guardian was finished, and that it was time to seek a new life in the west. She chose Italy because she wanted warm weather and beauty, and refused to follow the stream of Poles migrating to England. The grubby, slow bus to Rome had cost 50 eu-ros, and the room in a squalid student house in San Giovanni swallowed up a further 200 each week, as did the language-school lessons in Italian. Her adequate English meant she could get some bar work but only in tourist dives at what the owners called "the Polish rate"—four euros an hour, less than the legal minimum wage. She ate like a sparrow, pizza rustica, pre-cooked, often disgusting, but less than two euros a slice. She never went out and had yet to make a friend. Still each week the money from Uncle Hen-ryk went down a little further. She could not, in all conscience, call and ask for more.

"I know it's a song," the tramp replied with an unpleasant sneer on his half-hidden face. Then he crooned a line of it, in the voice of a long-dead American singer she'd heard when her mother and father played music on their cheap hi-fi to remind themselves of their days in the States, before they returned to a new, free Poland in search of different lives. The name of the singer came back to her: Dean Martin. And the tune too, so she played it, pitch perfect, from memory, improvising a little after the fashion of Stéphane Grappelli, putting a leisurely jazz swing on each inflected run of notes until the original was only just recognizable.

She was good at the fiddle. Sometimes, if she was bored or there seemed to be someone musical in her audience, she would pull out some sheet mu-sic stuffed into the case, ask a spectator to hold it, then play Wieniawski's Obertass mazurka, with its leaping fireworks of double stopping, harmonics and left-hand pizzicato. Both of her parents were musical, her mother a vio-linist, her father an accomplished pianist. Together they had provided her with a musical education from before she could remember, in a household where music was as natural and easy as laughter, right up until the black day they disappeared and she found herself under the wing of Uncle Henryk.

The tramp stared at her as if she'd committed a sin.

"You screwed with it," he spat. "Bad girl. You ought to know your place." He stared at his own clothes: a grimy overcoat that stank of sweat and urine, with a belt made, perhaps a little theatrically, out of rope. "One little step up from me. Nothing more."

Then he threw a single euro in her violin case and stomped off toward Largo Argentina, the open space where she used to catch the bus back home, fascinated always by the wrecked collection of ancient temples there—a ragged, shapeless gathering of columns and stones populated by a yowling community of feral cats, a piece of history only she and the passing tourists seemed to notice any more. She didn't like cats. They were bold, aggressive, insistent, climbing into her fiddle case when it was open to collect money. So she kept a small water pistol, modeled on something military, alongside her music and rosin, and used it to shoo them away when the creatures became too persistent.

The bum caught up with her four times after that. Twice at the Trevi Fountain. Once in the Campo dei Fiori. Once outside the new museum for the Ara Pacis, the peace monument erected by Augustus that now lived in a modern, cubist home by the hectic road running alongside the Tiber. She was surprised to see him there. It didn't seem the usual kind of place for street people, and she caught him staring through the windows, engrossed in the beautifully carved monument inside she had only glimpsed from the street too, since paying the entrance fee was beyond her. Homeless men rarely looked at Imperial Roman statuary, she thought. Most of them never looked much at anything at all.

And now he was back near her again—on this hot, sunny summer morning in the Via delle Botteghe Oscure at the weekly market her uncle had told her about. It took place at the foot of the Via dei Polacchi—the street of Poles—and made her homesick every time she went. This was where the poor, migrant Polish community gathered in an impromptu bazaar that was part economic necessity, part reaffirmation of their distant roots. There were cars and vans, all rusty, all belching diesel as they arrived bearing plates from Warsaw and Gdansk. Quickly, not wishing to draw the attention of the police, they threw open their doors and trunks and began selling all the goods that Polish immigrants could not find or, more likely, afford in their new home: spirits and sausage, ham and pastries; some clearly homemade, a few possibly illegal.

Felicia knew none of these people. But sometimes the poor were the most generous, particularly when they knew she was Polish too, alone in the city, still a little lost. The Berlin Wall had tumbled to the ground when she was 12 months old, an infant in some small apartment in a suburb of Chicago. She knew this because her parents had told her so often of the joy that followed. Of their own expectant return to the country they had fled in order to throw off the shackles of Communism.

There had always been a shadow in their eyes when they spoke of that decision. As she grew older she knew why. When they left Poland it was a world of black and white, and they returned to one that was a shifting shade of gray. The bad days before she was born was a time of secret police and cruel, arbitrary punishment of dissent, but no one had to travel thousands of miles to a distant country to earn a living. They said something good had been lost alongside the visible, more easily acknowledged bad. Talking to the old men and women who gathered at the foot of the Via dei Polacchi she had come to realize there was a gulf between them and her that could never be bridged, a strange sense of guilty loss she could never share. Yet there was a bond too. She was Polish, she was poor. When she played the right notes—a mazurka, a polonaise—there were misty eyes all around and a constant shower of small coins into the fiddle case.

And on this day there was the tramp too, with a hateful look in his eyes, one that said, she believed . . . shame on you, shame on you.

As she bowed a slow country dance she told herself that, if he continued with these attentions, she would upbraid him, loudly, in public, with no fear. Who was a tramp to talk to anyone of shame? What gave him the right? . . .

Then, feeling a hand on her shoulder, she ceased playing and turned to find herself staring into the amiable, bright blue eyes of a middle-aged man in a gray suit. He had a pale, fleshy face with stubbly red cheeks, receding fair hair and the easy, confident demeanor of someone official, like a civil servant or a school headmaster.

"You play beautifully, Felicia," he said in Polish.

"Do I know you?"

He took out an ID card from his jacket and flashed it in front of her face, too quickly for her to make much sense of the words there.

"No. I am a Polish police officer on attachment here in Rome. There is no need for you to know me."

She must have looked startled. He placed a hand on her arm and said, in a voice full of reassurance, "Do not be alarmed. There is nothing for you to worry about." His genial face fell. "I am simply performing an unhappy task which falls to this profession from time to time. Come, I will buy coffee. There is a small place around the corner."

The man had such a pleasant air of authority that she followed him automatically into the Via dei Polacchi, even though she couldn't remember any cafe in this direction.

They were halfway along when he stopped her in the shadow of an overhanging building. There was such sadness in his eyes, a sense of regret too.

"I am sorry," he said in his low, calm voice. "There is no easy way to say this. Your uncle Henryk has been killed."

Her stomach clenched. Her eyes began to sting. "Killed?"

"Murdered, as he worked. With two other people too. Such a world we live in."

"In Warsaw?"

He shrugged. "This would never have happened before. Not in the old days. People then had too much respect. Too much fear."

There were so many questions, and none of them would form themselves into a sensible sentence in Felicia's mind. "I must go home," she said finally.

The man was silent for a moment, thinking, a different expression in his eyes, one she couldn't work out.

"You can't afford to go home," he observed, frowning. "What's there for you anyway? It was never your country. Not really."

The narrow street was empty. A cloud had skittered across the bright summer sun casting the entire area into sudden gloom.

"I can afford a bus ride," she answered, suddenly cross.

"No you can't," he replied, and took her by both arms. He was strong. His blue eyes now burned, insistent, demanding. "What did your uncle give you? To come here?"

She tried to shake herself free. It was impossible. His grip was too firm.

"Some money . . . Two thousand euros. It was all he had."

"Not money," the man barked at her, his voice rising in volume. "I'm not talking money."

He turned his elbow so that his forearm fell beneath her throat and pinned her against the wall as he snatched her fiddle case with his free hand. Then he quickly bent down, flipped up the single latch with his teeth and scrabbled open the lid.

"This is a pauper's instrument," he grumbled, and flinging the fiddle to the ground. Crumpled sheets of music followed, fluttering to the cobblestones like leaves in autumn. "What did he give you?"

"Nothing. Nothing . . ."

She stopped. He had discarded the bow and her last piece of rosin, and now had her one remaining spare string, a Thomastik-Infeld Dominant A, in his fingers. He took away his elbow. Before she could run off, he jerked her back and punched her hard in the stomach. The breath disappeared from her lungs. Tears of pain and rage and fear rose in her eyes.

As she began to recover, she saw he had turned the fiddle string into a noose and felt it slip over her head, pushing it down until it rested on her neck. He pulled it, not so tight, only so much that she could feel the familiar wound metal become a cold ligature around her throat.

"Poor little lost girl," he whispered, his breath rank and hot in her ear. "No home. No friends. No future. One last time . . . What did he give you?"

"Nothing . . . Nothing . . ."

The Thomastik-Infeld Dominant A started to tighten. She was aware of her own breathing, the short, repetitive muscular motion one always took for granted. His face grew huge in her vision. He was smiling. This was, she now realized, the result he wished all along.

Then the smile faded. A low, animal grunt issued from his mouth. His body fell forward, crushing hers against the wall, and a crimson spurt of blood began to gush from between his clenched teeth. She turned her head to avoid the red stream now flowing down his chin, and clawed at the noose on her throat, loosening it, forcing the deadly loop over her hair until it was free and she could manage to drag it over her head.

Something thrust the gray-suited man aside. The tramp was there. A long stiletto knife sat in his right fist, its entire length red with gore.

He dropped the weapon and held out his hand.

"Come with me now," he said. "There are three of them in a car round the corner. They won't wait long."

"Who are you?" she mumbled, her head reeling, breath still short.

A car was starting to turn into the narrow street, finding it too difficult to make the corner in one go. The cloud worked free of the sun. Bright, blinding light filled the area around them, enough to make their presence known. She heard Polish voices and other accents, ones she didn't recognize. They sounded angry.

"If you stay here you will die," the tramp insisted. "Like your uncle. Like your mother and your father. Come with me . . . "

She bent down and picked up her fiddle and bow, roughly pushing them into the case, along with the scrappy sheets of music.

And then they ran.

He had a scooter round the corner. A brand new purple Vespa with a rental sticker on the rear mudguard. She climbed on the back automatically, hanging tight, the fiddle case still in her grip, as he roared through the narrow lanes trying to lose the vehicle behind.

It wasn't easy. She turned her head and saw the car bouncing off the ancient stone walls of the quarter, following them down narrow alleys the wrong way. She knew this area. It was one of her favorites for its unexpected sights and the way the buildings ranged across the centuries, sometimes as far back as the age of Caesar.

He was going the wrong way and she knew it but they were there before she could tell him. The Vespa screamed to a halt in a dead-end alley sealed off by freshly painted black iron railings, a view point over the tangled ruins around the Pescaria, the imperial fish market that led to the vast circular stump of the Theatre of Marcellus, like some smaller Colosseum cut short by a giant's knife. There was no road, only a narrow pathway down into the mess of columns and shattered walls.

They ran and stumbled across threadbare grass through the low petrified forest of dusty granite and marble. She could hear shouts behind and anguished cries in Polish. Then she heard a shot. The tramp's strong hand grasped her as she tripped over a fluted portion of shattered column. Panting for breath, she found herself in the angry mass of traffic beneath the looming theatre. He dragged her into the mob of vehicles. Halfway across the road there was a young man on a scooter, long black hair falling out from beneath his helmet.

The tramp kicked him out of the seat, then screamed at her to get onto the pillion.

She didn't need to think any more. She didn't want to. They wound a sinuous route through the snarled-up vehicles, found the sidewalk on the river side of the road, roared over the cobbles, out to the Lungotevere. The traffic was just as bad there.

She dared to turn. Over the road, fighting through the cars, were three men, guns in their hands.

She swore. She prayed. And then they were through, on the Tiber side of the road, rattling down the steps that led down to the water and the long broad concrete of the flood defenses.

Two days before she'd walked here, wondering, thinking, trying to work out where she belonged. Not yet 20, born in a country that had forgotten her, without parents. And now, she reflected, without her uncle who had come to her rescue when she found herself orphaned. She clung on, tears in her eyes, determined they'd be spent before this man who had both rescued and kidnapped her would look into her face again.

After half a mile, they raced up a long walkway and returned to the road, riding steadily through San Giovanni, past the street where she lived. In her head she said good-bye to the few belongings she had there: a Bible little read; some photos; a few cheap clothes; a music case with some much-loved pieces.

They found the autovia and she saw the sign to the airport. A few miles short of Fiumicino he turned the Vespa into the drive of a low, modern hotel, found a hidden space in the car park at the rear, stopped and turned off the engine.

She got off the scooter without being asked.

"You did well," the man said simply, staring at her.

"Did I have a choice?"

"If you want to live, no, you don't. Have you already forgotten you are in grave danger?"

She glanced at the scooter. "Is that what you are? A thief?"

He nodded, and she wondered if there was the slightest of smiles behind the matted, grubby beard. "A thief. That's correct, Felicia. We must go inside now."

He waved the key as they rushed past reception, and went to the first floor where he opened the door and ushered her into his room. It was a suite, elegant and expensive, the kind she had only seen in movies. There were two large suitcases already packed on the floor. The pillows of the bed were covered with scattered chocolates. He picked up a couple and gave them to her. She ate greedily. It was good chocolate, the best. The room, she understood, had been waiting here, empty, running up a bill, perhaps for weeks.

"Do you have a passport with you?" he asked.

"Of course. It is the law."

She showed him.

"I meant the other. You have dual nationality. This is important."

"No." She shook her head forcefully. "I am Polish only. That was an accident of birth."

"A lucky accident," he grumbled, and picked up a briefcase by the side of the bed. The man—she could no longer think of him as a tramp—pulled out a blue document, an American passport.

"Your name now is Joanna Phelps. Your mother was Polish, which explains your accent. You are a student at college in Baltimore. Remember all this."

She didn't take the passport, though she couldn't stop herself staring at the gold eagle on the cover.

"Why?" she asked.

"You know why, Felicia," he replied.

"I don't, really . . . "

His strong hands suddenly held her shoulders, shaking her slender frame. His eyes were fierce and unavoidable.

"What's your name? What's your name?"

"My name is Felicia Kaminski. I am nineteen years old. A citizen of the Polish Republic. I was born . . . "

"Felicia Kaminski is dead," he cut in. "Be careful you don't join her."

Stepping back, he said, "Do not answer the door to anyone. Eat and drink from the mini bar if you need something. I must—" he stared at the grubby clothes, hating them—"do something."

He took new clothes out of one of the cases and disappeared into the bathroom. She looked at the second piece of luggage. It seemed expensive. The label bore the name Joanna Phelps and an address in Baltimore. Felicia opened it and found that it was full of new jeans, skirts, shirts and underwear. They were all the right size, and must have cost more than she earned in an entire month.

When he came out he was wearing a dark business suit with a white shirt and elegant silk red tie. He was no more than 40, handsome, Italian-looking, with a sallow skin, clean shaven, rough and red in places from the razor. He had dark, darting eyes and long hair wet from the shower, slicked back on his head, black mostly, with gray flecks. His face seemed more lined than she felt it ought to be, as if there had been pain somewhere, or illness.

He had a phone in his hand.

"In an hour, Joanna, we will go to Fiumicino," he said. "There will be a ticket waiting for you at the first class Alitalia counter. You show them your passport, check in and go straight to the lounge. I will meet you there. I shall be behind you all the way. Do not stop after immigration. Do not look at me. Do not acknowledge me until we have landed and I approach you."

"Where are we going?"

He considered the question, wondering whether to answer.

"First to New York. Then to Washington. You must know this surely. How else would one get back to where you live from Italy?"

She said nothing.

"Where do you live, Joanna?"

She tugged at the label of the case he had provided for her. "I live at 121 South Fremont Avenue, Baltimore. And you?"

He smiled genuinely. In other circumstances, she might have thought she liked this man.

"That is none of your business."

"Your name is?"

He said nothing, but kept on smiling.

Felicia walked quickly to the second case, before he could stop her, and grasped the label.

It was blank. He laughed at her, and she was unsure whether this was a pleasant sound or a cruel one.

"So what do I call you?" she asked.

A theatrical gesture: He placed a forefinger on his reddened chin, stared at the hotel bedroom ceiling, and said, "For now, you may call me Faust."

3

JAMES GRADY

The jetliner glided out of the night to touch down at Washington's Dulles Airport 29 minutes early and 47 minutes before Harold Middleton killed a cop.

As soon as the plane's wheels grabbed runway, Middleton text-messaged his daughter.

She hadn't answered his calls from Europe, and state, county and city police had been vague about protecting a young couple just because a frantic father called from Poland. The D.C. suburban cops seemed skeptical of Middleton's promises that Polish badges and American diplomats would echo his alarm as soon as their chains of command argued out who should contact whom.

Middleton's text-message read: GREEN LANTERN EVAC SCOTLAND.

GREEN LANTERN: His then-wife Sylvia had scoffed at his family code word system to prevent their toddler from being deceived by two-legged predators, but little Charlotte judged the plan cool, especially when Daddy let her make their secret code his (and thus her) favorite comic book hero.

EVAC: Charlotte was nine when the Pentagon Military Intelligence Unit where Middleton spent most of his career ran an evacuation drill. She adopted the word EVAC as a mantra, with significant shifts in irony as she roared through her teenage years.

SCOTLAND: When Charlotte got married, Middleton let her use his suburban house for the wedding's staging ground while he rented another lonely room in a hotel near the Capital Hill garden for the marriage ceremony. Two nights before the wedding, father and daughter got drunk in the hotel bar as she introduced him to a hip single-malt Scotch. From then on, they called that hotel "Scotland."

Told her what to do, thought Middleton. Where to go. That it's really me.

If she got the message.

The seatbelt "ding!" launched Middleton into the plane's aisle. Looping the shoulder strap on his soft black briefcase across his sports jacket kept his hands free. He didn't know where the rest of his luggage was; didn't care. His briefcase held his work, his laptop, iPod and toiletries airport security let him take onto an airplane, plus a paperback copy of Albert Camus's *The Stranger*.

As Middleton was about to reach the plane's door, a couple from first class barged in front of him. The woman, who may have looked great 10 years and a million scowls ago, clutched a battered jewel case to suspiciously firm breasts as she and her sad-eyed husband shuffled up the jet way ahead of Middleton.

Middleton heard the wife huff, "I still can't believe that sister of yours thought she could keep your mother's jewels from me just by going to Europe!"

The husband's flat voice knew its own irrelevance. "We all make mistakes."

They bumbled ahead to Customs, where a surgical-gloved guard carefully examined the jewel box's glittering necklaces, bracelets and earrings, comparing them to a transit document the wife kept tapping with her crimson fingernails. When he was through, the first class couple trudged ahead of Middleton through the terminal.

Middleton's jagged nerves keyed him into a detached hyper-vigilance he'd not felt since returning to the Balkans' slaughterhouse. There, all he had to fear were the ghosts of strangers. Now he felt his own life crawl along the edge of a straight razor.

He smelled his fellow travelers. Damp wool scent of lived-in clothes. Deodorants' metallic perfumes. Stale beer from the Englishman who'd tried to drown his fear of flying.

Middleton heard a child whine, and sobs from a Spec 4 soldier, who was all of 20 years old, as he marched toward a flight to Germany with connections to Iraq. An unseen CD blasted drums and crashing guitars: Middleton recognized Springsteen, and then remembered that expanding his range of classic rock music was the only debt besides Charlotte he owed his ex.

Night filled the terminal windows. Ads landscaped its walls. The musician in Middleton found melody in crowd movements synced with his rhythmic march to a bus for the main terminal. From there, he'd find his car in Long Term Parking, race to Scotland, working his cell phone the whole way. He saw all that with the absolute clarity of what is and what would be.

Looming beyond the shuffling first-class couple, Middleton saw a cop hurrying toward him. Saw the cop's blue uniform. Saw his shoulder-holstered black automatic. Saw a second pistol on the cop's black-leather belt along with handcuffs, ammo pouches, an empty loop for a radio.

They were 10 steps apart when Middleton matched the cop's face to photos he'd seen in Poland of a murderer.

The fake cop unsnapped his hip holster.

Middleton shoved the first-class woman into the pistol-drawing cop.

The fragile jewel case popped out of her grasp and flew toward the cop, who knocked it away. The case burst open. Glittering objects rained on the airport crowd.

First-class woman clawed at the cop: "Mine! Mine!"

Her bumped husband fell into an empty chair.

The fake cop pointed his gun at Middleton's face, as the woman continued to flail at him.

The gunshot reverberated through the terminal to Gate 67 some 40 feet off to Middleton's left where FBI Agent M. T. Connolly was snapping a handcuff onto her own wrist. The handcuffs' other clamp already circled the wrist of Dan Kohrman, who wore a second set of handcuffs shackling his wrists in front of him. Connolly's close-cropped brass hair came up to the shoulder of the husky Kohrman who'd been apprehended in Chicago on a federal Flight To Avoid Prosecution charge and extradited to D.C. Chicago cops passed him off.

Connolly hadn't needed to double cuff Kohrman. True, he was a felony fugitive, but he'd embezzled funds as a lawyer. Not the kind of bad boy who'd give "14-years-on-the-bricks her" any trouble. No, she cuffed her left hand to his right hand because she didn't feel like talking to the scumbag. Easier to jerk him where she wanted him to go.

He'd protested his innocence as Windy City cops led him off the plane toward Connolly and a uniformed Virginia state trooper who had been assigned to accompany the FBI during custodial transferals through the state's jurisdiction to a federal lockup. After that . . .

Well, after that, the state trooper had the easy smile of a Dixie scamp. He seemed like a possible diversion from the storm of empty howling in Connolly. His eyes twinkled while they waited for the Chicago plane, indicating to her that he harbored similar thoughts. He introduced himself as George, and she knew he wouldn't be around long enough for her to need to remember his last name.

"Look," Kohrman had said as she clicked her handcuff on his wrist. "Have you asked yourself why I would be so stupid as to steal that money?"

As she tightened the handcuff on her left wrist, Connolly replied, "Like I care about why."

Then she heard the high-caliber pistol shot crackle behind her. Crowd reacting. Trooper George facing the sound source. Screams and she turned, her .40 Glock filling her right hand.

She saw travelers stampeding.

Sensed the taller, trooper-uniformed George draw his gun.

Glimpsed a thick, black-haired American crashing onto a cop.

The roar of the gun in Middleton's face deafened him. The muzzle flash novaed his eyes. But as the bullet cut wide, Middleton fell onto his would-be killer and the crazed woman from first class, and they crashed to the floor. The gun flew from the killer's hand as hordes of airline travelers panicked in a 21st century terrorism nightmare.

Middleton's vision returned. But why can't I hear? Why is there no noise?

He scrambled after a 9mm Beretta gliding silently across a jewel-strewn floor.

The fake cop chopped at the first-class woman's throat. Jumped to his feet. Reached for his shoulder-holstered second pistol.

Middleton heard only the hammering of his own heart. He grabbed the Beretta and fired at the man who was drawing a second gun.

A glowing green neon Starbucks sign exploded on a wall beyond as the fake cop to a marksman's stance and acquired his target. His black shoes crunched white pearls scattered on the floor.

The fake cop and Middleton fired at the same time.

His arm unsteady, Middleton's bullet missed.

The fake cop's bullet missed too because he slipped on pearls and tumbled back through the air.

Off to Middleton's left, State Trooper George saw a uniformed police officer in trouble. Saw the cop fall. Panicked civilians ran between Trooper George and the gun battle. George glimpsed his target—tapped out two snap shots.

Missed!

Middleton saw a nearby black plastic chair shatter.

Instantly knew why, whirled. His eyes locked on a man wearing a blue uniform like the enemy's. Middleton fired four slugs at that second uniform.

Connolly heard the whine of bullets, the roar of a gun.

As the fugitive Kohrman screamed, Connolly saw Trooper George. Flat on his back, a hole at the collar of the blue-uniformed shirt over his bulletproof vest. A red stream flowed from George's neck. His eyes stared at the ceiling

Connolly lunged toward the fallen trooper, but Kohrman jerked her handcuffed left arm and she tipped back toward him.

"I wanted to make it big!" screamed Kohrman. "All right? I admit it! Just don't shoot—"

"Shut up!" Connolly shouted as she broke his nose with the butt of her pistol.

Kohrman crumpled, dead weight she dragged to Trooper George bleeding on the floor. Dropped her gun, pressed her free right hand over the gushing hole in the trooper's neck.

"You're going to make it!" she screamed at the fallen officer.

But she knew that was a lie.

Can't hear!

Middleton saw the second uniformed man who'd tried to shoot him crash to the floor. Middleton whirled his deaf attention to the nearby fake cop, who scrambled to his feet on the floor's glittering debris and fled through an emergency exit door.

Get him before he gets me! Or my daughter!

Battling in a world of silence, Middleton saw men and women dive for cover behind waiting room chairs. He saw their muted screaming faces.

First-class husband slumped in a black plastic chair, his face contorted like a laughing clown, staring at the tiled floor where his buxom wife lay gasping for air.

Middleton's eyes followed the husband's focus.

Saw flecks of gold paint on the tiles.

Saw broken shards of red and green and white stones.

Saw glittering glass ground to dust.

Saw a fallen cell phone spinning to a stop amid the rainbow rubble.

Middleton scooped up the cell phone as he burst to the emergency exit, broke out to the night from a facility designed by Homeland Security to prevent people from storming into it and its planes, not to keep people from running away.

Swallowed by cool air, Middleton stood at the top of metal stairs leading to the vast fields of runways where jets taxied, landed, took off—all in terrible silence.

A baggage caravan rolled silently across the dark tarmac. No sign of the fake cop. Middleton suddenly realized he stood spotlighted by the door's white light—a perfect target.

He ran down the stairs. Ran toward the glowing swoop of the main terminal.

A jumbo jet dropped out of the sky, skimmed over his head as he staggered across a runway. He ran under a second airliner as it climbed into the night. The pressure changing wakes of those jet engines popped his gunshot-deafened ears.

Suddenly, blessedly, he heard jet engines roar.

Get to Scotland, he thought. Got to get to Scotland.

The strap of his briefcase boa-constrictored his chest as he gasped for oxygen. Sweat stuck his shirt to his skin. His leg muscles burned and felt as if someone smashed a baseball bat into his right kneecap.

He knew better than to try for his car. They—whoever they were— might be waiting for him in the parking garage.

Pistol shoved in the back waistband of his pants, Middleton loped to the front of the main terminal. No one paid much attention—people run through airports all the time. A long line of people stood waiting their turn for a taxi.

To his left, he saw a young couple exiting a Town Car. He burst between them, leapt into the back seat before the driver could protest.

"Go!"

The man behind the wheel stared into the rearview mirror.

"Two-fifty," Middleton said, digging into his pocket for U.S. currency.

He sank into the backseat cushion of the taxi as it shot away from the terminal. "Capitol Hill."

The driver let him out in front of the Supreme Court that glowed like a gray-stone temple across from Congress' white-castle Capitol. Middleton walked through a park and saw no one but the nocturnal outline of a patrolling Capitol Hill policeman and his leashed German shepherd.

Scotland was a hotel built back when visiting Washington wasn't a big business. Middleton passed through the hotel's glass doors, walked straight to the registration desk.

"No sir, no young woman by that name is registered. No Mister and. Missus either. No sir, no messages. Yes sir, I'll call you at the bar if anything changes. Oh wait, what was your name? Excuse me: Sir? Sir?"

In the dark lounge, Middleton told the bartender, "Glenfiddich, rocks."

After the ice melted in his drink, Middleton concluded that his daughter wasn't coming. Wasn't here. Wasn't where she was supposed to be.

He laid the cell phone he'd snatched off the floor beside his glass on the bar. A pre-pay. Not his. He fished his phone from his briefcase. Ached to call someone, anyone. But he couldn't risk a monster hacking and tracking his calls. Besides, who could he talk to? Who could he trust now? Maybe killers had infiltrated Uncle Sam's badges too.

Breathe. Breathe.

You're a musician. Be like Beethoven. Hear the full, true symphony.

Do what you do best.

Interpret. Authenticate.

Whatever this was started in Europe. Could still be evolving there with other assassins, other terrors. Started way back with Kosovo, a war criminal, and a phantom mastermind. Was worth killing for. Worth dying for.

From Poland, the fake cop rode the plane that Middleton was supposed to be on. He might have spotted an airport cop getting off shift, followed him to his parking spot, snapped his neck, stuffed the dead cop in the trunk of his own car, stripped the corpse of clothes, weapons and IDs. As a cop in uniform, the killer strolled into the airport to meet every plane from Paris.

But who were his partners?

Focus on what makes sense.

I know something. Or someone. That's why they wanted to kill me. I have something that somebody wants. Or am something. I did something.

But the truth is, I'm not that important.

Wasn't. Am now.

That new truth is calibrated in blood.

In his mind, Middleton heard random notes, not a symphony. He flashed on jazz. When asked how a musician could slip into a free form jam that he'd neither started nor would finish, legendary pianist Night Train Jones said: "You gotta play with both hands."

Middleton put his cell phone inside his shirt pocket.

Stared at the cell phone he'd found spinning on the floor in a combat zone.

The phone had been turned on when Middleton grabbed it. If someone could locate a cell phone just because it was turned on, they were already rocketing toward him. Middleton found the "recent calls" screen. On the inside front cover of the paperback Camus novel, Middleton wrote the phone number that this cell phone had connected to for 3 minutes and 19 seconds. That same number sent this phone one text message:

122 S FREEMNT A BALMORE

Baltimore, thought Middleton. A 40-minute drive from this bar stool. A train ride from Union Station kitty-corner to the hotel. A few blocks north of the train station was a bus depot from which silver boxes roared up Interstate 95 to Charm City where Middleton spent a lot of time at the Peabody Conservatory of Music.

Middleton wrote the address inside the novel's cover.

He went to the men's room and, in the clammy locked stall, counted his remaining cash: $515 American, $122 in Euros. Credit cards, but the second he used one to buy a ticket, meal or motel, he would pop up on the grid. He checked the ammo magazine in his scavenged Beretta: eight bullets.

Can go a long way and nowhere at all on what I've got, thought Harold Middleton.

Back on the bar stool, he realized he reeked of frenzy. The bar mirror made him flinch. He looked terrible. Burned out and all but buried. Worse, he looked memorable.

Middleton left enough cash on the bar, walked toward the night.

He turned away from well-lit streets, still not ready to risk a phone call or a train or a bus or shelter for the night. Walked past empty office buildings.

Out of the darkness loomed a man brandishing a butcher knife.

Middleton froze two paces from a blade that would've punctured his throat.

Butcher-knife man growled: "Give it up! Cash. Wallet. Hurry!"

So Middleton reached under his gray sports jacket and came out with Beretta steel.

"Go, baby!" yelled the robber to a waiting car. He dropped the knife.

"Freeze, baby," Middleton shouted, "or I'll blow his head off, then kill you too!"

Middleton kept the robber in his vision while turned toward the rusted car idling at the curb, its front passenger door gaping open like the maw of a shark.

Never heard it roll up behind me. Never saw it coming. Wake up!

The robber said: "We want a lawyer!"

Middleton jerked his head toward the open car door—but kept his gun locked on the robber. "Get in and you might get out of this alive."

The hands-high scruffy man eased into the shotgun seat of the idling car. Middleton slid into the backseat behind him, told the boney young woman with blazing eyes behind the steering wheel, "Do what I say or I'll blast a bullet in your spine."

"Baby!" yelled her partner. "You were supposed to beat it outta trouble!"

Not anger, thought Middleton, that's not the music. More a plea. And sorrow.

"Fool! He'd have lit you up! Word, Marcus: I ain't never gonna leave you go."

"'Knew you weren't meant for no thug life." Notes of pride. Sorrow.

"Where?" the woman asked the dark silhouette in her rearview mirror.

"We're going to Baltimore," Middleton said. "Drive."

4

S. J. ROZAN

Swift and silent as a cheetah after an antelope, the dust cloud chased the approaching Jeep. Almost, you could imagine it putting on a burst of speed, catching the Jeep and devouring it. Squinting over the sun-baked soil, Leonora Tesla gave in to an ironic smile as she found herself rooting for the dust.

Since she'd come to Namibia she'd seen this contest often, the predator running the prey. Conscientiously, she told herself not to take sides—they were all God's creatures, and they all had to eat—but her heart was always with the prey. And her heart was usually broken, because the predator usually won. Now she was on the other side, but—as usual, Leonora!—in a hopeless cause. The dust would lose this race, settling into defeat as the Jeep came to a stop in front of her hut.

At least this time, she wouldn't have to worry about heartbreak: This would not be a life-and-death struggle, only an annoyance in her day.

"He's a funder," her program manager had said over the village's single crackling telephone, calling from Windhoek, his voice equal amounts sympathy and command. "You will have to see him."

Leonora Tesla had come to the bush so she wouldn't have to see anyone, except the HIV-positive women she worked with. After The Hague, after the hunting—after the shock of being called together and told by Harold the Volunteers must disband—even the smaller African cities had been too much for her. So she'd gone to the bush, traveling from village to village, staying not long in any one place. Her mandate was to establish craft co-operatives, micro-financing women's paths to independence. The work suited her. Her days were filled now with distracting minutiae—finding hinges in one village so another's kiln door could be repaired; lending the equivalent of four American dollars so a group could buy paper on which to keep records of baskets sold. And with beauty: the color-block quilts, the Oombiga pots whose tradition had almost been lost. Beauty suited Tesla too. Visual beauty: the way the women weaved echoed the stark sub-tlety of the African landscape. And musical beauty: The only artifact of 21st century technology she'd brought into the bush was an iPod loaded with—among other things—Bach preludes, Shostakovich symphonies and Beethoven sonatas. Reluctantly, she removed it now, cutting off Chopin as the Jeep neared. She hoped this wouldn't take long. She'd ferry him around, this funder from . . . She'd forgotten to ask. She'd show him the kiln, the looms, the workshop. She'd rattle off her statistics on life-span ex-tension and self-sufficiency, give him her little speech about hope for the next generation. The women would present him with a quilt or a pot for which he could have no possible use and he'd be patronizingly pleased with them and inordinately proud of himself for making this all possible. Then maybe he'd go away and leave them in peace.

Oh, Leonora, at least try to smile.

The other Volunteers used to say that regularly, and precisely because their work gave them little to smile about, she'd try. She did it now, a polite smile for the angular blond man who stepped from the Jeep. He smiled back and slapped his hat against his thigh to shake off the dust. He took off his sunglasses: well trained in the art of courtesy, at least.

"Leonora Tesla? I'm Günter Schmidt."

He spoke in English with a soft accent she couldn't quite place. Not German, but no law said his German name meant he was brought up in that country. That's what the permeability of European borders was about. It was supposed to be a good thing.

They shook hands. Schmidt's was soft and fleshy, as befit someone who dispensed money from behind a desk. "You've had a long drive," she said. "Sit down. I'll get you something to drink." She indicated a stool on the hard clay under the overhang, but he followed her into the house. He'd learn, she thought. In Africa the indoor, though shadowed and appealing, was never cooler than outside.

Still smiling, Schmidt dropped himself onto one of the rough-hewn chairs at her plank table. She handed him a bottle of BB orange soda. In a hut without electricity, of course she had no refrigerator, but she'd learned the African trick of burying bottles in a box in the hut's clay floor, so the drink was relatively cool. "We'll be more comfortable outside," she suggested, resigned to try to be pleasant to this intruder.

"No," he said, "I'd rather stay here. Leonora."

She bristled at the odd way he said her name, but his expression was mild as he looked about her hut. So she shrugged, wiped her brow with her kerchief and sat beside him.

"You've lived here long?" Schmidt asked, taking a pull from his soda bottle.

"No. I don't live anywhere long. My work takes me many places."

"That would account for the . . . simplicity."

"And yet my possessions, few as they are, are more numerous than those of the women in our programs. When you're rested, I'll take you to see the kiln. We'll be covering a lot of ground today if you want to see the full scope of our work." She stood to reach her own Jeep keys on the hook by the door.

"No, I think we'll stay here. Leonora."

She turned sharply. His smile and the mild expression in his eyes were still in place, but his hand held a pistol, pointed at her.

Calm, Leonora. Stay calm. "What do you want?"

"Where is Harold Middleton?"

Tesla's heart, already pounding, gave a lurch. But she spoke calmly. "Harold? How would I possibly know?"

Schmidt didn't answer her. The gun moved slightly, as though seeking a better angle.

"Isn't he in America, in Washington? That's where he lives."

"If he were in Washington," Schmidt asked reasonably, "would I be here?"

"Well, I haven't heard from him in almost a year."

"I don't know whether that's true, though eventually I'm sure I'll find out. But it doesn't matter. Whether you've heard from him or not, you know where he'd go. If, say, he were in trouble."

In trouble? "No, I don't."

"When you worked together—"

"When we did, I might have been able to tell you. But I don't know anything about his life now. He teaches music; I don't even know where."

Neither of them had moved since Tesla had seen the pistol. Neither of them moved now, in the stretching silence. A breeze rustled the leaves in the acacia behind the hut. Sweat trickled down Tesla's spine.

"Who are you? What do you want with Harold?"

He laughed. "I suppose you had to ask that, but you know I won't tell you. But it's about your work, Leonora."

"The Volunteers?"

His smile was bitter. "Your work. So. You really don't know where Middleton is? Not even if I shoot you?"

A gunshot roar ricocheted off the tin roof and mud walls; Tesla stumbled, grasped the plank table for support as clay shards flew everywhere. She found herself staring into Schmidt's mild eyes. Wheezing a few breaths, quieting her heart by an act of will, she answered him.

"Even if you shoot me. I don't know."

Schmidt nodded. "All right. You don't know where he'd go if he were in trouble. I suppose then we'll have to depend on what he'd do, if you were in trouble." He stood. "Come."

"What?"

"As you said: We'll be covering a lot of ground."

She walked ahead of the gun out onto the uneven baked earth. The glaring sunlight was unforgiving; she did not turn, but waited. There: a stutter in his step, a whisper of plastic on fabric. Behind her, Schmidt reached into his pocket for his sunglasses, she dropped down and rolled into him. He stumbled; she yanked his ankle forward, threw her weight sideways into his other knee. Dust boiled as he thudded to the ground. Another shot screamed, but out here in the endless bush it didn't thunder, and she'd been prepared to hear it. The gun waved wildly, looking for her, but by the second shot she was in the hut and by the third she'd hurled a clay pot with the force and accuracy of Yaa Asantewa's spear.

In the whirling dust, Schmidt—and more important, the gun—was still.

Forcing her breathing even, Tesla crouched by the door, waiting. When all had been motionless for a full minute, she crept to the table, reached down for one of the soda bottles and flung it at Schmidt's head. On impact it smashed into glittering shards, but Schmidt didn't move.

Slowly, she rose. She made her way to where Schmidt lay in the settling dust. His blood trickled into the dry soil amid the shards of a once-beautiful pot. There, you see, Leonora? This time you were on the side of the dust. And the predator always wins.

Her first steps back inside took her to the plastic water bucket in her makeshift sink. She scooped with her hands, splashed water over her face and head as though here, at the edge of the Namib, water was hers to waste.

Then she made her way swiftly about the room, collecting the few things she would take. When her canvas bag was packed she used a knife to slit the seam she'd sewed on the thin mattress as she had on each mattress in each hut she'd stayed in. She extracted the envelope of American dollars and the small, battered portfolio she'd had with her since The Hague. She slipped them both into the side pocket with the iPod, zipped and she was done.

Getting Schmidt into the Jeep was harder. She was strong but he was tall, and leverage was a problem. Eventually, his head wrapped in a towel to keep bloodstains from the seat, she'd maneuvered him into the back, fished the keys from his pocket and started the engine. Driving along the dust track the way Schmidt had come, she saw ahead the spot she'd been thinking of, where the edge of the road fell off steeply toward the wadi. She passed it and turned around so the Jeep was headed toward her hut. Then, on the curve, she yanked the wheel sharply, opened the door and jumped.

Anywhere in the wadi would have worked, but her luck was better than she'd had the nerve to hope, and the Jeep smacked head-on into an acacia tree. When she reached it—limping slightly, she'd banged her knee—cracks spider-webbed the windshield. Excellent. Then came more sweat, strain and maneuvering, and finally Schmidt was half-in, half-out of the driver's seat. Though the crack in his skull was clearly not from this crash, he was unlikely to be found for a while—except by the hyenas that skulked along this dry streambed. Once they were through, no one would doubt what had killed Günter Schmidt.

Or whoever he was. And wherever he'd come from.

She walked back to the hut, hoping she could walk out the ache in her knee. Once there, she stripped and washed in the little water she'd left herself. She changed clothes, took what she'd been wearing and the bloody towel in a pillowcase. Slinging it and her bag into her own Jeep, Tesla paused. Though she'd lived in and left too many places to make a habit of goodbyes, she took a moment to stare at the hut, and then turned to salute the wide brown land. She'd thought this might be home, but now she doubted she'd be back.

The drive to Windhoek Airport took a little more than three hours. Once there, she used all four of her credit cards to withdraw as much cash as she could. With what she'd taken from the mattress, she'd be all right for a while. On one of the cards she bought a ticket on the connecting flight through Munich to Washington, D.C. Then she exited the terminal and boarded the long-distance bus to Cape Town.

She didn't know if her credit cards were being monitored, but she had to take the possibility into account. In Cape Town, she'd buy a ticket in cash.

To New York.

Where you could catch a train to Washington, Harold had told her, a dozen times a day.

Hugging her bag to her, feeling the portfolio's stiffness through the canvas, Leonora stared out the window at the dry land, the lonesome trees.

A dozen trains a day.

That ought to be enough.

5

ERICA SPINDLER

Charlotte Middleton-Perez cracked open her eyes, disoriented. Not home. Not the dining room at the Ritz.

Bright, antiseptic white. Shiny surfaces, stiff sheets. She hurt. Ached everywhere, especially her lower back.

The squeak and rattle of a cart broke the silence. Muffled voices followed. She shifted her gaze. Her husband Jack by the bed, head in hands. The picture of grief.

With a shattering sense of loss, she remembered: standing up. Seeing the blood. Crying out, then gasping as pain knifed through her belly.

She brought a hand to her abdomen, vision blurring with tears. She'd had a life growing inside her. A baby boy. She and Jack had begun picking out names.

Had. Past tense. Now, no life inside her. No little boy with Jack's blue eyes and her dark hair.

Her tears spilled over, rolling down her cheeks, hot and bitter.

He lifted his head. His eyes were red-rimmed from crying.

"Charley," he said.

The one word conveyed a world of emotion—despair and regret, love and need. For comfort. To understand—how could this have happened?

They'd reached the second trimester. Safe, they'd thought. Out of the woods. Common wisdom validated their belief.

Her fault? Working too hard? Not enough rest?

As if reading her thoughts, Perez stretched out a hand. She took it and he curled his fingers protectively around hers. "Not your fault, Charley. The doctor said these things . . . happen."

She shook her head. "That's not good enough. I need to know why."

He cleared his throat. "They're going to run some tests. On us. On our . . . The miscarriage. He suggested an ultrasound of your uterus, an x-ray, too."

She squeezed her eyes shut as he tightened his fingers on hers. "This is a setback. It really hurts, but we'll have—"

"No."

"—other childre—"

"Don't. Please." Her voice cracked. "I wanted this baby . . . I—I already loved him."

"I understand," he said with apparent sympathy.

And he always seemed to. She didn't know what she had done to deserve his love. They'd met at Tulane University in New Orleans. She had been stunned when he asked her out, when he pursued her. She wasn't an extraordinary beauty. Just pleasant looking—average face, average figure. And Jack was off the charts handsome. Smart. Educated. From an influential Louisiana family. His falling for her had been as much a mystery as a miracle.

"Have you heard from Harry?" she asked. She'd stopped calling her father Dad on her thirteenth birthday. She was Charley, he was Harry and her mother was perpetually horrified by the both of them.

"Not yet."

"You left a message—"

"At the restaurant. And just a bit ago on his cell phone. It went automatically to voicemail."

He was delayed, still in transit. "You didn't tell him—"

He squeezed her fingers again. "Just that we were here. To call on my cell. I left my number."

She swallowed past the sudden rush of tears. "Mother?" she managed.

"No answer, home or cell."

"Ms. Middleton?"

They turned. Two men stood in the doorway, expressions solemn. Both men, dressed in dark suits, were pin neat and pressed, despite the hour. She wasn't surprised when they introduced themselves as federal officers. "We need to ask you a few questions."

"Now?" Perez asked as he stood. "Here?"

"It's about your father," the taller of the two said, producing his Department of Justice ID.

"About Harry?"

"Harold Middleton, yes. When's the last time you spoke with him?"

The hair on the back of her neck prickled. "Before he left for Europe. A week or so before."

"Did he seem himself?"

"Yes. But why—"

"Did he express any concerns about the trip? Any anxiety? Unexpected excitement?"

"My father was a seasoned traveler, Agent—"

"Smith," he offered. "Did you get the sense this trip was different from others he's taken?"

"None at all."

"You planned to meet last evening? At the Ritz dining room?"

"Yes . . . But how—" She didn't finish the thought. The feds could find out anything. Harry had taught her that. "For a late supper. I didn't make it."

Her throat closed over the words. The agents seemed unmoved by her pain. "We're sorry for your loss, Ms. Middleton, but—"

"Mrs. Perez," her husband corrected, voice tight. "As I said, this is not a good time. Either tell us why you're here or leave."

Agent Smith looked Perez in the eyes. "Perez is a well known name down in Louisiana."

Perez frowned. "Meaning what?"

"It's a name we're familiar with, that's all."

Jack August Perez. His family, descendants of the original Spaniards that settled the New Orleans area, wielded both political and economic influence. In the era of Huey P. Long, they had exerted that power with an iron fist, nowadays with business savvy and brilliant connections.

Angry color stained Perez's cheeks. "What are you getting at?"

Don't let him get to you, she thought. Emotions lead to mistakes. Ones that could prove deadly. Another of Harry's pearls.

What the hell was going on?

She touched her husband's clenched hand. "It's all right, sweetheart. It's just a couple of questions."

"Thank you, Mrs. Perez. Has your father contacted you in the past twenty-four hours?"

"No. I expect his flight was delayed. I'm used to that sort of thing with Harry."

At her response, she felt her husband's startled glance. She didn't acknowledge it. "How did you know I was here, Agent Smith?"

He ignored the question. "I'm afraid your father's in some trouble."

She noticed that while Agent Smith spoke, his partner studied her reactions. She also noticed that every so often he rubbed the back of his hand against his leg, as if scratching at a bite or wiping at a stain.

Most un-fed like. Feds were trained to be as robotic as possible. Nervous twitches were not an option.

"Trouble? I don't understand."

"He was questioned in Warsaw concerning three murders in Europe."

"Harry?" That incredulous retort came from Perez. "You have the wrong Harold Middleton."

The agent's gaze flickered to Perez, then settled on her once more. "Your father was able to catch an Air France flight out of Paris several hours later. He arrived at Dulles—then he shot and killed a police officer."

She who couldn't hold back. "Impossible!"

"I'm sorry."

"That's not my father."

"I understand how you must feel. It's a shock, but we have witnesses—"

"My father couldn't have shot anybody. First off, Harold Middleton has spent his life fighting for what's right. Hunting down and bringing to justice the sorts of monsters who terrorize and murder. That said, where did he get a gun? He'd just gotten off an international flight. Who was this cop? Why would my father want to kill him?"

She held his gaze; the tense silence crackled between them. After a moment, the agent broke the contact, inclined his head. "Those are all questions only your father can answer. We need to speak with him."

The last thing she was about to do was help them find Harry.

The Feds were like buzzards on road kill—once they made up their mind someone was guilty, they'd move heaven and earth to "prove" it.

"What can I do?" she asked, sounding annoyingly earnest to her own ears.

"Let us know the minute you hear from him." Agent Smith handed her his card. She gazed down at it, adorned with the Bureau's familiar red, white, blue and gold seal.

He handed one to Perez. "That's my cell number. Call anytime, day or night."

"I will." She ran her thumb across the business card, heart pounding. "And if you find him—"

"You'll be the first to know."

"This is all a mistake. You're looking for the wrong man."

"For your sake, I hope so." As the two crossed to the door, Smith turned, meeting her gaze once more. Something in his expression made her skin crawl. "Thank you for your cooperation."

The moment the door shut behind them, she swung her legs over the side of the bed. "We're getting out of here. Now."

"Charley, what—"

"This whole thing stinks. And I'm going to find out wh—" She stood and a wave of dizziness swept over her.

Perez grabbed her arm, steadying her. "Harry's in some trouble, no doubt. But there's nothing you can do about it right now—and certainly not in your condition. I'll get the nurse to call Doctor Levine and find out when you're being released, and we'll plan from there."

She shook off his hand. "You don't get it. I'm not going to lie around here and do nothing when I know Harry's in danger."

"For God's sake, Charley. You're in more danger than he is. You just had a miscarriage. Doctor Levine said to expect discomfort and bleeding. That you'd be weak. He advised taking it easy for a couple days. I'm not letting you walk out of here without his okay."

"Try to stop me." She took a deep breath and looked her husband squarely in the eyes. "Those guys weren't FBI."

Without waiting for a response, she crossed to the room's version of a closet, a press board armoire. Her panties and trousers were bloodstained. The panties were ruined, she decided, so she would have to make do with the pads the hospital had provided. If she tied her jacket around her waist, her dark-colored trousers would do until she could replace them.

She glanced at her husband as he watched her. "Those cards 'Agent Smith' handed us were bogus," she said. "Take a good look. Cheap stock. Laser jet printing. Run your finger over it. The Bureau's cards are engraved. This one could've been printed from any home computer."

She stepped into the stained trousers, a lump in her throat. She swallowed past it. There would be a lifetime to mourn their loss. Right now, Harry needed her.

"The only number on Smith's card," she continued, "is a cell number."

Perez frowned, struggling to come to grips with what she was proposing. "So where's the Bureau's number?"

"Exactly."

He rubbed the bridge of his nose. "Charley, have you considered that you might be a little emotionally unstable right now? You've suffered a loss . . . It's been a shock. I think taking a step back and a deep breath might be a good idea. I'll check you out, we'll go home. See if Harry's there or left us a message. You need a change of clothes, something to eat. We'll sort everything out."

"Do you trust me?"

"Of course."

"Then help me. Please."

In the end, she wore him down. Worried that one of the bogus agents was watching the front of the hospital, she refused to allow him to officially check her out. The hospital would insist on a wheelchair—standard policy—and a front-door exit. Instead they took the stairs and slipped out the delivery entrance.

She waited while he brought the car around. Once they were both buckled in, he looked at her. "What's the plan?"

"We find Harry."

He smiled at her. "Good plan. How do y—"

The faint sound of a digitized version of the song "Brown-Eyed Girl" interrupted him.

Her cell phone's ring tone.

"It's in your purse," he said. "I locked it in the—"

"Trunk."

He shifted into park, threw open his car door and climbed out. A moment later he returned with her purse, cell clipped to it, message light blinking frantically.

A number she didn't recognize—perhaps her father had bought a prepaid for security. She quickly scrolled through a half-dozen missed calls and one text message waiting. All from Harry.

She returned the last call first, and it was answered on the first ring. "Dad, it's me. Thank God! I was so worried."

"Charlotte! Where are you?"

"Jack and I—"

She bit the words back, realization crashing in on her. Not her father. Her father hadn't called her Charlotte since the second grade."

"Charlotte? Sweetheart, are you—"

With a sound of distress, she hung up. "Drive, Jack. Now."

He did as she instructed. "What happened?"

"Someone pretended to be Harry. They wanted to know where I was."

"Check your messages."

She did. At the sound of her father's voice relief flooded her.

"Charley, I've been delayed. I hope to still make a late dinner. Love you."

She frowned at the second message. "Charley, there's a situation here. I'll explain everything when I get there. Look . . . Be careful. Stay with Jack. Don't trust anyone you don't know. My flight's due into Dulles at 7:10 p.m."

By the third and last message there was no denying the panic in his voice. "Where are you? I'm boarding the Paris flight. When you get this, dial back so I'll know you're okay."

She checked the text message next.

GREEN LANTERN EVAC SCOTLAND

She stared at those four little words, feeling as if all the air had suddenly been sucked out of the car's interior.

"What's wrong?"

"Change in plans. We're going to Capitol Hill. The Scotland—The St. Regis."

While he drove, she explained about the code. When she finished, he glanced at her. "This is a gag?"

"Hardly. Harry would never have sent that text message unless it was for real."

"Maybe he didn't send it?"

The thought chilled her, but only for a moment. "No, no one else would know our code. Even mother only knew part of it. Harry sent it."

"This makes no sense. It's like some cloak-and-dagger parlor game. Only you're telling me it's real." Perez pulled up in front of the hotel. "What is your dad, some kind of a spy?"

She flung open the car door. "Wait here. I'll be right back."

Moments later, she greeted the guest services agent. She dug a photo of Harry out of her wallet; the guy at the desk squinted at it, then nodded.

"He was here. Looking for some woman. You, I suppose. Went to the bar to wait."

She thanked him and hurried to the lounge. She saw right away that he wasn't there.

She crossed to the bar. The bartender was busy with another patron, a stunning redhead. While she waited for him to finish, her attention was drawn to the television behind the bar, the news story being broadcast. A shooting at Dulles. A police officer down. The grainy image of the suspect.

Harry. It couldn't be true.

"What can I get you?"

She looked at the bartender. She had the photo of her father out, ready to ask if the man had seen him, if he knew where he'd gone. Instead, she shook her head and slipped the photo back into her pocket. She couldn't chance him recognizing Harry and sounding the alarm.

"Nothing. I just remembered . . . Sorry."

She turned and quickly left, aware of the bartender's gaze on her. As she strode past the desk again, she glanced the attendant's way. He was on the phone; when he saw her looking his way, he quickly averted his eyes.

If those goons had what they wanted, they wouldn't have paid her the little visit in the hospital. That was the good news.

The bad news. Harry was wanted in connection with the murder of a cop. That part of the "agent's" story had been legitimate.

By now, the police knew who he was, where he worked and lived. Where she lived. They were amassing the names of friends and coworkers.

He wouldn't be able to use his credit cards or cell phone. His car would be off-limits, as would his home.

He had two groups after him—the fake police and the real ones.

Her husband was waiting for her at the hotel entrance, expression tight. "Any luck?"

"He was here. He's not now."

"Look, I was listening to the news and—"

"I know," she said, cutting him off. "I saw it on the TV. In the bar."

They hurried up the block to their BMW and slid inside. "Maybe those guys were real agents?"

"No way," she replied. "Mother lives close by. Maybe she's heard from him."

"Sylvia and your father hate each other."

Hate was a strong word, but she certainly wouldn't call them friends. A more mismatched union she couldn't imagine. Plus, her mother had never forgiven Harry for Charlotte liking him more than her. And for turning her only child into what she called a "do-gooder, spy-in-training."

The marriage's final straw had been the brief affair he'd had with one of his fellow Volunteers—Leonora Tesla.

"Let's try there anyway. At the very least, I can borrow a change of clothes."

Her mother would ask about the baby. They'd have to explain. She brought a hand to her empty belly. She didn't want to talk about it. She couldn't.

Falling apart was a luxury she couldn't afford right now.

They made her mother's upscale Georgetown neighborhood in less than 20 minutes. Easing to a stop in front of the two-story colonial, they climbed out of the car and hurried up the walk.

Her mother's Mercedes sedan was parked in the drive. The porch was dark, though light glowed in several of the windows.

Charley rang the bell. From inside came the frenzied yapping of Bella, her mother's Pomeranian.

"Mother!" she called, ringing again. "It's me!"

Maybe she'd gone out with a friend who had picked her up. Or she was on a date.

No. This wasn't right. She felt it in her gut.

Beside her, Perez dialed his mother-in-law's number. It rang twice, four times, six times.

Heart thundering, she dug in her purse for her key ring. She kept one of her mother's spares in case of emergency. She found it, fitted the key in the lock and eased the door open.

"Mom!" she called. Bella came running from the kitchen, across her mother's bright white carpeting. Leaving a trail of perfect little paw prints.

Red prints.

A cry slipped past her lips. With an order for her to "stay put," Perez started for the kitchen. She followed.

They stopped at the kitchen entry. Her mother lay on the tile floor. Face up, eyes open. Vacant. Seeping blood had formed wing shapes on either side of her torso. Bella had run around and around her mistress, through the blood, creating a bizarre, almost floral pattern on the white tile.

Her mother had been dressed for bed. She wore a teal-colored silk robe. The robe's flap had fallen open, exposing her legs and an edge of lacy lingerie. One hand rested on her chest, as if she had grabbed at her heart, the other at her side.

"Oh Mother." Whimpering, she took a step forward, then stopped, lightheaded, and grasped the counter for support.

Her husband inched toward his mother-in-law's body, careful to avoid the blood. He squatted and checked her pulse.

Struggling to come to grips with what had happened, she shifted her gaze. It landed on an item peeking out from under the cabinet. She blinked, focusing. A candy-bar wrapper. With the toe of her shoe, she nudged it out. Milka, a European brand, one difficult to acquire in the states. She tilted her head. This one was from Poland.

She stared at it, blood thundering in her head. Her father's favorite chocolate. His secret passion. One that they shared.

"She's dead, Charley."

"We've got to get out of here. Now." She snatched up the candy wrapper and stuffed it into her pocket.

"What are you doing? Charley, that could be evidence. We've got to call the police."

"They're going to try to pin this on Harry."

"Have you thought that maybe he did—"

"Never, not Dad. He sent me that text message because I'm in danger too. Mother was as well. I don't know why this is happening, but I trust him."

"With your life? With mine as well?"

"Yes." She pressed her lips together as the full meaning of what was happening set in. "We've got to find him."

"How?" Perez dragged a shaking hand through his hair. "We're not wanted by the police, but I'm sure they're looking for us."

She looked back at her mother, fighting back despair—and the urge to crawl into her husband's arms and sob. She was Harold Middleton's daughter. She would hunt down whoever had done this. And make him—or her—pay.

In the distance came the sound of sirens. "The lake house," she said, starting for her mother's bedroom and a change of clothes. "Eventually, Harry will look for us there."

6

JOHN RAMSEY MILLER

In the Dulles parking lot, FBI Agent In Charge M. T. Connolly watched homicide detectives process a policeman's corpse. A deep ligature mark around the murdered cop's neck and blossoms of red in the white of his eyes made cause of death obvious, the same way the security videos made just as obvious the identity of the man who killed him, stole his uniform and stuffed him into the back of a Jeep, where he now lay.

The detectives had arrived in response to the shooting of a state trooper in the concourse. Despite early reports to the contrary, Trooper George was still alive, but in grave condition. Three bullets had deformed against his bulletproof vest and one had gone high and deflected against the collar and severed an artery. He wasn't expected to live. If he did, he could have serious brain damage from blood loss.

Accompanied by homicide detectives, Connolly had gone from the parking deck to the security offices to view the video surveillance. She got a good look at the fake cop who'd fired at the passenger identified by customs as Harold Middleton. Middleton had taken away the assailant's gun and subsequently fired in self-defense. Trooper George assumed the cop was in the right and his target a felon—an understandable mistake. Initially, she had jumped to the same conclusion in the melee, but she had been shackled to her idiot prisoner and couldn't give pursuit until it was too late. She'd assumed that the fake cop had chased Middleton to capture

him, but it was now clear he'd run away from her and other security officers who'd come rushing at the sound of gunfire on the concourse. It was
also apparent that the fake cop had drawn his gun on Middleton right after
Middleton seemed to recognize him.

After Middleton captured the Beretta and used it to defend himself
from the trooper's gunfire, he'd fled through an emergency door. The fake
cop, wearing the purloined and somewhat ill-fitting uniform, had vanished
as had Middleton.

Her next reaction had been to use Bureau resources to find out all she
could about Middleton and the cop killer. She and the detectives had
agreed that Middleton would be identified only as a material witness who
had to be picked up immediately for his own protection. Unless the uniformed cop-killer got to him first. His description was circulated immediately to area law enforcement—picture to follow as soon as it could be
printed from the surveillance video—and he was identified as a wanted
cop-killer, which meant he'd only live through his apprehension if they
found him naked and lying face down on the pavement in front of live TV
film crews.

The airport terminal and parking deck teemed with angry cops, crime-
scene evidence staff and passenger witnesses. State troopers with dogs were
beginning a search of the airport, hoping to find the killer and Middleton,
but Connolly doubted they were still in the area. While the cops were
reacting like disturbed fire ants, Connolly was working the steps calmly—
something that came naturally to her.

She had found a business card lying on the concourse floor, which the
detectives had taken as evidence. They didn't know where the card had
come from, or if it had meaning to the case, until in watching the video of
the struggle between Middleton and the fake cop in slow motion, the card
was seen falling to the floor after Middleton's shirt pocket ripped. It read
"Jozef Padlo, Deputy Inspector of the Polish National Police."

It caught her like a hammer blow, and, if she hadn't believed in coinci-
dences before, she was a devotee now. Mere minutes later, certainly hours
before the detectives would get around to it, Connolly called the phone
number and, since it was six hours later in Poland, left the inspector a message on his office voice mail to call her ASAP. Next she tried a number that

wasn't on the card, but was in her cell phone, but again Padlo didn't answer. When the inspector's voice mail kicked in, she left the same message. This time she gave Harold Middleton's name figuring that if hearing her voice wasn't enough to get him to respond immediately, Middleton's name would.

When Padlo returned the call 25 minutes later, Connolly had already learned about retired Colonel Harold Middleton from the FBI's Intel group, and decided she was going to work the case come flood or tall cotton. Middleton had located the butcher, KLA's Colonel Agim Rugova, and brought him to trial at The Hague. Rugova had been murdered, so the possibility that the two events were connected thrilled her. Aside from terrorism, there was nothing sexier or better for a career than an international case. And she knew Padlo would cooperate fully with her.

Connolly met Padlo at Quantico three years earlier when he was a guest at the Bureau's law-enforcement classes offered to leading European investigators. As fortune would have it, Connolly had been one of the instructors, and she and Padlo had become close—very close. An image of a naked Padlo sitting cross-legged on her bed—a glass of wine in one hand and a cigarette in the other—as he told her in depth about a cold case he couldn't solve brought a warm smile to her lips.

Jozef Padlo wasn't especially handsome, but there was something about the lanky Pole that strengthened his appearance and negated his well-worn clothes. Connolly knew she wasn't a beauty either, but Padlo saw her as one. He was quick-witted, honest, intelligent, dedicated to his work, spoke fluent English, had big sad eyes, delicate hands and was an attentive lover. For the first time in her life, she hadn't minded the clouds of cigarette smoke. In the intervening years, they spent a few days vacationing together and spoke by telephone two or three times a week. Since both were dedicated to their careers, being together full time was impossible.

Connolly knew she was going to run the case—a cap-feather generator, probably an international one—and if the detectives got in her way, she'd sweep them aside. After all, she'd witnessed the shootout, connected Middleton to the ICCY and kept the cops from misinterpreting Middleton's actions and, possibly, killing him. And she had a working relationship with the foreign authorities. Plus it didn't hurt that she was the southern belle apple of the her boss's eye—they were both from Mississippi and, more important, she had a high-profile case closure rate second to none. It also helped that she never failed to give her superiors as much of the credit as possible.

Connolly looked across the security room at her annoying prisoner, whose wrist was now cuffed to a pipe. EMS had bandaged his nose and cleaned the blood from his face. To turn him over for processing, she'd been calling the U.S. Marshals Service every 10 minutes for an hour. Finally, she thought, as her phone rang. A callback.

"This is Connolly," she said. "Where the hell are my Marshals?"

"When and where did you last see them?" the Polish inspector asked.

"Well, hello, Inspector Padlo," she answered, softening her voice as she stepped outside.

"Hello, FBI Special Agent Buttercup," Padlo said. "Have you found Middleton?"

"Here's the deal," she said—and told him everything she knew. Padlo listened without interrupting.

When she was finished, he said, "Harold Middleton was the last person to meet with Henryk Jedynak, a collector of old music manuscripts who, along with two witnesses, was murdered here. I had Colonel Middleton picked up and I questioned him. From your description of his assailant, he could be Dragan Stefanovic. I made the Rugova connection to Middleton and showed him an array of photographs of men known to have associated with Rugova in the old days, displaced mercenaries who are now thugs for hire. Stefanovic's picture was among them, as was a man we know only as The Slav. Middleton said he saw The Slav at the airport—apparently waiting for the same flight to Paris that he was taking. The Slav made it out of Paris before we could get French authorities there. As you know, the French authorities generate more red tape than red wine."

"You don't think Middleton may have been somehow involved with Jedynak's death, do you?"

"No. Harold Middleton is one of the good guys, a devoted family man with firm moral fiber, and a man who has made sacrifices so he could right terrible wrongs. Now we have the death of Jedynak, the attempt on Middleton in public and the disappearance of Jedynak's niece."

"His niece. Is it related to his murder?"

"She is a talented violinist so I suspect all of this might be connected to something all three have in common—music. For Middleton and Jedynak, the link runs through rare music manuscripts, which may connect them to Rugova as well."

"Rare music manuscripts . . . "

"As you know, Rugova spent part of the war in Bosnia securing looted treasures from World War II. At St. Sophia, he stole forty-something crates the Nazis had hidden in a sealed chamber: paintings, drawings, golden figures, a few small but valuable bronzes, jewelry—and musical scores. The deaths of almost two hundred civilians got the attention at the time, rightfully so, but Rugova moved those crates. In time, he was eager to trade information on who received the looted art—in exchange for leniency."

"Middleton knew this," Connolly said.

"Middleton had a Chopin manuscript he said might be a fraud, but maybe it is part of this missing collection and he doesn't know it. Or maybe he does. I believed him when I interviewed him and I can tell you that he was suddenly very afraid for his family's welfare. This, I believe, is a valid fear."

Connolly said, "I hope the cop-killer hasn't found him."

"You can be sure that if it's Stefanovic, he isn't working alone," Padlo said. "I can send you photos of the men who served with Rugova. If one of them has killed Middleton, it is to keep the location of the hidden treasure a secret. We're talking millions, maybe even billions of euros here."

"Send the pictures to my email address at the Bureau and I'll send the cop-killer's to you."

"Of course, Buttercup."

She smiled. "You know, Jozef, maybe I can get clearances and have a ticket for you at the airport. I mean, you know these people better than we do, and your assistance could be invaluable."

"Amazingly, I've already told my commissioner that by helping you we can quite possibly help solve Jedynak's murder and bring the killer back here to justice. Maybe you can arrange to have someone meet me at Dulles?"

"I think I can arrange that, Inspector Padlo."

The Slav's name was Vukasin, which meant Wolf, and he was not pleased with how badly things were going. Waiting in a car outside the St. Regis for two of his men, he stiffened at the sight of the elegant woman who had climbed from a cab across the street. She approached his vehicle, opened the door and slid inside.

"Eleana," he said in their native tongue, "your timing is perfect."

"How could I pass up an opportunity to work with dear old friends? And it's Jessica, please."

"Jessica. Very American. Good."

The woman seated beside Vukasin was a Serbian national named Eleana Soberski who was now, thanks to forged documents, a U.S. citizen. Soberski had been a child psychologist before serving as an Intel gatherer assigned to Rugova's forces. The real Jessica Harris had been a volunteer nurse at the central hospital in Belgrade, a woman without close family in the States. She had become eel food in the Danube, compliments of the woman aspiring to steal her identity.

Soberski's primary duty with the KLA during the cleansing action had been interrogating captured enemy soldiers and civilians collected by Rugova's unit. Vukasin, one of Rugova's lieutenants, had seen her work and admired her interrogation methods and enthusiasm. A beauty without a sympathy gene, she rejected the soldiers' overtures and Vukasin came to believe she derived sexual pleasure only when she had utterly terrified people lashed to a table, a chair or hanging from the rafters in excruciating pain.

"Your target is here at this hotel?" she asked.

Vukasin took a picture of two men at a table in a restaurant out of his pocket and handed it to her. "The target is this one—Harold Middleton, who led the Volunteers that tracked Agim and found him."

Her expression hardened. "This is Harold Middleton? I thought he would be more impressive. Where is he?"

"We're not yet sure."

"And you believe he will come here. To a bar. In public."

Vukasin nodded. His ex-wife had been persuaded by his men to list places were Middleton might flee. The St. Regis was one.

"Do you have men inside there?" Harris asked.

"They're on the way." Vukasin smiled. "They're disguised as FBI agents. It will be effective: Middleton is wanted for shooting a policeman at the airport."

"A policeman?"

Vukasin explained.

"A fiasco," Harris said. "Where is Dragan now?"

"Deceased. What choice did I have? He put everything at risk."

"And why do we care about Middleton?"

Vukasin took the picture from her. "This other man is Henryk Jedynak, a collector and expert in rare music documents. Jedynak is no longer with us either. You can ask Middleton why."

"I will gladly do so," Harris replied. "But surely there is more to this than the death of music collector . . . "

Vukasin was tired, but it was the true she needed to know what the mission was. Now was a good time to tell her.

"Middleton was at St. Sophia with the peace keepers and he was among those given the task of cataloguing the musical manuscripts—the ones that remained at the church before we could remove them. Three years ago, Jedynak was asked to authenticate a few of the manuscripts Middleton left behind. When they were to be sold to a private collector, it was discovered that Jedynak replaced the manuscripts with fakes."

"The seller was Rugova," Vukasin added.

"And he expected a price sufficient to cover his costs of buying his freedom," Harris said.

"When I interrogated Jedynak, he admitted to his crime, but I could not persuade him to tell me where the original manuscripts were."

Harris smiled wryly. Vukasin knew only violence, and not the more subtle and sophisticated methods that were needed when interrogating true believers.

"He did tell me that Middleton was in possession of something he doesn't know he has, but would discover it soon enough."

"You squandered a valuable resource."

"I hardly need you to tell me what I have or haven't done."

But it was so. Jedynak had taken knowledge to the grave, and now his niece was gone too—stolen from under the noses of his men in Rome. What she knows remained a mystery.

Vukasin said, "I believe the key is somehow in a Chopin manuscript Jedynak gave to Middleton."

"Real or fake?" Harris asked.

Vukasin looked at her and raised an eyebrow. There was no reason to believe Jedynak could've known the real manuscript needed to be moved now. Vukasin had waited three years to seek its return.

Harris saw Vukasin bristle. "It was you who got to Rugova and his wife, wasn't it?" she asked, her voice rich with flattery.

Vukasin nodded. He was glad to tell her about how he'd accomplished the seemingly impossible.

"Colonel Rugova was desperate," he said. "Guards were bribed ahead of my visit, and I went in disguised as a lawyer from the Tribunal needing Rugova's signature on some documents. My fountain pen leaked, and the poisoned ink on the colonel's fingers did its job in seven or eight hours."

Vukasin smiled. "You know, the colonel was glad to see me. He was amused by my disguise, and very pleased when I told him we had a plan to get him to safety. He was unaware, of course, his wife had surrendered his journals—we had everything he was going to use for leverage. He even named the men who paid him for the treasures—his benefactors. In the end, the great Colonel Rugova was a simple coward without loyalty or honor."

"I wish I could have been there."

Vukasin lit a small cigar and watched as a car pulled up. His two men exited and entered the hotel side by side.

"Now we'll see if Middleton is inside," he said.

"And if he's not . . . ?"

"His daughter," he replied. "Charlotte. Pregnant, by the way."

"Once I have Charlotte in the same room with him . . . " She smiled at the thought and rubbed her long delicate hands together vigorously. "Does he love anybody else?"

"A woman he worked with named Tesla. Leonora Tesla."

"If we had the Tesla woman, that might almost be as effective—if he still cares about her. But a pregnant daughter is preferable."

7

DAVID CORBETT

The car's interior reeked of almost archeological skank, old greasy food wrappers gumming the floor, malt liquor cans cluttering the wheel wells, ashtrays brimming with stale butts. The air-conditioner stuttered and coughed, exhaling a mildewy coolness, while the three bodies added an additional tang of gamey sweat—not just Middleton but Marcus and Traci, his would-be muggers. He'd learned their names from the nonstop badgering back and forth, relentless recriminations salted with snapshot details from their shattered biographies—their fumbling needs, their aching wants, their pitiless crank habits, promises to amend, curses in reply, testaments fired back and forth in a fierce vulgar slang that Middleton could barely decipher. Meanwhile, the car bumped and rattled north toward Baltimore, a lone headlight pointing the way along I-495's rain-wet asphalt. A brief summer storm had come and gone, turning the night air cottony thick and hot, against which the dying air-conditioner merely chattered. Middleton's sport jacket clung to his shoulders and arms like a second skin, and he wiped his face with his free hand, the other damply gripping the Beretta.

Finally, if only to ward off his nausea, he broke into the front-seat argument with, "Turn on the radio," nudging Marcus's shoulder with the pistol.

The youth turned just slightly. His cheek was mottled with small white sores. "Hey, me and Traci got things to discuss here."

Middleton lodged the tip of the pistol's barrel into Marcus's neck. "I said turn on the radio. I can't think."

"Don't jump the rail there, Mr. Gray." This was Traci, at the wheel, eyeing him over her shoulder. "You kidnap us, threaten us, we doin' all you ask. Be cool now. Don't play. Not with that gun."

They'd been calling him that since he'd climbed in the car: Mr. Gray. At first he'd thought it referred to his rumpled appearance, which was only worsening with the strain, the need for sleep. But he'd caught an edge of racial mockery in it too. Wasn't it Cab Calloway, in his Hepcat's Dictionary, who'd referred to white people as grays? But that was so very long ago, before these two were born. Christ, before even Middleton himself was born . . .

"I'm not playing," he said.

"All I mean—"

"Turn on the damn radio!"

Marcus's hand shot toward the dash and punched the On button. Middleton recoiled at the instant blast of menace, a lilting growl of bragging bullshit warring with a jackhammer bass track and droning synthesized mush, all inflicted at ear-splitting volume.

"Change the station."

"Whoa, mack, you got a serious pushy streak."

"Change the station. Now!"

Marcus huffed but obliged, fiddling through crackling sheets of white noise, punctuated by sudden twangy cries, garbled Bible-drunk voices . . .

Traci said, "You need to put a chill on, Mr. Gray. Break it back, let the little shit slide."

Suddenly, the reedy cry of woodwinds broke through. A soprano lilting through a familiar bar of haunting Sprechstimme. Middleton shot forward. "There! Stop!"

Marcus looked like he'd been told to swallow a toad. "This?"

"Tune it in. Get rid of the static."

"No, no. Taking us prisoner, that's wack enough. You can't torture us too."

"Tune it in!"

The piece was Pierrot Lunaire by Schoenberg, 21 songs scored for five musicians on eight instruments, plus voice, with the lyrics half-sung, half-spoken, the first twelve-tone masterpiece of the 20th century. Incomprehensible noise to most people, but not to Middleton, not to anyone who understood, who could hear in it the last throes of Romanticism, with echoes of not just Mahler and Strauss, but Bach.

"Maybe you're the one who should chill," Middleton said, easing back in his seat a little. "You think your generation invented rap or hip-hop? Spoken word with musical background goes back over four hundred years. It's called recitatif. Here, though, Schoenberg's notes are scored, but in speech we never stay on a single pitch, our voices glide on and off a tone. That's what the soprano's doing. It's left entirely up to her how she does it. Meanwhile, the instruments are conjuring up the landscape: there's moonlight, insanity, blood . . . "

Traci was leaning ever so slightly toward the speaker, intrigued now.

Eyeing the Beretta with a newfound skepticism, Marcus said, "You a professor?"

"Sshhh." It was Traci. The gaunt young coffee-skinned woman with glowing eyes and mussed Afro was rapt. "Act like you got some sense."

Sulking, Marcus flopped back against the door, moodily scratching his scabbed arm.

Finally, they were quiet; Middleton had his chance to think. But the eerie music, with its tale of the moon-obsessed clown and his Freudian nightmares, only enhanced his dread. Where was Charley, was she safe? Who tried to kill him at Dulles, what was the man after? And what was waiting for him at 122 Fremont Avenue, in the city of Baltimore?

The possible danger to Charley only amplified the need to decipher the threat. His mind spun around and around like that, addled by the fatigue, his fear, thoughts careening against each other senselessly. Meanwhile:

> With a white speck of the bright moon
> On the shoulder of his black frock coat,
> Pierrot saunters off this languid evening
> To seek his fortune and look for adventure . . .

Nodding toward the radio, Marcus said, "Sounds like the same old screechy shit, over and over."

"Not if you understand German." Middleton rubbed his burning eyes. "And you're not listening to the accompaniment."

"It's edgy," Traci offered, striving for a compliment, though she'd clearly lost interest already.

Marcus sniffed. "Sounds like some kind of secret code, you ask me."

"Funny you should say that." Middleton stared out the grimy window at the blurring trees. "There were rumors during World War II that the Nazis were using twelve-tone music to send messages to sympathizers in the American cultural elite. There's no standard melody, people can't pick out a wrong note—"

"Sounds like nothing but wrong notes."

"Exactly. All the easier to hide a message in it. Who's going to know when the music is off?"

He flashed on the Chopin manuscript in his briefcase, the one he'd thought the Polish authorities had wanted when they'd stopped him at the Krakow airport. His conviction it wasn't genuine lay exactly in several passages of oddly discordant cadences, unlike the meticulously melodic Chopin. What if it's a code, he wondered. What if it's not the manuscript or the other music they're after, but something far more valuable, something only to be found by decrypting the counterfeit folios?

Inspired suddenly, he reached down for his briefcase to check the manuscript—only to realize the briefcase wasn't there.

No please, he thought. Dear God. He mentally backtracked to the St. Regis, remembered placing his cell phone in his pocket at the restroom sink, then shambling out to the bar, checking his ravaged, hopelessly memorable reflection in the mirror before dropping the cell phone into his briefcase, snapping it shut. Had he then just wandered off without it? How dementedly absent-minded. It was one more sign of how addled, scattered— moonstruck, like mad Pierrot—he'd become.

"Turn the car around."

Traci glowered over her shoulder. "Come again?"

"Turn the car around! We're going back to the hotel."

The two hapless thieves glanced back and forth. Marcus said, "Check out your eyes, mack."

Traci chimed in, "You beginning to scare me, Mr. Gray."

Middleton lifted the Beretta, placed the tip of the barrel against the back passenger-side window, and pulled the trigger. The thundering report in the small car, topped by the piercing hiss of shattered glass, deafened him again. Traci opened her mouth in a silent scream, hunching forward in terror as she fumbled to maintain hold of the steering wheel. Marcus clutched his head, staring at the gun with wide-eyed dread. The burnt sulfur smell of cordite, fanned by the sudden gust of black wet summer heat, finally masked the stench of the car's moldering interior.

Middleton reached forward, clutched Marcus's collar with his free hand while jabbing the pistol forward. As before at the airport, every sound came swathed in invisible muck, and yet from somewhere deep within his thrumming skull he heard the underwater roar of his own words, shouted at Traci: "I said turn the car around or I swear to God I'll kill him—I'll kill him, understand? Right here. I'll kill you too."

Struggling weakly in Middleton's grip, Marcus started to tremble uncontrollably. Reaching across the car, Traci tried to soothe him, the lilt of her gentling words finally beginning to register as, with a hateful glance over her shoulder, she merged right to make the coming exit.

Gradually, even the crackling radio, the abstract insistence of Pierrot Lunaire, returned. Middleton wondered: Who have I become?

Conrad the bartender held the manuscript, paging through it gingerly. It seemed very old—the paper faded and brittle, the notations handwritten, not printed like the ones he'd bought Jennifer before. She'd love this, he thought, feeling a surge of inner heat. Chopin. She'll throw her arms around his neck, press her cheek to his.

He lived to dote on his niece, buy her things—toys when she was younger, bits of modest clothing, sheet music now that she'd started piano lessons. A gifted girl, his sister's oldest, just turned nine. Growing a little awkward now that she was shooting up in height, leaving the baby fat behind, but still with that shimmering black hair, halfway down her back, the vaguely lost blue eyes, the porcelain skin. Black Irish, like her wretch of a father, wherever he might be. Prison. The grave. Back in Carrickfergus. Someone had to look after the girl, she needed a man in her life. And her uncle loved her. He loved her very much.

Her musical turn the past two years had proved a welcome change. He didn't have to just sit on the sofa and watch her gambol about on the floor in her school jumper and socks. He could sit there beside her now, turning the pages as she played the Schumann he'd bought her. Scenes from a Childhood. Album for the Young. With the vanilla scent of her shampoo thick between them, her hands faltering in painful discords across the keys, he'd gently nudge closer, until their thighs touched, the rustle of her sleeve against his. That was enough, he'd remind himself. No more, not yet. Content yourself with this. But someday. Perhaps. If she wants to.

Such thoughts, such images, so terrible, so welcome, like the devil whispering in his ear: It's what you've always wanted. He lived for that, too.

He let the warmth subside from his face as he rolled up the manuscript and put it in the pocket of his sport jacket, draped on its peg on the storeroom wall. As he returned to the bar, two men entered from the hotel lobby, dressed in blue sport coats and gray slacks, one of them tall with an edgy fluid rhythm in his gait. The other was broad and muscular, with a bull-like neck, small dead eyes. The tall one offered an empty smile and slid a business card across the bar. It bore the seal of the FBI. Behind him, the hefty one remained expressionless.

There was no one else in the bar. It had been deathly slow all night.

The tall one, leaning forward to read the bartender's nametag, said, "Good evening, Conrad. A middle-aged man came in earlier, probably a little uneasy, rattled. He shot a peace officer out at the Dulles airport, then fled the scene. We have some indication the shooting may be terrorist-related. His cell phone placed him here just a short while back. It's very important we track his whereabouts. You recall him, yes?"

Conrad knew exactly the man they were talking about, but he couldn't convince himself just yet that admitting as much was wise. "The description you just gave," he said, "that could fit just about every guy who's been in here the past few hours. I mean, I'd like to help, but—"

The tall one wasn't listening. He'd spotted the briefcase behind the bar.

It belonged to the stranger from earlier, the one who looked like he'd wandered in from a car wreck. A cop-killer, they said. Apparently, a musical one. Conrad had found his briefcase while straightening the barstools, and he'd glanced inside, hoping to find some identification, only to discover the Chopin instead.

The tall one refreshed his vacant smile. "Would you mind handing that to me?" He nodded toward the briefcase and held out his hand. "I'd like to take a glance inside."

Conrad hesitated, yielding to an inchoate fear of being found out.

"Just to be clear, Conrad. National security's involved. We have broad powers. So." He wiggled his fingers. "If you would please."

Conrad collected the briefcase and handed it across the bar, figuring he had little choice. The tall one took it greedily and immediately opened it up, searching the contents brusquely. His partner just stood there, a little ways behind, his huge arms folded across his massive chest.

"It's not here," the tall one said finally. He looked over his shoulder at his partner, then back toward Conrad. The empty smile was now pitiless. "Something's missing. But you know that already—don't you, Conrad?"

Conrad felt the floor sway beneath him, his viscera coiled. An inner voice said, They're going to find out your dirty little secret. Before he could think through the consequences, he heard himself say, "I don't know what you mean," his voice faltering. He pictured Jennifer sitting sad-eyed and prim on her shiny black piano bench, waiting for her only uncle, smelling of breath mints and aftershave, to settle in beside her.

"The sheet music, Conrad. It's supposed to be inside. It's not. Fetch it for us now. Before I lose my temper."

It was only then that Conrad realized what it was that bothered him about the man's voice. The accent. Canadian, he thought. Can Canadians join the FBI?

"Look, I'm not trying to be difficult, but I honestly don't know what you're talking about."

The tall one glanced past the bartender to the storeroom door; they'd seen him closing it behind him as they'd entered from the lobby. The agent nodded for his muscular partner to have a look.

"You can't go back there." Conrad felt a trickle of sweat feathering down his back.

"And why is that?"

"It's hotel property."

The tall man grinned. "And?"

The hefty one was behind the bar now. He gave Conrad a snide pat on the cheek, then opened the storeroom door.

His partner said, "It's in your best interests to offer full cooperation. I'm a little disappointed I have to explain that."

"You get out first."

Middleton waved Marcus onto the sidewalk with the Beretta. Opening his own door, he sent one last shower of broken glass tumbling, the spiny fragments toppling down his sleeve. Closing the door behind him, he told Traci through the jagged maw where the window had been, "Wait here. There's something I left behind. We'll only be a minute."

The young woman said nothing, just sat there gripping the wheel, seething.

Middleton plunged the pistol into his sport-coat pocket, taking Marcus's elbow and gripping it tight. "Come on. We'll make this quick."

They were halfway between the street and the hotel's revolving door when the car peeled out behind them. Both of them turned, watching Traci flee, Middleton feeling his jaw drop. The car reached the corner in one long burst of speed, then a squeal of brakes, a swerving turn. Gone.

Before Middleton could gather his wits, the youth shook off his grip and swept a cracking left across Middleton's jaw, then darted off, running as fast as his stick-thin legs could carry him. Reeling back on his heels, Middleton gathered his balance but then just stared, rubbing his stubbled chin as the scrawny boy vanished down the wet street.

An hour's gone by, Middleton thought, since I last stood here, this very spot. Nothing's changed. Except, perhaps, everything.

He entered the lobby wiping his face with his handkerchief, hoping he didn't look as raw and untethered as he felt. The desk clerk, recognizing him from earlier, smiled blankly. A well-dressed woman with a slim valise, possibly a call girl, waited at the elevator.

Finding his way to the small dark bar, Middleton crossed the threshold, then stopped. The bartender was wrestling with a man much bigger than he was, while another, taller man looked on. The two strangers were dressed almost identically: blue blazers and gray slacks, Oxford button-downs and forgettable ties, none of which matched their demeanor. The tall one looked on with a cold curiosity; sadism curdled his smile. He held Middleton's briefcase in his hand while examining a cell phone that Middleton quickly recognized as his. Meanwhile, the other one, who looked much stronger, had the bartender in a headlock, punching him brutally with his free hand. The bartender's arm was outstretched, the Chopin folio clutched tight in his fist.

As Middleton registered all this, the one with the briefcase turned toward him. You have no time, Middleton realized, as a scowl of recognition crossed the other man's face. Tugging the Beretta from his pocket, Middleton charged forward as the man dropped the cell phone and plunged his hand inside his sport coat. Middleton aimed and placed two quick shots into the fleshy center of the tall man's face, trusting the bullets would pierce the cartilage around the nose and lodge deep inside the brain.

The man tottered, his head jerking but his ugly expression strangely unchanged. Then he buckled and dropped.

Stunned by the gunshots, the thick man shoved the bartender aside and crouched, reaching for his own weapon. Middleton swung around, took a quick step forward, aimed and fired two more shots, close range, the soft center of the face again. The man wavered, visage threaded with blood, before dropping to one knee, grabbing at the edge of the bar, then sliding down in fitful spasms.

The bartender recoiled, horrified. Middleton heard steps coming from the lobby, the gasps of unseen onlookers, as he reached out his hand.

"Give that to me." He gestured for the manuscript. When the bartender merely stared, Middleton turned the gun toward him. "I don't have time."

The bartender hesitated, then dropped the mangled folio onto the bar, his face half terror, half desolation. Middleton snatched his briefcase from the floor, stuffed his cell phone then the manuscript inside, then headed toward the scattering crowd in the lobby, the Beretta still in his hand.

The well-dressed woman who'd been near the elevators earlier slipped up behind, tucked her hand inside his arm and clutched his damp sleeve. She guided him across the lobby. "Don't stop, Harry," she whispered. "Not if you want to see Charlotte."

8

JOHN GILSTRAP

Felicia Kaminski had always loved the idea of airports. As a child in a family that never went anywhere, she used to envy the friends who would take their holidays in places that were far enough away to be flown to. Trains were a thrill in their own right, but only at airports did you find people who are going far enough away to actually change their lives. Having dreamed of the moment for so long, she was finally about to climb on her very first airplane—to fly to the United States. In first class, no less.

Fiumicino International Airport teemed with travelers mingling in their common mission to check in and navigate their way to their departure gates. Felicia Kaminski—no, Joanna Phelps; she might have to remember that—found herself distracted by one family in particular as a mother and father did their best to herd six children toward the security lines. It looked a lot like pushing water up hill. She found herself smiling.

Then she forced herself to concentrate. After this morning's events, she needed to be vigilant. Clearly, she was a target and if another attacker wanted to hurt her, she would most certainly be hurt. It helped that every 10th person in the airport was a carabinieri with a machine gun slung over his shoulder. It seemed to her like a very bad place to attempt murder.

The afternoon's events were unfolding exactly as Faust had predicted. Freshly cleaned and redressed, he'd led her downstairs through the lobby of the hotel, where two Mercedes sedans stood waiting with their engines running. He ushered her to the first vehicle while he climbed into the back seat of the other. They'd pulled away from the curb together, but then split into different directions, her car going right while his went left, and she hadn't seen any sign of him since.

"I understand that you haven't traveled much," her driver said in passable Polish. She couldn't quite place the accent. "Do you know how the check-in process works?"

Kaminski hated the patronizing tone, but had to confess her ignorance. The driver—Peter, if he'd told her the truth—took her through the process step by step, from check-in at the ticket counter, to the passage through security, and on to the boarding process itself. The only real surprise came from the requirement to take her shoes off to go through the metal detectors. She was well aware of the detectors themselves, of course, but it just hadn't occurred to her that she would have to strip off articles of clothing.

"Are you going to walk through the process with me?" she'd asked when Peter had finished.

"No, Miss Phelps, I'm afraid that will not be possible. Security at the airport is very tight these days. I must stay with the car and drive away as soon as I drop you off. You will be on your own."

"Where is Faust?"

Peter's eyes found hers in the rearview mirror. For a long moment, he said nothing. "He will be where he needs to be at the correct time. What is most important is that you remember to show no sign of recognition if you see him again. Let him make that move."

"I remember," she said. I'm in no hurry to know him anyway.

Having arrived at the airport with nearly three hours to spare, Felicia moved quickly to get through the check-in process at the ticket counter, but then took her time heading for security. Befitting her first-class status, Faust had given her 300 U.S. dollars to fill her wallet, and she decided to put some of the windfall to good use at an airport coffee shop. She found a table at the edge of the concourse, one that offered a broad view of the security lines. It was a sea of people, shoulder to shoulder in a human corral.

On the far side of the crowd, she could see the first-class security area, where the crowds were much thinner and better organized, and that was where she concentrated her attention. It was there that she predicted that things were about to get exciting.

It took long enough that she had to order a second espresso—surrendering herself to the inevitability of being wide-eyed all night—but after 45 minutes, she saw what she'd been waiting for. Faust finally entered the line. In his business attire, he looked completely at home among the other wealthy travelers.

From 15 meters away, she watched as the man who'd saved her life shrugged out of his suit jacket and stepped out of his shoes. He placed his briefcase on the belt for the x-ray machine, then stepped through the narrow archway of the metal detector.

Kaminski's heart hammered against her ribs as she began to wonder if something had gone wrong. There should be a reaction by now. There should—

Suddenly, an alarm erupted and a red light strobed urgently over the security checkpoint. It was the kind of noise and light that guaranteed attention and made people instinctively want to run away. All except for the carabinieri, that is, who swarmed from all over the concourse to respond to the threat.

Biting the inside of her cheek to stifle any sign of the satisfied smile that might draw attention to her, Kaminski pushed away from the table and started walking toward the taxi stands at the front of the airport. Before that, she needed to find a cambio, where she could convert her windfall of U.S. dollars into more readily spent euros. She knew she had time—Faust would be busy with the carabinieri for at least a couple of hours, she imagined— and she hoped that even a short delay would provide enough time for her to do what she needed to do and then disappear.

Meanwhile, the officials at the airport would be turning Faust's luggage inside out as they looked for the pistol that showed up so clearly in the x-ray. Ultimately, probably in fairly short order, they'd find the source of their alarm.

She wondered if any of them would even smile when they realized that they'd mobilized dozens of policia because a businessman had covered a water pistol with a foil wrapper and stuffed it in one of the file pockets of his brief case.

Felicia Kaminski left the airport with none of her new clothes—none but what she wore, that is. Her fancy new suitcase was somewhere in the bowels of the airport, already checked and on its way to the aircraft that would dead-head it to New York. She kept the money too, but beyond that, she carried only those items that were rightfully hers—her backpack and her violin.

She had the taxi drop her at the foot of Via dei Polacchi, and she added a generous tip to the fare. What was the point of a windfall if it couldn't be shared with others? The driver thanked her effusively and offered three times to wait for her while she ran whatever errand she was on, but after she'd steadfastly refused, he finally understood that her insistent "no" meant just that, and he drove on.

She waited until the taxi was out of sight around the corner before she started walking up the hill. She'd never actually visited the shop she was looking for—La Musica—but she'd sipped coffee with Abe Nowakowski, the proprietor, several times since she'd arrived in Rome. Signor Abe and her uncle had shared a childhood, it turned out, living only a few houses away from each other in the old country. Uncle Henryk had asked his friend to look in on her from time to time. During their last meeting, at a cafe near the Pantheon, only a few dozen meters from the spot where she had first encountered the man who called himself Faust, Abe's demeanor had been different than it had been before. His easy humor seemed clouded by something dark.

During one of her visits, she asked, "Are you feeling all right?"

He'd smiled, but it wasn't convincing. "I am just getting old, that is all," he said. He paused a moment before adding, "I am concerned for you, Felicia."

So that was it. "I enjoy my life, Signor Abe. I understand that you worry about me, but as I've told you before—"

He cut her off with a dismissive flick of his hand. "I know what you have to say, so let's pretend that you have already said it and move on. I want you to promise me something."

She cocked her head, waiting. When dealing with her uncle's generation, it never paid to make a promise before all terms had been revealed.

"If anything happens to you, if ever you are in any trouble, I want you to come to me."

Looking back on the conversation now, she wondered if Signor Abe hadn't known something. Even at the time, she'd felt her pulse quicken with his sense of urgent mystery.

He'd read her expression exactly, and hurried to soothe her. "I don't mean to frighten you," he'd said. "As I get older I sometimes worry about things that perhaps I shouldn't. But if there ever comes a time when you feel as if you are in danger—or even if there comes a time when you merely feel lonely or hungry for some of my fettuccini—I want you to promise that you will come by the shop. I worry that I am not showing you the hospitality that I should. I don't want to disappoint my dear friend Henryk."

That conversation had taken place only two weeks ago. Now, as she walked purposefully up the hill, she forced her mind to think of music. If she could bridge the synapses of her brain with triplettes and chromatic scales, maybe there would be no room left for her fear. No room left for the looming grief that awaited her when she finally confronted the fact of her uncle's death.

She walked faster. The increased tempo brought to her imagination the sound of American bluegrass music—fiddle music instead of the violin—a music form that she'd never taken seriously until she'd listened to a CD that featured Yo Yo Ma bringing sounds out of his cello that she had never heard before. She heard alternating strains of joy and melancholy. She'd tried to recreate the sounds in her own violin, but could never quite discover them. It was as if those particular strands of musical DNA could not be found in an instrument played by a Polish girl whose childhood was steeped in classical training.

Kaminski saw the sign for La Musica from a block away, and instantly wished that the walk could have been longer. With a few more steps, perhaps she could have found the emotional strength she craved, the strength she needed before breaking terrible news to such a nice man. But it was not to be. She had arrived, and she could think of no reason not to enter the shop.

Passing across the threshold was like stepping backward a hundred years. Narrow, dark and deep, the shop reminded her of a cave; where there would be bats, dozens of violins and violas and cellos hung instead from the ceiling, each of them glimmering as if they'd been freshly dusted. Double basses lined the left-hand wall, and along the right, countless pages of sheet music peeked out from above their wooden racks. At the very back of the store . . .

Actually, she couldn't see the back of the store through the shadows that cloaked it.

"Felicia?"

The voice came from behind her—from the cash register she had not seen, hidden away as it was around the corner at the very front of the store. She instantly recognized the heavily accented voice as that of Signor Abe, but she jumped anyway as she whirled to look at him.

"Felicia, what's wrong?" Even as he spoke, he was on his way around to the front of the tiny counter, moving as quickly as his arthritic hips would allow him. "What has happened?"

The flood of emotion hit out of nowhere, all at once. "Uncle Henryk is dead," she managed to say, but her next words were lost in her sobs.

Abe Nowakowski locked the door to his shop at mid-day, something he'd never done before, and helped his beautiful young friend up the back steps to his flat on the second floor. There he fixed her some tea and listened to her story.

Kaminski hated herself for losing control of her emotions this way, but there were times in the next hour when she feared that her tears would never stop. They did, of course, eventually, but she sensed that Signor Abe would have sat with her for as long as he needed to.

"These things take time," he said. He was a little man, a round man, with leathery skin and thick white hair that could never be tamed by a comb. When he spoke softly like this, his normally strong voice grew raspy. "I lost my Maria six years ago now, and while sometimes it feels as though the hole in my heart has healed, there are days when the pain is as raw as the day she died. I've come to think of the pain as proof that I loved her as much as I told her I did."

The tea was awful, overly strong and overly sweet. "Did you know this might happen to my uncle, Signor Abe?" she asked.

The question seemed to startle the old man.

"The other day, when we met for coffee, you asked me to make a promise. I made it, and here I am. But I was wondering . . . "

She let her voice trail as Signor Abe let his gaze fall to his lap. The body language answered her question; now she hoped that he wouldn't dishonor her uncle's memory with a transparent lie to protect her feelings.

"I had an inkling, yes," he said. "Your uncle called me shortly before you and I met. He seemed . . . agitated. He spoke hurriedly, as if he were trying to get his message out before he could be interrupted. Or perhaps before he could change his mind." Nowakowski took a deep breath and let it go slowly. When he resumed speaking, his rasp had deepened. "He told me that he would be sending me a package for safe keeping. He said that it would be too dangerous for him to have the package with him and that by sending it to me it would truly be safe."

"Did the package come?"

He ignored the interruption. "I of course agreed, but then he called the very next day. This time, he was clearly frightened. He said that he hadn't thought things through very clearly before he mailed it and he was terrified that people might think that he had sent it to you instead. It's what people would naturally think of anything he sent to Rome. He asked me to check in with you more frequently and to try and find out if you had been in any danger. He wanted me to do this without alarming you, of course."

"What kind of danger?"

The old man rose from the table to return to the stove. "Before today, I wouldn't have been able to tell you. I think now we know. More tea, Felicia?"

She recoiled from the thought and tried to cover the reaction with, "I've been drinking coffee all day. I don't need my hands to shake more than they already do."

Nowakowski gave a knowing smile and limped back to the table. "Yes, I've been told that I make it a bit too strong. One of the hazards of not having very many guests, I suppose."

"About the package," she pressed. "Did you ever receive it?"

"I did." He spoke the words as if his explanation was complete.

"What was it?"

Signor Abe's gaze dropped again. Kaminski realized that this was his habit when he was embarrassed. "Dear Henryk asked me specifically not to open the package when it arrived. He told me that it would arrive double-wrapped, and that if anything ever happened to him, I was to open only the outer wrapping and then contact the name I found on the card taped to the inner wrapping."

"But you opened it anyway," she said, connecting the dots.

"Loneliness breeds weakness and curiosity," he replied sadly. "And I'm afraid that I have been particularly lonely."

"So what was in it?" She found the old man's embarrassment charming, but she'd have ripped it open in a second if she'd have been in his place. No reason for shame there.

He thought for a moment, and then rose again from his chair. He disappeared into what must have been the bedroom, and then returned less than a minute later with a thick, mangled envelope. "I tried to re-wrap it," he confessed, "but I'm afraid I made something of a mess."

The envelope was a large one, more suitable to construction blueprints than a letter. He handled the package gently, with reverence, almost, as he placed it onto the table between them. When Felicia reached toward it, he shooed her hands away.

"Please," he said curtly. "Allow me to do this."

She folded her hands on her lap.

The old man wiped his hands aggressively with a napkin, and then carefully slid the contents into the daylight.

Kaminski leaned closer. She saw a stack of papers. Her first impression was that it was very old—yellow with the kinds of marks that could only be made with an old style ink pen. As more of the contents were revealed, she squinted and leaned even closer. "It's a musical score," she said, recognizing the rows of staves.

Nowakowski allowed himself a conspiratorial smile. "Much more than that," he said. He gently placed it on top of the envelope and turned it so that she could better read his treasure.

My God. Could it be what she thought? There was no mistaking the long runs of sixteenth notes and the other musical notations, but as exotic as they looked written by hand, her eyes were drawn to the written signature at the top. In her circles, there was no more famous a signature.

"Mozart?" she gasped.

"An original," he beamed. "Or at least I think it is."

She didn't know what to say. "It must be worth a fortune."

"Three fortunes," he corrected. "Priceless, I would think. It's clearly a piano concerto, but I've searched the Koechel Catalogue and this isn't there. I think this is an undiscovered work."

She recognized the Koechel Catalogue as the internationally recognized indexer of Mozart's myriad compositions. If Signor Abe was right, then there truly was no way to estimate the value of the manuscript. "This is fabulous," she said. "But I don't understand why it frightened Uncle Henryk. This could have answered all of his wildest dreams. Honestly, this is the kind of discovery that he would have given anything to make. Why would he keep it a secret? Why would he send it away?"

"All very good questions," Nowakowski agreed. "But I have an even bigger one."

She waited for it while the old man slid the inner envelope out from under the manuscript. She saw a name, but there was no address.

He said, "Who is this Harold Middleton and how are we supposed to find him?"

9

JOSEPH FINDER

The moment her Nextel phone chirped, Special Agent M. T. Connolly had a bad feeling.

She'd just gotten into the elevator at the brand-new building that housed the FBI's Northern Virginia Resident Agency, on her way back to her office. It was a cubicle, actually, not an office, but she could always dream.

Glancing at the caller ID, she immediately recognized the area code and exchange prefix: the call came from the Hoover building—FBI headquarters in D.C. Not good. Only bad news came from the Hoover building, she'd learned. She stepped out of the elevator and back onto the gleaming terrazzo floor of the lobby.

"Connolly," she said.

A man's voice, reedy and overly precise: "This is Emmett Kalmbach."

He didn't actually have to identify himself; she'd have recognized the prissy enunciation anywhere. Kalmbach was the FBI's Assistant Director who oversaw the hundreds of agents in D.C. and Virginia who worked out of the Washington Field Office as well as her satellite office in Manassas, Virginia. She'd met Kalmbach a few times, enough to recognize his type: the worst kind of kiss-up, kick-down bureaucratic infighter. A paper-pushing rattlesnake.

Kalmbach had no reason to call her directly. At least, no good reason.

And why was he calling from the FBI's national headquarters, instead of from his office on Fourth Street?

"Yes, sir," she said. She sounded blasé, but she felt her stomach clench. She watched the brushed-steel elevator doors glide shut in front of her. The two halves of a giant fingerprint, etched on the elevator doors, came together. The fingerprint had been some government committee's idea of art, which was precisely what it looked like: art by government committee.

"Agent Connolly, who is Jozef Padlo?"

Ah ha. "He's an inspector with the Polish National Police and he's working a triple homicide in Warsaw that—

"Agent—Marion, if I may—"

"M. T., sir."

But he went on smoothly, ignoring her: "—Our legat in Warsaw just emailed me a letter rogatory from the Polish Ministry of Justice, requesting that we grant immediate entry into the U.S. to this . . . Jozef Padlo. He says you personally guaranteed him clearance. Our legat is understandably ticked off."

So this was what he was calling about. She hadn't gone through channels, so some junior FBI paper-pusher, who'd picked the short straw and had ended up assigned to the American Embassy Bureau in Warsaw, had gotten bent out of shape.

"Obviously there was some translation problem," she said. "I didn't guarantee anything to Inspector Padlo. He's provided invaluable assistance to us in a case at Dulles involving the murder of one, possibly two, cops. Since it seems to be connected to his triple homicide, he—"

"It 'seems to be connected,'" Kalmbach interrupted. "What's that supposed to mean?"

Trying to conceal her annoyance, she explained as crisply as she could. "Padlo was able to ID the shooter at Dulles as a Serb national and a war criminal who—"

"Excuse me, Agent Connolly. He ID'd the shooter based on what?"

"Surveillance video taken at Dulles."

"Ah. So Inspector Padlo viewed the video, then?"

She faltered. "No. I did. But Padlo made a positive ID based on my verbal description to him."

"Your . . . verbal description," Kalmbach echoed softly. Condescension dripped from every word.

"In fact—" she began, but Kalmbach cut her off.

"Do you understand how complex and involved the process is by which a foreign law enforcement official is granted entry into the United States? It involves weeks of legal findings and sworn affidavits by the DOJ's Criminal Division, the Office of International Affairs. It's a cumbersome and extremely sensitive legal affair and not one to be taken lightly. For one thing, there must be absolutely incontrovertible evidence of dual criminality."

Oh, for God's sake, she thought. The guy lived and breathed paperwork. It was a wonder he hadn't already died of white lung. "Sir, if Padlo's right then, those three homicides in Warsaw are tied to these police shootings at Dulles Airport and we've got a clear-cut case of dual criminality."

"A case built on a verbal description over the telephone, Agent Connolly? I hardly think that constitutes a finding of dual criminality. This is an awfully slender reed. I'm afraid we're not going to be able to grant a visa to Inspector Padlo."

Yeah, she thought. If Jozef wanted to get into the country quick and easy, no questions asked, he should just join Al Qaeda and enroll in flight school. We'd let him in without a second look.

But she said, "So you're saying that if we had a clear-cut ID of the shooter—connecting the Warsaw homicides to the Dulles ones—you'd have no problem letting Padlo in?"

"We don't have that, do we?" Kalmbach said acidly.

"No, sir," she said. "Not yet."

"Thank you, Agent . . . Marion."

"M. T.," she said.

But he'd hung up.

She'd been M. T. since the age of thirteen.

She'd always hated her given name, "Marion." Her father had also been Marion; but then, as he was always proud to point out, that was John Wayne's real name. In Gulfport, Mississippi, where Dad had been a part-time deputy in the Harrison County Sheriff's Department, the Duke was up there with Jesus Christ. Bigger, to some folks.

But to her, "Marion" was either a librarian or a housewife in a TV sit-com, and neither fit her self-image. She was a tomboy and proud of it. As tough as any boy, she had even beat up the seventh-grade class bully for daring to call her adored younger brother Wayne a "sissy."

So she insisted on being called by her initials, which to her ears sounded tough and no-nonsense and the exact opposite of girly-girl. Maybe even a little enigmatic.

Over the years, she'd learned about makeup, and she'd developed a pretty damned nice figure, and she worked out every morning at five for at least an hour. When she wanted to look hot, she could. And she knew that when she put on that slinky red jersey halter dress from Banana Republic she always drew appreciative glances from men.

At work, though, she downplayed her femininity as much as possible. The FBI was still a boys' club, and she was convinced that the guys took you a lot more seriously if you didn't arouse their libidos.

Like the guy who sat across from her right now. His name was Bruce Ardsley, and he was a forensic video analyst with the Bureau's Forensic Audio, Video, and Image Analysis Unit. The main FBI lab was in D.C., in the Hoover building, but they'd recently installed an outpost here because of all the demand on the Bureau since 9/11.

Ardsley wore thick aviator-frame glasses and had greasy hair and long bushy sideburns that might have been modish in the Swinging '70s, and he was notorious for trying to hit on all the female agents and administrative assistants. But he'd given up on her long ago. Now they got along fine.

His office, in the basement of the new resident agency building, was no bigger than a closet, jammed with steel shelves heaped with video monitors and digital editing decks and CPUs. Taped to one wall was a mangled poster of a man running up stadium steps. Above his blurred figure was the word PERSISTENCE. At his feet it said, "There is no GIANT step that does it. It's a lot of LITTLE steps."

She handed Ardsley two disks. "The one marked Dulles is from Dulles Airport," Connolly said.

"Clever."

She smiled. "The other has the photos from Warsaw." As he promised, Padlo had emailed her photos of Agim Rugova's henchmen. One of them was Dragan Stefanovic, the man Padlo thought might be the Dulles shooter who'd tried to kill Harold Middleton. Stefanovic had served under Agim Rugova, which made him a war criminal at the very least. After the war, Padlo said, he'd become a mercenary and had gone into hiding.

"High-def, I hope."

"I doubt it," she replied.

"Well, all I can do is my best," Ardsley said. "At least one thing in our favor is the new networked digital-video surveillance system at Dulles. The airports authority dumped a boatload of money on this a couple years ago. Bought a bunch of high-priced Nextiva S2600e wide-dynamic range IP cameras with on-board analytical software-based solutions."

"Translation, please," said Connolly.

"Meaning the facial-recognition software is still crap and the images are still fuzzy, but now we can all feel good about how much money we're throwing at the terrorists."

"And that's in our favor . . . how exactly?" she asked.

He pointed to the steel shelves lined with video monitors. "Once the Bureau realized how crappy the facial-recognition system is, they were forced to sink more money into toys for boys like me to play with. Remember the Super Bowl?"

She groaned. The FBI had put in an extensive surveillance system at the Super Bowl in Tampa in 2001 in order to scan the faces of everyone passing through the turnstiles and match them against the images of known terrorists. The ACLU pitched a fit—this was before 9/11, when people listened to the ACLU—but the whole scheme was a resounding flop anyway. The Bureau had rounded up a couple of scalpers and that was it. "You're telling me the technology's no better now?"

"Oh, it's better," Ardsley said. "Well, a little better."

Her phone chirped, and she excused herself and stepped out into the hallway.

"Connolly."

"Hey, M. T., it's Tanya Jackson in Technical Services."

"That was fast," she said. "You got something?"

She'd called the FBI's Technical Services unit and asked them to run a locater on Middleton's cell phone to find out where he was at that very instant.

Most cell phones these days, she knew, contained GPS chips that enabled you to pinpoint its location to within a hundred meters, as long as it was turned on and transmitting a signal.

"Well, not exactly," Jackson said. "There's sort of a procedural problem."

"Procedural? . . ."

"Look, M. T.," Jackson said apologetically, "you know we're no longer allowed to track cell phone users without a court order."

"Oh, is that right?" Connolly said innocently. Of course, she knew all about the recent rulings. Now you had to get a court order to compel a wireless carrier to reveal the location of one of their cell phones. And to get a court order, you had to demonstrate that a crime was in progress or had occurred.

But Jackson had done her favors before. She'd located cell phones for Connolly without the necessary paperwork. Why did she all of a sudden care about the legal niceties?

"Tanya," she said, "what's going on?"

There was silence on the other end of the line.

"You're getting heat on this, aren't you?" Connolly said.

Another beat of silence, and then Jackson said, "Five minutes after you called me, I heard from someone pretty high up in the Bureau. He reminded me that it was a felony for me to locate a cell phone without a court order. I could go to jail."

"I'm sorry I put you in that position," Connolly said.

"I just wanted you to understand."

"Tanya," Connolly said. "Was it Emmett Kalmbach, by any chance?"

"I—I can't answer that," Jackson said.

But she didn't have to.

"You're in luck," Bruce Ardsley said. He was beaming.

"Dragan Stefanovic is the shooter?"

He nodded.

"How certain can you be?"

"Ninety-seven percent probability of true verification."

"Bruce, that's fantastic." Take that, Kalmbach, she thought.

"The probability on the other one's lower, though."

"The other one?"

"Maybe seventy-eight percent probability."

"Which other one are you talking about?"

Ardsley swiveled around in his chair, tapped at a keyboard, and a large photographic image came up on the flat-screen monitor mounted on the wall in front of her. It was a close-up of a dark-haired man in his 40s wearing a dark, expensive-looking business suit. He had flat, Slavic facial features.

"Where was this taken?"

"A surveillance camera outside a men's room in Concourse D at Dulles."

"Who is it?" she said.

"Nigel Sedgwick."

"Who?"

Ardsley struck another key, and a second photo popped onto the screen next to the first.

"A British businessman. From Bromsgrove, in Worcestershire. That's England. Or so his passport said. Here in D.C. on a buying trip for his hot-tub business."

"Looks like it was taken at passport control," she said.

Ardsley turned around, shrugged modestly, smiled. "Right."

"How'd you get it?"

"I hacked into Homeland Security. Well, not hacked, really. Just used a backdoor into Customs and Border Protection's database."

"So who is this guy really?"

A third image appeared on the screen next to the other two. She immediately recognized the photo as one of the mug shots of Agim Rugova's men that Padlo had emailed her.

"Vukasin," she said.

"He entered the country last night on a British Airways flight from Paris. Using a British passport."

Connolly nodded. "I guess Homeland Security doesn't have facial-recognition software, huh? Or they'd have stopped him."

"Oh, they have the software, believe me," he said. "Plus, this guy Vukasin is on one of their watch lists."

"Maybe their software isn't as good as ours."

"Or maybe someone knew who he was and let him in anyway."

"That doesn't make any sense," she said.

"A lot of what Homeland Security does makes no sense," Ardsley said.

"What are you saying—you think he was flagged as a bad guy but let through anyway?"

"Yes," Ardsley said. "That's what I think. But I'm only a video tech, so what do I know?"

"Jesus," she breathed.

"So let me ask you something," he said.

She turned away from the flat-screen. "Go ahead."

"You ever free for a drink?"

"You don't give up, do you?" Connolly said.

He pointed at the ripped motivational poster on the wall. "Persistence," he said with a sheepish smile.

As Connolly approached her cubicle, she saw from a distance that a man was sitting in her chair. Another man was standing next to him.

The man in the chair was Emmett Kalmbach. The man standing beside him was tall and wiry, with horn-rimmed glasses and a receding hairline. She had no idea who he was.

Then the standing man noticed her, muttered something, and Kalmbach turned slowly around.

"Agent Connolly," Kalmbach said, getting to his feet. "Allow me to introduce Richard Chambers from DHS."

She shook hands with the man in the horn-rimmed glasses. His handshake was cold and limp.

"Dick Chambers," the man said. He didn't smile.

"M. T. Connolly."

"Dick is a Regional Director of Homeland Security," Kalmbach said.

"A pleasure to meet you." Connolly kept her tone and face neutral, as if she'd never heard of him. But in fact she had. His background was almost clichéd diplomatic track: Yale, OCS, and then State Department. He'd been posted to some of the worst hotspots in the world. After September 11, he'd gone to Homeland Security, resolved that no terrorist would ever show his face in the Mid-Atlantic region of the country. Chambers wasn't popular among the feds—an abrasive façade over an ego that wouldn't quit—but he was a man who took on fires that nobody else wanted to go near. And, without any hesitation to risk his own hide, he got them extinguished. That he was involved made her uneasy. Real uneasy. "Now will someone explain to me what's going on?" she asked.

"We can talk in the conference room," Kalmbach said.

"Agent Connolly," the man from Homeland Security said, "we seem to have a communications problem that I hope we can all work out in person." He'd taken a seat at the head of the mahogany conference table, wordlessly indicating his place in the hierarchy.

"What sort of 'communication problem'?" she asked.

"Agent Connolly," Kalmbach said, "what happened at Dulles Airport falls cleanly within the jurisdiction of the Virginia police. I thought I made it clear that the situation there is of no concern to the Bureau."

That wasn't what he'd said, of course. He seemed to be performing for the man from DHS. But she knew better than to argue with Emmett Kalmbach over what he had or had not told her.

"Actually," Connolly said, holding up the CD that Bruce Ardsley had made for her, "I think it's very much of concern to the Bureau. Our own facial-recognition software has identified two Serbian war criminals who've entered the country illegally, one of them using a false British passport under the name—"

"Why are you trying to locate Harold Middleton?" Chambers interrupted, taking the disk from her hand.

"Because he's a material witness," Connolly said. "In an international case that involves a triple homicide in Warsaw, and another one, or possibly by now two—"

"Was I not absolutely clear?" Kalmbach said, his face flushing, but the DHS man put a hand on Kalmbach's sleeve, apparently to silence him.

"Agent Connolly," Chambers said softly, "Harold Middleton's file is blue-striped."

She looked at him, then nodded. A blue stripe indicated that a file was sealed for national-security reasons. Part of Middleton's military record had been designated as codeword-classified. That meant a level above even top secret.

"Why?" she asked finally.

Kalmbach scowled and said nothing. The man from Homeland replied, "How do I put this in a language you'll understand? This is above your pay grade, Agent Connolly."

"Meaning I'm off the case?" she blurted out.

"No, Agent Connolly," Chambers said. "Meaning that there is no case."

10

JIM FUSILLI

Leonora Tesla stepped out of the yellow taxi on the busy northwest corner of Sixth Avenue and 35th Street, and hustled into Macy's. She emerged with her hair trimmed short and punked, wearing a black button-down blouse with the collar curled high, black slacks and black flats—in many ways, the opposite of what she wore 24 hours earlier when she killed Günter Schmidt. A new black-leather shoulder bag, tucked tight under her arm, held a change of underwear and what remained from the moment she steered Schmidt's body toward the ravaging hyenas down in the wadi: her sunglasses, cash, credit cards and passport, her portfolio and her most valued possession, her fully loaded iPod, a gift from Harold Middleton.

She called the Human Rights Observer from a payphone in Herald Square. An intern answered and told her Val Brocco hadn't come in. A flu, she reported; his message said he intended to spend a second day in bed. Tesla decided against giving her name and demanding his latest cell number, consoling herself with the thought that Brocco's bordering-on-obsessive sense of precaution might serve him well. It'd better: To find Middleton, they'd tried to kill her, sending an agent to Namibia for the task. No doubt they already had at least one agent in metro D.C., where Middleton and Brocco were based.

Next, from the lobby of Madison Square Garden, she tried Jean-Marc Lespasse in Parkwood, North Carolina. Mr. Lespasse, she was told, was no longer with TDD—Technologie de Demain, the company he founded. And, no, the receptionist added tersely, there's no forwarding information. Sure enough, the last cell number Tesla had for Lespasse was no longer active.

Downstairs into Penn Station, Tesla paid cash for a one-way ticket on the Acela Express to Washington's Union Station, though she planned to get off in Delaware. Checking the overhead departure board, she saw she had enough time to run to the newsstand for a pre-paid cell phone and an array of domestic and international newspapers for the two-hour train ride to Wilmington.

As she gathered her change, she looked up. There, on a TV above a rack of batteries and disposable cameras, was a grainy video of a gun battle at Dulles Airport. "Two Cops Killed," the zipper reported.

"Harold," she said, the word escaping before she realized it had.

She stared at the soundless newscast. The zipper under the video now told her the gunman hadn't yet been found.

For some reason, she took it as verification that he was still alive.

She wondered if the same could be said of Lespasse and, maybe, Brocco.

Twelve hours earlier, Harold Middleton left the St. Regis Hotel with the sadist Eleana Soberski on his arm and a Zastava P25 in his ribs. As he and Soberski walked west along K Street, they seemed like the kind of couple not unknown in the neighborhood: a disheveled middle-aged man in a business suit, briefcase swinging at the end of his fist, and an upscale hooker exuding cold impenetrability. Except they were moving away from a four-star hotel rather than toward one for a $500 an hour "date."

Middleton listened for police cruisers' sirens—no doubt the cowering bartender had called the D.C. police who, in turn, would notify the FBI. Lurching along, he wondered if he'd be saved by the people he'd been trying to avoid.

He said, "Where—"

The gun nozzle raked his ribs.

"Farragut Square," Soberski replied, "the statue. Charlotte is there."

Middleton stumbled, but Soberski kept him upright.

"The briefcase," he said.

"Yes, the briefcase," Soberski replied. "Of course, the briefcase. But the briefcase is not enough."

Middleton glanced around. K Street was empty, the sidewalks rolled up now that the dinner hour was through. In New York, Chicago, San Francisco, Krakow, Warsaw, there'd be dozens of people enjoying the night air, on their way to a new hot spot, their chatter and laughter a giddy prelude to what's next. In Washington, you could hear the joyless scrape of the guards' shoes outside Lafayette Park and the White House two blocks away.

"What do you mean 'not enough'?" Middleton asked as they turned north on 16th Street.

"To me, a piece of paper."

"My daughter—"

"Of course you would trade your Chopin for your daughter. But what else?"

They stood at the corner of Connecticut Avenue, pausing as a few taxis headed east. As Middleton caught his breath, he finally heard the wail of sirens, further off than he'd hoped, but drawing nearer.

"There's nothing else," he said. Fatigue clouded his thoughts. The men he'd shot in the bar were after the Chopin manuscript, weren't they?

"Colonel Middleton," she replied with a wry laugh. "Let's not be silly."

"But I don't know what you want."

She jabbed the gun deeper into his ribcage. "Then we will leave it that I know what you want—Charlotte and your grandchild."

Up ahead, the traffic light changed, and Soberski led Middleton off the curb and into the street.

"Anything," he said, as they reached the yellow line.

"Where is Faust?"

A Mercedes sedan eased to the end of the short queue of waiting cars, blocking their path.

"Faust?"

"We are aware of your relationship with Faust," Soberski said.

"'We'? Who's—"

Before Soberski could react, the driver of the Mercedes jutted his left arm out the open window and squeezed off a shot.

The lone round entered her face at an upward angle, penetrating a nasal bone and exploding the top of her head. Red mist filled the air above Middleton as Soberski collapsed in a heap, the Zastava tumbling from her hand.

"Leave it, Harry."

As sirens blared, Middleton saw his son-in-law staring up at him from behind the wheel of his ex-wife's sedan.

"Leave it and get in. Now Harry."

Seconds later, Jack Perez twisted the wheel and skirted the queue, bursting across the intersection. He raced through a yellow light at George Washington University Hospital, intent on reaching Route 66 before the cops responded to another shooting, this one on Connecticut Avenue.

"Charley?" Middleton asked. The briefcase sat flat on his lap.

"Safe," Perez said, tires squealing as he turned left.

"Sylvia?"

"No, Harry. They got Sylvia."

"Where is—"

"The lake house, Harry. Charley's at the lake house."

Middleton wiped the side of his face, then stared as his bloody palm.

"Before we get there, Harry, you'd better tell me what's going on."

"They're trying to kill me," Middleton managed.

"Trying, but you're not dead," Perez said. "Sylvia, two guys in the bar, two cops at Dulles—"

"Three people in Warsaw," Middleton heard himself say.

"And now the hooker."

"She wasn't—"

"That's nine, and none of them is you."

The ramp up ahead, and what little traffic there was flowed free.

"Jack, listen."

Perez lifted his right hand from the wheel and silently told his father-in-law to keep still. "I just undid a lifetime's worth of work reversing my family's reputation for you, Harry."

Middleton stayed quiet. He knew the Perez family had been connected in the '60s to the Genovese crime family through Carlo Marcello, but Army Intel said young Jack had tested clean. He never mentioned the off-the-books background check to Charley.

"In return," Perez continued, "you tell me what you're into."

"There's a Chopin manuscript in here," Middleton said, tapping the briefcase's lid. "It's believed to be part of a stash the Nazis squirreled away in a church in Kosovo."

"'Believed'?"

"It's a forgery. It's not in Chopin's hand. It's been folded, mistreated—"

"And yet somebody thinks it's worth nine lives?"

Middleton remembered the bodies strewn inside St. Sophia, and the dying teenage girl's desperate cry. "Green shirt, green shirt . . . please."

"A lot more than nine, Jack."

They were on the highway now and Perez slid the Mercedes into the fast lane, pushing it up to 70, the sedan riding on a cloud.

"So I'm telling you, Jack, that you and Charley ought to go on thinking I was in Krakow to authenticate—"

"A manuscript that some other expert will know is phony too. Suddenly, you, who's catalogued scores by Bach, Handel, Wagner—"

"Mozart," Middleton added.

"—are fooled by an obvious forgery."

"Jack, what I'm trying to say—"

"And with Charley ready to pop, you go to Poland. That's not you, Harry."

Middleton watched the maple and poplars trees rush by at the roadside. "Are you going to toss that Python?"

Perez had been driving with the .357 pressed against the steering wheel. "Hell no. At least not until you're straight with me."

Middleton sighed. "Better you don't know, Jack."

"Why?" Perez said, peering into the rearview. "You think it's about to get worse?"

Though toughened by a native cynicism and the hardscrabble life of a street musician, 19-year-old Felicia Kaminski was too young to understand that a sense of justice and a blush of optimism raised by an unexpected success were illusions, no more reliable than a promise or a kiss. Still energized by caffeine and the vision of Faust as he was hauled off by airport security, she'd headed from Signor Abe's La Musica shop to an internet café near the Colosseum—another sign of her cleverness: She fled Via delle

Botteghe Oscure and hadn't gone to the Pantheon or north to the Trevi Fountain, areas Faust had scouted; nor did she return to her home in San Giovanni. She'd begun to feel she was living a clandestine life, a purposeful life, in memory of her uncle Henryk.

Within the first minute at the computer, she'd learned Harold Middleton taught "Masterpieces of Music" at the American University in Washington, D.C.

Which was 40 miles—40.23 miles, to be precise—from the address in Baltimore Faust said was to be her new home.

There was a 6:45 flight from Fiumicino through Frankfurt that would arrive in Washington at 12:45. She could exchange her first-class ticket for a coach seat, and still have enough euros—no, dollars—to take a taxi to the college. Even if Professor Middleton was off campus, she could arrange to bring him back—the words "I am Henryk Jedynak's niece" would be enough to earn his attention.

She spent the night in a cheap flop on the Lido, resolute but feeling naked without her violin.

Remembering to use the Joanna Phelps passport Faust had given her, she swapped the ticket at the Alitalia courtesy desk in terminal B, sharing a conspiratorial smile with the young woman behind the counter when she explained that she didn't want to fly with the vecchio sporcaccione—dirty old man—who'd bought it in her name. Incredibly, the woman directed her to retrieve her luggage that had been pulled from yesterday's flight.

Her excuse played with security in baggage claim too, and she returned upstairs to a Lufthansa desk to turn over nearly 1,400 euros for a new ticket. She converted the remaining euros to dollars, paying an exchange rate worthy of a loan shark.

Three hours later, the ample jet was soaring above the Dolomiti on its way to its stopover in Germany. And miracle of miracles, as it departed Frankfurt, the two seats next to her in row 41 remained empty. She slipped off her shoes, grabbed a blanket from an overhead bin and stretched out, her last thoughts a prayer that Middleton would explain everything and a sense that she was about to discover that her uncle had died in defense of art and culture in the form of an unknown composition by Mozart.

She was in a deep sleep, dreaming of music, of a violin with quicksilver strings, of returning to the States—a glimpse of her father, who hadn't appeared to her in years, and the broad-shouldered buildings of Chicago's State Street—when she felt a tug on her toe. She awoke slowly, her mind unable to recall where she was. Opening her eyes, she scrambled to uncoil her body.

"Looking for this?"

Faust held up the oversized envelope that she had seen in Signor Abe's shop. No doubt it contained the Mozart manuscript.

She rose up on her elbows and, to her surprise, spoke in Italian. "Che cosa avete fatto con l'anziano?"

He nudged into the seat on the aisle, and placed a forefinger on his chin. "Old man Nowakowski is fine," he replied in English. "He may continue to be fine."

She stared at him. In a blue-striped business suit, white shirt and a blue tie that matched the sky over the Atlantic, he was utterly composed as he stroked back his long black hair.

"You are very lucky you were not killed last night," he told her.

"It wasn't luck." Her senses had begun to return.

"Well, you were hiding from me, I suppose, which is as good as hiding from them."

"Tell me what's going on."

Faust looked around the rear of the jet. Stewardesses were in the back cabin, preparing the beverage service.

"Think, Joanna," he said. "Your Signor Abe is alive and so are you. I have the Mozart your uncle wanted to protect. Knowing that, tell me how you can believe I am the enemy."

"You say nothing," she said as she sat up, crossing her legs under her. "Niente. Nic. Nothing."

"With the Mozart in my hand, I will go with you to meet Harold Middleton," he replied. "The last man to see your uncle alive—except for the killer, that is."

"You know who killed my uncle?"

Faust stood and held out his hand, beckoning her to leave the narrow row. "Of course," he said, speaking in Polish. "The traitor Vukasin. The lowest of the lows. It's a shame your uncle had to die in his presence."

"Where is he?"

"Vukasin? No doubt he is within a kilometer or so of Colonel Middleton."

Faust turned at the sound of the beverage cart rattling into the aisle.

"Come, Joanna," he said, reaching for her. "They serve Champagne in first class. And Bavarian bleu cheese with a pumpkinseed bread—before lunch. I'm sure the effects of the panzanella and cantucci you had last night have long passed."

Kaminski—no, Phelps—stood and wriggled her feet back into her worn shoes.

The arterial spray from Brocco's severed throat had already dried on his heartbreakingly meager kitchen table, and rigor had begun to subside. Curiously, only his left hand was tied behind his back; his right hung limply, fingertips just above the blood- and urine-stained floor. Tesla saw the outline of a standard-sized reporter's notebook on the table. Which meant the killer coerced Brocco to write something before he died. And getting Brocco to write something meant he was tortured before he was killed.

The killer also recorded Brocco's voice—how else could a dead man call in sick after he died? Clever; a way to buy some time.

But what had he wanted Brocco to write? Tesla had been asked one pertinent question by Schmidt: Where is Harold Middleton? There are four immediate answers Brocco could have given: Middleton's true location; a false one; a concession that he didn't know where he was—as Tesla had— or a refusal to say anything. All but the first would lead to escalating pain and, if Brocco hadn't known where his old boss was, he could have been compelled into speculation.

Tesla looked at her former colleague and, though his head was lolled back and his eyes opened wide and empty, she remembered tenderly his earnestness, his awkwardness around women, his passion for 18th century classical music, his unassailable belief in the power of a free press.

She peered into his mouth and saw that his tongue had been cut out. Which explained the dried blood on his lips and chin, and also whatever he wrote on the notebook's page.

Tesla went to the sink to retrieve a ratty dishtowel, and brought it to the old, newsprint-smudged yellow wall phone. She dialed 911, gave them

Brocco's address and then let the handset fall, the towel unraveling and landing on the worn linoleum.

As she turned to leave, she saw Brocco had five deadbolt locks on the door. His tattered khaki saddlebag, which hung from the knob, was empty.

The ultra-cautious Brocco had let the killer in. The killer stole Brocco's laptop.

Brocco knew the killer, and the email addresses stored in the laptop weren't enough.

Tesla hustled down three flights of stairs and stepped into the late-afternoon sun. Shaken, her thoughts occupied by Brocco's brutal murder as well as by speculation on where Harold might be, she momentarily abandoned the vigilance she applied when she stepped off the Acela in Wilmington, only to taxi to BWI, scurry through the airport as if she were late for a flight, and then pop back on Amtrak to Union Station, buying a ticket using a credit card issued to a woman who worked as an extra at Il Teatro Constanzi in Rome. Now as she hurried to catch the Georgia Avenue bus as it wheezed from its stop, she suddenly remembered, with a startling vividness, an unexpectedly satisfying afternoon she'd spent with Harold at a house on Lake Anna. Were she the type to blush, she would've.

Lake Anna, she told herself, unaware that she'd failed to see a man in an old sun-baked Citröen sitting directly across from Brocco's shabby building. He wore a black stocking cap atop his shaved head; the cap covered a black-and-green tattoo of the jack of spades.

When Tesla leaped onto the bus, the man turned the ignition key, folded the switchblade he'd been using to clean his fingernails, and eased the car out of the spot.

He was waiting when, 33 minutes later, the woman in black pulled out of the Budget lot at Union Station in a dark blue rental, sunglasses on her nose.

There was nothing else they could do. They had no choice.

The Mercedes had kicked up pebbles as Perez parked it at the side of the house. As Middleton hoisted his weary body from the car, Perez said, "Harry, no lights."

"She's sleeping?"

"Harry . . ."

No, of course not. Charley sent her husband to "Scotland" to rescue her father. If she wasn't pregnant, she'd have been there herself.

Perez pulled the Python.

Groping through darkness, they'd stepped inside the house, and as Perez climbed the stairs to the bedrooms, Middleton put down his briefcase and headed through the kitchen to the living room.

Through the picture window, he saw his daughter's silhouette on the porch. She was slumped in a wicker chair.

"Charley," he'd whispered. Then he said her name again, louder this time.

When she didn't respond, Middleton called to his son-in-law and raced outside.

Charley had his Browning A-Bolt across her lap.

Beneath the wicker chair was a tiny puddle of blood that had been dripping from between her legs.

Middleton recoiled.

"Oh Jesus," Perez said as he skidded to a halt. "Charley. Charley, wake up."

At that moment, Middleton understood that his daughter had lost her baby. He felt a muted sense of relief: For a moment, seeing the blood, he thought they had gotten to her as they had Henryk Jedynak, Sylvia and others—and had tried to kill him at Dulles.

Kneeling, Perez said, "She needs—"

"Yeah, she does."

And now Charlotte Perez was recovering at Martha Jefferson Hospital. A private room, IV drip in place, and her husband at her side, barely awake in a lounge chair with a .357 Magnum in his jacket side pocket.

Honey sunlight streamed through the windows. Treetops swayed in the gentle breeze.

Felt like hiding in plain sight to Harold Middleton.

To Jack Perez too.

11

PETER SPIEGELMAN

Felicia Kaminski collapsed on the vast sofa that sat before the window that filled the wall of a suite atop the Harbor Court Hotel. The fat, silk-covered cushions nearly swallowed her whole. Far below, the lights of Baltimore's Inner Harbor blinked yellow and white at her, and big boats bobbed like eggs on the black water. Was there something in the blinking lights—some pattern, a signal, a message meant for her? If there was, she was too tired to decipher it.

Beyond tired, really. She was spent—exhausted by fear and flight, and addled by too many time zones and Champagne that flowed freely in the first-class cabin. Faust had all but forced it on her, and he'd kept up with her glass for glass, all the while smiling like the Cheshire Cat. One bottle had led to another—so many bubbles—but the smiling Mr. Faust seemed entirely immune.

Kaminski closed her eyes, but she could still see his white teeth and those dark, stony eyes, could still hear that deep melodious voice speaking in Italian, then in French, in Polish, in German, and now in English as he addressed the hotel man. There was a rueful smile in his words. Without looking, she knew that the hotel man—not a bellman but the immaculate, blue-suited fellow from behind the desk—was smiling back and nodding. It was all smiles and nods and discreet bows for Mr. Faust, all along the way: on the airplane; in the executive lounge in Frankfurt as they waited to fly to the States; and from the man at Dulles who met them, retrieved their luggage and drove them in a shiny black BMW all the way to Baltimore. It was as if they all knew him, their oldest friend, dear Mr. Faust—who smiled and drank Champagne and spoke in many tongues, but answered questions in none of them.

Kaminski sighed and sank deeper into the cushions. Her head swam and the harbor lights blinked at her, even through her closed lids. She had smoked opium once, an oily black bead with that Tunisian boy—what was his name?—who played guitar near the Castel Sant'Angelo, and it had set her drifting like this. Floating, her worries no more than distant lights.

There was a sharp knock and she came to with a bump. She rubbed her eyes and sat up to see Faust opening the suite door. A man came in, squat and muscular, wearing jeans and a black-leather jacket. His hair was gray and cut short, and he greeted Faust in Italian, then glanced at his guest and switched to something else. Whatever it was sounded fast and harsh to Kaminski's ears—Slavic, she thought, but otherwise no clue. Faust listened and nodded and checked his watch. He said something to the man—an order, a dismissal—and the man nodded and left.

Faust looked at her. "Another trip," he said.

Felicia could barely find her voice. "What? Now? At this hour?"

Again the smile. "No rest for the wicked, Felicia, but we won't be gone long. If you wish to wash up first, I will wait."

She rubbed her hands over her face, rubbing life back into it. "No," she said. "I'm tired of being dragged around, and now I'm done with it. Sono rifinito. Non sto andando."

Even to herself she sounded like a child, but she was beyond caring. She looked at Faust, leaning so casually against the doorframe, his suit somehow without a wrinkle and every hair in place, as if he had stepped from a page in a fashion magazine.

He shook his head. "You are not staying here alone, Felicia."

Anger welled in her. "No? And why not?"

"It is not safe."

"I take care of myself."

"Yes, I saw how well back in Rome."

She said, "Screw you! I don't need a goddamn babysitter."

"You are the tough little urchin now, eh?"

"Tough enough," Kaminski said, grinding her teeth. "I didn't grow up in places like this, being waited on hand and foot."

Faust's smile widened. "You think that I did?"

"Let's say you don't look out of place."

He chuckled. "You haven't known the real romance of street life until you've experienced it in Buenos Aires, caught between the Montoneros and the Battalion 601 boys. Now those were charming fellows, and much more dedicated than your average Roman teppista."

Kaminski massaged her temples, trying to get her brain to function. Buenos Aires? Montoneros? What the fuck? She'd read something once about the Dirty War, but she couldn't remember what. "So you had it rough and now you're up from the gutter—a real success story."

"Something like that."

"Good for you. You've earned all this! And never mind that you're a thief or a spy or some kind of terrorist—someone who bullies old men, and kidnaps girls from the streets of Rome."

"I've told you, Felicia, your friend Abe is fine, and I am no spy. I have no taste for politics at all. If I had to describe my profession, I'd say I was a broker. I match buyers with sellers, and take a fee. A modest fee, all things considered."

"Buyers and sellers of what?"

Faust shrugged. "This and that. Odds and ends."

"Like stolen music manuscripts?"

"The manuscript is in the closet, Felicia, behind lock and key. My own musical inclinations run more to Sinatra than Mozart."

"Not music, then what—drugs, guns? Whatever it is, I'm sure it makes your family very proud."

Kaminski felt the air change, going silent and thick around her. The smiling Mr. Faust was no longer smiling, and those dark eyes seemed to look right through her. Defiance and anger drained from her, replaced by choking fear. This time, the knock on the door was a relief.

It was the squat man again, and he looked nervously at Faust. Faust said something to the man—she didn't know what—and walked out the door. The squat man turned to her.

"Come," he said in gravelly English.

She was not inclined to argue.

Faust hadn't lied about the trip. It was a short one in the back of the big BMW, through sodium-lit nighttime streets. Kaminski looked for signs and landmarks: Light Street, East Lombard, a big stadium off to the left, bathed in light and carpeted in impossible green, then a tangle of narrower streets, and old brick buildings. In 10 minutes, they pulled up in front of one of them.

Four stories and broad, the building looked to her like a warehouse or an old factory. And so it had been once upon a time, as she read on the shiny brass plaque near the modern glass entry: The Sail Cloth Factory— 1888. Just above that plaque another, with the address: 121 South Fremont Avenue.

Home, she thought, her anger returning as she followed Faust inside.

Exposed brick and ornamental wrought iron whispered of the building's industrial past; otherwise, the rest of the lobby—gleaming brass, etched glass and marble—proclaimed its current incarnation as a luxury apartment building. Faust crossed to the elevator and Felicia followed him in and then, on the fourth floor, out again. Around a corner, down a pale gray corridor, and to a black door at its end; Faust knocked twice. Then he took a key from his jacket pocket, worked the lock, and stepped inside. And stopped short.

Kaminski didn't see the wiry, bearded man pointing a Glock 30 at Faust's chest until she bumped into Faust's back. Then she gasped and gripped Faust's bicep.

"Jesus," she whispered.

The bearded man smiled at Faust, who smiled back. "*Qué tal*, Nacho," Faust said.

"*Nada*, Jefe," the man said, and slipped the Glock into a holster behind his back. "All quiet on the western front. Have a look for yourself."

Faust gently removed Kaminski's hand from his bicep and followed Nacho to a window. She let out a long breath and looked around. The large loft apartment—brick walls, high ceilings, exposed beams and ductwork, shiny plank floors, and little in the way of furniture: a card table, some folding chairs, a dim floor lamp, and heavy white drapes across the windows. There was plenty of technical equipment: three laptops; several cameras wearing long lenses; and two massive, tripod-mounted binoculars. They were pointed at a narrow gap in the drapes, and now Nacho fiddled with one of them.

"Got the image intensifier on this one, Jefe," he said as Faust bent to the eyepieces.

"When was the last delivery?" Faust asked as he looked.

"This afternoon. Maybe five o'clock."

"You know what it was?"

Nacho looked at Kaminski and switched to Spanish. She tried to follow it, but it came too fast and the accents were strange, and anyway it sounded scientific to her, chemical terms maybe. She walked slowly to the binoculars while Faust and Nacho spoke. The men saw her but seemed not to care. She peered into the eyepiece.

Outside, the world was tinted green, as was a brick building, low and long, that seemed very close. It had a lot of windows, all shuttered, and she thought it looked abandoned. There was a loading dock in the center of the image, and the only thing that moved was a plastic bag, blowing in the warm night breeze.

Nacho pulled the drapes and the outside images went black. He looked at Kaminski and nodded his head at a chair in the corner. She sat, still straining to catch the conversation. It was less technical now, Faust asking something about someone—does he know . . . Does he know what? Horario. Was that like orario, meaning schedule, timetable? And who was this he?

It seemed as if Nacho was uncertain too. He shrugged at Faust and moved to a large closet's double doors. He put his hands on the knobs. "Maybe you have better luck than me, Jefe," he said in English, and swung the doors wide.

Kaminski screamed.

The man on the closet floor stared at her, though he was bound with wire and gagged with duct tape, and bleeding from a gash on his shaved head, which, she noticed, was tattooed with the likeness of the jack of spades. Nacho pressed a forefinger to his lips and made a shushing noise at her.

She had no idea how long it was before her head cleared, but when it did she saw Faust kneeling by the tattooed man. His hand rested gently on the man's shoulder, and he spoke softly in his ear. The duct tape was off the tattooed man's mouth and Kaminski could see that the man's lips were split, and that he was crying. And speaking too, in urgent, terrified English.

"No, no—not weeks! It's days, a matter of days. Maybe less!"

Faust spread the duct tape over the man's mouth again and patted him, almost affectionately, on the back. Then he stepped away and shut the closet door. Nacho looked at Faust and smiled.

"Still got the touch, Jefe," he said.

Faust smiled minutely. "You call if there's any more activity," he said. To Kaminski, he added, "We return to the hotel."

She stood and followed numbly. As they were about to step into the corridor, she touched Faust's arm and spoke in a whisper. "What will happen to him—the man in the closet?"

"Nacho will see to him," Faust said. "Now come, we have dinner plans to make."

It was nearly black in the hospital room when Jack Perez came awake, the .357 in his hand. The only light came from the orange glow of the call buttons on the wall, the green digits on the blood pressure monitor, and the pinkish scatter of streetlight through the shaded window. It was nearly silent, too—only the sounds of his wife's steady breathing, the quiet whir of air in the vents, and the electric ping of some sort of warning bell reached his ears. About right for two a.m.

But something had woken Perez from his brittle sleep. His father-in-law going out? Someone in the corridor?

Perez wiped a hand across his eyes, rose from the lounge chair and crossed the room without a sound. He leaned against the doorframe with one hand on the knob and the .357 down along his leg. He took a deep breath and opened the door a crack.

Middleton was down the hall, his back to Perez, and he was talking quietly to a man and a woman. The man was lanky and pale, and his jaw was darkened by a three-day beard. His eyes were shadowed and darting. The woman was tall, tanned, and broad-shouldered, and her dark hair was cut short. Perez hadn't made a sound, but somehow Middleton knew he was there.

"Come meet some old friends, Jack," he said, without turning around. Perez pocketed the Python and closed the door to his wife's room behind him.

"This is Jean-Marc Lespasse and Leonora Tesla, former colleagues of mine. Nora, JM, this is my son-in-law, Jack Perez."

Lespasse nodded at Perez, and Tesla put out a warm hand. "Harry has told us all that's happened, Mr. Perez. I'm so sorry for what you and your wife have been through. Will she be all right?"

"She's lost a lot of blood, but the docs say she'll recover. All right is another story. I don't know that either one of us will be all right again after this."

As Tesla nodded sympathetically, Middleton said, "Nora and JM have been through the wringer themselves the past couple of days. A man nearly killed Nora in Namibia, and JM narrowly avoided abduction in Chapel Hill."

"Jesus, Harry, is all this about—?"

"We think so," Middleton said. "The man who attacked Nora was looking for me."

"I didn't hang around to find out what those clowns in the parking lot were after," Lespasse added in a raspy whisper, "but I heard them speaking Serbian, and they were carrying those cheap shit Zastavas."

"And this is all about . . . what? That fucking manuscript?" Perez asked.

Tesla and Lespasse shifted nervously. Middleton said nothing.

"For Christ's sakes, Harry . . . " Perez said, shaking his head. He looked at Tesla. "How did you two manage to find us?"

"We both saw the news reports of Harry's difficulty at Dulles and knew that he was . . . in flight. We both guessed that he might turn up at the lake house."

"I ran into Nora there," Lespasse said.

" . . . and nearly blew my head off."

"We saw the blood and thought the worst," Lespasse added. "We started checking hospitals, closest ones first, and there you were."

Perez turned back to his father-in-law. "Not too difficult. And the guys who are after you, whoever they are, seem fuckin' relentless. How much longer before they turn up here too?"

Any answer Middleton might have given was interrupted by the night duty nurse. "You and your father-in-law will have to quiet down, Mr. Perez, and your friends will have to come back during regular visiting hours."

Middleton seized the opportunity. "Yes, ma'am, and we're very sorry. I'll just see these folks out so Jack can sit with Charley."

He took Tesla's arm and led her and Jean-Marc toward the elevator, leaving Jack Perez grinding his teeth in the darkened hallway.

Outside, the air was warm and close. The hospital parking lot was nearly empty. Jean-Marc Lespasse lit a cigarette, inhaled deeply, and blew a column of smoke into the night sky.

Harry Middleton recalled the last time he'd seen Lespasse and Val Brocco. A blisteringly hot day at chaotic Kenyatta Airport. He remembered too his farewell to Nora Tesla. It had been somewhat after his final meeting with the two men and the location was much nicer—an Algerian-influenced inn on the Cote D'Azure—but the moment was no less difficult.

Events intervened . . .

She glanced at him once and then her eyes fled. Words seemed easier.

"Your family has no idea?" Leonora Tesla asked Middleton.

"No. I never told them—never thought I'd have to. I thought I could protect them from . . . all this."

She clutched his hand, an instinctive gesture, and released it fast. "This isn't your fault, Harry, but your son-in-law is right. It wasn't difficult for us to find you, and it won't be difficult for anyone else who's looking. It's not safe."

"It's safe enough for a little while—long enough for me to think things through. The Soberski woman asked about Faust. She thought I was into something with him."

"So you said, Harry, and I told you, Eleana Soberski was a sociopath and a congenital liar," Tesla said. "You have to assume that anything she said was meant to mislead and to manipulate. Faust was our boogeyman— our white whale—and she knew that. What better way to get your attention than dangle his name?"

"She didn't have to dangle anything, Nora. She had a gun in my ribs."

Blowing out more smoke, Lespasse said, "She thought she was going to be interrogating you, Harry. She was laying groundwork, putting you off balance. She—"

Before Lespasse could finish, Middleton's cell phone burred. He found it in a pocket, flipped it open and heard only static. And then a faraway voice, old and struggling in English.

"Colonel Middleton? My name is Abraham Nowakowski. I'm calling from Rome and I have a message from Felicia Kaminski—Henryk Jedynak's niece. An urgent message."

Harold Middleton listened intently for several minutes. Then he said, "Ciao, Signor Abe, mille grazie." Closing his phone, he let out a massive breath. Tesla and Lespasse looked at him expectantly.

"Speak of the devil, and the devil appears," Middleton said. "Faust. He's in the country, and close—up in Baltimore. He's got something Henryk Jedynak was holding for me, and he's got Jedynak's niece too."

"Baltimore? What the hell is he doing in Baltimore?" Lespasse asked.

"I don't know. Jedynak's niece managed to get a call out to a family friend in Rome—that's who was on the line. From what he said, it sounds like Faust has some sort of operation going on there, but the girl was cut off after a minute."

"Did she say where in Baltimore Faust is?" Tesla asked.

"No, but she did tell her friend where she and Faust would be tomorrow—check that—tonight. A place called Kali's Court, on Thames Street. Apparently the two of them are going there for dinner. Just the two of them. I'm thinking that maybe we should join them."

Tesla and Lespasse looked at Middleton. Tesla shook her head. "Join them? You can't be serious, Harry—with only three of us."

"We need backup for something like that, Colonel," Lespasse said. "Unless what you want is in and out, bang, bang, bang."

Middleton shook his head. "That's appealing, but not smart. No, we need to talk to this guy, and at length. So backup it is." Harry opened his phone again and clicked through his list of contacts. He stopped on an entry marked E.K. and hit dial.

The phone rang once.

The voice in Middleton's ear said, "It's about time you called, Harry. But then I guess you've had your hands full lately."

"I need a team, Emmett," Middleton said. "In Baltimore."

"Sure you do, Harry. And what about what I need?"

"We can talk about that too, after we settle Baltimore."

"We can fuckin' talk about it now."

"It's been real bad luck for people to run into you lately, Harry. We've got bodies at Dulles, downtown on Sixteenth Street and two assholes with fake Bureau IDs in a bar nearby. Okay, sure, self-defense. But you still have to answer questions. And we can't stop the local boys from bringing you in if they find out. Jesus, you should've told us from the beginning what was going on.

"Guess what, Emmett. Somebody forgot to send me an agenda. I didn't know what was going on. And I still don't."

"Be that as it may, we need to talk."

"No time, Emmett. My battery's running low."

"Not to worry, Harry, we can talk about it over coffee. Say in five minutes, in the hospital cafeteria." Middleton looked left, right, overhead. On the phone Kalmbach laughed nastily. "On your left," he said. "Across the street."

Middleton peered into the darkness and a pair of headlights of a Bureau-issued car winked once, twice at him. Emmett Kalmbach was still laughing. "Cream and two sugars for me, Harry."

In his suite at the Harbor Court Hotel, the man known as Faust answered the muted beep of a cell phone. The voice on the other end was faraway and old. Faust listened intently, and a small, satisfied smile played on his lips. "Well done, Signor Abe," he said.

Faust put his phone down and looked across the sitting room, into the smaller of the suite's two bedrooms. A splash of light fell across the king-sized bed, and in it he could see Kaminski's pale face on the pillow, and a spray of blond hair.

"Charming," he said again, to no one in particular.

12

RALPH PEZZULLO

There was something about Fells Point that put Harold Middleton in a foul mood. Maybe it had to do with the fight at The Horse You Came In Saloon that got him booted out of West Point. Maybe it related to the scar on his left temple left by a bar stool—the one that still throbbed whenever the thermometer dipped below 40.

This dank place changed my life, he thought, entering the fog that clung like bad luck to Baltimore's Thames Street.

Charley's miscarriage; his ex-wife Sylvia's violent death; the mayhem and destruction that trailed him since the meeting in Krakow: Now he was determined to right all that, coming on like St. George to slay the dragon as in the richly colored depiction by Raphael Sanzio he admired, even if Faust had chosen Kali's Court in some sort of a sick cosmic joke. He smiled to himself. Wasn't Kali the Hindu goddess of annihilation?

As he peered through the fog, Middleton reminded himself to focus. The forces aligned against him were vile and dark. The equation he followed was simple. He had come to slay evil, which had manifested in numbing complexity.

Nora Tesla's voice squawked in his earpiece. "Target's in. Alone."

That's strange, he thought, marching over the same cobblestones he'd been tossed to like trash so many years ago. "Kaminski isn't with him?"

"I said, 'Alone.'"

So you did. Middleton pushed his shoulders back, fixed the collar of his coat and entered the restaurant. A hostess with a frosted smile stopped him with hard blue eyes. "You have a reservation?"

"I'm meeting someone. A man. Mid-thirties, long dark hair, slicked back, tall. Just arrived . . . "

"I know him. Yes." Suddenly flummoxed, she managed to smile and frown at the same time. "He said he was dining alone."

"Not tonight, my dear."

Middleton's Dover Saddlery riding boots reverberated confidently across the walnut floor past Tesla and Lespasse in a nearby booth, along with an FBI agent and another man, ambiguously titled, but one whose job became clearer if you knew his phone number was an exchange near Crystal City, Virginia, the home of the Pentagon.

Outside, in a control van, were some other distinguished visitors: Emmett Kalmbach and Homeland Security's Richard Chambers.

Such seniority at a surveillance operation was unusual. But Faust was such a wild card, and the recent shootings so troubling, that both the major agencies responsible for tracking foreign threats within the U.S. wanted direct involvement. Middleton knew Kalmbach. The man could be spineless, but Middleton didn't care; all the easier to get what he wanted from the feebies on Ninth Street. As for Dick Chambers, the regional director wouldn't have much personal interest in Faust. The politics of the Balkans hadn't intrigued him. He'd made one trip to the region during the conflicts, apparently deemed it solvable by underlings and headed off for the Middle East—where he saw more of a threat to the U.S., about which he was right, of course.

But Chambers's presence here could be explained by a simpler reason: The DHS, the organization that brought us the color-coded threat levels and was charged with protecting our borders, had screwed up big time and, focused on people who's last names began with al-, had missed Vukasin, a known war criminal, and an unknown number of his goons sneaking into the country on phony papers.

Which wasn't necessarily bad news for Middleton. It meant that Chambers needed to protect his image and could bring resources to bear in a big way. Middleton was confident that all the pieces were in place for checkmate.

Spotting thick black eyebrows protruding over the top of the Racing Form, Middleton stopped and lowered his chin. "Good evening, Faust," he said deeply, placing the edge of his briefcase on the table. His heart was beating fast, palms moist. The man he'd been tracking for years was now in front of him. He seemed diminished, much smaller than Middleton expected, though he knew the physical details of the war criminal better than he knew his own.

"I rather liked Patty's Special in the eighth running ten to one," came the reply. Faust set down the paper and smoothed it carefully. "Colonel Harold Middleton."

The swarthy-skinned man with the lopsided grin looked up briefly, then snapped his fingers at the nervous waiter with the puff of blond hair. "Bring a glass for my friend." Then to Middleton, he said, "I hope you don't mind Beaujolais."

The American beamed at his quarry's attempt at gamesmanship. "I have you, Faust," he said as he pulled out a chair and sat. "We can do this anyway you want."

Faust folded the paper and fixed him with intense black eyes. "'Unhappy master, who unmerciful disaster followed fast and followed faster, till his songs the burden bore; till the dirges of his hope, the melancholy burden bore of Nevermore, of Nevermore.'"

"I deplore people who play with other people's lives."

"So do I."

"It's over."

"Let's hope not, Colonel." The man took a bite of food, which he seemed to relish. He then said, "One thing I've never thanked you for. My name."

"Your name?"

"That was your creation. I believe you found some documents in a volume of Goethe's masterpiece, and dubbed me after the hero."

"You think Faust was a hero?"

"Protagonist then." He raised his glass. "So here's to selling our souls to the devil."

Middleton let his wine glass sit, untouched.

They confronted each other's stare. Middleton wanted nothing more than to reach over and wring the younger man's neck.

Faust said, "The great Edgar Allen Poe died at Church Hospital, very close to here. Few grieved. The poor mad genius was placed in an unmarked grave. His last words: 'Lord help my soul.'"

"It seems you identify with him."

Faust shook his head. "I was thinking he was more like you. Condemned to walk the earth as a marked man. Walking down the avenue of life stalked by demons. Using his will to bend his torment into art."

Middleton drank down his wine then slammed his fist onto the table. "You're a criminal! A fiend! I still dream about the slaughtered children of Kosovo and Racak."

Faust laughed into his fist, adding fire to Middleton's anger. Then he held up his hand. "Easy, my friend. Why it is that you Americans always assume that everything is black and white?"

"In this case, it is."

"So if it has a pink ribbon tied around it it's a birthday present?"

"Maybe you didn't pull the trigger yourself, but you backed the man who did."

"Rugova was a pig. May he rest in—"

"I hope he's rotting in hell."

"He was useful."

Middleton stabbed a finger toward his rival's chin. "You stink of guilt."

"I like you, Colonel. I need you. That's why I must stop you from continuing to demean your own intelligence."

Before Middleton could reply, Faust snapped his fingers at the waiter, who skittered across the dining room. "My guest here will have the lacquered octopus to start; for me, the pear and caramelized walnut salad. We'd both like the whole Bronzini. No salt."

Faust lifted his glass. "Here's to the beginning of our partnership. Success!"

"What the hell are you talking about?"

"Tens of thousands; maybe hundreds of thousands of people are counting on us, but don't know it."

"Music lovers?" he asked darkly.

"I know a great deal about you, Colonel. I've studied you carefully. You're a man who is relentless in pursuit of what you consider a worthy goal. I hope you'll excuse me if I say that your goals so far have been wrong-headed."

The salad and octopus arrived and were soon treated to showers of fresh black pepper.

"I bet you the price of this meal that we'll be working together by the evening's end," Faust offered.

Middleton nodded his acceptance.

In a small bookkeeper's office in a corner of the lemon-and-brine-scented kitchen of Kali's Court, M. T. Connolly sat listening with desperate attention to the two men at the table not 50 yards from her, their voices traveling through an earbud.

Kalmbach. At his disposal were hundreds of Bureau agents and yet, in a display of typically unnecessary bravado, he drove to Martha Jefferson Hospital by himself, unaware Connolly was behind him. Now, hours later, Kalmbach, with Dick Chambers in tow, had led her to Middleton. And Faust, who was beginning the next phase of his dissertation with an anecdote about his father.

Connolly listened hard. The bug was under Faust's bread plate.

" . . . Invitations to dance made with simple nods," Faust said. "The intense courtship . . . "

She jumped as her cell phone rang. She stretched her leg and snapped it quickly from her belt. "This is Connolly."

"Hello, Buttercup."

She walked toward a corner, away from the kitchen staff's prying eyes. "Padlo," she said, her voice barely above a whisper. "Where are you?"

"Sono a Roma," he replied, his Italian accented with as much American English as his native Polish. "Someone wants to say hello."

"Josef, wait—"

"Oh, and by the way, his English is . . . Actually, it's non-existent."

Connolly sighed as Faust and Middleton continued in her other ear.

"Buona sera, Signora Connolly," an old man said nervously. "Il mio nome è Abe Nowakowski. Posso aiutarlo con il vostro commercio."

"I'm sorry—'Commercio'? I don't—"

"Business," Padlo said, taking the heavy black handset in the old man's shop. "Which is still finding Middleton, I presume."

"I've got Middleton," Padlo heard her say. "And Faust."

When Padlo repeated the names, the old man recoiled.

"They are together?" Padlo asked.

"Together, and negotiating."

Nowakowski, who had lived in terror since the moment he first saw the Mozart score, said, "Dove è il Felicia?"

Padlo saw that the old man trembled. "A young girl," the deputy said to Connolly. "Felicia Kaminski. Jedynak's niece." Recalling her photo, he began to describe her.

"She's not here," Connolly said.

"Harbor Court," the old man told Padlo.

Padlo repeated the hotel's name.

Not now, Connolly thought as she shut her cell phone.

Out in the dining room, Faust had made his play.

Faust said, "My father was a relatively old man when he married my mother. They met at a type of tango bar we call milangas in Buenos Aires. A scratchy Carlos Gardel record, seductive glances filled with subverted desire. Invitations to dance made with simple nods. The intense courtship begins with toe-tangling turns and kicks under crystal chandeliers. Before they speak, it seems to my father that they're making love."

"What's your father got to do with this?"

"As a young man, my father was a chemist in Poland. He said my mother reminded him of his first wife, a gypsy, Zumella. She died in Europe during the war."

"Along with million and millions of others. If we didn't stop that madman we'd all be speaking German."

"He called my mother Jolanta—violet blossom. He was a sentimental man. He met his first wife selling violet blossoms in Castle Square in Warsaw."

"I fail to see what this—"

"Colonel Middleton, in all your travels or investigations for the government have you ever heard the name Projekt 93?"

"I don't believe I have."

"Are you familiar with the work of Gerhard Schrader?"

Middleton shook his head.

"A German chemist who experimented with chemical agents. He invented Tabun, which was originally used to kill insects, then adapted as a lethal weapon against mankind. The Nazis produced twelve-thousand tons of the stuff at a secret plant in Poland, code named Hockwerk."

Faust dipped into a briefcase at his feet and removed a photocopy of a document from the Nuremberg Tribunal. "My father worked at Hockwerk. His name is fourth on this list."

"Kazimierz Rymut?"

"You'll note the asterisk, which refers to the footnote at the bottom. It might be hard to read so I'll quote it for you: 'This individual has been exculpated due to cooperation he provided regarding experiments conducted on human subjects.'"

"I'm not sure I know what that means."

"It means that my father heard that some of the chemical agents he was working on—agents that he assumed would be used to kill rats and other rodents—were being used on human beings. On October 14, 1944, Doctor Josef Mengele removed approximately five thousands gypsies from Sachsenhausen concentration camp outside Oranienberg and had them trucked into a wooded area near Rudna, Poland. There they were sprayed with Sarin gas. Within hours, every single man, woman and child died."

"Isn't that the same material that was used in the subway attack in Tokyo?"

"By the Aum Shinrikyo cult. Yes."

Faust's hand drifted toward his briefcase. "I have in my possession the official report, but will spare you the details. Suffice it to say, the results were ghastly. When rumors of this event reached my father, I'm sure he refused to believe them at first. He was a man, like many, who tried to insulate himself from the ugliness of the world around him. He listened to Vivaldi, tinkered with coo-coo clocks, baked pastries, wept at the faces of young children. He was not like us, Colonel. And yet when confronted with the horror of what was going on around him, he acted."

Middleton said, "Sounds like your father was a hero."

"He became a hero and a great example to me. I won't go into all the details of what he did except to say that he found a way to pass details of the chemical weapon program at Hockwerk known as Projekt 93 to the

Allies, which helped them target the plant before it could cause any more damage."

"Thank God."

The waiter arrived with the Bronzini, which gave off a faint scent of orange blossom under a delicate brown crust.

"Yes, thank God," Faust said as he sampled the fish, deeming it delightful. "The maniacs were stopped. But evil men have a way of rediscovering the most horrifying things."

Middleton nodded. "I do believe that evil is an active force in the world."

Faust leaned closer and almost whispered, "And you and I are going to stop it."

"How?" Middleton was confused. A part of him wanted to believe Faust; another part was hugely skeptical. "I still don't understand how this relates to us, here, tonight."

"Because, Colonel, some of the manuscripts that you found hidden in St. Sophia, in the Czartoryski Collection, were not about music. This is what your friend Henryk Jedynak was on the verge of telling you. That's why he was killed."

"Why?"

"Because encrypted in the musical notes are formulas for a number of V-agents—highly stable nerve agents that were developed at Hockwerk, many times more lethal that Sarin or Tabun. The most potent of these is known as VX. Scientists call it the most toxic synthesized compound known to man."

"If this is true—"

"It's undoubtedly true! I'll provide the supporting documents," Faust said. "I assume you'll thoroughly check out the story yourself."

"Of course."

"The clock is ticking, Colonel. We don't have much time."

"Why?"

"I don't think I need to tell you which formula is encrypted into the Chopin manuscript."

"VX."

"Correct."

Middleton's mind worked feverishly, tracking back over all that had happened since he first saw the manuscripts in Pristina.

Faust tore into a piece of bread. "Vukasin must be stopped!"

"The Wolf is behind all this? He thought of Sylvia, his ex; and Charley, who was still at risk.

"Absolutely. His plan is horrifying. Unimaginably cruel."

"But Rugova . . . Where did he fit in?"

"Sometimes one doesn't have the luxury to choose the most favorable allies. When I learned about the existence of the manuscripts, I hired Rugova to help me. He wasn't particularly reliable or sympathetic. I was, I regret to say, desperate. I'm even more desperate now."

Vukasin knew he was alone now—alone amid perhaps five police cruisers, nine uniformed cops and maybe twice as many in plainclothes who had come to the Martha Jefferson Hospital. Someone had been smart: They had told local law enforcement that Middleton, the man they believed had killed two policemen at Dulles, had been spotted at the hospital and would soon return. So right now Charlotte Middleton-Perez was as protected as anyone inside the Beltway. She could not be Vukasin's next victim. Too bad, he thought. He would have to draw out Middleton in some other way.

And he would have to do it. Andrzej, his last reliable agent in the States, had failed to contact him after trailing the Volunteer Tesla from the house at Lake Anna to who knows where; Vukasin imagined the killer and his shaved head, with its ridiculous jack of spades tattoo, had been served to pigs in the countryside. Soberski had failed too—getting her head blown off in the middle of the street a short walk from the White House. Briefly, he wondered what the sadist's last utterance had been.

Well, Vukasin thought, as he retreated in the forest behind the hospital. With all the work comes all the honor. Tens of thousands of dead Americans, and the credit will belong only to me.

But one last chore.

The Harbor Court Hotel, near the next Ground Zero, was only 150 or so miles north. Driving with caution, he'd be there in four hours.

He smiled at the thought of what would occur after he arrived.

13

LISA SCOTTOLINE

Charley Middleton-Perez floated in that netherworld between wake-fulness and sleep, anxiety tugging at the edge of her consciousness like a toddler at the hem of his mother's skirt. She knew at some vague level that she was in a hospital room, that her husband Jack was asleep in the chair beside her, and that the doctors had given her meds to help her rest. From outside in the hall came the faint rattle of a cart gliding over a pol-ished floor and people talking in low voices. She didn't care enough to eavesdrop. She remained in the drug cocoon, pharmaceutically insulated from her fears.

Unfortunately, it was wearing off. And no drug could quell these fears, not forever. So much had happened, almost all at once. In her mind's eye, she saw the scenes flicker backward in time, a gruesome rewind. Someone had tried to kill her. They'd murdered her mother, and she had seen her dead on the floor, her lovely features contorted and a blackening pool of blood beneath her head, seeping into the grains of the oak floor, filling its lines like a grisly etching.

Troubled, shifting in the bed, she flashed on her father running for his life. And her husband Jack had risked everything to save them both.

But there was one life he couldn't save.

She heard a slight moan and realized that it came from her. She was waking up, though she wasn't sure she wanted to. Closer to wakefulness than sleep, she felt an emptiness that she realized was literally true. She was empty now.

The baby was gone. The baby she had carried for the past five months, within her very body.

She had loved being pregnant, every minute of it. They had tried for the baby for so long, and she couldn't believe when they'd finally gotten pregnant. She'd memorized baby books, and from day one of her pregnancy, was mindful that every spoonful she put into her mouth and every sip of every drink, she was taking for them both. She ate plain yogurt, gave up her beloved chocolate, fled from secondhand smoke and refused anti-nausea meds when her morning sickness was its worst. Her every thought had been to nurture the baby, one they'd both wanted so much.

Jack, Jr.

She had decided to name him Jack, Jr., and Jack would have loved the idea. Now she would never tell him her plan. He hadn't wanted to know whether the baby was a boy or a girl, so she'd kept it from him too, though she was bursting with the news.

Surprise me, he had said, the night she had found out, a smile playing around his lips. And she had felt so full of love at his uncharacteristic spontaneity that she had thrown her arms around him and given him a really terrific hug, at least by pregnancy standards, which was from three feet away.

She shifted on the bed, and her eyelids fluttered open. She caught a glimpse of light from the windows, behind institutional-beige curtains. The brightness told her it was morning, though of which day, she didn't know. Before her eyes closed again, she spotted Jack, a sleeping silhouette slumped in a chair, his broad shoulders slanted down. His head, with his sandy hair rumpled, had fallen to the side; he would have a crook in his neck when he awoke.

She felt an ache of love for him, together with an ache of pain for their loss. His son. Their son. A son could continue to redeem a family name tainted by his grandfather's shady dealings. He had become one of the most respected lawyers in New Orleans, if not Louisiana, and his secret motive was to silence the whispered sniggering behind hands, the malicious talk of Creole mob connections and worse. He'd served on several committees to allocate Katrina relief funds, and his work to help the hurricane victims had gained him some national attention. For him, a baby son represented a new, brighter future.

I'll take one of each, Charley, he said one night, as she rested on his chest after they had made love. He had been tender with her in bed, even more so than usual, moving gingerly over her growing tummy. Neither wanted to do anything to hurt the baby, the two of them as spooked as kittens.

But now there would be no baby, no son, no redemption. Only emptiness.

She blinked, then closed her eyes, feeling tears well. She didn't cry, stopping at the edge of emotion, afraid to fall into the chasm of full-blown grief. The drugs were preventing feelings from reaching her, distancing her even from herself. She must be having some kind of delayed reaction. The night she'd miscarried, she'd been so scared when she heard that she was in danger and Harry, too, that she hadn't had time to react to losing the baby, much less to mourn him.

Her eyelids fluttered again, and the background noise grew louder. She was waking up; there was no avoiding it. She realized that the talking wasn't in the hall, but it was her husband's voice. He was saying, "Don't worry, she's asleep and should be up in an hour or so."

She looked over, her vision clearing, and realized that he hadn't been asleep, but on the cell phone, which was tucked in his neck.

"Okay, good luck," he said into the phone. "I'll keep you posted."

"Jack?" she asked, her voice raspy.

"Hey, sleepyhead." He closed the phone, rose, and came over to the bed with a warm smile. "How you feeling?"

"Fine." She didn't feel like telling the truth, not now.

"That was your dad, checking on you." He sat on the bed and stroked her hair back from her forehead. "Good news. He's fine. He's joined forces with some people he seems to have faith in. I gotta believe he knows what he's doing."

"He does." She felt relief wash over her. A professional, her father knew who to trust and who to run from.

Perez leaned over and gave her a soft kiss. "So all we have to worry about now is you."

Suddenly a burst of laughter came from the open door, and they both looked up in time to see a stout nurse in patterned scrubs bustle into the room, her hand extended palm-up. "Give it here, buddy!" she said to Perez. Her voice was louder than was polite, but she was laughing.

"No way." He laughed, too.

"We had a deal," the nurse shot back, and without missing a beat, she grabbed the cell phone out of his hand. "Your husband works too damn hard," she said. "I told him he can't use his phone in the hospital. Now I'm confiscating it."

Perez rose, mock-frowning. "Who are you supposed to be? Nurse Ratchett?"

"You know, your poor husband hasn't eaten since yesterday lunch," the nurse said. "He won't leave your side."

"Aww." She felt a pang of guilt. The nurse couldn't know that Jack was guarding her in case the killer came looking for them.

"All the other girls are crushing on him, but I'm impervious to his charms."

"Impossible," Perez said with a smirk.

She was feeling safer now that it was morning and her father was OK. Plus the hospital was waking up, the hallway increasingly noisy. "Jack," she said, "why don't you go get some breakfast? Take a break."

"No, I'm fine." He dismissed her with a wave but the nurse grabbed his arm.

"Go, get out. I have to check some things on your wife, and I'd throw you out, anyway."

Perez said, "You OK, Charley?"

"Yes. Please, go. Eat something."

Perez nodded, then eyed the nurse with amusement. "Gimme my phone, Ratchett."

"When you come back."

"But I need to make calls."

"Go and take a break."

"Sir, yes, sir." Perez mock-saluted as he left.

"So how are you doing?" the nurse asked. She had a pleasantly fleshy face, with animated blue eyes and a freckled nose, and she wore her wiry, reddish hair back in an unfashionably long ponytail.

"Fine, I guess." She wasn't about to open up about her feelings to someone she hardly knew. The nurse tugged over a rolling cart, slid out a digital thermometer, and replaced its plastic tip.

"Open wide."

She obeyed like a baby bird, and the nurse stuck the thermometer into her mouth.

"You slept well, and your color looks good. I need to check your vitals."

The thermometer beeped. The nurse slid it out, read it quickly, then replaced it in the cart.

"You're back to normal," she said.

"Great. Is that what you have to check out on me?"

"No, I just said that to give us some alone time." The nurse took the blood pressure cuff from a rack on the wall and began wrapping it around her patient's upper arm. "I wanted to see how you were feeling. Really feeling, I mean. It's tough, emotionally, I know. I missed once, myself."

Missed. That must be the lingo.

"You will get through this, I promise. Take your time." The nurse squeezed the black rubbery bulb, and the pressure cuff got tighter and tighter.

"Excuse us, ladies!" called a voice from the door. A doctor entered, and two interns followed like a flying wedge of white coats.

"You're early, doc," the nurse said, her smile fading. She let the cuff deflate rapidly.

"Our chief weapon is surprise," the doctor said, and the young interns laughed.

"Please, no more Monty Python." The nurse rolled her eyes, folded up the blood pressure cuff, and stuffed it back in the wire rack. "I can't take any more."

"Ha! And now for something completely different." The doctor approached the bed with a sly smile, and the interns laughed again.

"Get ready to fake-laugh, Mrs. Perez," the nurse said as she patted her arm. "They're men, so they'll buy it." She handed over a cell phone. "Oh, I almost forgot, here's your hubby's phone."

"Thanks," she said, not recognizing it as Jack's. He must have gotten a new one.

"See ya, wouldn't wanna be ya." The nurse hustled from the room.

"I'm Dr. Lehmann, and these are my interns, but you don't have to know their names. Think of them as Palin and Gilliam to my John Cleese."

She fake-laughed, and the nurse was right. He bought it. Dr. Lehmann had a square jaw and long nose, and he smelled of fresh cologne. His expression was warm—until it changed.

"Well, my dear, you've been through hell."

"Yes."

"We did get some reports back, which we need to talk with you about." Dr. Lehmann frowned almost sternly, a pitchfork folding in the middle of his forehead, under steel gray hair like Brillo. "Your blood work shows unusual hormone levels, consistent with certain medications. Have you taken anything we should know about?"

She blinked, confused. "No, not at all."

"Nothing?"

"Nothing at all. I won't even take a baby aspirin."

"Really?"

"Really."

"Well." Dr. Lehmann frowned at her over the steely top of his glasses. "I won't mince words. To be frank, your levels are consistent with someone who has taken RU 486."

She didn't understand.

"Mifeprex. It's best administered under medical supervision. But unfortunately, it's commonly self-administered by women who want to induce miscarriage, much later in their pregnancy. It's commonly known as the abortion pill."

She couldn't see where he was going. "Okay, but what does that have to do with me?"

"Perhaps you wanted to end your pregnancy."

"Me? No. No way." She felt stricken. "Never."

Dr. Lehmann eyed her, plainly doubtful. "Many people who administer the pill themselves in the later trimesters don't realize that it's very dangerous and could lead to extreme loss of blood, which is what happened in your case. You could have bled to death."

"You think I tried to give myself an abortion?"

"Yes, I do. You can tell me the truth or not. Up to you." Dr. Lehmann paused as if for a confession.

"Is that why I miscarried?"

"Yes."

"How can you be sure?"

"Your levels can be explained by only one thing. In fact, they suggest you took two pills. You wouldn't be the first woman to have thought of that, either. Still, it's very, very dangerous."

"No, that's not what happened! I did not take the pill, any pill. I never would. I wanted this baby."

"I'm merely telling you what your blood work reveals."

"Then it's not my blood work. There's been a mistake." She looked at his lined face, then the equally grave faces of the interns. "There must have been a mistake."

"Look, Mrs. Perez, this is your business. I want to emphasize to you that it would be unwise to ever do this again." Dr. Lehmann's expression softened. "No judgment here. I'm concerned only for your safety."

She tried to function. "How does it cause an abortion, this pill?"

"The bottom line is that after the pill is ingested, severe cramping occurs and the fetus is expelled. When medically unsupervised, as in your case, it necessitates a D&C to be complete." Dr. Lehmann checked his watch. "We must be going. Grand rounds this morning. We'll check on you later."

She watched them go in silence. After they had left, her thoughts tumbled over one another, fast and furious. She hadn't taken an abortion pill, much less two. But she'd had cramping that night, so severe she'd doubled over from them. The cramps had started sometime after dinner.

She thought back to that awful night. She and Jack had had their typical Friday night dinner, which he routinely cooked as an end-of-the-week treat for her. He'd made chicken with rosemary and mashed potatoes, her favorite. He even shooed her from the kitchen when she'd tried to help and had served it to her at her seat, doling out extra mashed potatoes, over her protest.

The memory made her heart stop.

No.

She shook her head. It didn't make sense. It couldn't make sense. The blood work had to be wrong. Any other possibility was unthinkable. Impossible. There had to be a mistake.

She tried to puzzle it out, turning the cell phone over and over in her hand. Its smooth metallic finish caught the light from the harsh overhead fluorescents, and she flipped it open on impulse. The tiny, multicolored screen showed the menu and on impulse, she pressed the button for the call logs. On the screen appeared a sharp-focus highlighting of the last call that had been received. It should have shown that it was her father, but the caller's name didn't read DAD or even HARRY.

Instead, it read: MOZART.

Huh?

Why would Jack call her father Mozart? Puzzled, she flipped through the menu to the address book and skimmed the address list. The names were in alphabetical order, and she skimmed them: BACH, BEETHOVEN, BRAHMS, CHOPIN, HANDEL, LISZT, MAHLER, MENDELS-SOHN, SCARLATTI, SCHUBERT, SCHUMANN, SHOSTAKOVICH, SIBELIUS, TCHAIKOVSKY, VIVALDI.

What?

They were all composers. But Jack didn't know anything about music; her father was the music expert. What was going on? It looked as if the names were some kind of code, on a cell phone she hadn't even known existed.

What was happening? Who was Mozart? Had Jack heard from Harry? Had he lied about that? Why would he? Was Harry really okay? Suddenly, she didn't understand anything. The miscarriage. The abortion pills. A secret phone with coded addresses. Her heart thundered in her chest. Her mouth went dry. She needed answers.

She pressed the button for MOZART, thumbed back to the call log, and pressed the button for the MOZART profile. It contained no real name, no email and no other information except for the phone number, which had too many digits. What did that mean? Then she realized there was a country code in front of the number. She didn't know which country it was, but she knew it was an international number.

She pressed the buttons for two more profiles, HANDEL and LISZT. Both profiles were international calls, too, with no other information, like real name, email, or home phones. Why would Jack have a cell phone entirely—and solely—of international numbers? He'd never even traveled abroad; she was the world traveler of the two.

What about the baby?

She pushed the button and recalled MOZART, whoever the hell that was. The phone rang three times.

"Vukasin," answered a man, in a thick accent she couldn't identify.

She pressed End, her heart hammering. Who was Vukasin? What was going on? She couldn't puzzle it out fast enough. Something was horribly wrong, and Jack would be back any minute. She didn't know what to do. Confront him? Then she realized that this Vukasin guy could call back and blow her cover.

There was only one thing to do.

She hurled the cell phone to the hospital floor with all her might. The phone's plastic back sprung open, and the slim orange battery flew out, skidding to the wall in front of the chair.

Just then Perez appeared grinning in the doorway. "Honey, I'm home!"

She arranged her face into a wifely mask and turned sheepishly to the door. "Please don't be mad," she said, willing herself to act natural. "The nurse gave me your phone but I dropped it."

"Damn, Charley." Annoyance flickered over his handsome features. "It was a new one."

"I noticed. Sorry." She eased back into bed, watching her husband with new suspicion. "Did you buy one of those insurance contracts for it?"

"No." He strode to the chair, bent down, and began picking up the pieces of the cell phone. "Looks like all the king's horses and all the king's men . . ."

" . . . can't put it back together again?" She finished his sentence with ersatz remorse.

"Nah, but that's OK." He slipped the plastic shards of the phone into his jacket pocket and turned to his wife with a smile she had loved so much it broke her heart.

Did you kill our baby?

Did you try to kill me?

But she wouldn't ask him anything, just yet. She had to calculate her next move. Until she knew more, the best course was to keep her mouth shut and her eyes open.

She wasn't Harry Middleton's daughter for nothing.

14

P. J. PARRISH

Kaminski stood at the window staring down at the inner harbor. A fog had rolled in and the lights of the buildings blinked back at her like eyes in the dark.

Her head was pounding—from bone-deep fatigue and the lingering effects of Faust's Champagne. But also from fear.

She had never really felt fear like this before. Not when her parents disappeared and she was left on her own. Not when she had felt the press of the violin string against her neck when the man tried to kill her in Rome. Not even after she found out Uncle Henryk had been murdered.

But an hour ago, seeing the tattooed man bound in the closet, his bald head pouring blood, the cold, hammering fear began. It built as she heard him whimper as Faust whispered in his ear, as she saw his terrified tears, smelled the stench of his urine.

Shivering, she now moved away from the window, rubbing her hands over her arms. She scanned the suite's living room, its oriental carpets and colonial furnishings. A mahogany bar dominated one corner, a gleaming baby grand piano the other. Off to the left, through open French doors, she could see one of the two bedrooms. Faust's Vuitton duffle sat on the four-poster bed.

After the trip to the apartment, Faust had dropped her back at the hotel, and without another word, locked the door behind him and left. The man he called Nacho had been told to watch her. When he finally dozed off in the chair by the door, gun in hand, Kaminski had thought of running.

But where would she go? Faust had taken her passport, the one with the Joanna Phelps name on it, and her money. She knew no one in this country.

No, that wasn't true. She knew of one person: Harold Middleton, who taught at the American University in Washington, D.C., and whose name was on the package containing the Mozart manuscript Uncle Henryk had sent to Signor Abe days before he was murdered.

Kaminski shut her eyes, Abe Nowakowski's offer of help echoing in her head. She had tried to call him again in Rome, but the operator told her there was a block on her phone. No calls in or out. And so she was Faust's prisoner, and she didn't know why.

Nacho stirred, but went back to his snoring.

Kaminski paced slowly across the living room.

Her eyes found the piano in the corner and she went to it.

She ran a hand over the sleek black surface then slowly lifted the keyboard's lid. The keys glowed in the soft light.

Suddenly, the image of her father was in her head. She could almost see his long fingers moving over the keys of the old piano in their home. Her little hands had tried so hard at her lessons to please him.

He had been so disappointed when she chose the violin, her mother's instrument. Almost as if she had chosen her mother over him. But it had never been like that. She had loved her father so much, missed him so much.

And when he died, Uncle Henryk had been there for her to take his place.

Now the tears came. Kaminski did not stop them.

She sat down at the piano.

She played one chord. Then a quick section from a half-forgotten song. The Yamaha had an overly bright sound and a too-light action. But it didn't matter. Just hearing the notes was soothing.

She played a Satie Gymnopedie then started Eine Kleine Nachtmusik, a piece Uncle Henryk had so loved.

She stopped suddenly.

Mozart.

She wiped a hand over her face. The Mozart manuscript Signor Abe had given her: Was this the reason Faust had brought her here?

She glanced over at Nacho, who watched her with tired eyes.

She went quickly to Faust's bedroom. He had said the manuscript was "safe," locked in a closet. She threw open its louvered doors. The closet was empty. She turned and spotted his slender black briefcase sitting on the bed near the duffle.

There was nothing in it but an automatic gun, with an empty clip nearby, and a copy of Il Denaro. She stared at the date: four days ago. She picked it up and unfolded the paper.

Several yellowed manuscript papers fluttered to the bed. Where better for a man like Faust to hide a priceless Mozart manuscript than in plain sight, bundled in the financial news?

She carefully gathered the pages. Back at La Musica, when she had first seen the manuscript, she hadn't had time to really look at it. But now everything registered. The black scratchings were unmistakable. The fine strokes of faded ink. The distinctive signature. And finally, in the left corner very small: no. 28.

Her heart began to beat fast. She knew there were only twenty-seven catalogued Mozart piano concertos. Many of the originals that had resurfaced after the war were now housed in the Jagiellonska Library in Krakow.

Where had this one come from?

And was it the reason her uncle was dead?

She took the manuscript back to the piano. She sat down, carefully setting the fragile papers before her. She began to play.

The first movement opened with throbbing D minor chords. She had to go slowly, the technical demands way beyond her skills. Her heart was pounding with excitement as she grasped that she might be the first in centuries to play this.

She was sweating by the time she reached the end of the first movement. She stopped suddenly.

My God. A cadenza.

She stared at the notes. Her father had taught her that Mozart himself often injected cadenzas—improvised virtuoso solos—into his music. But he never wrote them down. Modern performers usually filled the gaps with their own improvisations that tried to mimic the master's intent.

She began to play the cadenza. But her ears began to pick up strange discordant sounds. Odd little dissonances and patterns. She could suddenly hear her father's voice speaking to her from behind as she practiced.

With Mozart, my dear, with music so pure, the slightest error stands out as an unmistakable blemish.

Kaminski stopped, her fingers poised over the keys.

There was something very strange about this cadenza.

The restaurant was almost empty. Two waiters stood at discreet attention just beyond a red curtain. Middleton could see from their faces they wanted to go home.

Yet Faust seemed in no hurry to go anywhere.

"So you never suspected anything about the Chopin?" Faust asked.

Middleton wasn't sure how much to tell him. He still didn't trust the man.

He thought suddenly about his interrupted ride to Baltimore with the two dopers Traci and Marcus. How he had made them listen to a Schoenberg recitatif, and Marcus's crack that it sounded like nothing but wrong notes.

All the easier to hid a message in, he had told Marcus.

How hard could it be then to encrypt a code within the mathematical beauty of Chopin?

"As soon as I saw it, I felt something was wrong with it," Middleton said. "But I just chalked it up to a bad forgery."

"Jedynak didn't say anything?" Faust asked.

Middleton shook his head. "When we were going over all the manuscripts, he seemed very interested in the Chopin in particular. He insisted I take it back to the States for authentication. Even though I told him I was sure it was a fake."

"Maybe he was trying to get it safely out of the country. Maybe he was trying to keep it out of the wrong hands."

"Jedynak knew the VX formula was encrypted in it?"

Faust shrugged.

Middleton sat back in his chair. "So I was supposed to be some fuckin' mule?"

Faust said nothing. Which angered Middleton even more.

"Can I see it?" Faust asked.

When Middleton didn't move, Faust gave him a sad smile. "I told you. I am desperate. I need your help."

Middleton reached down to the briefcase at his feet and pulled out the manuscript. He handed it to Faust across the table.

Faust looked at it for a moment then his dark eyes came back up to Middleton.

"I know chemistry. You know music." He pushed it across the table. "Tell me what you see."

Middleton hesitated then turned the manuscript so he could read it. The paper and ink alone were enough for him to offer Jedynak his initial opinion that it was probably a forgery. A good one, yes, but still a forgery.

But now, he concentrated on the notes themselves. He took his time. The quiet bustle of the waiters clearing the cutlery and linen fell away. He was lost in the music.

He looked up suddenly.

"There's something missing," he said.

"What do you mean?" Faust asked.

Middleton shook his head. "It's probably nothing. This is, after all, just a forgery. But the end of the first movement—a piece of it is missing."

"But you're not sure," Faust asked.

"I wish I had . . . "

"You wish you had another expert eye?"

"Yes," Middleton said.

"I have one for you," Faust said. "Come. Let's go . . . But we go alone. Not with any visitors."

"Who else would go with us?"

Faust smiled and glanced toward the front of the restaurant, where Tesla and Lespasse awaited. "Alone . . . That is one of the immutable terms of the deal."

"I'll follow your lead."

Faust reached forward and tugged on Middleton's tiny wire microphone/earbud unit. He dropped it on the floor and crushed it. He then paid the bill. "Wait here." He made a phone call from the pay phone near the men's room then returned to the table. No more than five minutes later sirens sounded in the distance, growing closer. The attention of everyone in the restaurant turned immediately to the front windows. Then, in a flurry of lights and horns, police cars and emergency trucks skidded to a stop across the quaint street from the restaurant, in front of a bar. The bomb squad was the centerpiece of the operation.

Middleton had to give Faust credit. Not a single person in the restaurant or outside was focused anywhere but on the police action. They'd discover soon enough it was a false alarm, but the distraction would serve its purpose.

Middleton slipped the Chopin manuscript back into his briefcase and rose to his feet. Faust gestured to the kitchen.

"Through the back. Hurry. Time is short."

This was where Felicia Kaminski was, M. T. Connolly thought, and it was where Middleton and Faust would continue their rendezvous.

Connolly now knew what Middleton had that so many people had deemed valuable enough to kill for: a seemingly priceless manuscript created for pleasure but now corrupted with the possibility of mass murder.

Even sitting alone, outside this hotel, in the dark privacy of her own thoughts, she was a little ashamed to admit she was ignorant of the strange history of this Chopin score, and of the human value of such a find. More so, until tonight, she had been as unaware as most Americans about the tragedies at St. Sophia.

But she did understand a monster's need for glory, no matter how twisted and unimaginable it might be to a sane person. And it was an interesting side note to the events of the last few days. Her colleagues in law enforcement were looking for Middleton because they believed he killed two cops. But, thanks to Josef, her angel in Poland, she knew better. Middleton had in his hands a formula for mass destruction, and though he had formed an alliance with Kalmbach and Chambers, she believed he needed her help to keep it away from Vukasin. Kalmbach and Chambers she did not trust. In the core of her being, she believed the only way to stop a chemical attack within the borders of the United States was to keep Harold Middleton alive.

She took a quick look along the street and checked her watch. There was no sense in going inside the hotel until Middleton and Faust arrived—because it was only then that Vukasin would appear. She had left her previous post inside the restaurant only seconds before Middleton and Faust, sure they would come here to confer with Kaminski, who could help them solve their puzzle.

Now the street was asleep and silent, few lights reflecting life, except in the windows of the Harbor Court Hotel. A white BMW sat under a flickering streetlamp, parked where it could easily be seen. About 100 feet to the south, tucked into the shade of an old oak, was a charcoal sedan, its hood glittering with raindrops, its side windows fogged: Connolly's.

Vukasin was hidden in the generous gray shadows of a nearby building, watching her. He would not move until she did.

Nine minutes later, he was rewarded for his patience. An almost undetectable shift of the undercarriage told him she had readjusted to a more comfortable position. He was certain she had been in the sedan's quiet and security for too long.

Though he rather it had been Middleton or Faust behind the wheel, or even Kaminski, it mattered little who was in the car. It could be an innocent soul waiting for a lover, or a fool sleeping off the last taste of cheap whiskey. A minor distraction, at best. But one that had to be dealt with. He could not afford to be seen.

Vukasin slipped from his invisibility and made his way toward the sedan. He added a stagger to his walk and a slump to his shoulders to simulate the last journey of a drunk's long night.

The sedan jostled again as Vukasin neared it, the occupant coming to life. He could not see inside as he passed, but he heard the faint creak of wet glass moving as the occupant cracked the window a sliver to see who was passing.

He decided to play.

He ambled back to the sedan, arms spread. "Good evening, kind sir, could you spare a few dollars and direct me to the nearest bus line?"

"Go away," Connolly said, her thoughts on Middleton and the manuscript.

Vukasin moved closer. "I am harmless, I assure you," he said.

"Get the fuck out of here. Go."

The window slipped lower, exposing a pale feminine face, her hair brassy and close-cropped. "I'm a cop," she said. "Now get moving."

"So maybe you'd like a drink?" he asked, as he reached into his pocket. "I have a bottle of Russkaya—"

He saw something begin to crystallize in her eyes as he started to withdraw the automatic.

She knows, he thought, with a smile. She knows I'm not American and not a drunk just passing by.

Her eyes widened in complete understanding.

She knew who he was.

And when she saw the metallic glint of the Glock leveled at her head, she knew she was about to die.

He fired, the silenced shot sounding like no more than a small but powerful puff of hot air on the empty street.

15

LEE CHILD

They used the Harbor Court's main street door. Faust led the way to it and pulled it and let Middleton walk through first. Good manners, etiquette, and a clear semaphore signal to the hotel's front-of-house staff: I'm a guest and this guy is with me. A literal embrace, one hand holding the door and the other shepherding Middleton inside. A commonplace dynamic, repeated at the hotel's entrance a thousand times a day. The staff looked up, understood, glanced away.

Vukasin didn't glance away. From 40 yards his gaze followed both men to the elevator bank.

The elevator was smooth but slow, tuned for a low-rise building. Faust got out first, because Middleton wouldn't know which way to turn. Faust held his arms at a right angle, like a traffic cop, blocking right, pointing left. Middleton walked ahead. Thick carpet, quiet air. The muffled sound of a piano. A bright tone and a fast, light action. A Yamaha or a Kawai, Middleton thought. A grand, but not a European heavyweight. A Japanese baby, cross-strung. Light in the bass, tinkly in the treble. A D-minor obbligato was being played confidently with the left hand, and a hesitant melody was being played with the right, in the style of Mozart. But not Mozart, Middleton thought. Certainly no Mozart he had ever heard before. Sight-read, which might explain the hesitancy. Perhaps a pastiche. Or an academic illustration, to demonstrate the standard musicological theory that Mozart bridged the gap between the classical composers and the romantics. The melody seemed to be saying: See? We start with Bach, and 200 years later we get to Beethoven.

The sound got louder but no clearer as they walked. Faust eased ahead and repeated his traffic-cop routine outside a door, blocking the corridor, corralling Middleton to a stop. Faust took a key card from his pocket. It bottomed in the slot, a red light turned green, and the mechanism clicked.

Faust said, "After you."

Middleton turned the handle before the light clicked red again. Bright piano sound washed out at him. The melody again, started over from the top, played this time with confidence, its architecture now fully diagrammed, its structure understood.

But still not Mozart.

Middleton stepped inside and saw a suite, luxurious but not traditional. A lean, bearded man in a chair by the door, with a gun in his hand. His nickname, it turned out, was Nacho. A Yamaha baby grand, with a girl at the keyboard. Manuscript pages laid out left-to-right in front of her on the piano's lid. The girl was thin. She had dark hair and a pinched Eastern European face full of a thousand sorrows. The manuscript looked to be a handwritten original. Old foxed paper, untidy notations, faded ink.

The girl stopped playing. Middleton's mind filled in what would come next, automatically, to the end of the phrase. Faust stepped in behind Middleton and closed the door. The room went quiet. Faust ignored the man in the chair. He walked straight to the piano and gathered the manuscript pages and butted them together and left them in a tidy pile on a credenza. Then he stepped back and closed the lid on the piano's keyboard, gently, giving the girl time to remove her fingers. He said, "Time for business. We have a Chopin manuscript."

"Forged and faked," Middleton said.

"Indeed," Faust said. "And missing a page, I think. Would you agree?"

Middleton nodded. "The end of the first movement. Possibly not a whole page. Maybe just sixteen bars or less."

"How many notes?"

"That's an impossible question. It's a concerto. A dozen instruments, sixteen bars, there could be hundreds of notes."

"The solo instrument," Faust said. "The theme. Ignore the rest. How many notes?"

Middleton shrugged. "Forty, maybe? A statement, a restatement, a resolution. But it's still an impossible question. It isn't Chopin. It's somebody pretending to be Chopin."

Faust said, "I think that helps us. We have to second-guess a second-guesser. It's about what's plausible."

"We can't compose the end of something that didn't exist in the first place."

Faust opened his jacket and took a folded glassine envelope from the inside pocket. Unfolded it and smoothed it. Behind the milky acetate was a single sheet of paper. It had been torn out of a reporter's note pad. It was speckled with dried brown bloodstains. Small droplets. Not arterial spray. Just the kind of spatter that comes from small knife wounds, or heavy blows to a face. Under the stains the paper had been ruled by hand into music staves. Five lines, four spaces, repeated four times. A treble clef. E-G-B-D-F. Every Good Boy Deserves Favor. A 4/4 time signature. Sixteen measures. A melody, sketched in with deft untidy strokes of a pen.

Faust laid the page in front of the girl, on the piano's lid, where the Mozart had been. He said, "Suppose someone who had seen the missing page was asked to reproduce what had been there."

The girl looked at the spatters of blood and said, "Asked?"

Faust said, "Required, then."

The girl said, "My uncle wrote this."

"You can tell?"

"It's handwritten. Handwriting is handwriting, whether it's words or musical notes."

Middleton said, "Your uncle?"

Faust said, "This is Felicia Kaminski. Temporarily going as Joanna Phelps, but she's Henryk Jedynak's niece. Or, she was." Then he pointed at Middleton and addressed the girl and said, "And this is Colonel Harold Middleton. He saw your uncle in Warsaw. Your uncle was a brave man. He stole a page. He knew what was at stake. But he didn't get away with it."

"Who did this to him?"

"We'll get to that. First we need to know if he put the truth on paper."

Faust took out the rest of the first-movement manuscript and handed it to the girl. She spread it out in sequence. She followed the melody with her finger, humming silently. She raised the piano's lid again and picked out phrases on the keys, haltingly. She jumped to the bloodstained page and continued. Middleton nodded to himself. He heard continuity, logic, sense.

Until the last measure.

The last measure was where the movement should have come home to rest, with a whole note that settled back to the root of the native key, with calm and implacable inevitability. But it didn't. Instead it hung suspended in midair with an absurd discordant trill, sixteenth notes battling it out through the whole of the bar, a dense black mess on the page, a harsh beating pulse in the room.

The girl said, "The last bar can't be right."

Faust said, "Apparently."

The girl played the trill again, faster. Said, "OK, now I see."

"See what?"

"The two notes are discordant. Play them fast enough, and the intermodulation between them implies a third note that isn't actually there. But you can kind of hear it. And it's the right note. It would be very obvious on a violin."

Middleton said, "Chopin didn't write like that."

The girl said, "I know."

Faust asked, "What's the implied note?"

The girl played the trill for half a bar and then stabbed a key in between and a pure tone rang out, sweet and correct and reassuring. She said, "Two notes."

Faust said, "Sounds like one to me."

"The last note of this movement and the first of the next. That's Chopin. Who did this to my uncle?"

Faust didn't answer, because right then the door opened and Vukasin walked in. He had a silenced Glock held down by his thigh and from six feet away Middleton could smell that it had been used, and recently. Faust said, "We're all here." He made the formal introductions, one to the other, Vukasin, Middleton, Nacho, Kaminski. He let his gaze rest on Kaminski and said, "Colonel Middleton killed your uncle. He tortured that page out of him and then cut his throat. In Warsaw, after their lunch."

"Not true," Middleton said.

"True," Vukasin said. "I saw him leave. I went in and found the body. Three bodies. Two bystanders got in the way, apparently."

Faust stepped aside as Nacho took Middleton's arms and pinned him. Vukasin raised the silenced Glock and pointed it at Middleton's face. Then Vukasin lowered the gun again and reversed it in his hand and offered it butt-first to the girl. Said, "Your uncle. Your job, if you want it."

The girl got up off the piano stool and stepped around the end of the keyboard and came forward. Took the gun from Vukasin, who said, "It's ready to go. No safety on a Glock. Just point and shoot, like a cheap camera. There won't be much noise."

Then he stood off to her left. She raised the gun and aimed it where he had aimed it, at the bridge of Middleton's nose. The muzzle wavered a little, in small jerky circles. With the sound suppressor it was a long and heavy weapon.

Middleton said, "They're lying."

The girl nodded.

"I know," she said.

She turned to her left, twisting from the waist, and shot Vukasin in the face. He had been right. There wasn't much noise. Just a bang like a heavy book being slammed on a table, and a wet crunch as the bullet hit home, and the soft tumble of a body falling on thick carpet. Then nothing, just the stink of gunpowder and pooling blood.

The girl twisted back, and lined up on Faust.

"Middleton understands music," she said. "I can see that from here. He wouldn't need to torture that melody out of anyone. It was predictable. Like night follows day."

Faust said, "I didn't know."

"The two discordant notes," the girl said. "Making a phantom third. My uncle always called it a wolf tone. And Vukasin means wolf, in Polish. It was a coded message. He was naming his killer."

"I didn't know," Faust said again. "I swear."

"Talk."

"I hired Vukasin. Someone else must have gotten to him. Hired him out from under me. He was double crossing me."

"Who?"

"I don't know. I swear. And we can't waste time on this. The music holds more code than who killed your uncle."

"He's right, Felicia," Middleton said. "First things first. It's about nerve gas. It could make 9/11 look like a day at the beach."

"And it's coming soon," Faust said.

Kaminski nodded.

"Days away," she said.

She lowered the gun.

"Forty notes," Faust said. "Forty letters between A and G. It's not enough."

"Add in the Mozart cadenza," Kaminski said. "That's bullshit too."

Middleton said, "Mozart didn't write cadenzas."

Kaminski nodded. "Exactly. He didn't write twenty-eight piano concertos, either. The cadenza is part of the message. Same board, same game."

Faust asked, "Which first?"

"Mozart. He was before Chopin."

"Then how many notes?"

"The two things together, a couple hundred in total, maybe."

"Still not enough. And you can't spell stuff out using only A through G. Especially not in German."

"There are sharps and flats. The Mozart is in D-minor."

"You can't sharpen and flatten letters of the alphabet."

"Numbers," Middleton said. "It's not letters of the alphabet. It's numbers."

"One for A, two for B? That's still not enough. This thing is complex."

"Not one for A," Middleton said. "Concert pitch. The A above middle C is 440 cycles per second. Each note has a specific frequency. Sharps and flats, equally. A couple hundred notes would yield eighty-thousand digits. Like a bar code. Eighty-thousand digits would yield all the information you want."

Faust asked, "How do we work it out?"

"With a calculator," Middleton said. "On the treble stave the second space up is the A above middle C. That's 440 cycles. An octave higher is the first overtone, or the second harmonic, 880 cycles. An octave lower is 220 cycles. We can work out the intervals in between. We'll probably get a bunch of decimal places, which is even better. The more digits, the more information."

Faust nodded. Nothing in his face. He retrieved the Mozart manuscript from the credenza and butted it together with the smeared page in the glassine envelope. Clamped the stack under his arm and nodded to Nacho. Then he looked at Kaminski and Middleton and suddenly leapt forward, ripping the silenced Glock from her hand.

He said, "I wasn't entirely honest before. I didn't hire Vukasin. We were both hired by someone else. For the same purpose. Which isn't entirely benevolent, I'm afraid. We have ricin, and everything else we need. But we couldn't stabilize the mixture. Now we can, thanks to your keen insights. For which we thank you. We'll express our thanks practically—with mercy. Exactly ten minutes from now, when I'm safely away, Nacho will shoot you both in the head. Fast and painless, I promise."

The gun in Nacho's hand came up and rested level, steady as a rock. He was back in his chair, solidly between Middleton and the door. Kaminski gasped and caught Middleton's arm. Faust smiled once, and his blue eyes twinkled, and he let himself out.

Ten minutes. A long time, or a short time, depending on the circumstances. Ten minutes in a line at the post office seems like an eternity. The last 10 minutes of your life seems like a blink of an eye. Nacho didn't move a muscle. He was like a statue, except that the muzzle of his gun moved to track every millimetric move that Middleton or Kaminski made, and except that about once every 90 seconds he glanced at his watch.

He took his final look at the time and raised his gun a little higher. Head height, not gut height. His finger whitened on the trigger.

Then the door opened.

Jack Perez stepped into the room.

Nacho turned toward him. Said, "What—"

Perez raised his gun and shot Nacho in the face. No silencer. The noise was catastrophic. They left by the fire stairs, in a big hurry.

Ten minutes later they were in an Inner Harbor diner and Perez was saying, "So basically you told him everything?"

Kaminski nodded her head very ruefully and said, "Yes."

Middleton shook his head very definitively and said, "No."

"So which is it?" Perez said. "Yes or no?"

"No," Middleton said. "But only inadvertently. I made a couple of mistakes. I guess I wasn't thinking too straight."

"What mistakes?"

"Concert pitch is a fairly recent convention. Like international time zones. The idea that the A above middle C should be tuned to 440 cycles started way after both Mozart and Chopin were around. Back in the day the tunings across Europe varied a lot, and not just from country to country or time to time. Pitch could vary even within the same city. The pitch used for an English cathedral organ in the 1600s could be as much as five semitones lower than the harpsichord in the bishop's house next door. The variations could be huge. There's a pitch pipe from 1720 that plays the A above middle C at 380 cycles, and Bach's organs in Germany played A at 480 cycles. The A on the pitch pipe would have been an F on the organs. We've got a couple of Handel's tuning forks, too. One plays A at 422 cycles and the other at 409."

Perez said, "So?"

"So Faust's calculations will most likely come out meaningless."

"Unless?"

"Unless he figures out a valid base number for A."

"Which would be what?"

"428 would be my guess. Plausible for the period, and the clue is right there in the Mozart. The 28th piano concerto, which he never got to. The message was hidden in the cadenza. If the 28 wasn't supposed to mean something in itself, they could have written a bogus cadenza into any of the first twenty-seven real concertos."

"Faust will figure that out. When all else fails. He's got the Mozart manuscript."

"Even so," Middleton said. He turned to Kaminski. "Your uncle would have been ashamed of me. I didn't account for the tempering. He would have. He was a great piano tuner."

Perez asked, "What the hell is tempering?"

Middleton said, "Music isn't math. If you start with A at 440 cycles and move upward at intervals that the math tells you are correct, you'll be out of tune within an octave. You have to nudge and fudge along the way. By ear. You have to do what your ear tells you is right, even if the numbers say you're wrong. Bach understood. That's what The Well-Tempered Klavier is all about. He had his own scheme. His original title page had a handwritten drawing on it. It was assumed for centuries that it was just decoration, a doodle really, but now people think it was a diagram about how to temper a keyboard so it sounds perfect."

Perez took out a pen and did a rapid calculation on a napkin. "So what are you saying? If A is 440, B isn't 495?"

"Not exactly, no."

"So what is it?"

"493, maybe."

"Who would know? A piano tuner?"

"A piano tuner would feel it. He wouldn't know it."

"So how did these Nazi chemists encode it?"

"With a well-tuned piano, and a microphone, and an oscilloscope."

"Is that the only way?"

"Not now. Now it's much easier. You could head down to Radio Shack and buy a digital keyboard and a MIDI interface. You could tune the keyboard down to A equals 428, and play scales, and read the numbers right off the LED window."

Perez nodded.

And sat back.

And smiled.

16

JEFFERY DEAVER

"No leads."

Emmett Kalmbach and Dick Chambers were supervising the search of the suite at the Harbor Court, which had been rented by Faust under a fake name. Naturally, Middleton reflected sourly, cell phone at his ear; the man was a master of covering his tracks.

"Nothing?" he asked, shaking his head to Felicia Kaminski and Jack Perez, who sat across from him in the diner.

"Nope. We've gone over the entire place," Kalmbach said. "And searched Vukasin's body. And some bastard with a weird tattoo. Name is Stefan Andrzej. Oh, and that Mexican your son-in-law took out. But not a goddamn clue where Faust might've gone."

"The binoculars Felicia told us about?" Kaminski had explained about Nacho's game of I-spy out the window, and the bits of conversation that had to do with deliveries and technical information. "They were focused on a warehouse across the street but it was empty."

"So he's taken the chemicals someplace else."

"And we don't have a fucking clue where," the FBI agent muttered. "We'll keep looking. I'll get back to you, Harry."

The line went dead.

"No luck," Middleton muttered. He sipped coffee and finished a candy bar. He told himself it was for the energy; in fact, he mostly needed the comfort of the chocolate. "At least I gave Faust the wrong information about the code in the music. He can only get so far with the gas."

"But with trial and error," Kaminski asked, "he could he come up with the right formula?"

"Yeah, he could. And a lot of people'll die—and the deaths'd be real unpleasant."

They sat silently for a moment then he glanced at Perez. "You looked pretty comfortable with that Beretta." As he had with the Colt when he took down Eleana Soberski.

His son in law laughed. "I stayed clear of the family business in Lose-iana. "But that doesn't mean I wasn't aware of the family business." A coy smile. "But you know that, right?"

Middleton shrugged. "I ran a check on you, sure. You were marrying my daughter . . . If there'd been a spec of dirt in your closet, Charley wouldn't have a hyphenated name right now."

"I respect looking out for kin, Harry. I'll be the same way with my . . . " His voice faded and he looked down, thinking, of course, of the child they'd almost had. Middleton touched his arm, squeezed.

Kaminski asked, "My uncle knew you as a musicologist, uno professore. But you are much more than that, aren't you?"

"Yes. Well, I was. I worked for the army and the government. Then I had a group that tracked down war criminals."

"Like the man who killed my uncle?"

"Yes."

"You said 'had.' What happened?"

"The group broke up."

"Why?" Perez asked.

Middleton decided to share the story with them. "There was an incident in Africa. The four of us tracked down a warlord in Darfur. He'd been stealing AIDS drugs from the locals and selling children as soldiers. We did an extraordinary rendition—lured him to international waters and were going to fly him back to The Hague for trial. Then our main witnesses against him all died quote accidentally in a fire. They were in a safe house. The doors were locked and it burned. Most of them had their families with them. Twenty children died. Without the witnesses there was no trial. We had to let him go. I was going to head back to Darfur and make a case against him for the fire but Val—Valentin Brocco—lost it. He heard the man smirking about how he'd beaten us. Val pulled him out back and shot him in the head.

"I couldn't keep going after that. I disbanded the group. You've got to play by the rules. If you don't, their side wins. We're no better than they are."

"It looks like it bothered you very much," Kaminski said.

"They were my friends. It was hard."

And one of them was much more than just a friend. But this was part of the story Middleton didn't share.

His phone beeped. He glanced at the screen and read the lengthy SMS message. "Speak of the devil . . . It's Lespasse and Nora," he explained. "This is interesting . . . They talked to one of our old contacts. He found out that machinery that could be used to make a bio-weapon delivery systems was shipped to a factory in downtown Baltimore yesterday." He looked up. "I've got an address. I think I'll go check it out." He said to Perez, "You take Felicia someplace safe and—"

The man shook his head. "I'm going with you."

"It's not your fight, Jack."

"These are terrorists. It's everybody's fight. I'm with you."

"You sure about that?"

"You're not going anywhere without me."

Middleton gave him an affectionate nod. He then subtly pulled his service Glock from his waistband and, holding the gun under the table, checked the ammunition. "I'm short a few rounds. Let me see your Beretta."

Perez slipped him the weapon, out of sight.

Middleton looked over the clip. "You've got twelve and one in the hole. I'm going to borrow three or four."

"Ah, you don't have to pay me back," his son-in-law said, grim-faced. Then smiled. "Give 'em to Faust instead."

Middleton laughed.

They left the diner and walked Kaminski to a hotel up the street. Middleton gave her some money and told her to check in and stay out of sight until they called.

"I want to go," she protested.

"No, Felicia."

"My uncle's dead because of this man."

He smiled at her. "This isn't your line of work. Leave it to the experts."

Reluctantly she nodded and turned toward the hotel lobby.

Middleton climbed into the driver's seat of Perez's car and together the men sped over streets that grew progressively rougher as cobblestones showed through the worn asphalt.

He said, "The delivery was to Four Thirty Eight West Ellicott Street. It's about a mile from here." Middleton then glanced to his right. Perez was shaking his head, smiling.

The father-in-law squinted in curiosity. "What?"

"Funny. You and your friends."

"Who? Lespasse and Nora?"

"Yeah."

"What about them?"

The voice was now sharp with sarcasm. "Supposed to be so fuckin' good at your job. And here you are, chasing down a bum lead."

"What're you talking about?"

The Beretta appeared fast. Middleton flinched as he felt the muzzle against his neck. His son-in-law took the Glock, tossed it in the back, along with Middleton's cell phone. Then he undid his father-in-law's seatbelt, but kept his own hooked.

"What's going on?" Middleton gasped.

"The gas delivery system was shipped to Virginia, not Baltimore. We drove it up. Whatever's on Ellicott Street, it doesn't have anything to do with us."

"Us?" Middleton whispered. "You're with them, Jack?"

"'fraid so, Dad. Turn right here. Head to the waterfront."

"But—"

The black automatic prodding Middleton's ear. "Now."

He did as he was told, following directions to a deserted pier, lined with old warehouses. Perez ordered him to stop. The pistol never wavering, he directed Middleton out of the car and pushed him through an old doorway.

Faust glanced up as if they were guests right on time for a party. In overalls, wearing thick gloves, he was standing at a cluttered worktable littered with tools, tubing and electronic or computer parts. A pallet of gas tanks was nearby. There were 50 or so of them. "Danger—Biohazard" was printed on them in six languages.

Faust gave a fast appraisal of Middleton. "Search him."

"I already—"

"Search him."

Perez patted him down. "Clean."

Middleton shook his head. "I don't get it . . . Jack shot Nacho."

Faust grimaced. "We had to sacrifice the greasy little prick—so you'd believe Mr. Perez here and give us the real musical code. I doubted you'd be honest with me back there."

"He wasn't," Perez confirmed. "He claimed he wasn't thinking clearly. But I'm sure he was lying. He told me how it works." He explained what Middleton had said about adjusting the pitch of A and using a simple electronic tuning device to decode the formula.

Faust was nodding. "Hadn't considered that. Of course."

Middleton said, "So Jack coming to our rescue in the Harbor Court was all part of the plan."

"Pretty much."

"What the hell is going on?"

"I'm just a businessman, Colonel. The world of terrorism is different now. Too many watch lists, too much surveillance, too many computers. You have to outsource. I've been hired by people who are patriots, idealists, protecting their culture."

"Is that how you describe ethnic cleansing?"

Faust frowned. "Protecting them from impurity is how they describe it. You meddled in their country. You'll pay for that. A hundred thousand people will pay."

"And you, Jack?" Middleton snapped.

The young man gave a grim laugh. "I have my own ideals. But they've got commas and a decimal point. I'm making ten million to keep an eye on you and help them out. Yeah, I went to law school and gave up the family business . . . And it was the worst mistake of my life. Going legit? Bullshit." He gazed at his father-in-law contemptuously. "Look at you, Mr. Harry Middleton . . . The star of military intel, the musical genius . . . Faust led you all over the world like he had you on a leash."

"Jack, we don't have time," Faust said. "I'll try the adjustment to the formula. If it works and we don't need him anymore, you can take care of him."

Middleton said, "Jack, you're willing to kill so many people?"

"I'll donate some of the ten million to a relief fund . . . " A grin. "Or not."

Then he stopped talking. Cocked his head.

Faust was looking up too.

"Helicopter," the younger man muttered.

But Faust spat out, "No, it's two. Wait, three."

Faust ran to the window. "It's a trap. Police. Soldiers." He glared at Jack. "You led them here!"

"No, I did what we agreed."

Middleton could hear diesels of Jeeps and personnel carriers in the distance, closing in fast. Spotlights shone from on high.

Faust slapped his hand on a button on the wall. The warehouse was plunged into darkness. Middleton lunged for Faust but saw the man's vague form run to a corner of the warehouse, open a trap door and vanish. A few seconds later, a powerboat engine started up.

Hell! Middleton thought. He swept the light switch on. He ran to the trap door. Tried it, but Faust had locked it from below.

Sweating, frantic, Perez pointed his gun at Middleton. "Harry, don't move. You're my ticket out of here."

Middleton ignored him and started for the front door of the warehouse.

"Harry!" Perez aimed at Middleton's head. "I'm not telling you again!"

Their eyes met. Perez pulled the trigger.

Click.

Middleton pulled a handful of bullets from his pocket. He displayed them. When pretending to take just three or four bullets from the clip in the diner, he'd taken them all—and the one in the chamber too.

His eyes bored into the younger man's. "That text message I got earlier? It wasn't from Nora and Lespasse. It was from Charley. 'Green Lantern.' It's our code for an emergency. And she text-messaged me who I was in danger from. You, Jack. I knew you'd lead me to Faust. So I text-messaged Lespasse and Nora and told them to follow me from the diner."

Middleton leapt forward and slammed his fist into Perez's jaw, then easily twisted the automatic away. He dropped a round into the chamber, locked the slide, aimed at his son-in-law.

"Harry, you don't understand. I was just faking. Playing along to find out who was involved. I'm a patriot."

"No. You're a traitor who was willing to murder a hundred thousand citizens . . . " His eyelids lowered. "A hundred thousand and one."

"One?"

"My grandchild. Charley told me what you did. How could you do something like that? How?"

Perez's shoulders slumped. He looked down and gave up all pretense of lying. "A baby didn't fit my new lifestyle."

"And Charley didn't either, did she? So after losing the baby, my daughter was, what? Going to kill herself in despair?"

He didn't answer. He didn't need to. Middleton grabbed him by the collar, forced the trembling man on his knees, touched his forehead with the muzzle. He felt the pressure closing on his index finger.

This man killed your grandchild, was going to kill your daughter. We're in the middle of a takedown, he attacked you . . .

Nobody'll care if you take him out.

Now, do it! Before anybody comes in.

Perez squinted, sealing his miserable eyes. "Please, Harry. Please."

Green shirt, green shirt, green shirt . . .

Middleton lowered the gun. He shoved Perez to his belly on the floor.

The door burst open. A dozen soldiers and men in FBI jackets filed into the room. The agents cuffed Perez as a bio-weapon containment unit, looking like astronauts in their protective gear, headed straight to the gas tanks and equipment on the worktable, sweeping them with sensors. After a few minutes one of them announced, "Nothing's been mixed yet. There's no danger."

A grizzled man in a uniform with major's stripes strode into the room. Major Stanley Jenkins's face was grim.

Oh, no . . . Middleton deduced what the man had just learned.

"Colonel, sorry. He got away."

Middleton sighed.

Well, at least they'd secured the nerve gas. The city was safe.

And Faust would be the subject of one of the most massive manhunts in U.S. history. They'd find him. Middleton would make sure of that.

A half hour later, Jack Perez was in detention and Middleton was outside with Tesla, Lespasse and Jenkins—his former colleague from the Army. A car pulled up. Unmarked. Did the feds think people didn't recognize wheels like that? It might as well have had We Serve and Protect in bold type on the side.

Two men climbed out. One was Dick Chambers, the Homeland Security man, and the other FBI Assistant Director Kalmbach.

"Emmett."

"Colonel, I—"

Chambers interrupted. "I don't know what to say, Harry. Your country owes you a huge debt. You saved thousands of lives."

Middleton hoped Kalmbach was used to being snubbed. After stumbling and letting Vukasin and his boys into the country, Chambers was going to milk the win for everything he could.

He added, "We have to debrief you now. We'd like—"

"No," Middleton said firmly. "Now I have to go see my daughter."

"But, Colonel, I have to talk to the director and the White House."

But all that Chambers was talking to at the moment was Harry Middleton's back.

She would be fine.

Physically, at least. The mental battering from losing her child and the betrayal of her husband was taking its toll, though, and Middleton had whisked her away to the lake house.

They spent a lot of time in front of the TV, watching the news. As he'd predicted, Dick Chambers and other officials from Homeland Security took most of the credit for stopping the nerve-gas attack and finding the terrorists who'd slipped into the country—"owing to extremely well-done forged papers," he pointedly added. The FBI got credited in a footnote.

Harry Middleton was mentioned not at all.

Which was, of course, how this game worked.

The post-mortem of the case suggested that Faust was in charge of the plot to seek revenge against America for the peace-keeping operation. Rugova worked for him but got tired of prison and was going to bribe his way out with loot stolen to support the terrorists.

That's why he was eliminated by Vukasin. Stefan Andrzej, the tattooed man, who'd killed Val Brocco, was probably a traitor, and murdered for that reason—and for his incompetence.

The hunt for Faust was continuing at a fervid pace and several leads were beginning to pan out. He still had some unaccounted-for muscle in the country, and records from the prepaid mobile that Perez had called frequently, presumably Faust's, showed that he made repeated calls to pay phones in a particular area of D.C., where his cohorts apparently lived. Stakeouts and electronic surveillance were immediately put in place.

But Middleton was, at least for the moment, not part of the hunt. He was more interested in his daughter's recovery.

And in reconnecting with Nora Tesla and Jean-Marc Lespasse.

He'd invited them to the lake house for a few days. He wasn't sure that they'd show up, but they had. His daughter seemed to have forgiven Tesla for what she'd thought was the breakup of her mother and father—though she also had clearly come to understand that the divorce was inevitable long before Nora Tesla entered the picture.

But the other issues loomed and at first the conversations among them had been superficial. The subject of the past finally arose, as it often does, and they broached the subject of the Darfur warlord killed by Brocco and the breaking up of the Volunteers because of the incident.

There was no concession by anybody and no apologies but neither was there any defense, and through the miracles of the passage of time—and friendship arising from common purpose—the incident was at last put to rest.

Tesla and Middleton spent some time together, talking much about things of little significance. They took a long walk and ended up on a promontory overlooking a neighboring lake. A family of deer sprung from the underbrush and galloped away. Startled, she grabbed his hand—and this time didn't remove it.

Not long after the nerve gas was found Middleton got a phone call. Abe Nowakowski—presently under arrest in Rome—had cut a deal with U.S., Polish and Italian prosecutors. In exchange for a reduced sentence he would give up something.

Something extraordinary, as it turned out.

Overnight, a package arrived at Middleton's lake house. He opened it and spent the next two days in his study.

"Holy shit," was his official pronouncement and the first person he told wasn't his daughter, Nora Tesla or JM Lespasse, but Felicia Kaminski, who came to his house in person in reaction to the news.

He displayed what sat on the Steinway in his study.

"And it's not fake?"

"No," Middleton whispered. "This is real. There's no doubt."

In payment for his services to Faust, Nowakowski had been the recipient of what Middleton had now authenticated: a true Chopin manuscript, previously unheard of, apparently part of the trove unearthed by Rugova at St. Sophia church.

It was an untitled sonata for piano and chamber orchestra.

An astonishing find for lovers of music everywhere.

Also, Middleton was amused to learn that. Homeland Security officials had leapt on the news and, further brushing up the feds' image after their nerve gas victory, had pushed for a gala world premiere of the piece at the James Madison Recital Hall in Washington, D.C. Middleton called Dick Chambers personally and insisted that Felicia Kaminski be the principal soloist. He agreed without hesitation, saying, "I owe you, Harry." Violin was her main instrument, of course, but as she joked in her lightly accented English, "I know my way around the ivories too."

Middleton laughed. She grew serious then and added, "It's an honor a musician only dreams of." She hugged him. "And I will dedicate my performance to the memory of my uncle."

Nora Tesla, Lespasse and Charlotte would attend, as would much of Washington's cultural and political elite.

Several days before the concert, Charley Middleton found her father in the lake house study, late at night.

"Hey, Dad. What're you up to?"

Dad? Been years since she'd used that word. It sounded odd.

"Just looking over the Chopin. How are you doing, honey?"

"Getting better. Step by step."

She sat down beside him. He kissed her head. She took a sip of his wine. "Tasty." What he used to say to her after sampling her milk at the breakfast table, long, long ago, to get her to drink the beverage.

"It's amazing, isn't it?" she asked, looking over the manuscript.

"To think that Frederic Chopin actually held these sheets. And look there, that scribble. Was he testing the pen? Was he distracted by something? Was it the start of a note to himself?"

Her eyes were gazing out the window at the black sheet that was the still lake. She was crying softly. She whispered, "Does it ever get better."

"Sure, it does. Your life'll get back on track again."

And Harold Middleton thought, Yes, it gets better. Always does. But the sorrow and horror never go away completely.

Green shirt . . . Green shirt . . .

And a sudden thought came to Harry Middleton. He wondered if he'd used Brocco's murder of the Darfur warlord as an excuse—to back away from the fight that he used to believe he was born for. He couldn't save everybody, so he'd stopped trying to save anyone, and retreated into the world of music.

"I'm going to bed. Love you, Dad."

"Night, baby."

When she was gone, Middleton sipped his wine and examined the Chopin again, thinking of a curious irony. Here was a work of art written at a time when music was created largely for the glory of God and yet this piece he was looking at was part of a horrific plot to murder thousands, solely out of vengeful religious fervor.

Sometimes the world was simply mad, Harry Middleton concluded.

17

JEFFERY DEAVER

The men finished the work at midnight.

"I'm exhausted. Are we through?" The language was Serbo-Croatian.

The second man was tired too but he said nothing and looked uneasily at the third, his face dark, his black hair long and swept back.

The man who'd been supervising their handiwork—Faust—told them in a soft voice that, yes, it was all right to leave. He spoke in English.

Once they were gone, he walked through the basement, using a flashlight to inspect what they'd spent the last four hours doing: Running two-inch hose—it was astonishingly heavy, who'd have thought?—through access tunnels from three buildings away. Painstakingly, using silent hand pumps, they'd filled rubber bladders with gasoline, a total of close to 900 gallons of the liquid. Next they placed propane tanks and detonators between the bladders and, most difficult of all, rigged the electronics.

Alone now in the basement of the James Madison recital hall, Faust ran final diagnostic checks on the system. Everything was in order. He allowed himself a fantasy of what would happen later this evening. During the adagio movement at the world premier of the newly discovered Chopin sonata, a unique combination of notes would slip from the microphone above the soloist's piano and be electronically translated into numerical values. These would be recognized by the computer controller as a command to small motors that would open the propane tanks. Then a few minutes later, when the score moved into the vivace movement, another combination of notes would trigger the detonators. The propane would flare, melt the bladders and turn the recital hall instantly into a crematorium.

This elaborate system was necessary because radio, microwave and cell phone jammers were in use in security-minded public venues in D.C. Remote control devices were useless. And timing devices could be picked up in sweeps by supersensitive microphones.

Ironically, Felicia Kaminski herself would be the detonator.

Now Faust hid the bladders, tanks and wires behind boxes. He was satisfied with the plan. Middleton and the government had taken the bait Nowakowski offered them, the manuscript. And it was clear they believed the entire charade, all false information Faust had fed to Jack Perez and Felicia Kaminski—the code in the first manuscript pages, the nerve-gas attack, the binoculars at the Harbor court focused on a warehouse, the mysterious talk about deliveries and chemical formulas, the torture of the tattooed man in the closet . . .

His enemy's defenses were down. He thought of an apt metaphor: They believed the concert was over; they never suspected he'd arranged a spectacular, unexpected crescendo.

Faust now slipped out of the basement, troubled as he pictured Felicia Kaminski dying in the conflagration. He wasn't concerned about the young women herself, of course. He was troubled that, if she used the original score to perform from, the manuscript would be destroyed.

After all, it was easily worth millions of dollars.

The crowds began assembling outside early, the queue stretching well past a construction site next door to the James Madison hall. Many were people without tickets, hoping for scalpers. But this was a world-premiere of Chopin, not pre-season Redskins, so there were no tickets to be had.

Harold Middleton made a brief backstage visit to Kaminski, wished her well and then joined his guests in the lobby: Leonora Tesla, JM Lespasse and his daughter Charley.

He said hello to some of the music professors from Georgetown and George Mason, and a few of the Defense Department and DOJ folks from his past life. Emmett Kalmbach came by and shook his hand. "Where's Dick?" he asked.

Middleton gave a laugh and pointed across the hall to the head of Homeland Security. "Gave his ticket to his boss."

The FBI man said, "At least I appreciate culture."

"You ever heard Chopin before, Emmett?"

"Sure."

"What'd he write?"

"That thing."

"Thing?"

"You know, the famous one."

Middleton smiled as Kalmbach changed the subject.

The lobby lights dimmed and they entered the auditorium, found their seats.

"Harry, relax," Middleton heard his daughter say. "You look like you're the one performing."

He smiled, noting how she referred to him. The lack of endearment didn't upset him one bit; it was a sign she was recovering.

But as for relaxing: Well, that wasn't going to happen. This was going to be a momentous evening. He was bursting with excitement.

The conductor walked out on stage to wild applause. He then lifted his arm to the right and nineteen-year-old Felicia Kaminski, in a fluid black dress, strode out on stage, looking confident as a pro. She smiled, bowed and stole a glance at Harold Middleton. He believed she winked. She sat down at the keyboard.

The conductor took his place at the stand. He lifted his baton.

"Dick, something interesting here."

Chambers was in his office at the Department of Homeland Security, working late. He was thinking about the concert and wondering if his boss was appreciative he'd been given the ticket. He looked up.

"Might want to talk to this guy," his straight-arrow aide said.

The caller was a restaurant worker near the James Madison recital hall. As he was leaving work early that morning, he explained, he'd seen a man leave through the hall's side door. He'd gotten into a car near the site. Thinking it seemed suspicious—the hall had been closed all day—he took a picture of the car and the license plate with his cell phone. He meant to call the police earlier but had forgotten about it. He'd just now called D.C.

police and was referred to Homeland Security, since the concert would be attended by some high-ranking government officials.

"Nowadays," the restaurant worker said, "you never know—terrorists and everything."

Chambers said, "We better follow up on this. Where are you?"

He'd just gotten off work, the man explained. He gave the address of the restaurant. It was now closed so Chambers told him to wait in a park near the place. He'd have agents there soon.

"And thank you, sir. It's citizens like you that make this country what it is."

On stage at the recital hall, Felicia Kaminski was playing as she'd never played in her life. She was motivated not by the fact that this was her first appearance as a soloist at a world premiere, but because of the music itself. It was intoxicating.

Musicians grow familiar with the pieces in their repertoire, the same way husbands and wives grow comfortably close over the years. But there's something about meeting, then performing, a new work that's like the beginning of a love affair.

Passionate, exhilarating, utterly captivating. The rest of the world ceases to exist.

She was now lost in the music completely, unaware of the thousand people in the audience, the lights, the distinguished guests, the other members of the chamber orchestra around her.

Only one thing intruded slightly.

The faint smell of smoke.

But then she came to a tricky passage in the Chopin and, concentrating hard, she lost any awareness of the scent.

A dark sedan pulled up fast, near a small park in northwest D.C., where a middle-aged man in food-stained overalls sat on a park bench, looking around like a nervous bird.

He flinched when the car stopped and only after spotting the plate Official Government Use and the letters on the side, DHS, did he rise. He walked to the man who got out of the car.

"I'm Joe. From the diner," he said. "I called."

"I'm Dick Chambers." They shook hands.

"Please, sir," the worker said. He held up his cell phone. "I have the picture of the license plate. It's hard to read but I'm sure you have computers that can make it, you know, clearer."

"Yes, our technical department can work miracles."

A man climbed from the car. He called, "Dick, just heard a CNN report on the radio! A fire in the recital hall. It looks big. Real big!"

Dick Chambers smiled, then turned to the man who had just shouted to him from the car.

It was Faust. His two thugs stepped out of back of the car and joined him.

"There, he's the man I saw," cried the agitated restaurant worker. "You have arrested him!"

But then he shook his head, seeing that Faust's hands weren't cuffed. "No, no, no." He dropped the cell phone, staring at Chambers. "You're part of it! I am dead!"

Yeah, you pretty much are, the Homeland Security man thought.

Chambers asked Faust, "What's going on at the hall?"

"They are just preliminary reports. No one can see anything. The streets are filled with smoke. Fire trucks everywhere."

"The recital hall! You've blown it up?"

He crushed the restaurant worker's cell phone under his heel. "I'm afraid you were at the wrong place at the wrong time." He then glanced at Faust, who pulled out a silenced pistol and began to aim it at the worker.

"Please, sir. No!"

Which is when the spotlights slammed on, fixing Chambers, Faust and the others in searing glare.

The restaurant worker dropped to the grass and scuttled away as a loudspeaker blared, "This is Emmett Kalmbach, Chambers. We've got snipers and they're green lighted to shoot. On the ground. All of you."

The DHS man blinked in shock but he hesitated only a moment. He'd been in this business a long time. He was four pounds of trigger pressure away from dead, and he knew it. He grimaced, dropped to his belly and stretched out his legs and arms. The two thugs did the same.

Faust, though, hesitated, the gun bobbing slowly in his hand.

"You, on the ground now!"

But undoubtedly Faust knew what awaited him—the interrogation, the conviction and either life in jail or a lethal needle—and chose desperate over wise. He fired toward the spotlights, then turned and began sprinting.

The lanky man who'd made a job of running from the consequences of his actions got six feet before the snipers ended his career forever.

Harry Middleton walked forward into the lights set up by the FBI Washington field office crime scene team.

He glanced at Faust's body then shook the hand of the man who'd been their undercover decoy—the one who'd pretended to have seen Faust sneak from the recital hall.

"Jozef. You're okay?"

"Ah, yes," Padlo said. "A scrape on my palm getting under cover. No worse than that."

The Polish inspector was stripping off the restaurant worker's uniform he'd donned for the takedown. He'd flown in that morning. It was true that getting credentials for a foreign law officer to come into America was difficult, but red tape did not exist for men like Harold Middleton and his anonymous supervisors.

Padlo had learned that Faust was instrumental in the death of his lover M. T. Connolly and called Harry Middleton, insisting that he come help to find Faust and his co-conspirators. There'd be no extradition of any perpetrators to Poland, Middleton had said, but Padlo was willing to give the Americans evidence in the Jedynak murders, which could prove helpful in any prosecutions here.

Middleton joined Kalmbach and, flanked by two FBI agents, cuffed Dick Chambers, who was staring at the colonel.

"But . . . The fire. You were . . . " His voice faded.

"Supposed to die? Along with a thousand other innocent people? Well, a team disarmed the bomb this afternoon, pumped the gas out. But we needed to buy some time while we set up this sting. If there was no fire at all, I was afraid you might panic and stonewall. So we lit a controlled fire in the construction site next door to the hall. No damage, but a lot of smoke. Enough to get us some ambiguous breaking news reports.

"Oh, if you're interested, the concert went on as planned. The Chopin piece, by the way, was pretty good . . . I'd rate it A minus. I'm sure your boss enjoyed it. Interesting you gave your ticket to him, knowing that he'd die in the fire. Should have seen his face when I told him it was you who was responsible."

Chambers knew he should just shut up. But he couldn't help himself. He said, "How did you know?"

"Well, this story that Faust was the mastermind? Bullshit. I couldn't believe that. He was too arrogant and impulsive. I had a feeling somebody else was behind it. But who? I had some colleagues run a computer correlation on travel to Poland and Italy in the past few months tied to any connections in that part of D.C. where Faust called pay phones. Some diplomats showed up, some businessmen. And you—who worked for the agency that quote accidentally let Vukasin into the country. I found out you also called Nowakowski in prison the day before he offered to give up the Chopin manuscript.

"You were the number-one suspect. But we needed to make sure. And we had to flush Faust. So we set you up with a phony witness as a decoy. Jozef Padlo, who you'd never met."

"This is ridiculous. You don't know what you're talking about."

"Yeah, I do. Dick. As soon as I got the call from Poland about the first Chopin manuscript, I became suspicious and made some calls. Intelligence from Northern Europeans suggested possible terrorist activity originating in Poland and Rome. Music might have something to do with it. So I went along, to see what was up. The trail led to a possible nerve-gas attack in Baltimore. We got the chemicals and it looked like the end of the story, except for tracking down Faust.

"But I got to thinking about things the other night. An attack out of revenge for our meddling in the Balkans? No, the ethnic cleansing there was about politics and land, not religious fundamentalism. That didn't fit the profile. Maybe Vukasin bought into the ideology but the main players, Faust and Rugova? No, they were all about money.

"And codes of nerve gas in a manuscript? Just the sort of thing the intelligence gurus would love and keep us from looking at the big picture. But in these days of scramblers and cryptography, there were better ways to get formulae from one country to another. No, something else was going on.

But what? I decided I needed to analyze the situation differently. I looked at it the same way I look at music manuscripts to decide if they're authentic: as a whole. Did this seem to be an authentic terrorist plot? No. The next logical question was what did the fake nerve-gas plot accomplish?

"Only one thing: It brought me and the rest of the Volunteers out of retirement. That was your point, of course. To eliminate us. The Volunteers."

It was Kalmbach who asked, "But why, Harry?"

"Close to a billion dollars in stolen art and sculpture and manuscripts—stolen by the Nazis from throughout Europe and stashed in a dozen churches and schools in Kosovo, Serbia and Albania. Just like at St. Sophia. We knew that Chambers did a brief tour in the Balkans but got out fast. He must've met Rugova and learned about the loot. Then he bankrolled the operation and hired Faust to oversee it.

"A few years passed and they wanted to cash in by selling the pieces to private collectors. But Rugova preempted them—and he got careless. He didn't cover his tracks and word got around about the treasures. It was only a matter of time until the Volunteers started to put the pieces together. So Chambers and Faust had to eliminate Rugova—and us too. But to keep suspicion off them they had to make it seem like part of a real terrorist attack. They brought Vukasin and his thugs over here.

"Well, after I realized his motive, I just looked for what would be the perfect way to kill all of us. And it was obvious: an attack at the recital hall."

Now Middleton turned to Chambers. "I wasn't surprised to find out that you were the one at Homeland Security who suggested the concert, Dick."

"This is all bullshit. And you haven't heard the last of it."

"Wrong on number one. Right on two: I'll be a witness in your trial, so I'll be hearing a lot more of it. And so will you."

Kalmbach and two other agents escorted Chambers and Faust's two thugs away for booking.

Middleton and inspector Jozef Padlo found themselves standing alone on the chilly street corner. A light drizzle had started falling

"Jozef, thank you for doing this."

"I would not have done otherwise. So . . . It is finished."

"Not quite. There are a few questions to answer. There's one intriguing aspect I'm curious about: Eleana Soberski. She had a connection to Vukasin. But I think there was more to her. I think she had her own agenda."

He recalled what she said just before she was shot: "We are aware of your relationship with Faust."

"Ah," Padlo said, "so there's someone else interested in the loot. Or perhaps who has some of his own and would like to expand his market share."

"I think so."

"One of Rugova's men?"

Middleton shrugged. "Doubt it. They were punks. I'm thinking higher up. Someone highly placed, like Dick Chambers, but in Rome or Warsaw or Moscow."

"And you are going to find out who?"

"The case is my blood. You know the expression?"

"I do now."

"I'll keep at it until I'm satisfied."

"And are you going to do this alone," asked the Polish cop, with a clever gleam in his eye, "or with the help of some friends?"

Middleton couldn't help but smile. "Yes, we've talked about reuniting, the Volunteers."

Padlo fished in his pocket for a pack of Sobieski cigarettes. He pulled one out. Then frowned. "Oh, in America, is okay?"

Middleton laughed. "Outside in a park? That's still legal."

Padlo lit up, sheltering the match from the mist. Inhaled deeply. "Where do you think the stolen art is, Harry?"

"Faust and Chambers probably have a half-dozen safe houses throughout the world. We'll find them."

"And what do you think you will find there?"

"If the Chopin is any clue, it'll be breathtaking. I can't even imagine."

Middleton glanced at his watch. It was after midnight. Still, this was northwest D.C., a yuppie oasis in the city that often sleeps. "Will you join me for a drink? I know a bar that's got some good Polish vodka."

The inspector smiled, sadly. "I think not. I'm tired. My job is done here. I leave tomorrow. And I must get up early to say farewell to someone. Maybe you know where this is?"

He showed Middleton a piece of paper with the address of a cemetery in Alexandria, Virginia.

"Sure, I can give you directions. But tell you what . . . How about if we go together? I'll drive."

"You would not mind?"

"Jozef, my friend, it would be an honor."

PART II

The Copper Bracelet

1

JEFFERY DEAVER

Finally the families were alone.

Since the start of their vacation two days ago, they'd been in public constantly, taking in the sights in this touristy area along the beaches near Nice, France. They'd seen the museums in Antibes Juan-les-Pins, the fragrant perfume-making town of Grasse, the violet fields of medieval Tourettes sur Loup and nearby Cannes—a dull provincial village when emptied of filmmakers, paparazzi and actors.

And wherever they went: too many people around for him to move in for the kill.

Now, at last, the Americans were alone, picnicking on a deserted stretch of white sand and red rocks near le Plages de Ondes at Cap d'Antibes—a postcard of the South of France. Sullen autumn was on the land now and everyone had returned from holiday. Today the weather was overcast and windy, but that hadn't fazed the two families—a husband and wife in early middle age and a slightly younger couple with their baby. Apparently they'd decided to take the day off from sightseeing and strolling past the tabacs, cafés and souvenir shops, and spend the day alone.

Thank you, thought Kavi Balan. He needed to get the job done and leave. There was much to do.

The swarthy man, born in New Delhi and now, he liked to think, now a resident of the world, was observing the family through expensive binoculars from a hundred yards away, in the hills above the beach. He was parked in a rented Fiat, listening to some syrupy French pop music. He was taking in the gray water, the gray sky, looking for signs of gendarmes or the ubiquitous governmental functionaries that materialized from nowhere in France to ask for your passport or identity card and snidely demand your business.

But there was no one about. Except the families.

As he studied them, Balan was wondering too about a question much on his mind the past few days: how he would feel about killing a whole family. The adults were not a problem, of course, even the women. He'd killed women without a single fleck of remorse. But the younger couple's baby—yes, that murder would bother him.

He'd lain awake last night, considering the dilemma. Now, watching the young mother rock the infant's bassinette absently, he came to a decision. Balan had been instructed to leave no one alive, but that was because of the need to eliminate anyone with certain information. He hadn't seen the baby, but it couldn't be more than a year old. It could hardly identify him, nor would it have retained any conversation between the adults. He would spare the child.

Balan would tell his mentor that he'd grown concerned about somebody approaching as he'd been about to kill the child and had left the beach quickly so he wouldn't be detected. This wasn't unreasonable, and wasn't a complete lie. There were houses here, cars and trucks passing nearby. Even though the beaches were deserted, people still lived in the area year round.

There. He'd decided. Balan felt better.

And he concentrated more closely on the task before him.

The families were enjoying themselves, laughing. His ultimate target—the American husband in his fifties—joked with his wife, who was a bit younger. Not classically beautiful, but exotic, with long dark hair. She reminded Balan of an older Kareena Kapoor, the Bollywood film star. Thinking this, he felt a wave of contempt course through him at these people. Americans . . . they had no idea of the richness of Indian cinema (no American he'd ever met even knew that that Bombay supplied the "B" for Bollywood, which, they also didn't know, was only a part of the nation's film industry). Nor did they understand Indian culture in general, the depth of its history and its spiritual life. Americans thought of India as customer-service call centers, curry and "Slumdog Millionaire."

On the beach the two men jumped to their feet and pulled out an American football. Another shiver of contempt raced through him, as he watched them pitch the elongated ball back and forth. They called *that* a game, gridiron football. Absurd. Big men running into each other. Not like real football—what they called soccer. Or the most sublime game in the world: cricket.

He looked at his watch. Soon, he thought. Just one phone call away. He checked his Nokia to make sure it was working. It was. Balan was known as a fanatic about details.

He turned the binoculars on the families again. Since they were about to die, he couldn't help wondering where they were on the ladder of spirituality. A Hindu, Balan had an appreciation of the concept of reincarnation— the concept of returning to earth after death in some form that echoes spiritual justice for your past life. His philosophy was a bit at odds with traditional Hindu views, though, since he believed that though he devoted his life to death and torture he was doing higher work here on earth. In an odd way, perhaps by hastening the families' deaths—before they had a chance to lead even more impure lives—he might hasten their spiritual growth.

He didn't need this idea to justify what was about to happen, of course. All that mattered was that his mentor, Devras Sikari, had singled him out to kidnap the husband—and kill anybody with him—then torture the man to find out what he'd learned on his recent trip to Paris.

There are more than 300,000 deities in the Hindu religion, but Sikari, though flesh and blood, was higher than them all, in Balan's mind. In India, the social and economic caste system is impossibly complicated, with thousands of sects and subsects. But the religious text the Bhagavad-Gita defines only four castes: the highest are the Brahmin spiritual leaders, the lowest, the working-class Sudras.

Devras Sikari was in the Kshatriya caste, that of spiritual warriors and leaders. It was the second most spiritual class, below only the Brahmin. The Bhagavad-Gita says that those in the Kshatriya caste are "of heroic mind, inner fire, constancy, resourcefulness, courage in battle, generosity and noble leadership." That described Sikari perfectly. His first name, Devras, meant servant of God. The surname meant "hunter."

The man took the names when he was "twice born," a phrase that has nothing to do with reincarnation, but refers to the coming-of-age ceremony for Hindu youths. Balan believed a name was important. His own first name, for instance, meant poet, and he did indeed have an appreciation for beauty and words. Mahatma Gandhi's surname meant "greengrocer"—and was a perfect description of the mild-mannered commoner who changed the history of his country though peace and passive resistance.

Devras Sikari, the hunter chosen by god, would change the world too, though far differently than Gandhi. He would make a mark in a way that befit *his* name.

Balan now recalled the day he left for this mission. The dark, diminutive Sikari—his age impossible to guess—came to Balan's safe house in Northern India. Sikari was wearing wrinkled white slacks and a loose shirt. From the chest pocket blossomed a red handkerchief. (Red was the color associated with the Kshatriya caste and Sikari always wore or carried something red.) The leader had greeted him in a soft voice and gentle smile—he never shouted or displayed anger—and then explained how vital it was that he find a particular American, a geologist who had been making inquiries about Sikari in Paris.

"I need to know what he's learned. And why he wants to know about me."

"Yes, Devras. Of course." Sikari insisted that his people use his first name.

"He's left India. But find him. Kill anyone with him, then torture him," he said as casually as if he were ordering a cup of Kashmiri shir chai—pink salt tea.

"Of course."

His mentor had then smiled, taken Balan's hand and given him a present: a thick copper bracelet, an antique, it seemed. A beautiful piece, streaked with a patina of green. It was decorated with ancient writing and an etching of an elephant. He'd slipped the bracelet on Balan's wrist and stepped back.

"Oh, thank you, Devras."

Another smile and the man who had brought so much death to some and hope to others whispered one of his favorite expressions: "Go and do well for me."

And with that Devras Sikari stepped out the door and vanished back into the countryside of Kashmir.

Now, remaining hidden from the victims soon to die, Balan glanced down at the bracelet. He knew it signified more than gratitude: the gift meant that he was destined for some place high in Sikari's organization.

It was also a reminder not to fail.

Do well for me . . .

Balan's phone trilled.

"Yes?"

Without any greeting, Jana asked coolly, "Are you in position?"

"Yes."

"I'm up the beach road, a hundred yards." Jana had a low and sultry voice. He loved the sound. He pictured her voluptuous body. In the past few days, as they'd prepared for the attack and conducted their surveillance, she'd worn bulky clothes that had concealed her figure. Only last night, when they'd met in a café to survey the escape route, had she worn anything revealing: a thin t-shirt and tight skirt. She'd glanced down at the outfit and explained dismissively that it was just another costume. "I'm only playing tourist."

Meaning I'm not sending you a message.

Though, of course, Jana knew that he came from a country where the most beautiful women often wear concealing saris, even to the beach, and that Balan *had* to be aware of her body. So maybe there was a message.

But the killer had resisted even glancing at her figure. He was a professional and had learned to stifle his lust. Sikari always came first.

Jana now said through her untraceable cell phone, "I have the hypodermic ready for him."

The plan was that Balan would stun the American with a Taser and kill the others. Then Jana would race up in the van. They'd throw the man inside and inject him with a tranquilizer. She'd drive him to an abandoned warehouse outside of Nice for the interrogation. Balan would meet her there soon after.

"You'll kill the family," she said, as if this were something they'd argued about, which they had not.

"Yes."

"All of them."

"Of course." He resolved to keep to his decision not to harm the child.

But he couldn't help but wonder about her: How could a woman be so casual about killing an infant?

"Get to work," Jana said abruptly.

Because she was beautiful he didn't give her a snide response, which was his first reaction. Instead he simply disconnected.

Balan looked around for traffic. Nobody was on the wind-swept beach road. He climbed out of the car with a canvas bag over his shoulder. Inside was an automatic weapon with a sound suppressor. It could fire 600 rounds a minute, but he had it set to fire in three-shot bursts every time the trigger was pulled. This was far more efficient than fully automatic, and more deadly than single-shot.

The bullets weren't big—.22 caliber—but they didn't need to be. Sikari instructed his people to look at guns as an extension of more primitive weapons, like spears or knives. "Your goal," Sikari said, "is to open the flesh and let the life flow out. Let the body destroy itself."

How brilliant he is, Balan thought, his heart tapping hard with love and awe as he rubbed the copper bracelet and walked closer to the people whose lives were about to change so dramatically.

He crossed the sandy road and slipped behind a faded sign advertising Gitane cigarettes. He peeked out. The family was pouring wine and beer and setting out food.

Their last meal.

Balan looked over the older husband, who was fairly fit for someone in middle age. From here—50 yards away—he was handsome in a nondescript American way; all of them looked alike to him. And his wife was even more striking up close. The younger man, Balan now decided, wasn't their son. He wasn't young enough. Besides he didn't resemble either of the older couple. Perhaps he was a co-worker or neighbor or the American's younger brother. His wife, the mother of the baby, was blond and athletic. Recalling his thoughts about sports, he decided she looked like a cheerleader.

Balan reached into the bag and extracted the gun, checked again to make sure it was ready to fire. He then put on a powder blue jacket that said *Inspecteur des Plages* and a fake badge, slipped the gun's strap over his shoulder and hung the gun on his back so it wouldn't be seen from the front.

He thought of Sikari.

He thought of Jana, the cold, beautiful woman now waiting in the van.

Would she await him later that night? In her bed? Perhaps this was only a fantasy. But, as Sikari taught his followers, fantasies exist so that we might strive to make them reality.

Then standing tall, he walked toward the family with casual purpose.

One hundred yards.

Then 75.

Making slow progress over the fine white sand.

The American, smiling from something his wife had said, glanced his way, but paid Balan little attention. He'd be thinking, a beach inspector? Those crazy French. At worst I'll have to pay five euros for permission to lunch here.

Fifty yards.

Forty.

He would shoot when he was 15 yards away. Balan was a good shot. He'd learned his skill killing Pakistanis and Muslims and other intruders in his home in Kashmir. He was accurate even standing in the open with the enemy shooting back.

The younger woman, the mother beside the baby's bassinette, glanced his way without interest and then turned back to her music streaming into her ears through the iPod. She leaned forward on her beach chair, looked inside the carriage, smiled and whispered to the baby.

That will be her last image as she died: her child's face.

Thirty yards.

Twenty-five.

Balan kept a restrained smile on his face. Still, none of them was suspicious. Perhaps they were thinking that with his brown skin he was from Algeria or Morocco. There were many Frenchmen around here who had roots in North Africa.

Twenty yards.

He wiped his palms on his blue jacket.

Fifteen.

All right . . . Now!

But Balan froze as he gazed at the family. Wait . . . what was this?

The two men and the older woman were diving to the sand.

The woman with the iPod ear buds leapt from her chair and reached into the bassinette. She pulled from it a black machine gun, a Heckler & Koch MP-5, which she trained on Balan's chest.

Astonished, the Indian looked right and left, as two men in NATO olive-drab uniforms and two French soldiers, in dark blue, sprinted from what seemed like empty cabanas. They must have been hiding there all morning; he'd checked the beach carefully after the Americans arrived.

A trap! He'd been set up!

One of the NATO officers, a boy-faced blond—his name badge read "Wetherby"—growled, "*Atakana*!" in a perfect Hindi accent. This was followed by "*Arretez maintenant*!" Then "Freeze!" As if Balan needed an interpreter to explain that he was about five seconds away from dying if he didn't do exactly as instructed.

Brandishing a large pistol, Wetherby stepped closer and repeated the warnings.

Balan remained where he stood, his head swiveling from the officers on his left, to the Americans, then to the other soldiers on his right.

His eyes fell on the older husband who was climbing to his feet, studying Balan—with interest, but without surprise. So he was the one responsible for the trap.

And in this instant he understood too that a man so clever was indeed a serious threat to Devras Sikari.

He told himself: You've disappointed him. You've failed. Your life is pointless. Use your death to good purpose. Kill the American. At least any risk to Sikari and his plans will die with him.

Balan crouched fast and reached for the gun.

Which is when his world went mad. Yellow lights danced in his eyes. His muscles spasmed and pain exploded from teeth to groin.

He dropped to his knees, his limbs unresponsive. He glanced down and saw the Taser barbs in his side. It was the same brand of weapon that he'd brought with him to use on the American.

Balan's eyes teared from the pain.

And from his failure to "go and do well" for his beloved mentor.

He fell forward on the sand and saw nothing more.

"His name's Kavi Balan, sir," said Petey Wetherby, the younger of the two NATO soldiers assisting on the operation here. He spoke with a North Boston accent. The eager, crew-cut man, an interpreter by specialty, nodded at the prisoner, who sat with his hands and feet cuffed, slowly coming to, beside one of the concession stands closed for the season. He was beneath a large sign that said "Crème glacée! Pommes Frites! Hot Dawgs!"

"Balan. Never heard of him," nodded Harold Middleton, the man who'd been masquerading as the older husband in the sting operation.

Wetherby continued, "We found his car. Rented under a fake name and address, prepaid credit card. But we've got his real passport and we recovered a computer."

"Computer? Excellent." Middleton looked around the deserted beach, then turned to one of the French soldiers. In French, he asked, "Any sign of Sikari?"

"No, Colonel Middleton. But the perimeter . . . " The slim Frenchman gave a Gallic shrug and twist of his lip.

Meaning, Middleton understood, they didn't have the manpower to search very far. The French had been cooperative to a point but weren't all-hands-on-board for an operation that was primarily American and NATO, and would deliver the suspect not to the Palais de Justice in Paris but to International Criminal Court in the Hague—the tribunal with jurisdiction to try war criminals and other human-rights violators.

Middleton had doubted Devras Sikari himself would be here. While intelligence sources had reported that someone from Kashmir had traveled to the South of France to kill or abduct the "American geologist," it would be unlikely that Sikari would risk coming out of hiding for such a mundane crime.

The best he'd hoped for was to capture someone who could lead them to Sikari.

Which, it seemed, they had.

Middleton continued to the Frenchman, "He'll have an accomplice, though. You find any other cars nearby? Monitor any radio transmissions?"

"No," the Frenchman said.

"You?" Middleton asked Wetherby. The NATO officers had their own monitoring system.

"No, Colonel." He referred to Middleton's rank when he'd retired from the Army years ago.

Middleton preferred "Harry," but some monikers just stick and "Colonel" was better than some others he could think of.

It was then that Middleton's "wife" joined them. She was in reality

Leonora Tesla, a colleague. The intense woman, with a mane of dark Mediterranean hair, held up a Nokia. "Prepaid cell phone. Some local calls within the past half hour but they're all caller-ID blocked."

A flash of white in the distance caught Middleton's eye. It was just a van accelerating slowly away into the hills.

Tesla added, "JM's going through the computer now. He said it's password-protected but he's trying to bypass that."

Middleton glanced at where she was nodding. In the back of the unmarked NATO van, Jean-Marc Lespasse, the "husband" of the younger couple, was pounding away at the keys on the laptop. Athletic with spiky black hair, JM had been playing his role in the sting to the hilt, referring to his boss, who was only 15 years older, as "Dad" for the past two days and asking if he should cut up Middleton's food for him.

"What do we know about him?" Middleton nodded toward their prisoner, slumped on the ground, and only semi-conscious.

"I just emailed Interpol," Tesla told him. "They'll let us know soon."

The fourth member of the faux family approached: twenty-nine-year-old Constance "Connie" Carson, who like Middleton and Lespasse, was former military. She'd returned the "baby," the MP-5 machine gun, to the NATO van. Though they couldn't legally carry weapons without permission—which the French had not given them—Connie, with her muscular cowgirl's body and piercing blue eyes, wasn't the sort to say no to. She'd walked up to the NATO officers, pulled the machine pistol off the gun rack, chambered a round and tossed the gun into the bassinette. Ignoring their protests, she'd said, "Just gonna take her for a little stroll," in an accent that pinpointed her roots in West Texas.

She unplugged the walkie-talkie ear buds, disguised to look like they belonged to an iPod, and examined the roads. "Betcha he's not alone."

"That's what I think," Middleton said. "We can't find anybody, though."

Connie continued to scan for possible offensive threats. This was her nature, Middleton had learned.

"He's coming to, Colonel," the other NATO officer called, standing near Balan, sitting under the sign. It looked like a cartoon, with the words "Pommes Frites!" in a dialog balloon over his head.

"How long?" Middleton asked.

"Five minutes."

"What do you want me to do, Colonel?" Wetherby asked.

"Hang tight. I might need you to interpret."

"Yes sir."

Harold Middleton stretched and gazed out to sea, reflecting that he was a long, long way from his home in Fairfax County, Virginia, outside of Washington, D.C., where he'd been only last week.

He was a bit trimmer than he had been a few years ago, when he was living comfortably—"fat and sassy," he'd tell his daughter Charley—with two great jobs: authenticating music manuscripts and teaching music history. He'd taken them up after retiring from one that was considerably more demanding. As a military intelligence officer, Middleton had witnessed the results of war crimes, ethnic cleansing and other atrocities in many parts of the world. Determined to help bring the perpetrators of those offenses to justice, he'd left the service and started a nonprofit group called War Criminal Watch, devoted to tracking down human rights violators wanted by the International Criminal Court in The Hague and by other tribunals around the world.

Since they were not affiliated with any law enforcement agency or nongovernmental organization and made virtually no money for their work, they were known as the Volunteers. They gained a reputation throughout the free world for their brilliant detective work in tracking down elusive criminals.

For various reasons, the group had disbanded some years ago, and Middleton went on to his beloved music, Leonora Tesla to do relief work in Africa and the other Volunteers to their own lives.

But recently a vicious, wanted war criminal who'd eluded them for years surfaced with plans for terrible carnage. The Volunteers were forced out of retirement. They managed to apprehend the killer—though only after Middleton's ex-wife was murdered and his daughter was nearly killed by her own husband, who turned out to be connected with the criminal.

Realizing that he could no longer remain in academia while such evil continued to thrive, Middleton decided to start up the Volunteers once again. The group included three of the original members: himself, Leonora Tesla and Jean-Marc Lespasse. New to the group were Connie Carson and Jimmy

Chang, who now was back at headquarters outside of Washington, D.C. The slightly built Taiwanese-American had a miraculous grasp of languages, advanced degrees in computers and science and a love of research—Lespasse called him "Wiki" Chang after the on-line encyclopedia. Middleton's daughter also helped them out.

Glancing now at Balan, who struggled to sit up straight after the Taser jolt, Middleton sure hoped the interrogation was successful. They desperately wanted to capture the man's boss. Devras Sikari was a curious character. Born into a poor family in Kashmir, the disputed territory in the north of India, Sikari had somehow managed the impossible: He'd attended an elite school in England. A brilliant student, his mind sharper than many of his professors, he'd studied engineering and computer science.

There were rumors that he was being bankrolled for his entire education and living expenses, but no one knew who it might be; the source of his underwriting was anonymous. As soon as he left university, he'd shunned dozens of offers from large British firms and returned home to India, where somehow—no one quite knew how—he amassed some significant start-up capital. He began setting up engineering and computer companies and making millions in India's burgeoning high-tech world.

Then, having made his fortune, he disappeared from Mumbai and New Delhi, where his companies were based. "Not long after that he surfaced in Kashmir," Jimmy Chang had explained, "and became a combination warlord, insurgent and cult figure."

Chang had briefed Middleton and the other Volunteers about the Kashmir conflict. Formerly known as a "princely state," Kashmir has been the object of a deadly game of tug-of-war for more than half a century. India and Pakistan each control separate portions of the region, while China exercises authority over a smaller section of the northeast. But the partition is merely tolerated; both India and Pakistan claim that the entire state is theirs and have fought frequently to assert ownership. The massive, fertile area has been the basis for perhaps the closest nuclear confrontation between nations since the Cuban missile crisis in the 1960s.

Devras Sikari settled in Jammu, in the Indian-controlled and largely Hindu portion of Kashmir, and now lived largely underground, surrounded by hundreds of followers, though he was known to travel outside of the country frequently using false documents, diplomatic papers and disguises.

He'd spent the past several years orchestrating the slaughter, kidnapping and torture of Muslims, Pakistanis, Buddhists and Christians in Kashmir—anyone who wasn't Indian or Hindu and anyone he felt had no right to be in the region of his birth or a threat to Kashmir independence. He was suspected of massacres of entire refugee camps and villages, and he even made incursions into the Pakistani-controlled portion of Kashmir.

Prosecutors at the International Criminal Court had wanted to bring him to justice for some time but were stymied because India isn't a member of the Court, so Sikari's crimes, though horrific, couldn't be prosecuted at the ICC. But Middleton managed to find a loophole: The Volunteers discovered that Sikari had been responsible for committing murders in nations that *were* signatories, which made him subject to ICC jurisdiction.

The only problem was finding the elusive man. But finally they turned up a lead: a source at Interpol reported that Sikari was spotted in Paris making inquiries about buying sophisticated hardware and software used to find sources for underground water. This was odd, though. Kashmir was one of the few places in the world where water was plentiful. The name of the state, in fact, comes from the words *ka shimir*, meaning the act of "drying up water," referring to the draining of a primordial lake that covered much of the land. Many major rivers in India and Pakistan originated in Kashmir and other parts of the region—like perpetually drought-plagued China—and nursed whatever water they could from tributaries that sprung from there.

Middleton seized this chance—as he joked to the other Volunteers—"to flush" Sikari. He'd flown to Paris posing as an American geologist and tried to arrange a meeting with Sikari or his representatives.

But no one took the bait. So Middleton left a clear trail to the south of France, pretending to be vacationing with his wife and friends, in hopes that Sikari or an associate would try to find them. They'd been here only one day when NATO and French army surveillance units reported that they were being followed—by a dark-complexioned man who might be Indian.

Perfect, Middleton had thought. And he and Leonora Tesla set up the sting.

Now, the former colonel walked to Balan and crouched down. He said, "Water? Food?" Middleton believed in respectful, measured interrogation. There was no point in psychologically—let alone physically—abusing prisoners. That was, he'd learned, counterproductive.

"I want nothing from you people." He gave a faint sneer.

Middleton glanced up once more into the hills above the beach. He saw the white van again. Or perhaps it was another one. It was about a half-mile away, parked. There was glare on the windshield. He didn't know if anybody was inside or not. Perhaps it had no connection to Balan. But Middleton was suspicious. He called to one of the French troops. "Please, could you go check that van out?"

The man squinted. "It's just one van of many I've seen. They're very common here."

"If you don't mind."

"It is wise to separate our forces?"

"Please," Middleton said patiently.

The French officer shrugged and climbed onto his motorcycle and roared up the beach road.

Tesla's phone rang. She answered, then announced, "It's Interpol. They're going to brief me about Balan."

She turned away and jotted notes as she listened.

Middleton said to his prisoner. "Kavi, we know you were sent here to kidnap or kill me. And we know it was Devras Sikari who ordered it. Those are the facts and they're not in dispute. Now, you're going to jail for a long time. There's nothing that's going to change that. But I can make sure that the prison you go to is tolerable or is hell on earth."

"You can do to me what you want. You are all—"

"Shhh," Middleton said amiably. "I'm not interested in speeches. It's a waste of your time and it annoys me. Now, what I want to know is how can we find him? Sikari?"

"I don't know where he is." The man laughed. "And if I did, you'd never get the information out of me." He glanced down at his hands, cuffed in front of him and chained to a waist shackle that Wetherby had carefully locked around him. Middleton thought at first that he was going to complain about the handcuffs but, no, he was simply staring fondly at a wide copper bracelet on his wrist.

Balan's eyes shown fiercely as he continued. "You don't have any idea who you're dealing with. You're not worthy to even stand in his shadow. You'll see, though. You'll see."

Middleton wondered about this. Did he mean something specific? Or were the words just empty posturing?

He asked more questions, but the prisoner proved no more cooperative.

Middleton's radio cracked. The French soldier was calling to report that he'd found no one in the van. He was checking the registration. He signed off.

Maybe it was nothing. He thought of the officer's comment about dividing the forces. He looked around and saw no one on the beach.

Balan's phone, which sat in Middleton's pocket, rang. He pulled it out. On the screen: *Nombre Inconnu.* He said to Balan, "You're going to answer it. If it's Sikari, tell him you're a prisoner and I want to negotiate." He handed the phone to Petey Wetherby, "Let him talk. Tell me exactly what he says."

"Sure, Colonel." Wetherby did so.

The prisoner said something in Hindi.

"He's saying a greeting," Wetherby said to Middleton as he retreated. "It's the normal way to answer the phone in—"

Then a huge orange fireball erupted next to Balan's ear. A deafening crack of an explosion.

Knocked to his knees, Middleton squinted away the stinging dust and smoke and realized that much of the prisoner's neck and shoulder was gone, and blood was spraying in random patterns on the sand. Petey Wetherby's arm was missing as well, blown into tiny bits. Wide eyed, the soldier gripped the wound and fell to his knees as his spurting blood pooled with Balan's.

"No," Tesla cried, running forward and ripping off her belt to make a tourniquet for Wetherby. But the bomb in the phone had been so powerful that there was not enough arm left to bind.

Middleton shouted to the other French officer, "Call for backup. And medical!"

Connie Carson paid no attention to the torn-apart bodies. She grabbed the MP-5 again and did exactly the right thing, crouching into a classic defensive shooting position, sweeping the gun in the direction from which attackers might come. Lespasse snatched up a pistol and covered the south side of the beach. The other NATO soldier, holding his .45, covered the north.

Then from the hills came the sound of gunshots.

Middleton knew exactly what happened. The accomplice had slipped out of the van to spy on them, then made the phone call and, when the phone was near Balan's head, had detonated the bomb in the phone, then returned to the van and killed the French officer.

This was a nightmare.

Middleton was staring in shock at the carnage. Wetherby was now unconscious, his face white. Miraculously, Balan was still alive, though he was losing blood so fast he couldn't survive long.

The colonel crouched. "Tell me! Where is Sikari? Don't let any more innocents die."

The prisoner glanced at him once with fading eyes, then did something curious. He lifted his hands as far as the shackles would allow and bent down his head. He kissed the copper bracelet. Muttered a few words. And then went limp. He stopped breathing.

Middleton stared for a moment then glanced down at his feet and saw a tiny bit of cell phone.

A thought stabbed. He turned quickly to Lespasse, who stood at the printer next to Balan's computer. He cried, "JM, the computer! Hit the deck!"

The former soldier was programmed to follow orders instantly. He dove to the ground.

A second booby trap—inside the computer—exploded in an even larger ball of flame, showering the area with bits of plastic and metal shrapnel.

Connie Carson ran to him and helped him up, keeping her eye out for other attackers.

"You all right?" Middleton asked.

"I guess." Lespasse winced as he massaged his arm and neck. He joined the others.

Her voice choking, Tesla nodded at Wetherby. "He's gone."

Middleton was furious with himself. He should have anticipated the devices would be sabotaged. Now the cheerful, young officer was dead, all because of his carelessness . . .

But he didn't have time to dwell on the tragedy. He was looking at the hillside. The white van was speeding away. He glanced at Carlson, who was aiming the MP-5 at it. But the woman shook her head and lowered the gun. "Too far."

They'd give the information to the French but he knew that the van would soon be abandoned and the driver long gone.

And who *was* that partner?

The sour residue of chemical explosives smoke hung in the air and stung their mouths and noses.

Middleton then noticed Tesla, who was looking at Balan's shattered body. Something was on her mind, he could tell.

"What is it?"

"Something's odd here." She held up her notebook with her jottings from her conversation with the Interpol officer. "Kavi Balan's been with Sikari for years. He was his number-one triggerman, been on hundreds of jobs. Sikari was his mentor and he was grooming Balan for high places in his organization."

Nodding, Middleton said, "Sikari was so worried about us finding out something that he killed his favorite protégé to keep him quiet?"

"Exactly."

"What is it, do you think?"

Lespasse said, "Might have a lead or two." He gathered up some sheets of paper he'd just printed out and that had flown to the ground when the computer detonated. "I managed to beat the pass code and print out three emails before it blew. Two of them are street addresses. One's in London, and one in Florida. Tampa."

Middleton looked them over. Were they residences? Offices? "What's the third email?"

The young man read, "*Kavi, I am pleased that you like your present. Wear it forever for good fortune. When your project in the south of France is finished and you send me the information on the American, you must leave immediately. Time is very short. You recall what I have planned for the 'Village.' It has to happen soon—before we can move on. We only have a few weeks at the most. And be constantly aware of the Scorpion.*"

Lespasse looked up. "It's signed, DS."

Devras Sikari.

"Destroying an entire village?" Leonora Tesla whispered. "More ethnic cleansing?" She frowned. "And where is it? Kashmir?"

Middleton shrugged. "It could be anywhere. And it's in quotes. Almost as if it's a code word for something else altogether."

Lespasse said, "And what does he mean by 'before we can move on'?"

Carlson said, "Something we damn well better find out . . . And the Scorpion? Sounds like a person. But who?"

Many questions, no answers.

Tesla asked, "Should we call the powers that be?"

The Volunteers had no governmental authority. Their efforts had to be coordinated through the International Criminal Court, the European Union Force, NATO, the U.N. or local governments. Sometimes all of the above, and that took a lot of time and a lot of red tape.

Middleton was gazing at the body of young Petey Wetherby—the young man they'd gotten to know over the past few days. He recalled the times they'd laughed and drunk wine together, talked about sports and politics back in the States.

"We'll call 'em *after* we have Sikari handcuffed and in a plane headed for The Hague," Middleton muttered. He stabbed a finger at the sheets of dusty paper in Lespasse's hand. "Who wants Florida and who wants London?"

Silence for a moment. Then in her sexy Texas drawl, Carlson said, "Not sure how good I'd fit in over in Piccadilly, don't y'all think? Damn, looks like I'm stuck with Tampa."

"You've got it. JM, you go with her. Nora, looks like you and I are packing bags for London."

Though what, or whom, they were searching for in either of those places was a complete mystery.

Lespasse was looking over the third email again. "Wonder what Sikari gave him as a present."

"I think I know." Middleton recalled Balan's curious last gesture—kissing the copper bracelet. With a napkin he carefully removed the jewelry from the man's wrist. He examined it closely, making sure not to dislodge any physical evidence that might be contained in the intricate etchings. Around the edge of green-streaked copper was delicate lettering, probably Sanskrit or Hindi. And on one side, where the bracelet swelled into an oval, was an exquisite carving of an elephant. The animal was lifting its trunk and spraying water into the sky, toward the sliver of a new moon.

Carlson drawled, "Guess it wasn't such good luck, after all."

"Maybe not for him," Harry Middleton said. "But it might be for us."

2

GAYLE LYNDS

Pierre Crane had spent months working toward this moment. It was odd that it would end on the outskirts of Paris, but then the investigation had been difficult and strange from the beginning.

It was 10 o'clock at night, the black sky winking with bright stars. As the taxi sped him along the Boulevard Bargue in Montfermeil, Crane stared out alertly. It was said the two Frances met here: To his left spread tidy prewar family homes with neat gardens and carefully painted black steel fences, while to the right was his destination—a public housing project of big apartment blocks 10 stories high, sheltering thousands of immigrants and their French-born children, grandchildren and great-grandchildren.

The tenements were called Les Bosquets, "The Groves," evoking visions of lush natural beauty. But what Crane saw through his taxi window was an asphalt-and-concrete jungle awash with graffiti, broken sidewalks, thirsty weeds and deep shadows. This was the last stop before homelessness for those who could afford no other shelter, which helped to explain its unemployment rate perennially hovering around 50 percent.

The bleak scene only increased the oddity of Crane's presence: The man he was to meet was wealthy and powerful and about as likely to live in Les Bosquets as a nun in a Las Vegas whorehouse.

"*Nous sommes ici,*" Crane told the driver in perfect French. His mother had been French, and he had spent many happy childhood summers with her family in the Champagne country around Reims.

The driver responded instantly, pulling to the curb and announcing the fare. He stuck out his hand. "*S'il vous plaît.*" The expression on his worried face said it all—he was ready to leave *now*.

Pierre Crane handed over euros and climbed out into the night. Thirty-eight years old, he was tall and gangly with pasty skin, dull brown hair, a large nose and a long neck. Teased as a child because of his physical appearance, and called "The Crane" behind his back by his colleagues (he enjoyed the fact that he knew that), he had developed a quick sense of humor and an appreciation for being underestimated. In service to both, he also held a black belt in karate, about which few people knew—and had for 20 years.

Dressed casually in khaki trousers and a nylon jacket zippered up against a cool autumn wind, Crane turned slightly on the sidewalk as the taxi squealed into traffic. Keeping his gaze neutral, he watched as a half-dozen teenage boys reversed direction and headed toward him through a pool of lamplight, snapping their fingers and doing a pimp walk to Algerian hip-hop music blaring from the boom box one carried on a heavily muscled shoulder.

As they drew closer, Crane bent his knees slightly, found his balance and let his empty hands drift down to his sides, fingers unfurled.

The youths appraised him with stony gazes, their bodies still rolling and dipping.

He shrugged, grinned and touched the snap-brim of his cap.

A few seconds of surprise showed in their dusky faces. Then their tension seemed to lessen. But as they passed him, a warning drifted back— "Go home *Français de souche!*" The phrase literally meant "French with roots," slang for ethnic French.

He stared thoughtfully after them, the bulges in the hip pockets of their low-slung jeans revealing what he had suspected—they were carrying knives.

Feeling a chill, Crane reminded himself he had walked into more dicey situations than this. An investigative reporter for Reuters, he seldom talked about his successes, but back in the 1990s he had discovered vital information that helped lead to charges of war crimes against Radovan Karadzic, the alleged architect of Bosnia's holocaust. Later he uncovered the atrocity-filled Cosa Nostra background of a top Italian presidential candidate, creating headlines across Europe and sending the politician to prison. And last year, while working on a small story he had dug up a large prize—one of Saddam Hussein's secret caches of gold, despite having three mercenaries on his tail the whole time.

Remembering all of that, the journalist marched resolutely into Les Bosquets, his large feet eating up the distance among the towering maze of dilapidated cement tenements. Pole lamps were alight, the ones that were working. He watched women in hijabs and blousy clothing move languidly in and out of doorways, many holding babies. Radio news in Arabic chattered from an open window. High above, colorful desert robes were draped over balconies, ready to dry in the morning sun.

He sensed no danger, but still he slowed and looked around carefully. He knew he had made no mistake in the directions, but none of the buildings carried anything close to the number he needed.

He forged onward, heading toward the next corner. He turned it in time to see two youths with reckless faces negotiating a drug deal. Watching it from a front stoop was a man in a bushy black beard, who was openly cleaning a 9mm Beretta pistol. The man quickly shifted his gaze to Crane, his sharp brown eyes assessing, a hawk spotting potential prey.

Suddenly the scarred door of the facing building swung open, and three men in denim jeans and short-sleeved shirts swarmed out, cradling submachine guns. The weapons were Ingram Model 10s, short, compact and fitted with MAC suppressors, which reduced emergent gas velocity to subsonic level.

Pierre Crane froze.

The pair involved in the drug deal ran in opposite directions. The man with the Beretta vanished indoors. All that remained were the armed trio—and Crane.

As they stared at him, expressions grim, sweat slid down his spine. Hoping they were who he thought they might be, he said the Arabic words he had been told to say: "*ªaDetni ªa'rabba.*" I've been bitten by a scorpion.

The man to his right nodded. "The Scorpion will see you now." The words were in English, and the voice was low. It was the correct response, which was all that mattered to Crane.

The guards hustled him safely up the steps and inside. The door closed with a loud thud, followed by the clicks of a battery of locks thrown into place. Clearly this was no ordinary tenement, and now the Scorpion's insistence that the meeting be held in Les Bosquets made sense: Crane had been warned to come alone, and by walking through the labyrinth of buildings to an address that did not exist, the Scorpion's people had had plenty of time to observe him and make certain he was not only by himself but had not been followed.

He inhaled and looked around. The foyer was old but clean, with a low ceiling. Standing in the middle of it was a fourth man, unarmed and of an entirely different sort.

"Monsieur Crane, you're late. I trust you had no trouble." The man was older, somewhere in his mid-50s, with an angular face, a yacht tan, and a halo of salt-gray hair, every strand in place. Crane studied the cut and fabric of his suit—charcoal gray silk with a 24-carat gold pinstripe, estimated cost $10,000. And the shoes—by Berlutti, in alligator with natural seams—at least $1,500. The tie was Hermès and worth $5,000. But it was the watch that held his attention—Patek Phillippe, $200,000, not a centime less.

Crane raised his gaze. "So I meet the Scorpion at last."

Bright blue eyes twinkled back at him. "You're a smart lad." The accent was lightly British, and his manner was casually *noblesse oblige* as he looked past Crane to his men. "Search him."

Crane knew the drill. He lifted his arms and spread his legs. No one spoke as a guard patted him down, then a second ran an airport-style wand over him. They were inspecting him not only for weapons but for any kind of recording devices, which was fine with Crane. Over the years he had developed an extraordinary memory not only for documents but also for conversations. Few people knew he had those talents either.

"He's clean," the man with the wand reported.

The Scorpion had been looking away. Now he focused on Crane again. "We'll take the elevator."

With two of the security men leading, they stepped into the elevator cage, followed by the last man who touched the button that sent them not up into the apartments, but downward.

Crane asked, "When did you become involved in—"

He raised a hand, silencing him. "We'll discuss serious matters when we're in the limo. It's debugged and the windows are treated so no demodulating devices can read our voices. You look surprised I know about such things." He shrugged. "It's the world we live in, lad. Pity, isn't it?" Then he beamed. "But it does make for good business."

"Certainly for what I understand is your business." Crane kept his tone neutral.

The older man inclined his head. "As you say."

The elevator door slid open, revealing a traditional cement-floor cellar with trash bins and laundry and boiler rooms. To the right was a wide expanse of stalls walled with wire fencing, each gated, combination locks dangling. Storage of some kind. As Crane studied the area, trying to see more than cardboard boxes, a powerful car engine purred to life.

From the shadows emerged a long Mercedes limousine. It cruised toward them, its polished black surface gleaming in the florescent lighting like freshly spilled ink.

"Our chariot," the Scorpion explained.

While the chauffeur remained behind the steering wheel, two of the guards opened the rear doors then stepped back, standing at attention. Crane walked around to the other side and slid in, joining his host.

The car smelled of new leather and lemon wax. The driver wore a traditional mufti-brown uniform and flat cap with a stiff brim. From what Crane could see, he looked old—he had thin white hair and the skin on the back of his neck was pale and wrinkled. Covering his hands were short calfskin driving gloves that revealed a copper bracelet on his right wrist.

The bracelet caught Crane's attention. Some kind of words edged it. Even at this distance he could see the letters looked exotic, which of course was always intriguing. The bracelet must be very old, he decided, since the copper was such a rich color. In fact, it seemed to shimmer as if from some deep inner fire. The bracelet was a stunning bauble—that was why it had attracted his eye, and that was all there was to it.

Crane put on his seatbelt. The doors closed, and they were alone.

"Proceed."

The driver looked into the rearview mirror and nodded, acknowledging the order. Then he rolled the limo toward a driveway that rose up to street level and the stars.

Crane watched as his host settled back against the leather and said, "Before I answer your questions, you must answer mine. Tell me how you came to be interested in me. Start at the beginning."

It was a strange question, but it was possible the Scorpion did not know the whole story. "I was doing research for an article when I ran across something that had nothing to do with it, but I was intrigued. It was an anomaly."

"Go on."

"The anomaly was three brilliant young foreign students at Cambridge— an Indian, a Pakistani and a Kashmiri—who graduated with first-class honors in 1988. They were close friends. All were born poor, but their educational expenses in England, which began when they were ten years old, were paid for. Then when they left Cambridge, they started different businesses, again completely funded. Each was quickly successful. But the Indian died in New Delhi within five years, drowned in a flood, and the one in Pakistan died ten years later, poisoned by bad well water. And the third one, the Kashmiri—Devras Sikari—is still alive, but he's sold his company and is living in the bush as some sort of combination warlord and would-be saint. The whole situation seemed to beg to be looked into. So that's what I did. I discovered the three hadn't known each other before England, all were Hindu and none had ever named their sponsor. The one clue I turned up about that subject was in an obscure Hindu journal. In it, Sikari is quoted as saying that the benefactor was 'holy, but of this world.'"

"Yes, I've heard parts of that. Do continue."

Crane allowed himself a brief smile. "Sikari's quote was tantalizing. Why would a benefactor want to hide his generosity? After all, he educated three impoverished children and his story might inspire others to be equally generous." Unless the person wasn't altruistic at all, he thought to himself. Unless he had a far different—and far less admirable—motive. "I was finally able to track down the name of the company that paid their expenses. It was a front, leading to more front companies. But one thing was constant. Their security was provided by BlueWatch Global Services."

Headquartered in Dubai, BlueWatch was the real deal, a private security and private investigation agency with a special division servicing very deep-pocket clients. "Naturally I asked for an interview with the president and board chair, Mr. Francis Xavier Kimball."

From everything he could tell, Kimball did not exist. Still, Crane was not ready to point that out, at least not yet, because it was his probe into Kimball's identity that had ignited the Scorpion's emails that had ended with the invitation to meet. He had never heard of the Scorpion, but one of his sources who was well connected in the underworld of international crime had described him as rich, dangerous, of unknown name and origin, and never seen. Shortly after that, Reuters's IT security team reported to Crane that the Scorpion's emails had been routed through multiple countries, including China and Russia, and their signals were untraceable.

As he finished speaking, Pierre Crane looked out, realizing they were long past Les Bosquets. They appeared to be in a lovely residential section of outer Paris where swaying trees, autumn flowers, and luxuriant moonlit lawns showed on both sides of the car. High hedges and pastel-painted walls appeared, lining it. The occasional driveway was sealed by ornate gates that were really high-security barricades.

"Where are we?" Crane asked.

"Nowhere in particular. It doesn't matter really, does it now? In fact, I don't know either. We're simply being driven. The point was for you and me to have a quiet, uninterrupted conversation. And that we're having indeed. You've just related an entertaining tale, Mr. Crane." He dusted an imaginary annoyance from the sleeve of his superb suit. "And what do you plan to do with it?"

"I'd like to write a story about the brilliant young Kashmiri who turned his back on the West and became an independence fighter. The benefactor who funded his education and was then betrayed when Sikari returned to Kashmir is part of that story. The name 'the Scorpion' came up in several conversations. So, will you confirm that you are the benefactor? The Good Samaritan who was betrayed?"

"There are occasions when it's far better for everyone to remain anonymous," the man replied. "Besides, as you said yourself, with two of the men dead and the third likely gone mad, I hardly think anyone would want to take credit for the experiment."

"The 'experiment'? That's even more intriguing. What did you hope to accomplish?"

"No, no. I wasn't the one. If I were, and I didn't want you to know, I'd simply dodge your questions. I had nothing to do with any of it." He held up a manicured hand. "Please, let me finish. At the same time, I'd like to know more, too."

"Why?"

"A man can't have too much knowledge. If I give you the address of a place where you're likely to uncover new information, will you promise to let me know in detail what you discover?"

Crane was surprised. He had expected the Scorpion to try to stop him, and any help he got from the mysterious rich man would have to be wormed—or tricked—out of him.

"Why don't you go yourself?" Crane demanded.

Again there was a twinkle in the older man's blue eyes. "Through you, I will. It is, shall we say, more discreet this way. From everything my people tell me, you're a man of your word. What's your answer?"

"All right, I'll give you a report. After that, I make no promises."

"Be very careful when you go there. There's a man who's pursuing Sikari. He's former U.S. Army, in fact former military intelligence. Well-trained and ruthless." He slipped his hand inside his suit jacket and brought out a color photograph. "This is him. His name is Harold Middleton. Be cautious of him at all times."

Crane glanced at the photo, but when he looked up he stopped listening. He was riveted by the scene on the other side of the car window—another black limo had appeared and was running without lights next to them on the cramped, two-lane residential road. It was keeping perfect and very dangerous pace, its front fenders aligned with their limo's front fenders. Cold moonlight reflected off the darkened side windows. He could see no one inside. His lungs tightened.

The chauffeur spoke. "I've been watching it." Crane liked the sound of him—there was authority in the voice, a man who knew how to get things done.

The chauffeur floored the gas pedal. The limo's tires spun and screeched, and the acceleration threw them deep into their seats.

As they left the other limo sucking their exhaust, the chauffeur commanded, "Get out the weapons."

Crane saw his host jab a button on his plush armrest. A door dropped open behind the driver's seat. He pulled out an MP5 submachine gun and quickly slid it over the seat to the chauffeur. Then he grabbed the other gun for himself and rested it gingerly on his lap.

"It's Jana," the driver said angrily. "I could see her through the windshield. How did she find us?"

"How should I know?"

"It's your job, dammit! You've screwed up!"

Crane was stunned. The chauffeur was questioning the Scorpion. He was giving the Scorpion orders. He was telling him he had failed. And the Scorpion was doing nothing to take back control.

As the limo raced onward, Crane noticed that the window between the front and rear seats had remained open the whole time. The chauffeur had heard everything. Crane thought back quickly, remembering when he saw the man in the tenement foyer and asked whether he was the Scorpion. 'You're a smart lad,' he'd said, and that was all he'd said, which was no answer at all. He had dodged the question.

Crane felt his heart pound. The disguise of chauffeur was perfect to conceal the Scorpion's legendary secret identity while carrying out business. There was only one answer that made sense—the chauffeur was the boss. Could the chauffeur be the real Scorpion?

The second limo pulled up again and the window on the front passenger side rolled down. Crane looked inside. He caught a gauzy image of the driver—a beautiful woman with long lustrous dark hair dancing in the slipstream. Her left hand was on the wheel. Her right, out of view.

She glanced at Crane and he felt a shiver—from her beauty and from what he saw as a fanatic's fire in her eyes. Captivating, terrifying. Then she lost all interest in him and instead focused on the other two men in the vehicle. Something about her gaze as she looked at the driver registered disappointment. She hesitated only a moment then lifted a machine pistol. Perhaps an Uzi, perhaps a Mac-10. As Crane gasped and cringed, a firestorm sprouted from the muzzle and, like amplified hail, the bullets slammed in the windows, flicking loudly but ineffectively off the armored sheet metal and bulletproof glass. Dismay spread on Jana's face and she wrenched the wheel to the right, forcing their limo into a grassy shoulder, where it bounced to a halt.

Jana's vehicle vanished into a cloud of dust.

"How did she find us?" the driver snapped.

"Followed him?" The man in the backseat glanced at Crane, who noticed that he held his pistol firmly in a steady hand. He wondered if he was about to die.

The driver spun around and snapped, "You can never underestimate anyone in this. Never."

The man beside him said, "What do we do about him?"

The driver considered. "Mr. Crane, there's a train station at the end of that road there. You see it?"

"Yes."

"You can get a train that will take you back to Paris. I'm afraid we have other concerns."

"Yes, of course."

"Follow the London lead. But be careful. Whatever you do, be careful."

Crane climbed out of the limo, which rocked out of the soft shoulder and made a U turn, the opposite of the direction Jana had sped in.

The reporter, now shaking and breathless from the incident, began hiking toward the road. His reporter's instinct gave him an important message: The woman had been intent on killing the Scorpion but the frown of disappointment when she saw the men in the limo told him that neither man was, in fact, that reclusive character.

Anyone with common sense would walk away from this story. It was beyond dangerous, but somewhere deep inside him he, the Crane, loved that. He was ugly, but his mind and spirit were beautiful. His curiosity was inflamed, and like a lover in the first fiery flush of requitement, he would see himself skinned and beheaded before he would let go of this amazing story.

He pulled out his cell and ran down the street. In the distance, police sirens screamed. He ignored them. His mind was on London and what he would find there.

3

DAVID HEWSON

Felicia Kaminski was playing Bach—Partita number two in D minor, the Chaconne, some of the most difficult solo violin music ever written—when the man with the gun burst through the door.

There was a woman behind the frantic, worried figure moving forcefully into the front room of the little terraced cottage on London's Lamb's Conduit Street. She was tall and elegant, with long dark hair and something that looked like a machine pistol—Kaminski wished weapons were not so familiar—extended in her right hand.

The young Polish musician placed her Bela Szepessy fiddle and bow on the antique walnut table by the window and said, "Harold. Leonora. So nice to see you again. How is the music business these days? Slow or fast? Looking at you at this moment it is difficult for me to judge. Are you here for my debut at the Wigmore Hall? If so . . . " She placed a slender finger, the nail trimmed down to the quick, on her cheek. "I have some sartorial issues, I must say."

"Oh crap." Middleton put away the weapon and Leonora Tesla followed suit, if a little more slowly. He slapped his forehead theatrically. "I'm sorry, Felicia. We saw there was someone inside. I forgot you had the keys."

"They shoot burglars in London, Harold? Such a beautiful little house. You don't remember who you lend it to?"

Middleton glanced at the woman with him. "I said Felicia was welcome to use the place. For her . . . " He stumbled over the details.

" . . . for my debut at the Wigmore Hall," Felicia repeated, picking up the fiddle and showing it to them. "I thought you wanted to see me play this. It cost you a lot of money."

Harold Middleton—she refused to shorten his first name since she wasn't, Felicia wished to say, a colleague—had proved a good friend of sorts. He saved her life on more than one occasion when she was enmeshed in the deadly game of terror and crime that should have ended in a massacre at the James Madison Recital Hall in Washington, D.C., while she performed as the principal soloist for a newly unearthed work by Chopin.

There had been many more favors in the intervening two years. Over that time she ceased to be an impoverished young Polish émigré, without friends at first, without parents, and had began slowly to adjust to the life of a professional musician, taking the first steps on the international orchestral ladder, occasionally and only when absolutely necessary, using Harold Middleton's many connections. She was grateful. She was also intensely aware that a part of his generosity stemmed from some private, inward guilt for introducing her to the dark and violent world to which he had now returned, one a million miles away from the music which he truly loved.

"I will see you play," Middleton insisted.

"We both will, Felicia," Leonora Tesla added.

Middleton winced when he failed to remember the date of the recital.

"Tonight," she interrupted with a scowl. "Seven o'clock. I texted you. I emailed . . . "

"I'm sorry. Give me time, please. Life's a little . . . "—he exchanged looks with his colleague—" . . . hectic right now."

Middleton strode over to the tall wardrobe in the living room, a hulking, ugly piece of furniture—the only out-of-place item in the room and one hidden in shadow so that it couldn't be seen from the long double window that gave out onto the street. The cottage was in a narrow Georgian lane in a backwater of Bloomsbury, walking distance from the West End and the concert hall where she was due that afternoon for a final rehearsal. It was a quiet, discreetly wealthy part of central London away from the crowds and the tourists, a village almost.

When he threw open the wardrobe's doors, Felicia found herself looking at the object she had found there when she was poking around the place two days before, after arriving from New York—a black, heavy-duty metal security cabinet with a rotary combination lock, like that of an old-fashioned safe. Middleton dialed the numbers then pulled on the handle to open the door. Felicia caught her breath, though in truth she knew she shouldn't have been surprised. A small armory—pistols, rifles, boxes of ammunitions, other items she didn't recognize—was neatly lined up inside.

Leonora Tesla put down her shoulder bag, joined him and starting picking at the hardware. Middleton had brought two grey hold-alls for their booty. The two of them looked like a couple in a fancy chocolate store, trying to decide what delicacies to take away with them.

"So the Volunteers are back in business," Felicia said.

"Supply and demand, kid," Tesla replied, taking down what looked like a pack of small metal balls. Grenades of some kind maybe. "Be grateful you're in a nicer business."

Middleton and Tesla were so utterly absorbed Felicia didn't feel too bad about poking around at something else while they were so preoccupied.

After a minute, she said, "I am grateful. Yet still, in your new job, you find time to buy nice jewelry. Nora, is this for you?"

They stopped packing weaponry into the soft grey cases and turned to look. In her delicate pale fingers, Felicia held the glittering object that had caught her attention as Leonora Tesla placed her bag on a chair by the dining table, the top half open. The article was enclosed in a transparent plastic evidence packet and tagged with a NATO label bearing the previous day's date, and what sounded like a French name. It occurred to Felicia that they must have been in a hurry indeed if they sought weapons before delivering what must, she imagined, have been something of importance.

"You know, when we first got to know one another I don't recall you being in the habit of going through people's things," Middleton told her.

"I got older, Harold. Quickly. You remember? With the company you introduced me to it seemed to make sense. What is this?"

She opened the evidence bag and removed the gleaming bright bracelet, studying it closely. When she was done she examined the two other items that had been alongside it: a slip of paper and a recent Indian passport in the name of Kavi Balan. The photo inside showed an inoffensive-looking Indian man perhaps 30 with a bland, perhaps naïve face. He had, she thought, very prominent and unusual eyes and wondered whether they had noticed. Probably not. Harold Middleton and Leonora Tesla were both intelligent, hardworking officers, trapped, Felicia had observed, inside an organization they seemed unable to leave. But small details often escaped them. They possessed neither the time nor the inclination to look much beyond the obvious.

"Our business, not yours," Middleton announced.

"He's dead, I imagine," she said, and they didn't reply. "Didn't you notice his eyes . . . ?"

She was stalling and they knew it. As she spoke, she scanned the sheet of paper. The writing was in Harold Middleton's hand, easily recognizable for its cultured yet hurried scrawl.

It read: *Kashmir. Search for water. Geology. Copper. Bracelet. Scorpion. Devras Sikari.*

"It sounds like a puzzle," she said. "I love riddles. I never knew you did . . . "

"I hate them."

"What does Scorpion refer to?"

"It was a reference in an email from Sikari. I think it's a person, but I don't know if he's allied with Sikari or is a threat to him."

"The bracelet is beautiful."

It looked like copper, though the color was lighter, more golden than most bangles of its type. In Poland, copper wristbands were popular among the elderly who believed they warded off rheumatism and disease. The jewelry she saw hawked around the cheap street markets in Warsaw looked nothing like this. The metal here was softer, paler, as if it were some kind of subtle alloy, the edges, flecked with green, more finely worked, with a line of writing in a flowing, incomprehensible Indian script, and, most curious of all, an oval feature like a badge, a mark of pride for its wearer perhaps.

"What does this mean?" she asked.

"I wish I knew," he replied. "We think it's from Kashmir. An identity bracelet, maybe denoting membership in a gang, a cult, an organization of some kind. Presumably the emblems stand for something. It could be connected with India. Or Pakistan. They've been fighting one another over

Kashmir for half a century. I need to get it to the lab, get the inscription translated."

Felicia stared at it and frowned.

"You have any ideas?" he asked.

"What? Some little kid Polish musician? What would I know?" She looked at the copper bracelet again. "You never do crosswords do you?"

"I told you. I hate puzzles."

"That's because you think logically, in one direction only. Crosswords are like Bach. Or jazz. They demand you think in several different directions simultaneously. Call and response, question and answer, all in the same moment."

She examined the bracelet again.

"The point is . . . All the information you need is there. In front of your face. Nothing is missing. You just have to make the links."

Middleton looked interested. It was the mention of Bach that did it.

"My problem," she added, "is I still think in Polish, not English. I love crosswords but they're too hard for me in your language. I used to wish you could see them instead of read them. You know what I mean? Look at cross *pictures*. Not words. That way language isn't so important."

They had what weapons they wanted. They were ready to go. Middleton held out his hand and she passed to him the note and the photograph of the dead Indian with the curious eyes. He placed them back in the evidence packet and slipped them into his carryall. She clung to the copper bangle, waiting for the question.

"If the pictures on the bracelet were a crossword," Middleton asked, "what do you think they might mean?"

Leonora Tesla shook her head. "We're giving these to a bunch of forensic people, Harry. Not a crossword expert."

"That's a shame," Felicia said.

They looked at her.

"Because? . . ." Middleton asked.

She pointed at the moon on the bracelet

"This would be the answer, I think. The part that is calling. See how it's separate, and the other two elements are subsidiary to it, as if their response somehow answers everything. The elephant. The way he blows his trunk comically into the sky, like a fountain, except that the liquid doesn't go very far, does it? The stream falls to earth so quickly, as if it weighs more than it should. This seems obvious to me."

"Obvious?" he asked.

"Look! It's an elephant. The biggest land animal on the planet. What's he doing? Trying to spray the moon, and failing. Two words. Maybe it's me being crazy but remember: I was born in the year of Chernobyl. We weren't far away. Five hundred kilometers maybe. At school they came along every six months and took our blood to see if the explosion had done something bad to us."

That blunt needle, the same one they used on everyone, hurt which was why she had read so avidly to understand its cause.

She put her finger on the carefully carved beast on the bracelet and said, "Heavy."

Then she indicated the fountain of liquid rising from the beast toward the sky and falling back again, too quickly. "Water."

Felicia Kaminski couldn't help but notice that Harold Middleton went a little paler when she said that.

"Chernobyl happened because there was no heavy water," she said quickly. "The Russians used some cheap and useless method of their own to produce a nuclear reactor which was why the plant exploded. I'm sorry. This is doubtless just me . . . As to the moon, I've no idea."

They didn't say anything for a moment as Middleton looked at her, his benign, bland face creased with concern.

"You're practicing here for the rest of the day?" he asked.

"Practice, practice, practice. After a while . . . "

"Stay indoors. I'll arrange a cab to the Wigmore Hall and a hotel for you this evening. Pack your things. Leave your bag here when you go to the concert. We'll pick it up for you later."

"But . . . "

They didn't wait for anything except a few short pleasantries. Felicia Kaminski watched them go, wishing they could have stayed a little longer. She knew no one in London. She felt a little lonely and bored.

"Practice," she hissed. "If I practice one more time I'll go mad."

As the door closed, she picked up a piece of paper and scribbled down the words she remembered from Harold Middleton's note.

Some forensics people would be running through every last one to try to forge a link. Maybe—she was worried, slightly, by the look on Middleton's face when she threw in her idea about the bracelet—they would be looking to see what the term "heavy water" meant in relation to India, Pakistan and the Kashmir question. Quite a lot, possibly, not that she wanted to think much about that. The dark shadow Chernobyl had cast over Eastern Europe had never quite lifted from her.

She looked at the grandfather clock by the fireplace. Two hours remained before she had to leave, a little less if she packed as Middleton had wanted. She had time. There was something else she could use too, something she felt sure Middleton and Tesla would never have countenanced.

Felicia Kaminski went to her laptop computer and pulled up the web page for Bicchu, the new search engine she'd stumbled upon only a month ago. It was all the rage in the social networks. The answers were sharp and relevant, almost as if someone were reading the question then thinking about its context and perspective before responding. It felt smart and human, not part of some dumb machine. Best of all, Bicchu promised to pay you for being online, for typing in queries and following through on the results. Just a few cents but it was something. For all the glamour of an appearance at the Wigmore Hall, she still felt like a music student when she looked at her bank balance. It would be years before she could even hope to command a reliable income.

Felicia glanced down and typed in the words on her scribbled note.

Kashmir. Search for water. Geology. Copper. Bracelet. Scorpion. Devras Sikari.

Then she added a phrase of her own: *heavy water.*

And another: *copper ring around the eyes.*

It took longer than normal for the answers to appear. A good 10 seconds. Must have been Middleton's broadband connection, she thought.

He sat in the restaurant near Piccadilly Circus, glued to the iPhone they'd given him, working the private application that linked through the mobile network, securely, privately, to the field HQ. He'd no idea where that was. In Kashmir. In Paris. Two doors away in the heart of London. It was irrelevant. The days of fixed bases, of dangerous safe houses and physical networks capable of penetration . . . all these things were in the past. It was thirteen months since he'd last met another comrade in person. As far as he knew anyway. Orders came via secure encrypted email delivered to a series of ever-changing addresses. Plans and projects arrived as password protected zipped pdfs, read, absorbed, and then deleted forever. This was the way of the world. Everything was virtual. Nothing was real. Except, he reminded himself, blood and money.

A YouTube video had just begun—the trailer for some new Bollywood movie—when the phone throbbed and flashed up an alert. It took a second or two for the signal to deal with the amount of data that followed. Then, as the little handset caught up, he watched as a series of web search requests were mirrored to his little screen. The results narrowed constantly. The scope and scale of the queries made him realize why they'd got in touch. A small window in the upper right hand corner showed the IP address of the source. It was in central London, somewhere near the British Museum. He tapped a few buttons. There was a pause then he found himself in the My Documents folder of the remote computer. A long list of correspondence was stored there. It was all encrypted. He hunted around the remote hard drive until he found the folder where the word processor stored its templates, unseen, often forgotten by those who used them. Sure enough when he got there he found a single file marked "personal letter." It was open, unsecured by encryption, just text.

He clicked the icon and the document drew itself on the screen of the phone. Dragging his finger across the letters he managed to copy the address into a note. Then he clicked a button in the private app marked "keylog all remote." Every letter and number typed on the distant machine would now be echoed directly into a file somewhere in the Bicchu system then passed on discreetly, encrypted from beginning to end, to his phone where the private app would decode the text automatically.

After that he copied the house number and street in the heading and pasted them into Google Maps. He knew the general area. It was no more than ten minutes away on foot. Pocketing the iPhone he walked back into the kitchen. It was full of the familiar smells, cumin and turmeric, a tandoori oven and scorched spiced chicken.

The sous chef watched him come in, as if half expecting what was about to happen. The little man from Bangladesh was staring mutinously at an office lunch booking for sixteen. It had been pinned to the order board just thirty minutes before.

"You can cope," he said, taking off his apron and his stained tocque. Then he walked out of the back, stopping only to collect his little Walther pistol on the way.

Bicchu was feeling talkative. Soon the answers began to come so quickly her head started to spin. She thought of the fearful years after Chernobyl, the pain, the uncertainty. And the school friends she lost, two, who died slowly, almost in front of everyone, day by day.

This was the world of the past, or so she'd thought. A world of hard, cruel science, in the thrall of men who didn't care about the consequences of their actions. Watching the hints and clues and links begin to assemble as minutes turned to an hour, she felt herself both repelled and attracted by what she was uncovering. This was important, she knew. And forbidden, terrible knowledge.

After one significant breakthrough, she tore herself away from the computer, made herself a cup of green tea, felt briefly guilty about neglecting her instrument and chose, instead, to listen to one of her favorite renditions of the piece she would play later. A fellow Pole, Henryk Szeryng, playing his famed Guarneri del Gesu "Le Duc" for Deutsche Grammophon in 1968: fourteen and a half minutes of bliss.

Then she went back and looked at what she'd found. A lot. Too much. It made her mind turn in on itself, craving the peace and simple faith of the music.

She called Middleton's cell phone. There was no answer. There wasn't even the chance to leave a message.

"That's not your real number is it, Harold?" she said to herself, half listening to Szeryng tackle the music with a studied assurance she hoped one day she might possess.

He wondered what would happen in the restaurant with him gone. The Bangladeshi was competent but slow. It was still a business, still a place that needed to look after its customers.

Later, he thought. The top end of Lamb's Conduit Street, after the pubs and shops, was deserted. Everyone had gone to work. This was good. The only vehicle around was a large black van with opaque windows on a meter at the park end of the street. Children leapt and danced in the little playground on the other side of the road. He glanced at the van and shook his head. London mothers. They wouldn't let their precious little princes walk half a mile any more.

She typed what she'd discovered into an email for Middleton and made sure to mark it for encryption, adding the digital signature he'd convinced her to use always on the net. No one could read what she'd written once it traveled beyond her computer and Middleton could be assured the message really came from her, not some imposter who knew how to spoof an email address.

"Fact one," she wrote, and she shivered as she was unable to force the true import of her words from her mind. "The picture of the dead man, Kavi Balan. What you didn't notice was the very peculiar green brown tint to his eyes. That may be normal. But it may be a symptom of copper poisoning, due to very heavy exposure to the metal. Look up Kayser-Fleischer ring for more information. The discoloration is caused by copper deposits in the eye."

She looked at her notes then checked her watch. Six minutes to the end of the Bach. Then she really would practice.

"Fact two. India is the world's largest producer of heavy water. This is a very resource-intensive exercise. Depending on the process it can take up to 340,000 tons of ordinary water, H_2O, to make one ton of heavy water, D_2O (that's deuterium, Harold—look it up). Maybe this is why your people are looking for new sources."

The tea was getting tepid.

"Remember what I told you about Chernobyl and heavy water? You don't always need it. But if you want to produce weapon-grade plutonium it's a wonderful way of bypassing the uranium enrichment process, which involves a lot of technological infrastructure that's impossible to hide. Not that heavy water is easy to manufacture but the process is a little like distilling cognac from wine. The difference is the conventional process uses a phosphor-bronze system to handle the distillation process whereas liquor is traditionally made using a copper still."

She looked at the words on the page and felt proud of herself. Or, more accurately, of Bicchu, which had thrown up the answers so quickly she could scarcely believe the ease with which they had been assembled.

"Fact three. Eleven years ago, a patent was filed in the U.S. for a new heavy-water development process. As far as I can see it's never been put into industrial production because some of the technology isn't in place to go large scale yet. The patent was lodged by the U.S. subsidiary of an Indian company that appears to be a shell outfit. At least I can't see any financial filings for it in the U.S. or in India." She'd retrieved the entire submission from the U.S. Patents Office database for free and saved it as a separate document.

"Sikari's name is on the patent too, along with a couple of other people. According to the patent submission the process would halve the amount of feed water normally needed to distill heavy water, shorten the process considerably and allow for minimal startup costs. You could almost see it as a DIY kit for making the raw material for a plutonium plant. And . . . "

Always save the best for last. The dead Henryk Szeryng, bowing away at his Guarneri in the background, did.

"The particular circular piping structure used for the process is at the heart of the patent. It's what makes it unique. The filing calls it 'the copper bracelet.' Except this one happens to be thirty feet tall."

She finished the cold tea and listened to the music enter its final, closing phase.

The doorbell rang as she hit send. Felicia cursed the interruption. One of the less attractive aspects of Lamb's Conduit Street was the number of people who came to private houses trying to sell everything from fake DVDs to Chinese paintings. Middleton had a little sign by the front of the house: no hawkers. It was useless. This being England, he didn't have a door video camera. There was trust in a quiet, upper-class street like this, along with big powerful locks and a high-tech alarm system.

The bell rang once more while she was walking out of the living room into the corridor.

"I don't want any," she shouted, and was surprised to hear an American twang in her voice. Two years in New York did this to you, she guessed.

She unlocked the latch and half opened the door. A stocky man of Middle Eastern appearance was standing there. He was no more than 30, wore a Chelsea football shirt under a jacket, a trendy slicked-back haircut and the kind of stupid self-satisfied grin some young London men liked to sport when they encountered the opposite sex.

"I don't want any," she repeated with a sigh.

He looked pleased with himself and held up what looked like a brand new iPhone. Her email to Harold Middleton was there, with the last few paragraphs including the words "except this one happens to be thirty feet tall" visible in large black lettering. Puzzled, Felicia Kaminski blinked.

"You got it anyway," the man said.

She drew back to slam the door in his face. The wood hit something along the way. She heard a yelp of pain but he was through, and there was no way of getting him outside again. A glancing blow struck her cheek and she stumbled toward the living room and grabbed the wooden inner door, sending it flying behind her.

He got struck hard in the face a second time and yelled again. Anger. Hurt. She liked both of them.

She propped herself against the sofa, trying to think, trying to locate something that might pass as a weapon.

"Hey," he said.

He had his hands up and looked offended. His right eye had gone purple from where the door had caught him.

"We just want to talk," he said. "That's all."

"Who wants to talk?" she asked, still looking, feeling behind the sofa with her right hand.

"Some big guys. They don't mean you no harm. They told me that. They just want you to visit."

"There are nicer ways to ask."

He reached into his jacket with his free hand and took out a handgun.

"There are nastier ones too. Alive isn't the same as undamaged. You choose, little girl. One way or another you're coming with me."

Szeryng was playing one of her most cherished passages. Felicia Kaminski hated this anonymous man for ruining it.

She looked him in the eye and said, "They won't hurt me? That's a promise?"

"A promise."

He still had the iPhone in his left hand. She watched the way he held it. The obvious affection he had for the thing.

She put a hand to her head and let down her long brown hair she had fastened for practice. He watched her, smiling again.

"Isn't that, like, the new version?" she asked, pointing at the phone. "The one with GPS or something?"

They all loved them. Sometimes it seemed there was nothing more precious on the planet.

"Yeah . . . " He held it a little higher and pressed a button. A video of MIA began to play on the screen. "I got . . . "

She was wearing the pointed leather boots she'd bought in a Gucci outlet place near San Giovanni. Those needle-like toes were going out of fashion but she liked them. She took one strong step forward, let her right leg fall back a little to gain momentum, then let loose with a kick, as hard as she could manage—right where it hurt most.

He screamed. The gun went sideways. She took his wrist and punched it back against the sharp edge of the wardrobe that contained Harold Middleton's armory. The weapon clattered to the floor. The iPhone he held on to, but not after the second kick. By then he was on the ground, squirming, looking madder than ever.

If he gets up, I'm dead, she thought.

Her hand strayed to the nearest available object. She felt it and wanted to cry. It was the precious Bela Szepessy that Harold Middleton had bought for her. The finest musical instrument Felicia Kaminski had ever owned.

She smashed the bone-hard composite chin rest hard into his face. The bottom of the fiddle tore away from the body immediately. It was gone and she knew it. So she took the neck in both hands swung the century-old instrument round like a mallet, dashing the jagged wood into his head until he fell once more to the floor, his nose a bloody mess, his eyes filling with pain and fear.

There was an old vase, big and heavy within reach. She let go of the ruined violin, picked up the vase and threw it at his head, hitting him square on the temple.

He went quiet.

Quickly, efficiently, she snatched a set of spare metal strings from her fiddle case, kicked him over onto his chest, put one knee on his spine and bound his hands behind, then his feet.

By the time she'd finished he was coming to again. He wasn't moving anywhere. She was thorough. Just in case, she bent down, retrieved his gun and held the weapon tightly in her right hand, hating the feel of the thing.

With tears beginning to well in her eyes, she looked at the ruined remnants of her fiddle and then the crushed man on the floor and said, "I am not little. And I am not a girl."

A noise made her look up. The front door was still open. She could see it from the living room and cursed herself for being so stupid. A tall, gangly man with exceptionally pale skin and an ugly face was marching through the door, looking both scared and determined at the same time.

Felicia Kaminski wanted to say something but at that moment her mind locked. Szeryng's luscious rendition of the Bach Partita was reaching its final note, a delicious D played double stringed, one open, one fingered with vibrato, then dying into silence. She loved that touch and had wished for so long that one day she might emulate it. Tonight, maybe, in the Wigmore Hall. Tonight . . .

It took Pierre Crane one strike to knock the weapon out of the fingers of the slender, pretty-plain young woman, and a second to render her unconscious as she stood dumb-founded over a man who lay bound on the floor, face swollen yet still visibly terrified. She crashed down in a heap next to him. Crane's eyes strayed around the room. There was no one else in the little house. He could sense this.

Crane made a fast search of the flat—which belonged to Harold Middleton, the American that the driver of the car outside of Paris had warned him about. He found what looked like a gun safe and scanned through a number of documents and notes on the desk.

"Find anything helpful, Pierre?" said a female voice behind him, one so calm and unflustered it made his blood turn cold, sent his hand dashing for the gun in the holster beneath his jacket.

Something stabbed into his shoulder before his fingers got halfway.

"Don't be foolish," she said.

He turned and saw the woman he now knew as Jana. She held a long black handgun with a lengthy silencer. A professional weapon. She looked at him carefully, her gaze reminiscent of what had passed between them on that deserted two-lane road outside of Paris not long before. "We meet again, Pierre."

Crane gave a faint laugh, though he shivered at the memory of the bullets snapping against the windows of the limo. "You know me?"

"You do your background work as a reporter," Jana shrugged. "I do the same in my line."

Which told Crane that she had indeed followed him to the meeting outside of Paris with the man posing as the Scorpion.

"Where's Middleton?" she asked.

"I don't know."

"The woman he works with? Tesla?"

Crane shook his head. "I don't know her."

In the distance, the urgent bray of a police siren grew closer. Had someone reported a disturbance? Seen a weapon? She grimaced, looking at the flat and apparently realized she had no time for a thorough search.

Jana ordered, "Take the girl outside. There's a van there." She hesitated. "Go with her. I will join you in a moment."

"You don't think I'll run?"

A smile. "No."

"Why?" he asked, trying to see some window of attack, realizing, from her careful stance and the steady gaze in her eye, this was impossible. Nor was he sure he wanted to; something—the journalist within him? Or the man?—told him to simply go with what was happening.

"Because you're after the truth, aren't you, Pierre?"

Jana reached out and removed the weapon from his jacket. Then she watched as he picked up the unconscious young woman in his arms and walked outside.

There was a Mercedes van with opaque windows by the front door and a driver in a black uniform, gloves and a cap, sliding open the rear door.

As Crane reached the gate with the girl in his arms he heard the sound from behind, and recognized immediately what it was. The low, explosive growl of a silenced weapon, followed by a curt, agonized shriek of pain, one that lasted a second, no more.

4

JIM FUSILLI

A gray morning in Paris had given way to a lovely, tranquil afternoon, and as she crossed the Place de la Concorde and entered the pebbly pathway that cleaved the Jardin des Champs Élysées, she reviewed her day: an early jog along Avenue George V across the Seine at Point d' Alma, back through the Parc du Champ de Mars and under the Tour Eiffel; a shower in her room at the Hotel Queen Elizabeth on Pierre 1er de Serbie; and in a thin, peach v-neck sweater, jeans and a short, buttery leather jacket she'd bought for a small fortune in USD at a shop on Boulevard Saint Germain, a walk around the corner to the Hotel George V for a bowl of oatmeal sprinkled with brown sugar as she read *The Wall Street Journal Europe* and *USA Today*. Then she went back to the Queen Elizabeth, sat on the floor with her back to her unmade bed and sobbed.

It wasn't working. "Come to Paris," her father had said. "You need a little magic." "Thanks, no, Harry. Too many memories," she'd replied. "Charley, maybe you'll make new memories," he said gently, taking her hand. "We need you among the living. We really do . . . "

But everywhere in Paris reminded her of what she'd lost: her baby, the miscarriage induced by, of all people, her late husband who was part of a conspiracy that took her mother's life as well. Every day was a relentless replay of what could've been and what would never be. Even now, as she strolled through dappled sunlight under leafy trees whose branches crowned the pathway, she saw young children toddling comically as they chased pigeons, their contented mothers smiling as they watched. Nothing else existed for her at that moment, neither the dignified old men in their brown suits who chatted knowingly, the businessmen and women on the Champs Élysées who were making their way back to their offices nor the tourists wandering toward the Obelisque and Jardin des Tuileries. All she saw were stout, laughing children and their beaming mothers, and she felt the weight of hopelessness and a profound, hammering sense of loss. She knew she would never be whole again and would never trust any man enough to love him. As for a child of her own, she feared she would never be able to provide the sense of security and optimism the child would need to thrive. She was counting her days, wondering when she would be consumed by the void inside her.

And so all that remained for Charlotte Middleton—she'd returned to her maiden name when she learned the extent of her husband's participation in a plot to kill thousands in Washington, D.C.—was the work she was doing for the Volunteers. Her father had told her he needed her. It was possible that he did. Protesting, she'd said, "Harry, I can't. Given how pointless, how empty . . . Damn it, I wish I could explain so you'd know." "Charley," he replied, "when I think about what my life would be without you, I know."

At a kiosk near the Théatre Marigny, she bought a sandwich of thin slices of ham, a sliver of gruyere and salty butter on crunchy bread, and a bottle of Badoit, and sat on a bench in a stream of sunlight, the Étoile and the Arc de Triomphe in the distance, the relentless traffic coursing along the cobblestone. In an attempt to dispatch her thoughts, she recalled some of the research she'd done for the Volunteers. Her mind wandered to Connie Carson and the bravado instilled in every task undertaken by that little Texas firebrand, and then to Wiki Cheung's fascination with Second Life and how the adorable 19-year-old computer geek had given himself a black avatar with a '70s Afro and chiseled body any athlete would kill for. "Try it," Wiki had suggested. "Everybody needs someplace to be somebody new." As soon as the words passed his lips he recoiled in embarrassment. "I'm not saying your life is not good, Charley. No, what I'm saying—I'm saying, Charley, the game—Maybe you'll make new friends— If you want new friends, Charley . . . Ah damn it . . . "

Around the same time, Leonora Tesla, who she admired more so now that she understood what the Volunteers had achieved, had asked her to join her for a drink after hours. They'd gone to a Latin lounge in Dupont Circle, where they were surrounded by careless singles floating between youth and responsibilities, six fresh faces crammed at tables for four. Giddy conversations rose over bubbling music. "Charley," Tesla shouted, "here's my advice: Don't take any advice. Listen to your own heart in your own time."

Now on the Champs Élysées, reflecting on those memories four-thousand miles away, Charley watched a tour bus scored with Hangul script wheezed to a halt, blocking traffic. She grimaced as taxi horns blared, and then returned to her solitude.

Perhaps 30 yards behind Charlotte Middleton in the park was a self-satisfied man in his 50s, tanned with salt-and-pepper hair. His blue suit, cut to perfection, was impressive even in the *arrondissement* that hosted the houses of Saint Laurent, Dior, Chanel and Lacroix. As he sat, he removed a silk handkerchief from an inner pocket and wiped the sides of his Berlutti shoes, removing a coat of dust. His cell phone vibrated as he returned the kerchief to its post.

"I'm on Middleton's daughter," he said. "In Paris. I'll stay with her." He hung up without waiting for a response.

Ian Barrett-Bone had gotten over the shock of nearly being gunned to death on a road outside of Paris. He and his employer were used to wielding money and threats of violence—and violence itself—to force people to do the most despicable things. Many of them sputtered and swore and promised to get even. But few did.

Jana was different, of course.

Barrett-Bone himself was motivated by money and thrill. He considered a desk job the purest of tortures.

But Jana? What drove her?

Idealism, he supposed. How childish a motive. How meddlesome.

Yet her appearance on that road outside Paris was a sharp reminder of the danger everyone was facing.

How many other deaths would occur—all because of the copper bracelet?

He watched as Charley rose from the bench. She took a long, final swig of the sparkling water and tossed its green plastic bottle in the trash, along with the heel of the bread. Then she thought better of it, retrieved the bread, crumpled it and offered the crumbs to pecking pigeons.

"She couldn't be more American if she tried," Barrett-Bone muttered to himself as he regarded the attractive woman with a measure of disgust.

He glanced at his Patek Phillippe wristwatch as he resumed following Middleton's daughter from a discrete distance. He imagined she would continue to wander aimlessly, her guard down, defenses non-existent.

Felicia Kaminski, now conscious, and Pierre Crane sat side by side in the back row of the Mercedes van, their wrists cuffed together with plastic, their ankles tied to each other's. The driver had managed to shackle them in seconds while Jana trained her gun at the two captives.

A double beep of a cell phone sounded. Jana answered. She spoke in a language Crane took to be Hindi. Then she spun to face the prisoners. "I have just learned," she said in thickly accented English, "that you are not Charlotte Middleton."

Felicia said nothing.

Jana barked at Crane. "Who is she?"

"I have no idea. I can ask her, but it will have to be in English. But I don't think she speaks French."

"You," Jana said in halting English. "What your name is?"

"Felicia."

Jana looked at Crane. "Is French," she said in English.

"Is Polish," he replied in French. He was going to mention her accent, but knew Jana couldn't detect it, no more than he could distinguish between an Algerian or a Moroccan when they spoken French. "She may be his maid."

"A maid who can fight."

"I think she was defending herself. A lucky blow with the instrument. You have the wrong girl."

Crane knew they were heading southeast.

"I think she's a little off," he added. "Incompetent. You know . . ."

Felicia seemed to will herself not to stare at him, not to stomp his foot.

Jana had Crane's gun in her lap.

"Let her go," the reporter said.

The driver glanced at Jana.

"Let her go and I'll help you." Crane was after a story. He was after Jana. He had no quarrel with the young woman.

"How? How can you help me?"

"I'm searching for the Scorpion. And so are you. I know things about him. I saw your face when you noticed the men in the limo. You were disappointed neither of them was him."

"Give me a fact. Something I can use."

"And you'll let her go?"

She stared at him. "Maybe I kill you *and* her," Jana replied.

"Or maybe I help you and nobody dies."

"Pay for one life. Yours or hers. Give me a fact."

Crane thought for a moment. What would be dear to her yet not give too much away? "There's a Dubai connection."

"Dubai? What?"

"That's all I'll tell you for now. For my own protection."

Jana debated. Then she turned to the driver and spoke in Arabic. "Dump her by the O2," she said. "We keep him."

Middleton stood on the driver's side of his car, his head hung in frustration. The London address Jean-Marc Lespasse found on Kavi Balan's computer was a mosque just south of Tufnell Park, a thriving neighborhood in North London populated by hundreds of Muslims and far, far fewer Hindus. The mosque had a noxious reputation its new, moderate leadership couldn't quite erase: Before his conviction for murder and racial hatred, its previous imam advocated jihad with suicide bombing its primary form—no one seemed to doubt his involvement in the 7/7 attacks. Supporting al-Qaeda's violent activities, it had offered training in assault weapons and served as a clearinghouse for untraceable telecommunications equipment.

"A ruse," he said. "A joke."

From the opposite side of the car, Tesla replied, "Not necessarily. Maybe someone here"—she nodded toward the mosque and the squat brick buildings that lined the street—"knows of an attack on the mosque. It might not be a dead end."

"But it's a lead that will take weeks of infiltrating to develop. We don't have the time. Not with what's going on."

Tesla tugged on the car door, but it was locked. "You're right. We need to strategize."

Middleton dug into his pocket and tossed her the keys. "Take the car," he said. He gestured in the direction of the Tufnell Park Underground station. "I'm going to Wigmore Hall to see Felicia. It was damned thoughtless of me to forget her recital. Lose the weapons and catch up with me, if you'd like. We can talk to Connie and Jean-Marc once they get settled in Tampa."

Middleton emerged from the Underground at Oxford Circus, amused by how quick the trip had been, even with the transfer at Euston. He imagined Nora still on the 503 motorway, if traffic was lurching. By instinct, he checked his common cell phone first. One message from Felicia, probably chiding him for failing to remember her recital or his lack of interest in crossword puzzles, cryptograms and such. When he looked at his encrypted phone, he saw he had no messages—nothing from NATO, the French, Interpol or the ICC as a post-mortem on the Cap d'Antibes operation; nor from Charley, Nora, Jean-Marc, Connie or Wiki. As he crossed the park at Cavendish Square, he thought for a moment of Wetherby, the bright NATO officer who gave his life to help prevent another godless execution of innocents. To steel himself from grief, long ago Middleton learned to shift his thoughts quickly to the mission at hand: to complete it would honor the likes of young Wetherby. Sikari and fresh water. Devras Sikari had developed an interest in fresh water. What could it mean?

Middleton left the park and as he waited for black cabs to pass, he saw a crowd milling under the hall's glass-and-filigreed-iron marquee. Ticketholders, he assumed, waiting to enter. Not that he would've delayed: He loved the hall's alabaster-and-marble walls, the painting in the cupola over the stage in which a figure representing the Soul of Music stared in awe at a fireball that stood for the Genius of Harmony. The Wigmore stage was an altar and the music represented an offering to the Heavens. For Middleton, music was mankind's link to divinity. It was his respite, his relief from the ugly, banal truth of the world of anguish and hatred in which he found himself while pursuing the likes of Devras Sikari. Only watching Charley blossom had given him a feeling of contentment and transcendence as had the music he loved.

"Is there a problem?" he said to the first patron he saw, a middle-aged woman dressed against the threat of rain.

"They aren't opening quite yet," she replied, "but they haven't said exactly why."

Middleton thanked her and headed toward the artists' entrance around the corner on Wimpole Street. He'd never known Felicia to be an overly demanding artist, so he assumed the problem was with the house. Perhaps the pianist had taken ill.

His encrypted phone rang, its call an old-fashioned American bell chime rather than an identifying ring tone like the Chopin he'd had on his other line.

"Harry," Tesla said.

"Nora—"

"Harry, you'd better come home."

Jean-Marc Lespasse caught up with Connie Carson on the concourse at Tampa International Airport. He smiled as he saw her volley, with a sweet smile, the attentions of one of the men who had tried to woo her on the flight from Nice through Paris. From his seat several rows behind her, Lespasse watched as one male passenger after another found a reason to approach her. Connie wasn't the only appealing woman on the flight, but she glowed with that sort of naïve, fun-loving self-confidence men were drawn to like bees to bluebells. As was her way, she managed to tell each one to buzz off with so much charm that they hadn't realized they'd been swatted.

"There you are!" she cheered as Lespasse approached.

The last man quickly withdrew and Carson lifted her bloated leather satchel, hoisting the strap on her shoulder. She hooked her arm in his and they strode off, the picture of a happy couple.

"Check your PDA?" she asked.

"So, I guess I'm the lucky fellow—"

"Don't start, Jean-Marc. A few of those boys had me searching for a parachute." She released his arm.

"You get the same message from Wiki?"

She nodded. "Big files."

"I'll use a computer in the executive lounge," he said.

"And I'll get the rental car. Give me your bag."

"Connie—"

"Give me the damned bag."

Lespasse had seen Carson dislocate a man's nose with a blow so swift he would've sworn her hand never left her side.

"Yes, ma'am," he replied.

They met 30 minutes later, Carson leaning against the hood of a Prius in a No-Standing zone. "Where to?" she asked, as she opened the passenger door.

When Carson jumped behind the wheel, Lespasse read from his notes. "Get on Interstate Two Hundred Seventy-Five East."

She laughed as she pulled from the curb. "I love how you say that. 'Interstate Two Hundred Seventy-Five East.' All formal and such."

"I-Two Hundred Seventy Five East is better?"

"Two Seventy-Five East will do. How long have you lived in America, Jean-Marc?"

"Almost ten years," he said. He slid on his sunglasses as they drove into stark sunlight beyond the airport grounds. Tampa was as bright as Nice had been.

"Ten years and it's still 'Interstate' and all that?"

"Tired, I guess. Anxious."

"Same," she said. "You came here to work with the Colonel?"

"Well, I had worked with him before. But, yes, Harold Middleton was the reason I came to America."

"You could've stayed in France."

"My wife preferred North Carolina."

"Your wife? Jean-Marc, I didn't know you were married." She looked at the third finger on his left hand. No ring.

"We worked together at Technologie de Demain—"

"Your company."

"She began as a systems analyst—which was not the reason I noticed her, I can tell you. But Johanna was very clever, very precise. Soon, she was invaluable to me. And of course, I was in love."

"She was too—if I'm hearing you right."

"Lucky for me . . ."

Carson checked the passenger side view and eased toward the highway.

"The first exit," Lespasse said. "Don't get on Inter—Don't get on Route Four."

The Prius took the ramp with ease.

"Jean-Marc, I see you're not wearing a ring . . ."

He undid the top buttons of his Oxford and withdrew a chain he wore around his neck. It was looped around a gold wedding band.

"Jean-Marc . . . "

"She was killed. On September 11, at the Pentagon. A new-business presentation scheduled for 10 in the morning. She was early, as usual. We had no chance for the business, of course. But that was Johanna. A fighter. Very American. Like you, Connie."

Carson saw his bittersweet smile.

"Jean-Marc, I'm so sorry."

"As am I. Thank you." Lespasse peered through the windshield. "There's the exit."

Carson tapped the blinker.

"Cookie-cutter," she said as they approached the long, one-story building in the corner of an industrial park just short of McKay Bay. "Glass and steel. They throw down a foundation and drop 'em out of the sky."

"Yes, but this one has palm trees," Lespasse said.

There were FedEx, DHL and UPS boxes out front, and a tin box labeled Doolittle Diagnostics with a warning that it contained blood products. On the first floor, drawn blinds revealed an empty lunchroom with vending machines and newspapers scattered on tabletops.

Carson and Lespasse entered the vestibule to look at a blackboard dotted with white plastic letters.

"Sindhu Power & Electric," he said. "Twenty-six South. So they're still here."

"Unless no one cared to change the sign."

"We can imagine Sikari has been here. Perhaps he returned."

"OK. But I don't guess we'll find him at a desk."

"No," Lespasse said, as he continued to study the board. "But let's see what we can see."

They stepped toward the receptionist, a young, brown-skinned woman who was hiding a college textbook under the crescent-shaped desktop. She greeted them with a warm smile and a Cuban accent.

Lespasse said, "My wife and I have an appointment with Dr. Faraday."

Carson nodded. "We know the way."

The receptionist hesitated. "You can go," she said finally.

As they turned onto a long carpeted corridor, Carson said, "Dr. Faraday?"

"His office is Eighteen South."

"Ah."

The wooden doors to each office were closed, muting the buzz of activity. At the end of the hall, two women were using a smaller reception area to review a presentation on a laptop. Lespasse followed Carson along a dogleg turn and soon they passed Dr. Faraday's office.

Twenty-six South was at the end of the hall and Carson realized its windows faced the parking lot, which teemed with cars glistening in the afternoon sun. "What's the play?" she said.

Lespasse dug into his wallet and pulled out a Technologie de Demain business card. "A cold call," he said. "I will ask for the head of IT."

"You think they'll have staff here? I mean, this office is probably the biggest on this side of the building. But it's a shell, if anything."

"I suppose you can file a patent from a post office box. Why go to the expense of opening an office if you don't intend to use it?"

Carson reached for the door. "Ready?"

He held up a finger. "Forgive me, but I will put on a heavy accent. Maybe it will explain why I'm so . . . so wrinkled."

She smiled. "At least you're wearing slacks. I'm in jeans and a T-shirt."

"Yes, but your T-shirt is the same color as your boots, and no one wears jeans like you, Connie. Maybe 100 men on our flights will swear to that." He didn't mention the make-up she applied at the airport nor the lipstick she refreshed before they left the car.

"Well, to be safe, I'm calling you 'boss.'"

"*Très bien*," Lespasse replied.

Carson swung open the door, and Lespasse stepped inside.

The office was empty.

Thin wires dangled from displaced ceiling panels and a few telephone handsets sat on the floor. There was room for perhaps 10 desks, but there were none in sight. The air-conditioner had been turned off.

As Carson passed him, Lespasse switched on the overhead lights. They flickered, then glowed. "Someone paid the bill," he said.

Carson had stepped into a private office. It too was empty, its carpet musty and soiled, its closet flung open and bare. "So much for Sindhu Power & Electric . . . "

Across the office space was another closet, the kind that held paper products, out-of-date files in cardboard boxes, maybe a space for jackets and personal effects. Someone had started to clean it—probably to get the place ready to lease again.

Together, Carson and Lespasse went through it and found nothing enlightening—except for a blank label from an international shipping company she'd never heard of. She also found a discarded Post-It note: *Call Moscow. 14.00 hours.* Carson jotted down the information. "That's it," she sighed. "When someone skedaddles, they usually leave *something* behind."

She looked around. The blinds were drawn tight, but under the overhead lights, she could see there was dust everywhere—on the ledge below the windows, on the phones on the floor. Every door inside the suite was flung open. Except for another closet door.

"Maybe they have," Lespasse said as he approached it, "Let's see what we—"

As Lespasse pulled open the door, an explosion burst from the closet, rattling the building. The force flung him across the room, a fireball trailing him as the windows shattered, throwing glass and debris onto the parking lot.

Carson awoke under the flood of water raining from the overhead sprinklers. Through ringing ears, she heard sirens drawing nearer. She tasted blood in her mouth. She tried to stand to find Lespasse, but couldn't manage. Collapsing, she lost consciousness again and dropped to the damp carpet.

5

JOHN GILSTRAP

Felicia fought to control her hammering heart, and by so doing control her racing head. She didn't understand what her captors were saying, but she easily comprehended the body language. They were angry, but in a way that went beyond whatever prompted them to take her. Twice while the woman was on the telephone jabbering in what she assumed to be an Arabic dialect, the word *Charlotte* rose above the gibberish and each iteration brought increased levels of ire.

The pieces fell into place easily. They'd thought she was Charley Middleton. And why wouldn't they? She was in Harold's house, after all, and she and Charley were close enough in age that it would be a simple conclusion that she was his daughter.

Oh, God, my Bela Szepessy, she whined silently. Of all the potential weapons at her disposal, why did she have to choose something so valuable—something so close to her soul?

After the bitch with the gun hung up her phone, the heated discussion with her fellow captive confused her. They seemed to have the kind of knowing—if uneasy—relationship that comes of people who have worked together before. Why, then, was Felicia bound to this man and why did he continue to speak to his captor in tones that were as cordial as they were laced with fear? Each in turn looked right at her as they spoke. Clearly, she was the focus of their disappointment.

Felicia knew she was in trouble when the woman talked directly to the driver. It was something about the way she made a tossing movement with her head, at once dismissive and definite. A moment later, the driver changed lanes and headed for an off-ramp. They were going to get rid of her.

They were going to kill her. At this point, given all that had happened, what choice did they have? Hadn't they already killed one of their own back in Harold's flat? Murder was murder in the eyes of the law, whether you killed one or twenty. If they were done with her—and she was certain they were—they'd be crazy *not* to kill her. It was just a matter of when and how.

Her heart continued to slam itself into her breastbone as she weighed her options. The clarity of her thinking shocked her even as she determined that she in fact had no options.

Carson dialed back slowly into her surroundings. There was light and there was pain, though considerably more of the former than the latter. As she climbed out of the dark well that was her unconsciousness, she had the odd nonsensical thought that she was living in a bowl of red Jell-o. The light had a certain red tinge to it, so that was part of the illusion, but she could talk herself into believing that her head had been crammed with the stuff as well. Hearing was muted and her sinuses felt as if they had been stuffed with cotton.

Closer to the mouth of the well the light grew brighter still and the buzzing drone of which she'd been barely aware fine-tuned itself into voices.

" . . . any time now. I can't say for certain, of course, but I don't think—"

"I need to speak to her as soon as possible."

Who? Who did they need to speak to? What was the urgency and why wouldn't Man A allow Man B to do whatever the hell he wanted?

As the voices clarified, so did the pain. It was as bright and red and piercing as the light and, now, equally inescapable. It radiated from the base of her neck, down her right arm to the ends of her fingernails and inward toward her belly button. With that kind of pain, you'd think you'd have some idea where it came from. Maybe that's what they wanted to talk to that other person about. Maybe she could tell them all why she felt as though she'd rolled in razor blades and swum in alcohol.

It was a terrible image, but something about it amused her. Razor blades and alcohol. Throw in a little fire to boot.

Fire.

There'd been a fire!

Jean-Marc. She had to warn him. He was in danger. She opened her mouth to scream, but the well wouldn't let her. Not yet. Yelling as loudly as she could, all she could produce was a moan. *Look out!* she shrieked. But there was no sound.

"She's stirring," a voice said. "She's waking up."

Yes! Tell her about Jean-Marc. Warn him!

"Connie?"

Yes! I'm here!

"Connie, can you hear me?"

The light grew brighter still and some of the color drained away. *Help me! I'm here! Pull me up! Jean-Marc is—*

"She still out of it, Doc?" another voice asked. This one wasn't as friendly. Wasn't friendly at all, in fact.

"She's coming to," the first voice said. "Hello, Connie, I need you to wake up for me."

Wake up. Wake up from what?

From the explosion.

Oh, Jesus, Jean-Marc was taken by the—

She returned to consciousness with a giant gasp. The sheer effort of it made her jump and the jumping added more alcohol to the razor blades. The light turned to white and surrounding the white, there was even more white.

And then a face staring down at her, his silhouette mercifully casting a shadow over her eyes. "Hello, Connie," the face said. He spoke English, but with a thick accent that she knew she recognized, but couldn't quite place. It was Indian. Maybe Pakistani. Just where the hell was she?

"Jean-Marc!" she said. To her own ears, her voice sounded normal, if distant, but the angle of the man's head told her that she was wrong. "Save Jean-Marc!" she insisted. She tried to sit up, but that proved impossible the instant her wounds flashed again.

"Connie, you're fine," the face said. "You're in a hospital. I am Doctor Ahmed. You've been in an accident."

Fragments of a thousand accidents raced through her mind. How did she get to India or Pakistan? "Where am I?"

"You are in Tampa General Hospital. You were flown here by helicopter."

"Tampa," she said, testing the word. "Tampa, Florida." It was coming back to her. The abandoned office. The dust. The closet.

"Is Jean-Marc OK?" she asked. But as her head cleared even more, the true imagery of that moment crystallized for her. There was no way he could have survived that blast.

"Ms. Carson," another man said from off to her left. It was *the* other man who'd seemed unfriendly as she was climbing out of the Jell-o well. "My name is Detective Langer with the Tampa Police Department. I need you to answer some questions for me."

She moved to look at him, but another stab of pain stopped her. "What happened?"

"There was an explosion," Langer said.

Carson snapped, "I know there was an explosion. I was there. I meant what happened to me? Why do I hurt so badly?"

"You broke your right arm," the doctor said. "In three places. And there are some burns."

Her stomach flipped. "Bad burns?" she asked. It was the injury that she feared perhaps more than any other. The pain. The disfigurement.

"You'll need some surgery."

"But I need to talk with you first," Langer interrupted. "A bomb like this, we need as much information as quickly as we can get it."

"You can say no if you don't feel up to it," the doctor said.

"Actually, you can't," Langer said. "Not if you want to avoid obstruction of justice charges. Either one of you."

All over the world, police forces drew their personnel from the same breed. "Then why don't you stand where I can see you?" Carson said.

Langer turned out to be a Ken doll. Six-one with a head of thick blond hair, he wore khaki slacks and a blue knit shirt that made her wonder if her misfortune hadn't pulled him off the golf course. "Tell me what happened," he said.

It took all of two minutes to relate the facts. When she was done, she concluded, "Jean-Marc is dead, isn't he?"

Langer nodded. His eyes showed pity, but she sensed that it was manufactured. "Yes, I'm afraid he is. You never said why you were there."

"I know," Carson said. "That's a longer story."

"I have time."

"Apparently, I don't." She glanced toward the doctor, who recognized it as his cue to move ahead with his treatment plan.

Langer raised his hand to freeze the action. "Don't push me, Ms. Carson. Right now you're the only living person found at the scene of a bombing. That makes you a suspect."

"I'm not going far," she said.

"She has a point," Dr. Ahmed intervened. "Speak with her now, speak with her in twenty hours, after surgery and recovery. What difference does it make?"

"It makes a lot of difference," Langer said. "This wasn't just any bomb, Doc." He shifted his gaze to Carson. "This was a thermobaric device, much more—"

Carson gasped. She hadn't intended to and if it weren't for whatever meds she was on, she never would have shown her hand like that.

"That mean something to you, Ms. Carson?" Langer asked.

Hell yes, it meant something to her. Thermobarics were a class of explosives that allowed low-density charges to produce high-density yields. Whereas standard explosives contain chemical oxidizers in high concentrations to allow the mixture to consume all of its fuel in a single instant, thus producing its blast effects, a thermobaric device has relatively low levels of oxidizer, but is packed with highly combustible, often exotic fuels. When the charge detonates, the finely divided fuel is dispersed over a wider area and the oxygen in the air performs the role that the chemical oxidizer performs in standard explosives. In effect, the disbursed cloud of fuel continues to detonate, often at higher temperatures, thus expanding the kill radius tremendously.

"Not a thing," Carson lied.

"I don't believe you."

"Then arrest me."

"Consider it done."

"Excellent," Carson said. She turned to the doctor. "Can I go to surgery now?"

Dr. Ahmed smiled. "Absolutely."

"Consider her to be in custody, Doc," Langer said. But he seemed suddenly flummoxed, as if this new turn had been totally unexpected.

"It will be foremost on my mind," the doctor said.

Three minutes later, they were on their way to the elevator—all three of them, plus a couple of nurses and seeming hangers-on. Langer made a point, it seemed, to always be within Carson's eyesight. The elevator took them to a set of double doors over which a sign read: SURGERY. AUTHORIZED PERSONNEL ONLY. Below that was a smaller sign with an arrow that directed everyone else to the waiting area.

"You cannot go in," Ahmed said to Langer.

The cop seemed to be struggling for words. "She's your responsibility, then," he said. He probably wanted it to be a more withering threat than it turned out to be.

On the far side of the double doors, Carson and the doctor exchanged victory smirks. "I often don't like police officers," Ahmed said.

"He was only doing his job the best he knew how," Carson said, surprised at her own maternal tone. If Lespasse had been there, he would have been shocked to hear such forgiveness.

Lespasse. She'd seen too many friends die over the years to mourn them one at a time anymore, but she wished him well on this next leg of his Great Journey.

"Doctor, I need a telephone," she said.

Their shared moment collapsed in his expression to more confusion. "Excuse me?"

"A telephone. It's an urgent matter."

"Your health is the most urgent matter at the moment," Ahmed said.

Carson grabbed the hem of his scrub shirt with her good arm, igniting a lightning bolt of pain from her bad one. "Doctor, please stop." The gurney glided to a halt. "It's really not," she said. "I love my own health as much as the next person—probably more, in fact. But in this case, it's nowhere near as important as the phone call I need to make."

Gun Bitch and the driver spoke with each other again and Felicia knew that the crescendo was about to begin. It was their manner of speaking, the conspiratorial tone. When Gun Bitch looked at her at the end of their exchange, Felicia knew that it would be bad for her.

The driver clicked the turn signal and started drifting toward the left—a shift in the natural order of a right-handed world to which she didn't think that she could ever truly adjust—and as they slowed, Gun Bitch reached into her purse, looking for something. Felicia's heart rate quadrupled. What could she possibly pull out?

It turned out to be a pair of clippers that looked like pliers and for a moment she thought she was looking at the instrument of her upcoming torture. When her captor leaned forward, however, and reached toward Felicia's zip-tied ankles, she sensed that the bad ending to this adventure was at hand.

Felicia heard a *snip* and instantly her feet began to regain sensation that she hadn't even realized they'd lost. She thought about kicking out at her captor, but then what? With her wrists bound to the man seated next to her, what would her next move be? Even if she knocked the bitch out with a kick to the head, she still wouldn't be able to save herself.

"Don't be stupid," Gun Bitch said in English. She leveled her pistol an inch from Felicia's forehead. "Move, I shoot."

She pulled roughly on Felicia's left shoulder to pivot her to the right. When she was facing the door, her arms stretched painfully beyond their limits, she first felt the closeness of her captor's shoulders, and then the coldness of the clippers against her flesh as the tiny jaws slipped between the flesh of her wrists.

Snip.

She was completely free and she knew without doubt that she was seconds away from death. The instant her hands belonged to her again, Felicia knew it was time to act; just as she knew that her window to do so could be measured in seconds, not minutes.

Her first kick caught Gun Bitch in the stomach, triggering a cry that was equal parts pain and surprise. But the punch that landed squarely on her captor's nose launched a shriek that was all pain and a fountain that was all blood.

The car slowed instantly, as if the driver himself had been the recipient of Felicia's attack. That instant of inattention opened another window of opportunity. She lunged for the door handle and pulled, introducing a hurricane of wind and road noise.

Clearly still blinded by the blow to her nose, Gun Bitch swiveled her weapon in the direction of the noise and issued a command in a language that Felicia did not understand, yet whose meaning was universal: "Stop or I'll shoot!"

Felicia punched the woman's wrist, connecting squarely with the tendons on the soft underside and sending the pistol spiraling into the lap of her co-captive, who grunted reflexively on impact.

The vehicle slowed even more as the driver pivoted to see what was going on, but when Gun Bitch barked another order, he whipped back around to face front and acceleration forces kicked in again.

Felicia dove for the racing pavement.

Middleton knew that the urgency in Tesla's tone had been driven by the presence of a corpse in the middle of his flat. His wrecked flat.

The body was a concern, of course, but Middleton had seen way too many of them over the years to get overly spun-up about one more. With a dead body, you got analytical. You could take your time. Someone dead today would still be dead a week from now, so the urgency was gone. The spattered blood and brains were literally and figuratively custodial matters—troubling annoyances to be cleaned up later with a little time, patience and detergent.

Far more troubling to him was the shattered violin on the floor. Resting as it was, scattered among the flotsam of overturned furniture and broken trinkets, Middleton knew in an instant why the concert had been postponed. It wasn't a missing pianist or a technical problem. It was the missing star of the show.

"Who took Felicia?" Tesla wondered.

Middleton muttered, "Whoever left a dead man in my foyer."

"They didn't just leave him here. They shot him here," Tesla said. "We need to notify the locals. Now that there's a murder, we need to get them involved."

"Fine." Middleton couldn't have cared less. Where the hell was Felicia? Why would anyone attack her like this?

"You say that so easily," Tesla said, trying to draw him into the present. "But they're going to ask some damn difficult questions."

Middleton scowled at her and cocked his head, as if he'd just heard a foreign language being spoken. "What?" Then it fell into place. "Oh, OK. Fine. Whatever. Let them ask their questions. Nora, we need to find her."

She shook her head. "No, we need to find *them*. They come as a package deal."

But where to begin? With so many moving parts, how the hell were they supposed to—

His cell phone chimed in his pocket. "Jesus," he spat, and as he looked at the caller I.D. display and didn't recognize the number or even the exchange, he almost hit the ignore button. But then he thought better of it. When this much was going so wrong so quickly, you never knew where the next turn was going to lead. He brought the phone to his ear. "Middleton."

"Carson."

He recognized the difference in her voice and his gut tightened. "Are you all right?"

"Lespasse is dead," she said. The simplicity of the delivery could have seemed harsh, but in this case, he sensed that by saying the words aloud, she'd freed herself of a burden.

"Dead! How?" At the exclamation from her colleague, Tesla's head whipped around.

"Tampa was a trap. Place looked like it'd been empty for weeks. They had a bomb planted for us."

His landline rang. He ignored it. "For *you*? How could they plant a bomb for you? They couldn't know that you were coming."

"If not for us, for someone. Jesus, Harry, cut me a break on the grammar, OK? I'm on my way into surgery."

So Carson was hurt too. He hadn't thought of that. "What happened to you?" The landline cycled through its third ring and Middleton nodded for Tesla to answer it for him.

"Some burns and broken bones. Not too bad, I don't think."

Despite her words, he could hear the pain and fear in her voice. "Is that what you say or does that come from the doctor?"

Carson said, "I didn't call for sympathy, Harold. I have important news that I need to share before I go under the knife."

Across the room, Tesla covered the mouthpiece with her hand and waved at Middleton.

Still stunned by the news of the death of his comrade and friend, Middleton stared at her blankly as he tried to focus on his own call. "Hold on, Connie."

Tesla said, "It's about Felicia."

"Is she OK?"

"This is the police on the line. They say that she wandered into the station bruised and bloodied and saying something about diving out of a moving car. They've sent her to the hospital."

"Who snatched her?"

"A woman. Youngish. Pretty. Tough . . . Middle Eastern maybe. Indian, Pakistani. Sri Lankan. Harold, what should I tell the police?"

"That you'll call them back."

He returned his attention to Carson. "OK, Connie, go ahead."

The Texan was explaining her own urgent matter. One phrase jumped out and refocused him entirely on his cell phone.

"Wait a minute," he said. "Did you say thermobaric explosive?"

"I did," Carson said. Even through the phone, he could hear her pleasure that he'd connected his own set of dots. "Just like all those we dealt with in Kosovo. Just like the ones the Afghanis have been disarming for a decade."

Thermobarics were perfected by the only nation he knew of whose troops regularly deployed them. "So you think there's a Russian connection?"

"Sure could be. I found a note about calling Moscow. No number. And a shipping label in the trash. Blank, but they may have records." She gave him the name, her voice quivering in pain.

He thanked her. "Connie, I'm sorry."

Toughening her drawl, she said, "Later, Harry. I've got to see a man about a knife."

The phone sagged in Middleton's hand. He turned to Tesla and inhaled deeply. Then he shared the terrible news about Lespasse.

"No! My God, no!"

"And Connie's been hurt." But then he controlled the emotion and continued, telling her what Carson had explained about the thermobarics."

"Russia?"

"Possibly." Then he nodded at Tesla's phone. "What about Felicia?"

"She told the police that her kidnapper was angry that they'd taken the wrong person. She thinks they were actually after Charley."

Middleton felt the color drain from his cheeks. "Sure, Felicia's young and was in my apartment. They thought she was my daughter. Then they realized she was Polish, not American. They were probably going to kill her. Thank God she got away."

"She's still in the emergency room—they won't let her call. But she sent a message. You should read your email."

He lifted his cell phone, furious at himself for not opening Felicia's message immediately. "Jesus," he said as he read, "Sikari patented technology for a new heavy-water system for making nuclear material."

"What she was telling us about heavy water . . . "

"Right."

Middleton pulled out his encrypted cell phone and placed a call to the Volunteers' office outside D.C. He took a deep breath and when a man answered, he said, "Wiki . . . "

"Boss? What's wrong?"

"I have something to tell you." After a moment's hesitation, he delivered the news about Lespasse.

"No, Harry . . . Oh no."

"I'm afraid so. Connie was with him. She's in surgery in Florida right now. I need you to stay on top of what's happening down there."

"You bet. Of course . . . Boss, I'm sorry."

Then Middleton shoved aside the memories about his dead colleague and consulted his notes. He said, "I need you to crack into the shipping records of Continental-Europe Transport Ltd. Find all the deliveries to and from Sindhu Power in Tampa. Connie found their shipping label."

"And that's the outfit in Florida where Connie and JM were?"

"Yeah. The address on Balan's computer."

Middleton clicked his phone shut and turned to Tesla. "OK, Nora, if they snatched Felicia thinking she was Charley—"

"It means Charley's in trouble. You want to go to Paris, Harold?"

"No, I want you to. The email on Balan's computer said whatever was going to happen in the 'village' was going to happen soon. Our Florida operation's been derailed. Given that Connie found a note about calling Moscow, Russia's our only lead—that's the only country selling thermobarics on the black market. I've got to get there as fast as I can."

Stepping over the body, he snagged his suitcase, which he hadn't had a chance to unpack.

Tesla looked at the body. "The police. I have to call them back. What should I tell them?"

Middleton paused for a moment to think. "Tell them anything," he said. "Everything, if you'd like." He started walking toward the front door. "We won't be around when they get here anyway." A nod at the body. "He's their problem now."

6

JOSEPH FINDER

At just after three o'clock on a gloomy afternoon, the Boeing 727 touched down on runway number 3 at Moscow's Domodedovo International Airport.

The reverse thrusters kicked in with a loud whine and before long the roar of the engines subsided as the plane was powered down.

For several minutes, the pilot and his three-man crew just sat there, waiting patiently for the tedious rituals to begin—border control and customs, clearing first the crew and then the cargo. Hours of forms and questions but most of all *waiting*. The Soviet Union was no more, but its bureaucracy lived on. Rain thrummed against the Plexiglas cockpit window, which slowly began to fog up.

And they waited.

Since this was a cargo plane, there were no passengers to deplane. The main cabin was a cavernous cargo bay packed with eleven containers of cargo—igloos, they were called in the business—which were in turn jammed with boxes. Everything from flat-screen TVs to iPhones, from Armani suits to Armagnac.

Seated along the bulkhead in the small compartment aft of the cockpit, the second officer spoke quietly to the new man, who had been added to the crew at the last minute, just before takeoff in Frankfurt.

"You don't talk much," the second officer said. He hadn't stopped talking since they departed Frankfurt.

"Yeah, well," said the other man.

"Ever been to Moscow before?"

"Once or twice. Long time ago."

"You won't recognize the place."

"So I hear."

"Well, you got one whole night to see Moscow before we turn around and fly out of here in the morning. I know a couple of awesome nightclubs. *Smokin'* hot Russian babes."

"Thanks anyway," the new man said. "I thought I might just do a little sightseeing."

"Come *on*, man. What're you gonna do, go see *Lenin's tomb* or something? This place I'm going to, it'll totally blow your mind when you see the way these Russian babes—"

"I'm good," said the new man. "I'm wiped. I'll probably just walk around, see what Moscow's like these days."

"Well, be careful, buddy," the second officer said. "They got street crime now, you know. Some parts of the city you don't want to walk around at night, being a foreigner and all."

"I'll keep that in mind," said the new crew member.

The second officer stood up and said, "I gotta use the john."

When he emerged from the lavatory, he heard a sharp rap on the plane's exterior. A beefy uniformed agent from FSB Frontier Control came aboard.

"Passport," the Russian barked.

The second officer handed his passport over and watched as the agent scanned it with a handheld device.

Then the second officer turned to look at his colleague, but the other pull-down seat was empty.

No one was there.

As the Russian entered the cockpit to check the passports of the pilot and co-pilot, the second officer looked around, bewildered. He got up, glanced into the cockpit, but the new guy wasn't there either. He yanked open the door to the cargo compartment, but there was barely enough room for someone to squeeze in between the rows of igloos.

The guy wasn't there.

Very strange.

Colonel Harry Middleton strolled along the Old Arbat, a cobblestone street that had been converted into a pedestrian mall crowded with shoppers and peddlers, bearded minstrels playing strange-looking guitars and teenagers just hanging out. There were souvenir shops selling ornate lacquer *palekh* boxes and Russian nesting dolls painted with the faces of foreign leaders and pop stars.

He'd visited Moscow once before during the height of the Cold War. Everything looked and felt different now: colorful instead of gray; boisterous and teeming instead of quiet and ominous. The rusty old Volgas and Zhigulis had been replaced by Ferraris and Bentleys. But the immense Stalinist tower that housed the Ministry of Foreign Affairs was still there, at the end of the Arbat, just as it was half a century earlier. Maybe the changes didn't really run all that deep after all.

The last twenty-four hours had been tense and exhausting, but he suspected the next twenty-four hours would be even worse.

Just getting into Moscow had involved calling in a stack of chits. Like an old friend from his time in Kosovo, an Apache helicopter pilot with the U.S. army's 82nd Airborne Division who'd taken his retirement from the army and risen up the ranks of an international air-freight company—and was willing to add a fourth crew member to a Moscow flight. And another old friend, a wily KGB careerist named Ruslan Maksimovich Korovin, who'd been in Kosovo at the same time and became one of Middleton's most-valued sources inside Russian intelligence.

They'd gotten him into Moscow, but Middleton knew that if anything went wrong, they wouldn't be able to get him out.

Now Middleton found himself staring at the display window of an antiquities shop across the street from the old Praga Restaurant. The shop window was a jumble of dusty curios—brass kaleidoscopes and bad copies of icons and Russian-made Victrolas and shabby oil paintings.

He wasn't inspecting the antiques, of course. He was watching the reflection in the plate glass. But so far he hadn't detected any followers. It was only a matter of time before Russian intelligence took notice of a foreigner walking the streets of Moscow. A foreigner who'd somehow managed to slip into Russia without leaving any fingerprints in the databases. If he were brought in for questioning . . .

Well, it was better not to think about that possibility.

Middleton pulled opened the heavy front door. A shopkeeper's bell tinkled pleasantly. No electronic entry alert here. The place looked, even smelled, a century old, musty and mildewed. Middleton half expected to see Aleksandr Pushkin, who once lived on this very street, browsing the wares.

Behind a crowded dusty glass counter was an elderly man with a pinched, severe face and oversized round black-framed glasses.

"*Dobryi dyen'*," the clerk said.

"Good afternoon," Middleton replied. "I'm interested in icons."

The clerk raised his eyebrows, and his big round glasses rose along with them. "Ah? Anything in particular, sir?"

"I'm particularly interested in the Novgorod school."

The flash of recognition on the old man's face disappeared quickly. "Yes, of course, sir," he said. "They are some of our finest. But there are very few and they're quite costly."

"I understand," Middleton said.

"Please," the clerk said, gesturing toward a maroon velvet curtain that divided the front of the shop from his back office. "Please to follow me."

It was dark in there, and even mustier, and dust motes swam in an oblique shaft of light that came in from between the curtains.

The Russian took out a battered leather briefcase from a file drawer and popped open the clasp. Inside, the case was lined with black egg-carton shell foam. Set snugly in a cutout at its center was a brand-new SIG Sauer P229, a compact semiautomatic pistol, with a matte black finish.

Middleton checked it quickly, pulled back the slide and was satisfied. "Chambered for 9mm," he said.

The old clerk nodded, pursed his lips.

Middleton peeled five hundred-dollar bills from the roll of cash in his front pocket and set them on the counter. The Russian scowled and shook his head. He held up two fingers. "Two thousand," he said.

"That was not the deal," Middleton protested.

"Then I am so sorry that we cannot do business today," said the Russian.

Middleton sighed, then put down another fifteen bills. He hated being held up this way, but it wasn't as if he had a choice. "I assume you'll throw in a box of ammo," he said.

The Russian produced an ancient-looking, dog-eared box of Winchester cartridges from another drawer. About twenty or thirty bucks back home. "Today we make special deal," the clerk said. "Only five hundred dollars."

Ruslan Maksimovich Korovin was a Russian bear of a man, short and rotund, with a neatly trimmed goatee that adorned a fleshy, ruddy face. He extended his short arms and gave Middleton a hug.

"Garrold!" Korovin exclaimed. This was as close to "Harold" as Korovin was able to say. He escorted Middleton into a large, comfortable room that looked like an English gentleman's club. Oriental carpets covered the floor; here and there were leather chairs in which doddering old men snoozed behind tented copies of *Pravda*. Except for the choice of newspaper, it could have been Boodle's in London.

Actually, it was a men's club of sorts, only the men were old KGB officers. In this nineteenth-century townhouse on a narrow street off Pyatnitskaya Street, former and retired Russian intelligence officers gathered over vodka and sturgeon and cabbage soup to reminiscence about the bad old days.

"Ruslan Maksimovich," Middleton said, stumbling slightly over the unwieldy patronymic. "Thanks for seeing me on such short notice."

In a lower voice, Korovin said, "I trust my friends at the airport treated you with the proper deference."

Korovin, who'd spent more than three decades in the KGB, was a legendary operative who knew how to pull strings that most people didn't even know existed. His web of contacts extended even into the facilities maintenance operations at Domodedovo Airport, where a refueling crew had smuggled Middleton off the cargo plane and into central Moscow. A risky infiltration, to be sure, but Middleton knew he could trust Korovin to make the plan go off flawlessly.

The old KGB man's directions had been precise. And they'd been relayed to Middleton using the simplest, yet most modern, of all spy tradecraft techniques: Korovin had written an email, but instead of sending it, he'd saved it as a draft, on a Gmail account for which both men had the password. The email account was one of many set up by Wiki Chang, back at the Volunteers' small office headquarters in Virginia. Intelligence agents no longer needed things like microdots and burst transmitters, not when they could use the good old Internet.

"It went far more easily than I expected, to be honest," Middleton said.

"From me you should expect only the best," Korovin said. "And I hear you made a purchase at Volodya's shop on the Arbat, yes? He has the finest selection of icons in all of Moscow."

"Pricy, though," Middleton said.

"Well, after all, it *is* a sellers' market, my friend," Korovin said.

"I didn't dicker," said Middleton.

Korovin led him to the dining room, dark and dismal and mostly empty. They sat at a small table, which was already set with *mineralnaya voda* and dusty-looking tumblers and shot glasses.

A waitress shambled over with a tray. An old crone with thinning white hair and pale gray eyes who looked to be in her eighties, she wore a long black shirt and a long-sleeved white blouse. Probably, Middleton thought, a pensioner from some back office at the Lubyanka. With fumbling hands, she set down an assortment of *zakuski*, Russian appetizers like beet salad and mushroom "caviar," smoked fish and pickled onions. Then she unsteadily filled their shot glasses with a domestic brand of vodka.

Korovin slid a cigarette from a pack of Marlboros, lit it with an old Red Army lighter and then offered a toast to their work in Kosovo. The two intelligence operatives had played a behind-the-scenes role in that ugly conflict a decade earlier, a role the world would never know about.

Ten years ago, they'd seen how close the Kosovo conflict had brought the two superpowers to war. The Russians backed the Serb guerrillas, and NATO and the Americans defended the ethnic Albanians, even though there was plenty of "ethnic cleansing"—that grotesque euphemism—on both sides. When Russia finally agreed to abandon the Serbs in exchange for a separate role in the peacekeeping process, NATO reneged on the deal. The Russian forces found themselves taking orders from a U.S. general. They felt humiliated and double-crossed. The tensions could well have boiled over into a war between two nuclear powers were it not for the quiet, back-channel efforts of a few intelligence officers like Korovin and Middleton.

Now, the two men drank and then Korovin poured again. But before he could offer another flowery toast, he gave Middleton a sideways glance. "I thought you were retired, Garrold."

"I thought I was too," Middleton said.

"Yet you needed to enter my country off the books. Which tells me that you have gone active again."

"In a manner of speaking." He gave his Russian friend a quick, sanitized version of the work that the Volunteers had been doing and then told him about the bizarre incident on the Côte d'Azur that had activated the Volunteers once again. "I need some information."

"Ah." Which might have meant yes, absolutely. Or the opposite.

"Information about thermobarics."

"It's easier to get you the explosives than it is to get you information about the explosives. Safer, anyway."

"Well, let me ask, in any case," Middleton said. "I had my associate look into the records of a shipping company that delivered some merchandise to an outfit in Florida. I think it was explosives. He contacted me on the flight and told me that a number of shipments labeled 'construction items' were sent from Albania to Moscow to Mogadishu to Algiers and finally to the U.S. The company realized he was into their system and blocked him out, but not before he got me the names of all the freight forwarders involved."

"You're looking at me rather knowingly, friend. I believe I am nervous now."

Though Korovin didn't look nervous. He looked amused in that indulgently conspiratorial way former Soviet army officers and KGB operatives slip on their faces like bank robbers do a ski mask.

"And you want to hear a funny coincidence?" Middleton asked.

"No, I do not."

"All the shipping companies were incorporated by a single law firm in Moscow. And guess who they also represent? Your boss, Arkady Chernayev."

Arkady Chernayev was the richest man in Russia, perhaps in the world. He divided his time between his estate in Knightsbridge, London, and a mansion on the outskirts of Moscow. Not to mention a dozen other properties around the world, several private planes and three obscenely large yachts. Chernayev had gotten rich in the oil business during the free-for-all in the last days of the Soviet Union.

"No, not boss." A scowl.

"Ruslan, you've done private security work for him. Don't even bother trying to deny it. My sources on this are impeccable."

Korovin looked away, then busied himself by sectioning a herring with the delicacy of a cardiac surgeon performing a coronary bypass. He placed each slice of herring atop squares of black bread, then looked up. "That was long ago," he said finally, his expression hardened. "Why is this so important to you?"

"Because if Chernayev is behind this, which I'm beginning to believe, I think he's channeling money or explosives or both to a dangerous fanatic named Devras Sikari. The point of contact for their interests was Tampa, Florida."

"Then let's say, for the sake of argument, that you are correct. This is why you wanted a weapon? Because you think you will shoot your way in to Chernayev's dacha? Do you know how many bodyguards this man has surrounding him at all times? And just one of you?"

Middleton shrugged, said nothing.

"And for what? You plan to *kill* Chernayev and hope to survive?"

"Kill him? No, of course not. I need to talk to him. Can you tell me anything about him?"

"He's grown reclusive. He had some financial problems."

"The richest man in the country?"

"Not any more. Wealth comes and goes like the tide, my friend . . . but he's on the rebound now, we hear. No one knows what his good fortune is. I can't give you first-hand knowledge . . . Tell me, what is this about?"

Middleton had a thought—Sindhu Power. Lowering his voice, he went fishing. "Because of the copper bracelet."

A nervous smile flitted across Korovin's face, then disappeared. "I have no idea what you are talking about."

"I think you do."

Korovin snubbed out his cigarette, then slid another one from the pack and lighted it. When he next spoke, it was through a mouthful of smoke, his voice muzzy. "The copper bracelet," he said. "This is nothing more than what we call *skazki*. Folk tales. What you call old wives' tales. Stories told by frightened old men to inflate their own importance."

"Try me," Middleton said.

"No. The copper bracelet is no more. That snake was killed long ago. *Decades* ago."

"Amuse me."

"It originally described some old scientific process. But then the name came to refer to a cult. A cult of madmen—fanatics, as you say—that rose from the ashes of the Second World War. You know of the Norsk Hydro plant?"

Middleton shook his head.

"This was a factory in Norway jointly owned by Norsk Hydro and I. G. Farben."

"The giant Nazi corporation."

"Yes. It was destroyed by the Allied forces and the Norwegian resistance movement. One of the most remarkable sabotage acts of the war."

"What did the factory make—weapons?"

"In a way, yes. The copper-bracelet system produced heavy water. It was a revolutionary way to produce nuclear material."

Middleton thought immediately of Felicia's insights and her encrypted message to him. Heavy water. Sikari's patents.

"The Nazis needed it to make an atomic weapon. But once the factory was destroyed, the Nazi atomic bomb program was ended. The story, Garrold—the *skazka*—is that the plant may have been destroyed, but some of the records of the technology survived. A group of Russians and Germans—successors to the Nazis, you could say—have been hoping for someone to reconstruct the science behind it."

"Connection to Chernayev?"

"None that I've ever heard of."

"Well, I need to find out. How can I reach him?"

"I—" Korovin fell silent as the doddering old waitress approached. She said something to him in a quiet voice.

"You will please excuse me," Korovin said, rising from the table, his knees cracking. "There is a call for me on the house phone."

Ruslan Korovin followed the waitress across the dining room and into the small antechamber next to the kitchen. There, in an antique wooden booth, an old black phone was mounted on the wall. Korovin picked up the phone, heard nothing. He depressed the plunger a few times, then turned to the waitress and said, "The line is dead."

"Yes," the waitress said. Her voice sounded strangely deeper, stronger. "It is dead." She slid a latch on the kitchen door, locking it.

Suddenly she lunged at him, vising his neck in the muscled crook of her elbow. Korovin struggled, gasped, but this woman—who was surely not an old woman, he now knew—had overpowered him. She twisted his head one way, his torso another.

There was a terrible loud snap and Korovin sank to the floor, and the last thing he saw was the copper bracelet on his attacker's left wrist, barely visible under the dainty ruffle of her sleeve.

7

LISA SCOTTOLINE

Devras Sikari needed time to think, and when, as now, he wasn't in his beloved Kashmir, he would come here to his second favorite place in the world—his colonial farmhouse in rural Pennsylvania.

Specifically, to the chicken coop.

Sikari was sitting in his director's chair in the pasture, watching his chickens enjoy the sun. He loved his little farm, some ninety acres, with its backyard quarter horses and tiny flock of pullets, and though he was Indian by-way-of Belgravia, he felt his most relaxed in this unlikely spot. Here he could shed his dinner jackets and Hermés ties, take off his clothes like so much costuming, and finally become himself. It made little sense, even to him. Sikari wasn't raised in the country, but to him, this farm was home away from home.

The air had a raw October nip, but his baggy jeans and old flannel shirt kept him warm, with a waxed jacket still dusty from the morning's ride. When he crossed one leg over the other, a red cashmere sock peeked from the top of his scuffed Blundstones. In his hand was a Phillies mug with bad coffee, which he had brewed himself. His housekeeper could make coffee the way he liked it, but it was her day off, so Sikari was stuck with his own swill. He took a sip and it tasted bitter and now, cold. He shook his head at the irony. He had patented a formula that would stump most nuclear physicists, yet he was defeated by Dunkin' Donuts.

SQUAWK! went one of the hens, startling Sikari from his thoughts. His attention shifted back to the brood.

"Settle, Yum-Yum," he said softly, though the pullet only blinked in response, a flash of a perfectly round, golden eye. Yum-Yum was an Araucana, an ill-mannered bird with brilliant plumage of russet, rich brown and flecks of black. Sikari kept three Araucana, because of their unusual greenish-blue eggs, and he also had a pair of brown Sussex's that reminded him of England, as well as some docile Bard Plymouth Rocks, a spoiled American breed, and a dramatic black-and-white Wyandotte named Princess Ida. All of his hens had been named for his private passion, the operettas of Gilbert & Sullivan, though the Bard Rocks looked so much alike that he simply called them the Women's Chorus. His farm manager tolerated his naming the hens, thinking Sikari an eccentric multimillionaire, which suited his purposes. His staff believed he was an international reinsurance executive, and he paid them well enough to ask no questions.

Sikari eyed the chickens and the sight cheered him. Some of them clustered together on the soft dirt around their coop, roosting together wing-to-wing, their feet tucked under them and their chubby feathered breasts forming a scalloped edge. Others were lying flat on their sides, their heads resting in the dirt as if it were an earthen pillow, their yellow feet splayed out straight. Sikari had never known that chickens did such a thing. The first time he'd seen them lying down that way, he'd thought they were all dead. It made him think again of Kavi Balan, and for a moment he watched the chickens without really seeing them, deep in thought, his coffee forgotten.

Sikari had to deal with the fact that things had not been going well for him. Everything had been in place—the geology, the personnel, even the Scorpion—but Middleton was still alive and Kavi Balan was dead. That alone was a major disruption. Sikari had been grooming Balan to be his number one, but now his plans had gone awry, the past nine years wasted. The situation was unstable, which threatened his future and his fortune, and stole his peace of mind. He had been mulling over the solution, but had yet to come to a final decision. Time had passed without him acting, but he trusted that his path would become clear, in due course. Sikari was a deliberate man, and that was one of the reasons he was so successful. Put simply, he planned, where others did not. His modus operandi was goal-oriented behavior, whether his goal was losing weight or building weapons of mass destruction.

He always reached his goal.

He took a sip of cold coffee as Princess Ida blinked herself awake and rose to her feet, stretching one yellow foot out behind her, then the other. Sikari smiled at the sight of his poultry diva, craning her feathered neck to stretch it out, too, making herself taller and more powerful. Princess Ida was the dominant hen, and he watched her ruffle her wing feathers, then settle them back into place, the simple motion bringing Yum-Yum, Peep-Bo, and the Women's Chorus to their feet, where they all began scratching and pecking at the brownish grass, following Princess Ida's lead. It reminded Sikari that all of nature had a pecking order, which insured stability.

He thought to himself, *Stability will be restored once my pecking order is restored. That's all. It's that simple.*

It made his decision for him and there was no time to delay. He set his coffee mug on the ground, reached into his moleskin pocket, extracted his cell phone, then pressed one letter. When the call was answered, he said into the phone, "Come to the coop. And bring your brother." He closed the phone with a snap and re-pocketed it, his gaze falling on Princess Ida.

The hen looked back at him, with approval.

Ten minutes later, his twin sons stood before him, with identical half-smiles, and as always, the sight pleased him. They were part of the plan, too. He couldn't say exactly that he loved them, for he traveled too much to know them, but he liked the notion that he had two such bright, active, good-looking sons. They were six feet tall and with their curly dark-blonde hair, round blue eyes, and confident grins, Archer and Harris were almost impossible to tell apart. They couldn't have looked more different from Sikari, but of course, he wasn't their biological father. He had bought them as babies on the backstreets of Prague; he had no idea where they had come from and it didn't matter anyway. He had told them, his farm staff and the tutors who home-schooled them that he was their godfather, a dear friend of their deceased French parents because he knew that passed for exotic here in the boondocks.

"Aren't you two cold?" Sikari asked, because neither wore coats. They were dressed in a way that people used to call preppy: turtlenecks, khaki pants and navy crewneck sweaters.

The boys shook their heads. "No, Dad," they answered, almost in unison. They were more than each other's best friend; they were so close they were almost the same person. It was the way Sikari had wanted it, essential for what would be expected of them someday. They had been trained in the martial arts and were both remarkably gifted, schooled especially in geology and the sciences; their IQs tested even higher than his. They both were slated to enter Harvard next year, but that would change now. College couldn't teach them what he could; he could offer them the world, literally. They'd be too young to succeed him, even in ten years time, but Balan's death had left him with no choice. Sikari would be around to guide them for the next thirty years or so and if he started grooming them now, they'd be ready ultimately to take the helm.

The problem was, he only needed one of them.

He had known this day would come, which was why he had bought twins, so he'd always have a back-up, the heir and the spare. But now he had to choose one and he wasn't sure how. They were doppelgangers and their temperaments were the same, as far as Sikari could tell.

"When did you get home, Father?" Archer asked, his tone casual, and duplicate sets of blue eyes looked at him.

"This morning. You boys were in the gym. Listen, we have a problem."

"What?" Archer asked.

Harris cocked an eyebrow. "Arch did it," he said, and the twins laughed, echoing each other.

Sikari smiled, for show. "Listen to me. This is serious. You have been preparing for this day your whole life. You just didn't know it."

The two boys fell silent and blinked at exactly the same time, which Sikari found eerie. They'd had their own language as toddlers and he'd always wondered if they were talking about him.

Princess Ida began to peck at Archer's loafer, but the boy didn't notice.

Sikari said, "I need one of you to succeed me in the family business, when the time comes. But I need only one of you. I assume you both want to ascend."

"Of course," they both answered, and suddenly neither looked over at the other, their gaze fixing on Sikari.

"So how do I choose between you?'"

Archer smiled crookedly. "Whoever can catch Princess Ida gets the job."

"Great idea!" Harris clapped his hands together, like punctuation at the end of a sentence. "How about it, Father?"

"Ha!" Sikari laughed, and this time it was genuine. They had no idea of the enormity of the position they were vying for. It was like drawing straws to become President of the United States. For some reason, the absurdity of the notion appealed to him. He smiled to himself. "But nobody can catch Princess Ida."

"I can," Archer said.

Harris gave him a playful shove. "So can I, you loser."

Archer's mouth dropped open. "I'm the one who catches them at night."

"Not without my help," Harris shot back.

"Whoever catches her first then," Sikari said, standing up. He had no better way to choose between them and it may as well be arbitrary. If the twins were that much alike, either would do. He raised his right hand. "When I say 'Go.'"

Archer and Harris planted their feet in the dirt and bent their knees slightly, a perfect footballer's stance. The chickens reacted instantly, sensing something afoot. Princess Ida flapped her wings, signaling to the Women's Chorus, and Peep-Bo and Pitti-Sing clucked loudly, rousing from their dirt baths and scampering around.

"Ready, steady, go!" Sikari said, bringing his hand down.

"On it!" Archer cried, taking off, but Princess Ida ran full tilt toward the chicken coop, with Harris sprinting after them both. The clever hen veered to the left before she reached the little door to the coop, which sent Archer crashing into the wall, and Harris gave chase, bolting after Princess Ida, his legs churning and his arms pinwheeling comically. The speedy hen dodged this way and that, half-running and half-flying from the boys, squawking loudly in alarm and protest, refusing to be caught.

"Go, Ida, go!" Sikari heard himself shout, lost for a moment in the spirit of the contest. It charmed him to see these two strapping young men laughing and running, prime specimens in the fullness of their youth and promise, their golden hair blazing in the sunlight, and Sikari found himself wishing he had been a real parent to them.

"BAWKKK! BAWWKK!" Princess Ida screamed, as the two boys chased her toward Sikari, and he stepped back so they wouldn't barrel into him. The twins ran neck-and-neck next to each other, their faces alive with the thrill of the battle, and just as Sikari was about to shout again, he noticed Archer's expression darken as if a storm cloud were passing over his features. In one unexpected movement, Archer raised his right arm and whipped it backwards into Harris's neck.

"No!" Sikari heard himself cry, and the sound was drowned out by a sickening guttural noise that emanated from Harris's throat. The boy's eyes widened in shock, his hands flew reflexively to his crushed Adam's apple, and bright red blood spurted in an arc from his gaping mouth.

Sikari couldn't believe his eyes. He was accustomed to violence, but not here, not at home, not now. He couldn't process what was happening. He watched in horror as Harris crumpled to the ground, his legs bent grotesquely under him, his face crashing into the dirt. Instinct drove Sikari to the stricken boy's side and he threw himself on the ground calling, "Harris, Harris, Harris." He turned the boy over by the shoulders, but Harris was already dead, his eyes fixed at the sky, his mouth leaking his life's blood. Cradling Harris, Sikari looked up in shock and bewilderment. Above him stood Archer, with Princess Ida tucked under one arm.

"I win," Archer said simply, and Sikari found his voice.

"Why?" he asked, hushed.

"Because I'm stronger, smarter and better than him. And because my time has come."

"But . . . He was your brother."

"So? Don't worry, Father. I can handle the responsibility. I know what's required of me. I know everything."

"What? How?" Sikari asked, astonished.

"I've been through your papers. I've hacked into your computer. I even broke the code on your passwords. I know everything I need to know. You understand what that means?"

Sikari understood, but he went for his holstered Berretta a split-second too late. The last thing he saw was the tip of Archer's loafer, kicking forward to drive his nose into his brain.

Devras Sikari realized that his successor was now in place and that the new king was smarter, stronger, younger and even more ruthless than the old one.

And as he died, he thought: What have I unleashed upon the world?

8

DAVID CORBETT

Harold Middleton regarded the crumpled butt of Korovin's Marlboro, mashed into his plate of *zakuski*, and for some reason it brought to mind Felicia's rebuke that he too often lacked the time or inclination to look beyond the obvious. He would have very much liked a view beyond the obvious at that moment: Bits of tobacco flecked the pickled onions; the charred aroma of cold ash lingered with the vinegary jolt of stewed beets and smoked herring.

A glance at his watch—what sort of phone call would demand so much time? Perhaps, Middleton thought uneasily, his secret entry into Russia at Domodedovo was no longer secret. Perhaps Korovin was being dragged across the coals by a younger, more officious and less forgiving man, his replacement in Russia's new intelligence megalith, the FSB.

Then again, maybe poor Ruslan was merely arguing with his wife. Or his lover—and Azerbaijani perhaps, or a sultry Uzbek.

Look beyond the obvious, he reminded himself.

He sank into a guilty humor. Felicia had barely escaped death in London, the cost of her staying at his apartment. How much misfortune can you visit upon a friend, he thought, before the friendship twists into a curse? And what of Charley—hadn't he inflicted the same jeopardy on her, insisting she join him on this quixotic crusade? What kind of father does that to his daughter?

The questions lifted him from his overstuffed chair and sent him ambling ruminatively toward the window. The distant reaches of Moscow sprawled beneath layers of urban haze fouling an ashen, moonlit sky. His impression of a transformed Russia had vanished. Trash fires dotted the less central reaches of the cityscape, surest testament to the country's lingering Third World status. The putrid stench of the rancid smoke filtered through the window glass: shoddy glazing, one more relic from the worker's paradise.

The gloss of prosperity he'd glimpsed on his way into Moscow was no more substantial than the paint-on-rust veneer of the Soviet era, the main pretense to wealth being the surge in petro revenues the past few years. Even that was suddenly at risk with plummeting oil prices—so much so, even oligarchs like Arkady Chernayev had to seek bailouts from the government. Just last week, he'd been literally moments away from losing his chief subsidiary to European banks.

Oil, Middleton thought. The mephitic sinkhole of modern politics. Correction, he told himself: oil and drugs. Those were the two gluttonous wants that kept the U.S. beholden to tinhorn despots like Putin, Chavez and Ahmadinejad, kept it tied to dubious friends like Saudi Arabia and Colombia or perpetually failing states like Nigeria and Mexico. Somewhere during the course of my life, he mused, the country I grew up in, the land of self-reliance and initiative, devolved into a daytime talk show populated by the obese, the whiny, the addicted. It was enough to make a patriot weep.

Which brought him back to Felicia—Polish by birth, she was in truth a gypsy. He suddenly felt the shock of an impossible and poignant envy, in which he sensed that what promise the future held belonged to the Felicias of the world—those with talent for a passport, as long as they kept moving, maintaining an ever fluid distance from men with patriotic obsessions and idealistic whims—men like Devras Sikari. Men like Harold Middleton.

The door to the back room swung open and Middleton turned to greet Korovin returning at last from his interminable phone call—except it wasn't his bearish friend who approached. It was the ancient waitress. Perhaps it was because he'd just had Felicia on his mind—or more to the point, her reproach of his inattentiveness—but he detected now what he should have noticed before, something artificial in her shambling gait, a subtle vigor in her movement that belied the woman's age. And the snowy white hair, off-kilter just slightly: a wig.

Middleton intuited instantly that his friend, Ruslan Korovin, was dead, the insight slamming home at the same instant his gaze met the imposter's pale gray eyes.

He reached inside his jacket, tugged the SIG Sauer P229 from his belt as the waitress lost all pretense of disguise and lunged forward. Middleton thumbed the safety down, pulled the trigger, point blank range: nothing. The gun didn't fire. In an instant of adrenalin-compressed recollection he wondered whether he'd loaded it, remembered that he had—no, the clip was full, he'd even chambered a bullet. By then the fake waitress was upon him, delivering a kick to the chest that sent him reeling backwards into the room, crashing against the low serving table with its tray of *zakuski*. The attacker's wig fell free, her real hair was closely cropped, a manlike burr. She pulled a knife from inside the shabby white blouse. Middleton struggled to his feet, slipping in the briny mess, changing his grip on the pistol to use it as a club, sensing vaguely that the ex-KGB officers in the room were stirring, ready to rise.

The attacker hadn't bargained on Middleton's discernment. She'd hoped for a quick kill, a darting escape. She lunged, not slashing with the knife but thrusting with it, no hesitation, no squeamishness—slashing was for cowards. Middleton fought off the blow with the pistol, parrying it, but the woman responded with a thundering left that caught him at the temple—his vision went white, his knees buckled. His mind coughed up a single word: Charley.

The unmistakable pop of a Makarov PM erupted seemingly inside his ear—from somewhere close behind him, one of the old *apparatchiks* had stirred to action, choosing at least for now the side of the American whom one of his old cohorts had befriended.

Through the watery film his field of vision had become, Middleton saw the waitress clutch her shoulder, tumble back a step, crumple to one knee.

The old KGB man stepped forward and murmured something brief and blunt in Russian. The knife fell from the shorn woman's hand. The man kicked it across the room where one of the others shuffled hurriedly to retrieve it.

The woman was panting, clutching her shoulder, pale hand over the growing bloodstain.

The old KGB man looked down at Middleton, eyeing the worthless SIG Sauer in his grip. His lips curled into a withering smile as, in syrupy

English, thickly accented, he said, "An excellent icon. The Novgorod school, yes?"

"Nothing speaks to good old Anglo-American homesickness like a bowl of oatmeal."

Charley glanced up from her *Wall Street Journal Europe*. The man addressing her was the same natty stranger who'd been tailing her yesterday as she'd walked along the Champs Élysées, lunching in the sunlight with the Étoile and the Arc de Triomphe in the distance. He was handsome in an aging, rough-trade sort of way, tanned, fit, salt-and-pepper hair. He dressed expensively, conspicuously so, like a social climber hoping to escape the inescapable, his class. So British, she thought. Too British.

Why, she wondered, does he want to kill me?

He said, "Might I join you?"

His accent had a flat Mersey drag to it that she recognized from specials on the Beatles. She hadn't understood then that John Lennon's accent wasn't perfectly upper crust—or lardy, as they said. If the Beatles weren't nobility, who was?

"Please do," she said, resisting a glance toward Leonora Tesla who sat across the hotel's elegant dining room. She'd flown over from London to warn her that her life was in danger and to watch over her. Felicia Kaminski had been kidnapped from Middleton's Bloomsbury apartment in the mistaken belief she was Charley.

The dapper Brit pulled back the opposite chair, sat down. "Ian," he said charmingly, extending his hand.

"Charlotte."

"I know."

A dark-skinned busman appeared—Algerian perhaps, maybe a Turk—bearing a coffee pot. Barrett-Bone declined.

Charley, affecting an ingénue's innocence: "You know my name?"

"You're in considerable danger, Ms. Middleton. I'd like to help—"

Leonora materialized behind him, nudging the back of his chair. One hand rested inside her pocket, the other settled gently on his shoulder. The hand in her pocket held a pistol, with which she gently prodded the back of his head.

He broke into a helpless smile. "You Yanks . . . "

"It would appear," Charley responded, gesturing for the check, "that there's considerable danger all around."

"That wasn't really necessary, you know."

They were seated in the back of a taxi, driving aimlessly through the Eighth *arrondissement*, the cabby's *rai* music turned down so they could talk. Prayer beads strung from his rearview mirror rattled with every turn. Ian Barrett-Bone sat between the Volunteers; Leonora Tesla still had her pistol trained on him from her coat pocket. Glancing out the back window, Charlotte Middleton watched for trail cars.

Tesla demanded, "What do you want with Charlotte?"

She was concerned, but not overly so. She'd gotten his name from his British passport—it was one of several, of course—and called somebody in another country; he could tell that from the number of times she punched the keypad. The information that came back was, as he knew it would be, that Ian Barrett-Bone was a business consultant without any criminal record and did not appear on a single watchlist around the world.

"There's a lot of money at stake in this matter."

"What matter?"

"Oh, Sikari's efforts, his companies . . . I would like to participate in a little of it. To that end, I'd like to get a message to Harold Middleton." He was perfectly calm, vaguely amused. "I might be able to spot him a few details on Sikari."

"Such as?"

"You can understand why I might want to share that solely with Colonel Middleton."

"And you can understand why that won't happen."

Barrett-Bone feigned a sulk. "Pity."

"You'll talk to us."

"And if I don't? Please don't throw out idle threats. Your reputation precedes you. That's the problem with being honorable, you know. Damn hard to scare people."

Tesla took his face in her hand, squeezing till his lips pursed. "You tried to kill an innocent woman."

He shook off her hold, but for a moment his insouciance wavered. "Ah, that's where you're wrong. The people I represent and I had nothing to do with that. That was Sikari's cock-up. A woman on his payroll named Jana. South Asian lass, lovely to look at, nasty disposition. None too trustworthy, either."

"And what people do you represent?"

"I think you missed a subtle hint in what I just said. This Jana, she's none too trustworthy. She's a bit of a loose bird. She's playable, if the conditions dictate. And the price is right."

"Why should we believe you?"

"Well for fuck's sake, luv, why should anyone believe anybody?"

Tesla leaned close. Whispering in his ear, she said, "If you call me luv again, I'll shoot you for the sheer pleasure of it."

He regarded her with mock horror. "What is it with American women?"

"What people do you represent?"

"Look, I've already put a few cards on the table here."

"Who's the Scorpion?"

He withdrew behind a mask of coy bemusement. "I'm not sure I know who you mean. Sounds like a comic book hero to me."

"A villain, I'm betting."

He shrugged. "The narcissism of minor differences."

The driver honked at a wayward cyclist, who responded with a handflick to the chin. Tesla said, "You work for him. The Scorpion."

"I'm here, talking to you, on my own graces. And just to confirm my bona fides, I'm going to fill you in on a little detail that should make it clear I know of what I speak."

He cocked an eyebrow. The two women waited.

"You've seen a bracelet, no doubt. You took it off the body of a poor sod named Kavi Balan. Jana was the one who blew him up—the old exploding cell phone ploy. Understand she damn near got you with the laptop."

"So she was the one at Cap D'Antibes."

"That's right. The bracelet has a certain significance, a meaning, if you will. The elephant, the spray of water—"

"The moon," Tesla said.

"Quite."

"Tell me what the moon means."

Barrett-Bone cocked an eyebrow. "And you'll . . . ?"

"I'll consider your request to speak with Colonel Middleton more mindfully."

He sighed. "You're a tough one, miss."

"The moon. Tell me."

"Well, I'm sure you've realized it has nothing to do with Islam. Sikari being Hindu and all."

"Go on."

"The crescent moon as a symbol predates Islam, actually. Byzantium chose it long before Mohammed ever came upon the scene, as it were. It represented the goddess Diana. She was a huntress—stop me if you know the story—but she was also a protector of the weak and vulnerable. A heavenly light in the darkness, oh my." He fluttered his hand, a music hall wave. "Sometimes you see her as a torchbearer, lighting the way for others. She was regal, proud, majestic, driving her chariot through the wilderness."

"What does that have to do with Sikari?"

He shook his head. "The question you should be asking is: What does it have to do with Jana?"

"Well?"

"She's looking for the Scorpion. Everyone's looking for the Scorpion."

"Sikari too, I assume."

"What if I were to tell you that Sikari's dead?"

Tesla struggled to conceal her shock. The man who was the center of the Volunteers' mission—dead!

Barrett-Bone continued, "And killed by his own son, it seems. But Jana's still a loose cannon."

"Looking for the Scorpion."

"And maybe that's not all."

"Go on," Tesla snapped. "Tell us."

"Look, one more hint, then I'm finished. Have you heard about the Baglihar hydroelectric dam?"

Despite herself, Charley Middleton stiffened. Wiki had been hacking and cracking nearly round-the-clock the past few days, trying to break through encryption codes and fending off countermeasures—Trojan Horses, root kits, backdoors, key loggers, bots, zombie attacks—in an attempt to determine what Sikari's next move would be. That effort had revealed the existence of the Scorpion—though no details about him—as well as turning up mentions of the Baglihar dam.

Tesla shrugged. "It's a dam being built in India."

"Kashmir," Barrett-Bone corrected. "More precisely the Jammu region of India-administered Kashmir."

"The area Sikari comes from."

"Quite."

"What about it?"

"You know there's a bloody serious dispute over the thing."

Pakistan had protested to the U.N. that the dam threatened irrigation from the Chenab River, on which the country's agriculture relied. It even went so far as to accuse India of deliberately going ahead with the project simply to deprive Pakistan of the water it needed to survive. Negotiations between the two countries had broken down over the issue of Islamic terrorism in the region, and so the World Bank, which brokered the 1960 Indus Water treaty for Kashmir, had appointed an arbitrator to review the dispute. Just recently the arbitrator had issued his determination: India, which claimed the dam was needed to provide much-needed electric power, was fully within its rights to finish the project, with a minor concession of lowering the spillway five feet.

Tesla said, "What does the dispute have to do with Sikari? His side won."

"Did it now?" Barrett-Bone sank back into the seat, arms crossed, winking. "I'm afraid that's all I'm prepared to say. For now. Till I get my face-to-face with the fabled Harold Middleton."

As prison cells went it wasn't half bad—one of those vast drafty rooms in some provincial estate house on the outskirts of Moscow, or possibly out in the neighboring countryside, a relic from the Romanov era, showing all too well the inevitable wear and principled neglect of the socialist century.

The floorboards were dull and pitted, the walls dingy and water-stained. The windows had been sealed up, leaving a musty smell of mildew and rot, tinged with the scent of wood smoke seeping in from somewhere. Not here—no wood in the fireplace, no warming blaze, just a ridiculously claptrap space heater resembling a helmet with a red-hot face behind the grille.

It gave off about as much heat as a nightlight. Except for three rickety chairs, it was the only piece of furniture in the room.

Middleton gathered his coat tight around his body, breath purling out from his nostrils in airy plumes. His lips felt numb.

How many hours had they kept him here? How many more to go—and what then?

At least there'd been no torture, not for him. He'd heard the cries from elsewhere in the large house—the woman with the buzz-cut hair, he supposed, his attacker. Ruslan's killer. They'd spare her no excess. The questioning would almost be secondary.

He glanced up at the ceiling, a stained expanse of yellowing plaster blistered and cracked to the point it resembled a contour map. He'd sat there staring up at it for hours at a time, creating an imagined landscape, tracing the rivers, the feed-streams and tributaries, the floodplains, the drainage basins, the terraced hillsides and marshy wetlands and vast beckoning steppes. Where would the cities reside, he wondered, where the outlying villages? From which direction would the Mongol horsemen—or the Nazis' vaunted Sixth Army—invade?

When this manner of passing time faltered, he closed his eyes and tried to mentally reconstruct the late Beethoven sonatas, the *Hammerklavier* in particular, with its echoes of Bach in the fourth movement fugue—which of course only reminded him of Felicia.

And this was his third manner of passing the time: He wondered where she was, if she was all right. If she was alive. His guilt quickened into rage that melted into fatherly concern that dissolved into hopeless sorrow. In time the despair would slither on to Charley, then Leonora—named for Leonore, heroine of Beethoven's only opera, *Fidelio*—which would return him to his mental reconstruction of the sonatas, until at last the ceiling beckoned once more.

He tried not to think of Ruslan. The bearish Russian had known the risks, they all did. Even so . . .

The room's lone door opened. Mealtime, he supposed. Breakfast? Lunch? Supper? He'd lost all sense of time. But instead of the hunched and ferret-faced crone—a real one this time—who'd delivered his tray of borscht and black bread earlier, served with a raw quartered onion and a glass of vodka, a tall and well-dressed man appeared: vigorous, vaguely military, with that chiseled Slavic bone structure, the uniquely soulful eyes. He wore a simple black suit beneath a heavy wool overcoat; his bluchers were muddy. Entering alone, he closed the door behind him, to the clatter of deadbolts from the hallway outside.

"Mr. Middleton," the man said, his English suggestive of British tutelage, not American. "I trust you've not been too terribly inconvenienced?"

His smile seemed sincere, his tone matter-of-fact. Middleton thought of the screams he'd heard through the walls just hours before—inconvenienced? "Not in the least." He wrapped his coat tighter and glanced up at the ceiling. "I've been admiring the view."

The stranger obligingly followed his eyes. "My apologies for the delay. We wanted to be sure we had the facts before troubling you."

The facts. Of course. That's what torture provides, the troubling facts.

"I suppose it would be impertinent of me to ask who, exactly, you mean by 'we,'" Middleton said. He assumed the old KGB men who'd saved him had fobbed him off on some shadowy element within the security apparatus. Gangsters, maybe. Perhaps both.

The stranger smiled, pulled up one of the other two skeletal chairs, brushed its dusty surface, sat. "I'm at liberty to tell you this: There are several groups very interested in—how to put it?—acquiring you, let's say. Considerable sums have been offered. Tempting sums. But we—and no, I will not tell you any more about who 'we' are—do not concern ourselves so much with financial reward as the singular satisfaction provided by one thing and one thing only: information. We like knowing what's going on. It's our reason for being."

Bingo, Middleton thought. Remaining poker-faced, he said, "Would it be too much to have your name?"

"Yes. I'm sorry." The smile remained rigidly in place. "No names. We're prepared to protect you, Mr. Middleton, from those who would gladly pay for the privilege of your company. People who would, I'm afraid, most definitely make things very difficult for you. But in return for this protection we are offering, we expect something in return."

The Man with No Name's voice trailed off into the void. He extended his hands in either direction, to suggest the vast store of knowledge—the information—he expected to receive.

"Several groups," Middleton said. "I can think of just two who might be interested."

"You underestimate your worth."

"This interest is current?"

"No. Some of it appears to go back a ways. You have made your share of enemies, Mr. Middleton. I find that admirable, incidentally. But yes, two groups originally found their way to a back channel, contacted us, inquired. Then a third came forward—same realm of interest, let's say. The others seem to bear old grudges, but once they learned there was a bidding war, they were spectacularly obliging."

Three, Middleton thought. Sikari, the Scorpion and who else? Chernayev? But why would he bid against Sikari? And how could he know that Middleton was interested in him? "It appears I have little choice."

The impish smile lingered, even as the man shrugged. "As Sartre says, one always has a choice, if only in how to die."

Middleton considered it. He could hand himself over to his enemies, but why? They would suffer no hesitation. They would most certainly *make things difficult.* They would *inconvenience* him. He shuddered, picturing it. He knew he had his virtues, knew himself to be selfless and moderately brave, but he lacked certainty on the issue of withstanding torture hour after hour, day after day, week upon week. Perhaps he would have the spine to lie, buy time. But when there was no more time to purchase, what then?

And it wasn't just his own torture to consider. The old KGB *apparatchiks* had taken both of his cell phones, the encrypted one and his regular one. All it would take is one call to Wiki, Leonora, Felicia, Charley—the signal would pinpoint their locations.

Middleton chafed his hands together to warm them. "How shall we do this?"

You would have thought he'd just praised the man's taste in lovers: The smile turned gracious, his sad eyes shone. "Well, don't laugh, but I prefer the dialectic approach."

Who is this character, Middleton wondered. "Fire away."

"Let's start simply. You are interested in Devras Sikari. Correct?"

Middleton didn't hesitate. "Yes."

"Very good. And why did you come here in that quest? To Russia?"

That wasn't a question. It was a test. "One of my people was killed, another badly wounded, by an explosion in Florida at a location linked to Sikari. The device used was thermobaric, which suggested a Russian source, given the army's use of such weaponry in Chechnya and—"

The man raised his hand. "Please, Mr. Middleton, do not insult me." The smile faded. "U.S. Marines have used thermobaric weapons in Iraq. They were used extensively in the second battle for Fallujah. The device is called a SMAW, shoulder-launched multi-purpose assault weapon. It was used against fortified positions—houses, mosques. You think we don't know this? Good God, a six-year-old who can Google could tell me as much."

Middleton replied, "And did *you* think I wouldn't have other leads?"

"I'm serious, Mr. Middleton. If you are not candid with me, your value plummets. Especially vis-à-vis the sums of cash being offered."

Middleton pulled the collar of his overcoat tight against the chill. "If you'll let me finish? This Russian connection was Arkady Chernayev. I hope to speak to him. I want to know about these explosives."

The man's smile vanished entirely. "You were going to talk with Arkady Chernayev."

"I had to try."

"To accomplish what? Do you hear what you sound like?"

"The group I represent does not have much but persuasion in its arsenal."

"You hoped to *persuade* him."

"Yes."

"You're either a fool or a liar."

For a moment Middleton wondered if he'd been wrong. Perhaps this man wasn't some rogue intelligence agent after all, but one of Chernayev's operatives—though his protestations had a vaguely theatrical ring. He was vamping, trying to goad a response. And what would Middleton tell him—the truth? That he believed Chernayev and a great many other Russians saw an arms race on the subcontinent as inevitable. Worse, that China, before that arms race proceeded much further, would invade Kashmir from its own controlled areas in Aksai Chin and the Trans-Karakoram Tract, doing so for the water, contriving some pretext for the offensive such as protecting an otherwise expendable ethnic minority. Russia could either get drawn into a ground war with China or let proxies wage the fight for it—enter Chernayev. The reason his company had been bailed out during the recent financial crisis was because of his pledge to use his private army to facilitate the development of a friendly force in Kashmir—nationalists perhaps, rabid idealists no doubt, but still susceptible to simple bribery. Would they remain so with a secret source of heavy water, a cache of nuclear arms? Was Chernayev aware of the copper bracelet? Were his Russian facilitators?

All of this went through Middleton's mind as he pondered the man's question: Why would Chernayev involve himself in such an outlandish scheme?

But in any case, Middleton needed information. He decided to play the man right back. He took a gamble. "I didn't have any choice but to come here. My leads to the Scorpion dried up. Chernayev was all I had left," he bluffed.

The reaction was subtle but telling. Trying not to sound eager, the man said, "What do you know of the Scorpion?"

"So he's not bidding for me?"

No answer.

Middleton had a flash. And tried another gamble. "I don't know much," he said. "But I'll tell you it was confusing. We couldn't figure out how one individual could pay for all of Sikari's education and then stake him after he graduated with start-up capital for his corporations? It had to be companies or foundations that were involved."

The man replied as if the Scorpion's support of Sikari were common knowledge. "You never thought that the companies he, or she, owns ultimately were set up as subterfuge. Layers upon layers of companies. Like BlueWatch."

"BlueWatch?" Middleton frowned. "The security outfit in Dubai?" Blue-Watch had been the subject of a number of investigations following the shooting deaths by overly enthusiastic employees around the world. Most of the investigations had ended without any prosecutions—some said the company had intimidated prosecutors and judges, forcing them to drop charges.

The man said, "But the cash ultimately came from one individual who controlled all the companies. The Scorpion."

So he'd not only confirmed the Scorpion had paid for Sikari's education and financed his companies but that, for some reason, No Name and his organization, whatever it was, had been following the Kashmiri's story very closely. And undoubtedly they too were eager to find the Scorpion.

Which told Middleton that he—or she—was the answer to everything.

"Well," he told his captor, "like I was saying, we weren't successful in finding the Scorpion."

No Name continued, "Do you know Sikari's own description of his benefactor? He said he was 'holy, but of this world.'"

"Yes, but I think that was a corrupted translation. The words Sikari used were *jnana* and *vijnana*. The prefix *vi*, when added to a noun, tends to diminish or invert the meaning of that noun. *Jnana* is spiritual knowledge. *Vijnana*, then, is practical or profane knowledge. Sometimes *vijnana* and *jnana*, used together, are meant to suggest knowledge and wisdom. All he meant was the man had not just a worldly but philosophical bent."

No Name shrugged. "What more do you know about this Scorpion? Tell me and I'll make your life here easier."

"Not much . . . " Another gamble. He thought of Felicia's email to him. "Aside from the copper bracelet, of course."

No Name's attempt to conceal his surprise was futile. His reaction was even more pronounced than at the reference to the Scorpion. As if unable to stop himself, he asked, "And the relation between the Scorpion and the copper bracelet? How do you mean, Colonel?"

Middleton wanted to play the man out longer, but he knew that if he told too much, he'd use up whatever value he had. "I think I've said all I'm going to for the time being."

The man leaned forward, persisting. "Do you know about the technology involved? What have you learned?"

Middleton smiled and shook his head.

No Name studied him for a moment, then rose and turned toward the door.

Staring at the back of his heavy wool coat, Middleton felt an odd premonition, as though life itself were about to leave him there alone. He'd established his value and learned some facts, but had he inadvertently exposed himself to long bouts of torture to learn what else he knew?

"What now?" He tried not to sound frightened. "I've cooperated. How much longer do you intend to keep me here?"

The man rapped gently on the door. The deadbolts rattled open. Without looking back over his shoulder, he said, "Regrettably, that's not for me to decide."

Ian Barrett-Bone stood outside the L'église de la Madeleine, leaning down so his face was level with those of Charley Middleton and Leonora Tesla. He said, "You're making a mistake, you know."

"You can always talk to me," Tesla said.

He sighed laboriously. "Not acceptable. How many times—"

"I'll pass word on to Colonel Middleton then. If he wishes to contact you, we have the number you provided."

He leaned closer, laying a hand on the roof of the cab. "The offer stands till midnight, not a tick longer. After that, I'm afraid, the race is on. And you're at a distinct disadvantage, you know. Been a step behind the whole time. I can change that. Truly. But I'll expect a certain recompense, you understand. Only fair."

"As I said, I'll pass that along." She signaled for the cabbie to drive on. "Thank you for your . . ."

They were out of earshot before she knew how to finish. The two women watched through the rear window as the dapper, thuggish, enigmatic Englishman grew smaller, staring right back at them through a ghostly plume of black exhaust.

Tesla tried her phone yet again, but was unable to reach Middleton. A call to Wiki Chang revealed that he'd sent their boss information on some shipping companies suspected of sending explosives to Florida from Russia, and that Middleton was investigating that lead in Moscow. But the tech expert had been unable to reach him either.

The taxi turned onto the Place de la Concorde and merged with traffic funneling onto the Champs Élysées. Charley turned toward the front, her voice an empty whisper. "Know what I admire most about you, Nora?" Lacing her fingers together, she stared at her folded hands in her lap as though not quite sure to whom they belonged. "You convinced that man, and quite possibly yourself, that my father is still alive."

9

LINDA BARNES

The four-poster dominated the room like a throne on a dais. Royal blue drapes floated over ivory walls. A turquoise satin coverlet turned the bed into a shimmering pool. Fat cherubs chased each other around the intricately carved molding. Outdoors, lovers who shared a kiss as they watched the brightly painted dhows cruise by on the Creek could be jailed. Here, in one of Dubai's finest hotels, a mirror was mounted to the ceiling over a bed large enough to sleep four.

Jana found the decadence both disturbing and provocative. Her long-sleeved navy sheath was conservative in cut, as befitted a woman traveling in the Middle East, the kind of dress an airline hostess might have chosen, or a nun, although neither would have cinched it with a wide leather belt.

She located the BlackBerry with no difficulty, tucked in the corner of the middle drawer of the bureau to the left of the bed, as arranged. At exactly eight, she pressed the keys. The connection took time, but the voice, when he answered, was clear. The right voice.

Archer had learned Hindi from the man he called father, Devras Sikari. They conversed in that language, Jana proud of her fluency in her mother's native tongue. She rarely spoke it aloud, letting others see her as the ignorant South Asian, almost equally tongue-tied in English and French. The assumptions of others wearied her, particularly the assumptions of men.

"Yes," she said, "he is with me. He's assured me there's a lead and I believe him." She listened awhile, nodding her head, all the while wrestling with the news Archer had just delivered rather casually—the death of his father Devras Sikari. It was inevitable, of course, though the particular circumstances had turned the matter into more of a Shakespearean tragedy. Her heart pounded hard as she considered the implications of the man's death. There were many of them.

"Is there news of Middleton?" she asked.

"Detained by the Russians. I doubt we need concern ourselves further with the amateurs."

"They beat us with Balan," she replied, "but we made that work to our advantage, no?"

It was the overhead mirror that betrayed Pierre Crane. Jana might not have noticed the journalist if she'd been scanning the room at eye level, but reflected in the ceiling mirror, the slight movement of the door to the suite's living room was clear, as was its cause.

She neither lowered her voice nor changed her tone. "So then, when do we move the equipment?"

Archer said, "Soon. It is set. It will be done. The wise control the world."

"The wise control themselves," she said quickly, pressing the button that ended the call.

Jana returned the BlackBerry to the drawer and, as she unpacked her small duffle, thought of Crane, who lurked in the next room. She had mixed feelings about the reporter. Her sources had given her a lot of information about him. He wasn't about money or power. He was about journalism and the Story—with a capitol "s." Which meant she could trust him up to a point. Jana, though, never believed in trust; daughters whose fathers are murdered rarely do. But Crane had access to important facts.

And in this murky business, facts were what she needed.

Besides, the gawky reporter was lusting after her and therefore it would be easy to tap the spigot of what he knew about the Scorpion, Middleton and the others.

After the girl she thought was Charlotte Middleton had escaped in London, Jana had cut Crane free and he'd behaved just as she knew he would: like a puppy with no desire to stray from his mistress, leash or none. She'd tried to charm from him what information he had but he'd continued to withhold details, other than the lead was centered in Dubai. Jana had immediately sized up what was going on and suggested that they go there together. She'd find the connection to the Scorpion first hand while he continued his research for the story.

It's what he'd been hoping for all along. He immediately agreed.

Now, Crane approached with deliberately noisy steps and knocked.

"Come in."

"You people do yourselves well, Jana," he said in French. "The bedroom on the far side of the living room is spectacular. Plenty of room. Lovely view, too. You can see all those odd little boats." He changed gears quickly. "Tell me about yourself."

"Questions," Jana said, "always questions."

"I gave you Dubai. You promised me the truth for my story. So?"

"Really, Pierre, yet another question? Can we concentrate on something other than talk? We've been on airplanes for hours." Jana let her voice fall, but kept her eyes steady. She knew how to play this game, a matter of tone and body movement rather than words.

Crane took the bait. "You are a very attractive woman, Jana."

"A compliment from a man who tells lies for a living—what is that worth?" Again, her words meant little.

"I'm a journalist. I don't lie . . . Well, not very often. Besides, beautiful women don't need compliments from homely men."

"So now I am beautiful?"

"You know perfectly well you are."

"Ah, but you call yourself homely? That's absurd. To a woman, being handsome is about making a woman feel like a woman. I think you understand what I mean." Smiling, Jana folded her arms under her breasts, giving them an unnecessary boost.

"Well, we do tend to try harder," Crane said.

"But how could you and I achieve mutual trust?"

Jana's eyes, Crane noticed, had flecks of caramel, almost gold, in the iris. Her lashes were long and thick, like her hair. "Perhaps we would have to start by searching each other," he said.

Jana lifted her chin and lowered her lashes. "Really?"

"If you wouldn't mind."

She held his eyes for a moment, then slowly turned her back, lifting the heavy hair from the nape of her neck with her left hand, exposing the thin zipper that ran like a snake down the length of her navy sheath. "Women, as you know, must be carefully and thoroughly searched."

The third time Connie Carson woke, she didn't feel nauseous. She was aware she was recovering in a hospital room and the cool white light no longer terrified her. Nor did the lack of feeling in her right arm, an absence so strong she'd been afraid to look down, sure she would see nothing but a stump.

But she was startled by a face peering down at her. Langer, she thought, the Ken-doll cop.

"Do you think you can stand? Move?" he asked hurriedly.

The quiet intensity of his voice flooded her system with adrenaline.

"You sure stirred up a hornet's nest." He looked around as if he anticipated action. "Come on. We've got to go."

If she hadn't needed all her strength to sit up and swing her legs over the side of the narrow bed, Carson would have said, that's exactly what I meant to do. Her phone call, and Middleton's response, must have grabbed somebody's attention.

"Let me help." Langer reached for her left elbow.

"I can, thank you. Does Dr. Ahmed know you're—"

"Ahmed's way too interested in you already. He's not our friend." Now that she was standing on her own, Langer tossed her a robe, then quickly grabbed her chart from the end of the bed and tucked it into a carryall. "He's been on the phone to friends in Pakistan."

The room didn't spin exactly. It did a lazy half-circuit, an aborted pirouette.

"Whoa, come on, Connie, stay with me." Langer jumped to her side, arm around her waist, helping her don a blue chenille robe twice the size of her slender frame. "We're on the third floor. We turn right out the door, twenty steps to the second door on the left, three flights down, handrail all the way. You hear me? Push-bar door at the bottom opens directly outside. There's a black van at the end of the path. The back doors will open as you approach. There are clothes for you inside."

"Why?" Carson whispered as she sank back onto the bed, deciding for the moment not to press the button that would summon a nurse. She was wondering whether Langer could be trusted—whether she had hallucinated the entire episode. Suddenly the door opened and he was back, this time pushing a gurney.

"Get on."

"You didn't answer me."

"What was the question?"

"Why should I trust you?"

Langer lifted her like she was a three year old and set her firmly on the gurney. She had already parted her lips to scream by the time his response reached her ear.

"Wiki Chang."

"Wiki—"

"We're trying to save your life, Connie."

In bed, Jana thought of herself not as the girl in the movie, the slut who spread her thighs for any hero, any villain, but as the great film director. She was the girl, yes, but she was completely in control. Sometimes the girl looked like Jana's own reflection, a sultry twin with shiny dark hair. Sometimes she was a younger Jana, a Jana as she had once been, the naïve younger sister of brothers who'd taught her too soon what girls like her were good for. Sometimes she was a remote ivory-skinned blonde. The director in Jana rarely enjoyed the kind of opportunity afforded by the Dubai suite: champagne glasses on the bedside table; satin sheets glinting in softly diffused light. This was no cheap porno reel, but a James Bond-like thriller, an upscale fantasia.

Crane, she admitted to herself, hardly looked the part. His long limbs were fish-belly pale. His hair was dull, his nose long, but he was surprisingly muscular, very sturdy. Jana watched the reflection in the ceiling mirror, studied the splay of Crane's limbs as he lay across her dark skin.

There was little Jana would change about her body. She was pleased with the swell of breast and hip. She wished her nose were shorter, a touch more *retroussé*. More than that, she wished she did not sweat. The movie girl always looked glossy and cool in bed, during and after the most passionate of exertions. A Bond girl shimmered and glowed. Jana sweated; it interfered with her close-ups, making them uncomfortably real.

Crane snorted. Jana tightened her hand at the base of his spine, murmuring in his ear, rotating her hips slowly, encouraging him to stay longer. Film directors, she found, concentrated on the man's pleasure. Jana, the director, concentrated on her own. Why not? she thought. She had time to kill.

Crane considered himself so clever, so subtle with his veiled questions about the Scorpion, about Ian Barrett-Bone. As if they were important, as if they were the movers and shakers, the planners and undertakers of the mission. It was like the Buddha said, in the ancient Sanskrit motto engraved on the copper bracelet: *The irrigators direct the water, fletchers fashion the shaft, carpenters bend the wood. The wise control themselves.*

Perhaps Archer had been right to alter the last phrase, *the wise control themselves*, making it *the wise control the world*. Already he had altered the second phrase: no longer the *fletchers fashion the shaft*, but *the archer shoots the arrow*.

Jana smiled at the conceit. Then her thoughts of Archer faded and an image of Devras Sikari soon followed.

Her mood changed instantly. She faked a second, more theatrical, orgasm. When she squirmed her discomfort, he dismounted and lay beside her, one ungainly arm draped across her belly.

He seemed entirely pleased with himself, a schoolboy who'd passed his final exam with flying colors. When he caught his breath, he said, "Now, don't you think I deserve the answer to a question or two?"

"Certainly, Pierre." That's what any pliant Bond girl would reply. "But I must use the bathroom, darling."

If he had any doubt that he'd won her over, this was the danger point, this was when the man would protest, try to grab her, or flee. Jana, the director, watched the action on the overhead screen.

"Hurry back," was all Crane said.

Clanging bells announced the elevator. Turning her head to the side, Carson read a sign warning hospital staff against discussing patient care in public places. Langer had his SIG Sauer P226 under the top sheet where he could retrieve it quickly. Carson wondered whether she'd be able to reach it—Langer had convinced her she might need to.

She watched the white light as the elevator descended. Each time they passed a landing without interruption, Langer said, "Steady, Connie. We're closer. Closer."

At the basement level, Langer pushed the gurney out of the elevator, his eyes searching left and right. "This corridor leads to a loading dock," he said.

Carson stared helplessly at the ceiling.

"Ready?" Langer asked.

Her throat dry, Carson nodded.

Suddenly, Langer began to run, speeding the gurney along the endless corridor. The whoosh of automatic doors preceded warmer air, the scent of ocean, sunlight.

As they rolled down a ramp, Carson saw a black Chevrolet Express waiting at the end of the path.

She heard the squeal of tires in the near distance.

Langer raced her toward the van where Jimmy Chang, the man Jean-Marc Lespasse had christened "Wiki," waited near the open hatch. He called to her, waving his hand frantically, his eyes wide.

A black town car bounded toward the loading dock.

She knew it was someone connected to Sindhu Power. The company might be defunct but the people who wished to keep its secrets were alive and well.

The detective said, "Here's where we say goodbye, Connie."

"What?"

"Don't think my jurisdiction includes wherever you and your people are going to follow up leads in this case. The best thing I can do is play defense here. Now get moving!"

He pulled out his SIG and turned to face the oncoming Lincoln.

The car slowed.

"Langer . . . "

"Go!"

"Thank you."

Chang jumped out and lifted Carson from the gurney, her injured body stiffening in his arms. He bundled her inside and the van took off, roaring toward the exit.

"Hey, you look great," Chang said as he settled into a seat.

Carson could only imagine how she looked standing there with no makeup, a huge bathrobe, bare feet. She felt a tingling in her right arm.

"I mean, you're just like your picture. I mean, you're pale but otherwise . . ."

The van's bay was converted to a cross between an ambulance and a computer lab, a workspace for Wiki that came complete with a cot. Along one side, three glaring widescreen LCD monitors and a couple of gooseneck work lamps nested on a long shelf twined with cables. Small green lights pulsed.

Chang said, "Do you want to get into bed? Dammit, that sure didn't come out right. What I mean . . . I mean, there's a cot . . . Because of your operation. Your arm must hurt like hell."

"I'm glad to see you, Wiki." He looked like his photo, too, not at all like his glamorous well-muscled Second Life avatar. In person, Chang was like an elongated twelve year old, with a round face, oversized spectacles and a bad haircut. "Whatever you did to that cop, you turned him into a pussycat. I thought he was gonna arrest me as soon as I revived."

"Langer's not bad. His people were keeping an eye on the industrial park, the one—"

That blew up. The one where Jean-Marc died.

Chang seemed to hear her thought. "Yeah, Tampa PD had information that one of the outfits in the park was a front for a bunch of Mexican narco-traffickers from the Juarez cartel. They had it under surveillance. The department even put someone on the front desk."

An image of Jean-Marc danced before Carson's eyes. "Too bad the man didn't—"

"The operation was shut down months ago, before Sindhu Power and Electric cleared out. The Tampa cops say Sindhu seemed like an ordinary business."

"But if they had someone on the front desk, they must have noticed something."

"Better than that; they kept copies of everything, shipping manifests, stuff like that. They searched through the Dumpsters, you know, looking for stuff on the drug runners, but pretty much going through all the garbage. Folks at Sindhu were avid shredders, Langer told me, but one day the surveillance team found a disk. Musta fallen under a desk or something and the cleaning crew tossed it."

"And you've got it?"

The van sped toward 275. "Langer tried to read the thing, said it was encrypted all to hell and back, figured with a name like 'Sindhu' and them clearing out, somebody ought to check it. So he notified a pal in Homeland Security. Guy might have gotten back to him in four or five years."

"But you've got the disk?"

"I sure do. Yeah, you bet."

Her arm throbbed; she was thirsty and exhausted, but Carson had to smile at his enthusiasm. Then she remembered Jean-Marc and a lump rose in her throat. Chang was so young. Though she was only a few years older, she felt ancient by comparison.

She said, "Fill me in. What's our next move? Who's driving this rig?"

"A friend. He's cool. He was an army medic, too, in case you—"

"You thought of everything."

His grin was infectious. "If you're up for it, we're heading to a military airbase."

"MacDill? Middleton's orders?"

The young man's face grew grave. "Not exactly . . . Connie, Colonel Middleton's gone missing."

"What?"

"No phone to trace, nothing. Headed to Russia and then vanished."

"You haven't heard anything from him?"

"Not a word. Tesla will fill you in."

"You won't be going with me?"

"I'm supposed to hold down the fort here."

"Right. You're not supposed to leave the lab, are you?"

"Hey," he said, smiling expansively and waving his arms at the interior of the van. "I brought it with me."

On the whole, Pierre Crane thought he had not done badly. He was alive. He was—if no closer to the secret of who had financed Sikari's education or the riddle of the Scorpion—at least closer to the woman who was in some way entwined in the Scorpion's life. Who wanted him dead or wanted to use him. The woman who was, quite possibly, his equal. He had acquitted himself well in bed. Casanova, he had heard, had been, if not an ugly man, a man of no particular physical distinction.

He assessed the danger at the moment and found it minimal. Their lovemaking had proven that. And besides he knew himself to be more than a match for Jana physically. He was an expert in several forms of unarmed combat, after all, and he was confident that it wouldn't come down to a matter of firearms. Hadn't he been with her when she'd disposed of her pistol before entering the terminal at Heathrow? Hadn't he sat beside her on the long flight and accompanied her in the taxi directly to the hotel? And she was naked now . . .

He was wondering what she might shed on the story of the three young South Asians staked to an education and start-up capital, what he thought of as his "anomaly story." The story of the Scorpion. As a journalist, he honored the maxim "follow the money." The Scorpion raised money, had money, but it galled Crane that, after all these months, he was still no closer to knowing who exactly the man was. That he was a man of no particular allegiance was a given; such men operated across national borders. Money and the economy were global, so crime was global as well. Perhaps he should be paying less attention to figures of political intrigue, more to those of organized crime. Organized crime had the networks international terrorism needed, the smuggling routes, the purveyors of forged documents, the weapons and money-laundering connections. Money moved with lightning speed and money begat more money, the kind of wealth that could build palaces in the desert, entire cities like Dubai. Whose money was behind such rapid development? Oil money, yes, but he had heard tales of the wealth of powerful Russian oligarchs.

Crane heard the water running in the bathroom.

He thought again of Jana's body.

And thoughts of the Scorpion slipped from his mind.

Wiki Chang flicked on an overhead light. Carson blinked, fluttering her eyelids until her irises adjusted to the bright fluorescence. The interior of the black van, that's where she was—a van speeding toward a military airbase—and she was lying on a cot, not unlike the gurney on which she'd escaped from the hospital, except this one was bolted to the wall opposite the computer screens.

"Did I—?"

"You tried to take a nap standing up. I caught you before you fell and carried you here. I'm stronger than I look." Chang's face flamed scarlet. "Not that you're heavy, that's not what I meant, uh, I hope you don't mind."

Really, Carson thought, he was totally adorable.

"No, no, don't get up," he insisted when she tried to sit. "You should be lying down. I researched your post-op care, but having your chart really helps. In about twenty minutes, you'll need your pain meds. I've got those ready. Your antibiotics will be—"

"I'm sure you've got it under control," Carson said. "Please, go back to work. You said the disk was encrypted—"

"A real bear."

"You haven't been able to decode it?" Carson didn't know how long she'd been unconscious, so she tried to keep the disappointment out of her voice. Everyone said Wiki Chang was the best, but if Langer, a hobbyist, and Tampa PD hadn't been able to crack it, and his pal at Homeland Security, a pro, had already given it a whirl . . .

"No, I've got the disk decoded. See?" As if the other three monitors were only for show, Chang held up a slim laptop, tilting the screen until she nodded her approval.

"I'm not even sure what I'm looking at."

"It's a ZIP file, an archive containing a bunch of other files. I opened it using 'fcrackzip,' this terrific brute-force ZIP cracking program for Linux. I mean, it really didn't have a terribly complicated password and even if it had been way more complex, there are tons of cryptanalysis tools I could have used. The encryption in ZIP files just isn't all that good."

"I'll take your word for it," Carson said.

Chang hurried on, pointing at the screen with an index finger for emphasis. "Now the coded files are all picture files, see? They were taken by a Nikon. Except for this one. This one's pretty cute. It's not a photo—it's a diagram, see, a blueprint of a hydroelectric dam. I matched it to the architectural drawings and schematics for the Baglihar dam project."

"In Jammu and Kashmir."

"Right. Good old J&K, but see this? The blueprints have been altered."

"Altered?"

"Added to. These look like plans to set up a heavy-water reactor at the core of the dam. In a kind of subterranean chamber."

Carson couldn't keep the excitement out of her voice. "But that could be what we've been looking for, what Sindhu Power and Electric was shipping overseas, the parts for the heavy-water reactor. Does it say when the reactor will go online? Does it give a date? We've got to get in touch with Middleton."

"Hold on, Connie. The plans—the alterations—to accommodate the heavy-water reactor . . . I've been looking at them, and excuse me, but they're either bullshit or they're incomplete. The way they are now, they're like a high-class con, a way to justify some incredible expenditures, but they won't actually do the trick. There's a reason the patent for this stuff was applied for, but never granted. This whole 'copper bracelet' technology seems to be built around faulty assumptions."

"Copper bracelet?"

"Yeah, because of the shape of the copper pipes," he said.

"Okay, so the reactor won't actually go online?" Light glinted off Chang's oversized lenses and Carson shifted her head to get a clearer look at the screen.

"Doesn't seem it will," the young man said. "There could be a way to fix it, but nobody seems to have the technology to do that at this point. In any case, there's no heavy-water generator at the dam . . . Connie, this whole thing doesn't smell right."

"You think the files are some kind of trap, like the one set in the office?"

"I think this disk is *more* than it seems."

"What do you mean?"

"The picture files, take a look at them." Chang flashed a series of images on the laptop screen.

Carson would have shrugged if her arm and shoulder had functioned. "It looks like an office, the office at Sindhu." The image of the place was seared on her retinas, along with a picture of Jean-Marc, lying there, eyes staring blankly into space.

Chang said, "Do they look like anything you'd want to encrypt? A picture of a desk, a chair, a table?"

"Maybe they were just keeping them on the same disk."

"Maybe. Or they might be something else. I mean, why put these innocent-looking photos in with a file that's so complex? I decided there must be another layer, beneath the images."

"But how would you find out if—"

"Steganography," Chang said. "It can embed information into a file, but getting it back isn't just a matter of running a simple cracking program—you have to figure out how it was done, because there are so many different ways. I tried a couple of approaches while you were out of it, and I finally got a handle on it with the Digital Invisible Ink Toolkit, and there's definitely embedded information in this picture. So I've got it, but it's encrypted, too."

"And you don't have the encryption key." Wheels within wheels, Carson thought. How many layers would they have to penetrate?

"Not yet," Chang said. "This is an old-style pencil-and-paper cipher—you can tell because it's just letters—but, wait a minute, look at the letter frequencies! I haven't seen one of these in years, but I think this might be a Playfair cipher."

"Playfair?" Carson said. "Spies used it, a long time ago—in World War II, right? How do you find the encryption key?"

"If it's Playfair, it'll be a group of 10 to 15 unique letters. It could be a single word, but sometimes it's, say, a long phrase in a book, a song lyric—"

"A phrase all the members of the group would have to know."

Chang nodded. "Anyone who needs to decode messages."

"Wiki, you called the technology, for the heavy-water reactor, the 'copper bracelet.' Right?"

"Yeah."

"When we were in France, the 'copper bracelet' was an actual physical copper bracelet. Jewelry." As she spoke, Carson tried to circle her left wrist with her right hand. The effort made her gasp. "There were words engraved on it, in Hindi, or—"

"Sanskrit. Do you want your pain meds now? It's a little early, but . . . "

"I'll wait. You've seen it? The bracelet?"

"With the elephant and the moon? Sure. Middleton sent it to me at the lab. I've got it with me."

"You know what it says?"

"Yeah, sure. It's a quotation, from the Buddha. *Irrigators direct the waters; Fletchers fashion the shaft, Carpenters bend the wood. The wise control themselves.*"

"Where's it from, the quote?"

"A text called the *Dhammapada*. It's a compilation of the Buddha's words."

"Could that be the key word? Dhamma-whatever?"

Chang shook his head. "Too many repeating letters."

"Well, could the quote itself be the encryption key?"

"It's a long enough phrase," Wiki said. "Let's give it a whirl."

"I think I remember how to do this," Carson said. "You make a five-by-five grid, right?"

"Yeah. The most common way to do it is to take the first letter of each word in the phrase. So we'd start out 'I', 'D', 'W', 'F', then 'A', from the second letter of 'fashion', since we've already used the 'F', then 'H', 'S', and so on. You arrange the letters at the beginning of your grid, one to a square, followed by the rest of the letters in the alphabet, in order, with the Q, or sometimes the J, omitted. And if the first letter in each word doesn't work, you try the last letter, or—"

"So there are a lot of possibilities. This could take a while."

"Take me a few minutes to write a tiny Perl program. Really, it's way quicker than filling in the grid hit or miss."

"Perl?"

"Sorry. It's this really easy computer language—I'm boring the hell out of you, aren't I?"

"No, Wiki, I love puzzles." She stopped. The pain was waking in earnest now; fire blazed down the length of her arm. "Maybe you better give me a pill or two?"

"Hey, I'm sorry. I forgot."

Chang disappeared from Carson's view with a clatter, using the wheeled desk chair to scoot around the van's interior. He retrieved a vial of pills from a satchel, a paper cup and a bottle of water from the monitor shelf, before returning to the side of the cot. "You lie back and relax, okay? You're turning paler every second."

"But I—"

"Hey. Doctor's orders."

Obediently, Carson swallowed the pills. Chang scooted his chair back to the shelf, turned a gooseneck lamp to focus on his laptop keyboard, flexed his fingers and went to work.

"Not the first letter of every word," he said. "Not the last. Dammit."

Carson closed her eyes. It had felt right, basing the encryption key on the quote from the bracelet. "So much for hunches. Now what do we do?"

"Hey, come on. If they can code it I can crack it. Hey, wait a sec. I've got it! Just the thing, it's perfect, a little gem of a program I once wrote for a puzzle contest."

"A puzzle contest?"

"Yeah, it's kind of embarrassing, right? For the American Cryptogram Association. Bunch of retired crossword addicts and a few computer geeks too. I never thought this thing would come in handy but lemme see now . . . Yeah, this won't take longer than a minute or two. It'll run way faster on this baby than on the computer I used when I wrote it."

Chang's fingers flew across the laptop's keys.

"How're you doing, Connie? Pills working?"

"Yeah. I think so." The fire was subsiding; Carson welcomed the throbbing in its stead.

"Hey, hey, we nailed it. Whoa, look at this sucker, fourth letter in every word."

"What's it say?"

"Oh shit," Chang murmured under his breath. "Dammit to hell."

"It didn't work . . . " Carson felt utterly deflated by the letdown. She heard the chair wheels cross the floor.

Chang's dark eyes peered down at her from behind his spectacles. "No. It worked, all right," he said, "but here's the thing: they're not planning to go online with the heavy-water plant. There is no heavy-water reactor, never was a heavy-water reactor. Sindhu didn't send any 'copper bracelet'. The 'copper bracelet' is the organization, not some shortcut to a nuclear reactor."

"But what about those shipping manifests? Sindhu sent something."

"You know where the plant is, right?"

"On the Chenab River."

"It's an Indian-funded project, but the location is in disputed territory, between Pakistan and India."

"I know," Connie said impatiently. "Traditional enemies."

"With nukes," Chang added.

"Yeah. So?"

"So they didn't send copper piping and coils. They sent thermobaric explosives. They're going to blow the Baglihar dam sky high."

Just as the BlackBerry had been pre-planted in the drawer, the Browning Buck Mark .22 was taped inside the toilet tank. Jana appreciated the compliment. The .22 was a marksman's gun. A larger weapon would have been overkill.

The bathroom was easily as large as the room she had shared with her brothers growing up. White veined marble surrounded the tub and steam shower, aqua tile gleamed on the walls and floor.

She used the facilities quickly, flushed the toilet and turned on the hot water in the Jacuzzi, using the noise to cover the sound as she screwed the Gemtech Suppressor to the threaded end of the Trail-Lite barrel.

She jutted her head into the bedroom. Crane was naked on the bed, scanning the room service menu.

"Pierre," she said. "Come here."

Crane looked over the menu. "I was going to order us—"

"This is better," she said over the rushing water.

"In a moment," he replied as he reached for the telephone.

He ordered something.

She set the pistol down temporarily on the edge of the Jacuzzi, opened a jar of bath salts, the source of the jasmine aroma, and inhaled deeply. On the edge of the tub, white towels were folded into a thick stack.

She checked her appearance in the mirror over the twin sinks, rearranged her hair. "Please, Pierre."

Crane rolled from the bed and opened the door. He stood naked in the frame. "I've ordered us a bit of caviar—"

Jana stopped him just inside the doorway by aiming the silenced pistol at his knee. Not so close that he could move in and grab it away in one of his karate moves.

Shock registered in Crane's eyes.

"You're surprised, Pierre? This is what it's come down to. If you want to live, answer me. First, what do you know about Harold Middleton?"

A flash of recognition in his eyes. The man didn't try to bluff. "He's former U.S. military intelligence. Maybe a killer. I'm not sure. The implication is that he has some connection to the Scorpion. That's why I ended up in London. Look, I'm on your side."

"Where is he?"

"I don't know. I swear."

"What else do you know about him? Tell me."

"I didn't have much time to find out anything, if you recall. You stopped me at his flat."

"You're lying."

"I—"

"Tell me." She said it calmly, and that she didn't thrust the weapon forward theatrically seemed to scare him all the more.

"I did see something in his flat. A note. About his daughter."

"What about her?"

"Where she's staying in Paris. The Queen Elizabeth Hotel. Registered under her mother's maiden name."

Jana knew that the daughter sometimes worked for the Volunteers. She filed this new information away.

"The name?"

"Rosewald. I think."

"All right. Now tell me everything you know about the Scorpion. No games. No pillow talk. Facts."

His eyes were searching for his play. But he was naked and too far away to try marital arts. His look of betrayal was feigned; he hadn't trusted her to start with. And in any case, he knew deep down that she wasn't one to be moved by hurt looks or pleas for compassion.

"He bankrolled Sikari and a few others. Anonymously. But I'm not sure what he wanted from them. He's in it—whatever *it* is—for the money. If he's a he. I'm not even sure he is. He might even be a group. Think about that."

"What's the Dubai connection? Why are we here?"

He regarded her eyes and his lost their playfulness completely.

"The Scorpion is connected with BlueWatch," Crane said as calmly as he could. "Which is headquartered here."

Her eyes glowed at this information. "The security company. Yes . . . Tell me more."

"Their—and presumably the Scorpion's—interests currently involve India and Pakistan."

"And what are those interests?"

"I don't know that. I don't."

The reporter was now showing fear. She wondered if he'd start to cry.

"I'm asking you again: Do you know anything more about his identity?"

"No, I swear. Please, Jana . . . "

She believed him. "Another question: In the limo that night outside Paris, who were those men?"

"I thought you knew. You tried to kill them."

"I tried to kill them because I didn't recognize them. Tell me."

"I was led to believe one of them was the Scorpion. I was wrong. They never identified themselves other than that. They were trying to get information out of me, I assume. They sent me to Middleton's flat in London. But I don't know why."

His tone and delivery convinced her that he was being truthful.

Crane gave a weak smile. "Now I've done my part. Your turn to answer some of my questions." He reached for a towel to cover his nakedness.

She knew instantly this was a feint—his submissive pose gave him away. So she was fully prepared when he flung the towel in her direction and leaped forward in what must have been some classic karate move, swinging his long arm and knife-like flat hand directly at her throat.

She only had to step back two feet and pull the trigger several times.

The recoil was negligible.

10

JENNY SILER

Something was happening, Harold Middleton thought, listening to the muffled sounds emanating from the world beyond the cracked plaster walls of his cell. After so much uncounted time in solitary confinement, Middleton was like a blind man, his senses as finely tuned as the strings on Felicia's beloved Szepessy. He had learned to distinguish the various footsteps in the hall outside his door and what they meant: whether his meal of rancid soup would be served with an angry smirk or merely an apathetic one; if there was a purpose to the questions about to be posed to him or if the impending interrogation was merely a way of passing the time.

But this was different. There was an urgency to the raised voices and hurried movements that he had not heard before. From somewhere outside the boarded windows came the faint but steady thrum of an engine and the unmistakable hint of diesel fumes.

They were getting ready to move him: Middleton was almost certain this was the case, though why was less clear. Had one of the factions interested in him finally placed a winning bid? Or had the Russians grown impatient and decided to wash their hands of him—permanently? Given the circumstances, neither possibility boded well for his survival. If he was going to get out of this alive, Middleton decided, he would have to act now.

Quickly, he glanced around the room, searching for anything that might function as a weapon. His eyes lit on the ancient space heater and he lunged for it, kicking the cover with the sole of his boot, feeling the rusted screws that held it to the wall give way. Another kick and the cover swung open to reveal the glowing heating element, a crosshatch of naked metal. Sharp and hot, Middleton told himself as he delivered a third kick, knocking the element free in a shower of sparks. He could only hope it would be more effective in his hands than at its intended purpose.

There was a flurry of footsteps in the hallway just outside the door and Middleton recognized the voice of the sad-eyed Russian who'd visited him earlier. Pulling the sleeve of his jacket down over his hands, he picked up the red-hot element, slipped it into his pocket and hastily kicked the heater closed, praying the man would be in too much of a hurry to notice the mangled cover.

Almost instantly, the door swung open and his inquisitor, accompanied by a shorter, beefier and decidedly meaner looking compatriot in a black leather jacket and stiff jeans strode into the room.

"Out!" the brutish man commanded, producing a pistol from the waistband of his pants, motioning toward the door.

"What's going on?" Middleton demanded, taking note of the man's choice of weapon—a Russian military issue Yarygin PYa.

The sad-eyed man took a black cloth bag from his pocket and handed it to Middleton. "If you could be so kind as to put this on," he crooned in his cultured accent.

Middleton hesitated, feeling the weight and heat of the metal in his pocket, contemplating his options. If they were, in fact, moving him to another location he'd do better to wait until they were outside to use his makeshift weapon.

"I have other ways of asking that are not so nice," the Russian reminded him.

Reluctantly, Middleton took the bag and slipped it over his head.

A hand grabbed him roughly by the arm and he felt himself propelled forward, out the door and down the corridor, then down a narrow, twisting flight of stairs. In his blind state, he stumbled on a riser and pitched forward, his shoulder slamming painfully into the wall.

"Up! Up! Up!" the man with the Yarygin yelled, cursing Middleton in Russian, prodding him with the pistol. He smelled of fried onions, cheap tobacco and the saccharine stink of half-metabolized vodka. In the confines of the stairwell, the stench was overpowering.

Trying not to retch, Middleton staggered to his feet and resumed his hurried descent. He could hear more voices now, urgent shouting in Russian. *Hurry! Hurry!* and that engine again, louder and closer. Then, suddenly, there was a blast of frigid air and they were outside.

Middleton took a deep breath, trying to gauge exactly what was going on around him. Dim early morning light filtered in through the mask. The air was heavy with the odors of fast-food grease and industrial pollution. From the movements around him, he guessed that there were at least four men, possibly more, no doubt all armed. Still, if he could get the Yarygin away from his captor he might stand a chance. It was now or never.

Slipping one hand into his pocket and grabbing the heating element, Middleton reached up and pulled the bag off his head.

Before the Russian could react, Middleton whirled around, jamming the jagged end of the metal element into the man's eye. The makeshift weapon found its mark with a sickening thwack, lodging itself firmly in the guard's upper cheek.

The man groaned in pain. Middleton caught his gun hand and wrenched it backward. Delivering a sharp blow to the Russian's ribs with his free elbow, he pried the Yarygin free, then pivoted to face the others.

A split-second was all the time Middleton had to survey the situation, but it was long enough for him to realize that he was seriously outgunned. He'd been right about the five armed men, who were loosely gathered around a battered Niva, a low-rent Russian version of a Range Rover. What he hadn't anticipated were the other four guards manning the tall iron gate that blocked the entrance to the villa's courtyard. All were carrying light machine guns, Israeli Negevs from the looks of them.

One of the men by the Niva fired first, initiating a hail of gunfire. Fueled by a jolt of adrenaline, Middleton dove for the only cover available: the doorway he'd just come out of. Out of the corner of his eye he saw the beefy guard hit the ground, his chest riddled with bullets.

Crouched in the darkness, Middleton briefly considered his dwindling options. Fighting his way out of the courtyard, he knew, would be tantamount to suicide. The men had just shot one of their own; they'd kill him as soon as he stepped out the door. The only alternative was to head back into the villa, though this didn't seem any more promising. Already he could hear footsteps above him. Desperately, he rose up on the balls of his feet, willing himself to act.

But before he could do so, a deafening roar filled the air. It was a sound Middleton knew all too well, the unmistakable snarl of an incoming RPG. There was a flash of white-hot light and a single, thunderous clap. The force of the blast knocked Middleton off his feet, slamming him into the wall behind him, showering him with plaster. The villa shuddered, swaying and pitching like a boat on a swell. There was a sickening snap as one of the beams holding the ceiling up gave way. Then, in an instant, everything went black.

"Can't sleep?"

Leonora Tesla turned from the glowing screen of her laptop to see Charley Middleton framed in the doorway to the hotel suite's bedroom. "Looks like I'm not the only one. You should try, you know."

Charley smiled weakly. "So should you," she retorted, padding across the room, settling herself on the sofa. "Besides, it's morning."

Tesla glanced at the clock in the bottom corner of her screen and was surprised to see that it was almost five. "Barely," she said.

"What are you doing?"

"Just following a hunch."

"You want to fill me in? I'm not going anywhere."

The Queen Elizabeth Hotel, with its friendly, lived-in atmosphere and compliant staff, was a charming cage if ever there was one, but it was, for the time being at least, a cage nonetheless. After their confrontation with the well-dressed Brit, they were reluctant to venture outside the walls of the hotel. If that man could find them, Tesla knew, others could as well.

"I found out more about what your father was telling us about Sikari's younger days," Tesla said. "When he was a teenager, he was chosen, along with two other boys, to go to school in England. The whole thing was financed by an anonymous source. Six years at boarding school, then Cambridge. And after they graduated they were each given start-up capital. We haven't been able to figure out why, but we think it was some kind of social experiment. All three boys were Hindu, but one was Pakistani, one was Indian, and one—Sikari—was Kashmiri."

"Social experiment sounds kind of ominous," Charley remarked. "What makes you think it wasn't just plain old philanthropy?"

"That's what we thought before we found out that Sikari was the only one of the three still alive. The Indian, a man named Sanjiv Das, drowned in New Delhi twenty years ago, and the Pakistani, Santash Grover, died after drinking bad well water a few years later. Are you starting to see a pattern?"

Charley looked skeptical.

"That's not the only thing," Tesla continued. "Guess what all three studied at Cambridge?"

"Don't tell me."

"You guessed it: engineering, energy and hydrology."

"So who's the source?" Charley asked.

"There doesn't seem to be one. So far all Wiki's been able to find is an impressive collection of shell companies. But that's not what I'm interested in."

"No?"

"There's been so much focus on Sikari that no one's bothered to find out about the two dead men," Tesla explained. "I figured it wouldn't hurt to do some poking around."

Charley Middleton sat forward on the couch, propping her chin on her palms. "And? What did you find?"

Tesla scowled. "Not much so far. But then I don't have a lot to work with."

Charley pointed at black and white photograph of a group of people displayed on the screen. "What's that?"

"It's a ground-breaking ceremony. Some project Santash Grover's engineering firm was working on. I just pulled it up from the *Daily Dawn* archives." She pointed to a slim man in a western suit holding a shovel. "That's Grover."

"Who's the little girl?" Charley asked, leaning closer to get a better look at the lithe teen who stood slightly apart from the group. The intensity of her expression was disarming.

Tesla squinted to read the caption. "That's odd . . . "

"What?"

"This says she's Grover's daughter, Jana. But nothing else I've found so far has mentioned anything about him having a child. His obituary in the *Dawn* didn't list any survivors."

"Maybe it's a mistake."

Tesla looked from Grover to the child and back again. The girl's curly hair and mostly Mediterranean features were distinctly out of place in the predominantly South Asian crowd. But at the same time, her resemblance to Grover was uncanny. They both had the same high forehead, the same full lips.

"Or just maybe she's gone to great lengths to conceal her identity."

"What are you looking at?" Jana snapped as she ducked into the back of the limousine outside Le Bourget airport in Paris. Her young Moroccan driver had not been able to take his eyes off of her since they'd met outside customs, but now he quickly averted his gaze, looking down at the tips of his cheap dress shoes.

Normally, Jana might have welcomed the flattery, even from a mongrel like him, but she was in no mood for it this morning. She was furious she'd been forced to kill Crane and hadn't able to interrogate him further.

She'd spent hours trying to learn what she could about the connection between the Scorpion and the BlueWatch security company. Curiously, despite her considerable talents, she'd been able to find out very little; the company was shrouded in layers of corporate disguise, like a Russian *matryoshka* doll. Fortunately, though, one of the reasons she hadn't made much headway was that many BlueWatch employees had left the U.A.E. for a big mission. This in itself was an important find—all the more so when she learned that the flight plans had taken them to Mumbai and New Delhi.

She wasn't sure what to make of this yet. But she had some ideas.

She fought exhaustion. But in just two days, Jana reminded herself, she'd have all the time in the world to sleep. But for now it was imperative that she focus on the task at hand. She and Archer agreed to follow one lead that Crane had provided: Jana would fly to Paris and take Charlotte Middleton, preferably alive, to neutralize any danger from her father and find out what information the man had. She'd convinced Archer that Middleton was indeed a threat. At the very least, she could kill the woman; her death would distract Middleton and perhaps make him give up his mission altogether.

"Avenue Pierre 1er de Serbie," Jana barked as the driver climbed in behind the wheel, giving him the street address of the Hotel Queen Elizabeth. The man nodded, then pulled away from the curb, merging with the gleaming black stream of corporate limousines leaving Le Bourget and heading into Paris. Jana pressed a button on her leather armrest and raised the partition between them.

A French breakfast was laid out on the small bar: a selection of pastries on a china plate, a thermos of *café au lait*, butter in the shape of a rose, tiny jars of lavender honey and apricot conserves flanked by delicate silver spoons. Enough to feed a small nation, Jana thought, the excess making her suddenly uncomfortable.

Ignoring the food, she reached under her seat and pressed a small and discreetly placed lever. Immediately, the armrest popped open, revealing a Hawlen 9mm with a matching silencer and a half a dozen spare clips. Jana took the pistol from its hiding place and fingered it lovingly. Here, at last, was a luxury she could appreciate.

Harold Middleton opened his eyes to a roiling cloud of greasy black smoke. He couldn't have been out for more than a minute or two, but in that brief amount of time the drafty villa had been transformed into hell on earth. The ceiling, where it still existed, was crawling with flames, the walls baking hot to the touch. The air smelled faintly of burning flesh.

Middleton struggled to his feet, trying to orient himself. He'd lost the Yarygin in the explosion, but that was the least of his problems. The stairway he'd come down just moments earlier was gone, replaced by a gaping hole. A burning beam lay across the doorway, his only exit. Moving quickly, Middleton sloughed off his jacket and tossed it across the beam, hoping to temporarily douse the flames and create a narrow passageway for himself. The tactic worked, if barely. Seizing the brief window of opportunity, he leapt over the beam and barreled out the doorway.

The situation outside was only slightly less dire. Looking around him, Middleton was reminded of the puzzles Charley had loved when she was a little girl: drawings where everything was slightly off, where you could look and look and still not see the man wearing the shoe on his ear or the bicycle wheel that was really a button. Bodies lay scattered across the courtyard, several of them burning, one missing its head, another an arm. The Niva was engulfed in flames. Shards of glass and other debris from the villa littered the ground. The tall iron gate at the courtyard's entrance had been blown off its hinges.

An ordinary explosive device couldn't have caused this much destruction, Middleton knew, his brain slowly beginning to function once again now that he was out of immediate danger. No, this much damage had to be the result of a thermobaric bomb.

As he picked his way through the debris, heading for the gate, Middleton listened for the sounds of approaching emergency vehicles. It was only a matter of time before the fire department arrived and he didn't want to be there to welcome them. But, strangely, he didn't hear any sirens.

In fact, he suddenly realized, he couldn't hear anything. Not the roar of the inferno. Not the howls of pain from the guard by the gate with the metal rod stuck in his thigh. The explosion had numbed his eardrums.

Fighting back a wave of panic, trying to focus on anything besides the fact that he was stone deaf, Middleton forced himself to put one foot in front of the other and keep moving.

"Wait here," Jana told the driver as they pulled to a stop outside the front door of the hotel.

The man reached for the key, but Jana stopped him. "Keep it running," she said, opening the door for herself, swinging her black leather boots out onto the curb. "I won't be long."

It was not quite six o'clock when she stepped into the Hotel Queen Elizabeth. Her timing, if not perfect, was propitious. Half an hour later and she would have had to contend with a doorman and a bellhop, but at this early hour there was just a lone receptionist behind the front desk.

"May I help you?" the man asked, glancing up from his computer screen as Jana made her way across the small but elegant lobby. He used the formal *vous* to address her, but the tone of his voice was pure contempt.

Jana knew exactly what he was thinking: *What is this Arab whore doing in my hotel?* He was about to find out.

"Give me the key to Charlotte Rosewald's room," Jana demanded, approaching the front desk.

The receptionist raised a single black eyebrow. "Would Madame also like the combination to the safe?" he asked, with caustic sarcasm.

"The key!" Jana snapped, pulling the Hawlen from beneath her jacket, raising the silenced barrel to the level of the man's heart. "Now!"

Calmly, he glanced at the gun. "We don't use keys," he said, holding up a plastic card for Jana to see. His nails were perfectly manicured, coated with a thin layer of clear gloss. "I will have to program it for you."

"Do it," Jana told him, keeping the 9mm trained on his chest.

Charley put her ear to the bathroom door and listened with satisfaction to the sound of the shower running. She understood Leonora's reluctance to leave the hotel, but she was starting to go stir crazy. If she didn't get out and get some fresh air soon, she felt like she might hurt someone.

She wasn't asking for much, just a quick run and a stop at the patisserie across Avenue George V for something other than the disappointing croissants the Queen Elizabeth served. Once Tesla tasted a real *pain au chocolat*, all would be forgiven.

Besides, it wasn't like she was sneaking off. She'd left Leonora a note explaining where she'd gone and that she'd be back in an hour or so with breakfast. Still, she felt a twinge of guilt as she slipped into her running clothes and let herself out into the hallway.

The elevator was just outside the door of their room, but it was notoriously slow and creaky. More often than not she opted to take the stairs instead of waiting for it to creep upward. But for some unknown reason—lack of sleep affecting her brain, perhaps—she pushed the call button. Somewhere far below in the bowels of the building, the aged mechanism rattled to life.

The receptionist tapped the keyboard a few times, then swiped the card through the encryption device next to the computer before handing it to Jana.

"The room number?" she asked.

"Two nineteen," he sneered.

"How many guests?"

"Two women. One older and Madame Rosewald."

He was still sneering when Jana pulled the trigger.

Shoving the receptionist's body out of sight behind the desk, Jana headed for the stairs, sprinting for the second-floor landing. As she stepped in the hallway, she heard the elevator door slide shut. An early riser, she thought testily. No doubt there would be others. She'd have to work quickly.

Methodically, she made her way down the corridor, checking the room numbers as she went: 215, 217. Stopping in front of 219, she paused to listen. She could hear the elevator laboring noisily downward. And inside the room, the faint whine of water running.

With her left hand, Jana slid the pass card into the electronic lock and watched the light change from red to green. Keeping the 9mm ready, she turned the brass handle and let herself inside. So two occupants: Charlotte Middleton and presumably some babysitter her father had brought in.

Jana closed the door softly behind her and made her way across the small sitting room, moving toward the sound of the shower. Her wrists were locked in place, her finger light on the trigger of the Hawlen, her mind sharp. She nudged open the half-closed bedroom door and stopped, scanning the room, the two unmade beds.

Unless they'd taken to showering together, only one was here now.

Suddenly, the shower stopped. Jana heard the curtain slide open and the sound of someone climbing out of the tub.

"Charley?" a woman's voice called out.

The babysitter, Jana thought, squaring herself with the bathroom door, aiming for the height of an average woman's head.

"Charley?" The tone was slightly more urgent.

The door swung open to reveal a dark-haired woman, older but far from old, in a white bath towel. Seeing Jana standing there with the gun, she drew back slightly.

"Where is Charlotte Middleton?" Jana demanded.

The woman didn't answer. Her eyes were hard on Jana, searching for something. Then, suddenly, a look of recognition flickered across her face. "You're Santash Grover's daughter," she said triumphantly.

Jana flinched. It was impossible that this woman should know about her father and yet she did. "Where is Charlotte Middleton?!" she asked once again, reminding herself that any knowledge the woman had would soon be irrelevant.

The woman smiled. "Go to hell."

"You first," Jana told her, pulling the trigger.

11

DAVID LISS

The smoke, the heat of the fires, the falling debris, the ash that caked his mouth and choked his lungs—all these things were near unbearable, as was the clutching fingers of death at his heels, but what pained him most as he ran through this scene of destruction was the belief that for the rest of his life—whether the rest of his life spanned decades or minutes—he would never again hear the music he loved so much. His hearing was gone. No ringing. No hum. Nothing. Harold Middleton felt as though he were trapped in a horrible, violent snow globe, able only to peer helplessly at the world outside. He ran through the shattered compound, leaping over crumbled walls, scattered furniture, dead bodies, trying to find his way out of the destruction, holding on to the strange and childish notion that if he could escape soon enough, perhaps his hearing would be restored as his prize. He felt battered and bruised and hot but other than his hearing, no injuries seemed serious or permanent and for that he was grateful.

In his right hand he clutched a battered AK-47 he'd found among the ruins, scarred but its metal was not superheated. He'd fired off an experimental round—strangely disorienting in its silence—before heading off again, and now Middleton was glad he had picked it up, for as he turned a corner around a ruined, toppled wall, he saw two panicked Russians heading directly toward him. Behind them, a shattered wall spat out hot tongues of fire like an angry demon. One of them stopped in his tracks, as though stunned by the presence of another living being, the other better maintained his composure. He raised his weapon and began to fire off bursts of silent gunfire.

Middleton hit the ground, rolled and took shelter behind a twisted mass of metal and stone. He felt broken glass slice into his palm and in his silent world, the pain was somehow more vivid, more real than it would have been before. He felt rather than heard the impact of the rounds against his shelter and he crouched low, assessing his situation. He was protected here. He was safe for the next few seconds. He could form a plan.

It was all so absurd. Yes, he'd done high-risk work before with the Volunteers, but it was not that long ago he had been a professor of music, a man who investigated and verified musical manuscripts. Now here he was, in a destroyed, burning compound somewhere outside Moscow, fired upon by men whose affiliations and allegiances were a mystery to him. It was all a mystery to him. So much had happened since that day on the beach in the south of France and none of it made any sense at all.

In a dreamlike state that accompanies the loss of one of the senses, Middleton peered over his shelter. One of the Russians stood with his feet wide apart, his shoulders hunched, moving his weapon back and forth. He had a crazed, desperate look in his eye and at once it became clear that the Russian believed that if he could kill Middleton it would somehow lead to his safety, just as Middleton believed that if he could escape quickly enough, his hearing would return.

Middleton squeezed off a short burst, and the Russian went down. Now the second Russian, who had stood still and impassive, raised his own assault riffle. Middleton began to duck, but his shirt caught on a protruding piece of metal. It took only a second to disentangle himself, but that second should have been his end except the Russian went down in a spray of ash and blood.

Middleton felt it before he saw it, the faint *whump whump whump* of a helicopter. When he looked up it was hovering perhaps fifty feet above the wreck of the compound, perhaps two hundred yards from his current position. One man in the helicopter squatted with his weapon, scanning the chaos while another threw over a rope ladder and waved Middleton on. He shouted something, but Middleton could not hear over the noise of the chopper.

But he could hear that noise. His hearing was returning, along with the ringing, but his hearing was coming back.

Middleton had few choices. He could attempt to find his way out of this burning mess, fighting off more Russians as he found them, or he could take the escape offered by the helicopter. That seemed to be the better of the two options. He would worry about the chopper's BlueWatch logo later.

In her Paris suite, Leonora Tesla had fallen to her knees. She pressed her right hand against the wound in her left shoulder. It bled horribly, but it was not a life-threatening wound—certainly not if she could get medical attention soon. It hurt like hell and she tried to think clearly through the pain, see clearly through the tears of agony that clouded her vision. She still wore nothing but an oversized bath towel wrapped around her and absurdly she felt embarrassed. She should have worn something more appropriate to her own shooting.

Above her hovered the daughter of Santash Grover, the man who had studied with Sikari. Jana was tall for a South Asian, beautiful, dark in complexion, and she moved with a kind of ease and grace that Tesla could not help but admire. She was also very cruel. Tesla could see it in her eyes.

"That," said the woman in her accented French, gesturing with her weapon toward the wound, "is to let you know that I am serious. Nothing more than that. You may think you are in pain, but it is nothing compared to what you will feel if I shoot you in your knee. In addition, you will have the knowledge that you will never walk unaided again. Think of what will happen, then, if I shoot you in both knees. Take a moment to consider these things and then I will ask you again."

"I don't believe I will ever walk again in any case," Tesla replied in French, trying to think of something, anything, to give her more time, to throw this woman off balance. "You won't leave me alive. I suspect it is the way you work, but even if it weren't, I know you are Grover's daughter. You think you can kill me to contain the secret, but the secret is already out. I've already sent a dozen emails."

Something dark crossed the woman's face, but it was followed by a cruel smile. "Then I will have more questions to put to you. I only hope you will answer easily. Once I put bullets into your knees and elbows, any place else I shoot will have little effect. I've seen it happen that way."

"I'm sure you have," Tesla said with a grunt. Her eyes scanned the room around her, looking for something she might use as a weapon: a lamp, a phone, a phone cord, a chair. In truth, Tesla did not know how much torture she could endure before betraying what she knew. She supposed it was a good thing she knew so little. Apparently Charley was no longer in the suite; she had impulsively slipped out. Well, good for her. But she would be back. That was what Tesla knew or perhaps assumed. Charley would, sooner or later be back, and what would she find upon her return? Tesla's dead body, and this assassin waiting?

Jana held up her silenced pistol. "You do not get to ignore my question without me destroying your kneecap, so I hope you are prepared to answer me. Where is Charlotte Middleton?"

Tesla forced herself to grin broadly. "Why, she's right behind you."

The ploy ought not to have worked, indeed it would not have worked, had Tesla not looked so supremely satisfied when she spoke the words. All of this woman's training and instincts—and Tesla did not doubt they were considerable—failed in the presence of what seemed to be real human emotion. She turned and looked.

Though it caused her the greatest agony she had ever known, hoped she would ever know, Tesla sprang to her feet and slammed into the woman with her good shoulder, ramming into her like an American football player. She struck the assassin just below the ribs, and the pain was fierce in itself, but it reverberated throughout her body and felt as though someone had thrust a hot poker into her bullet wound. Tesla cried out, but so did the assassin.

The dark woman stumbled back and collided with a chair, which she tripped over, falling and hitting her head hard upon the carpeted floor. The carpet was not thick and the concrete below was heavy. Tesla heard the woman's teeth snap together and a trickle of blood began to flow at once from her mouth; Grover's daughter had undoubtedly bitten into her tongue. She still held onto the gun, however, and Tesla could not afford to wait to discover how stunned the assassin might be. In a sweeping gesture, graceful and excruciating, she raised the wooden chair as far as the wound would let her and smashed it down against the assassin's back. She wanted to stun her, to incapacitate her, but hopefully not to kill her. She wanted the woman alive and able to answer questions, but Tesla would kill her if she had to.

The pain rocked through her and she thought she might faint, but she willed herself alert, willed herself to ignore the agony. She hardly noticed that her towel had fallen off. She lifted the chair again, this time no higher than her waist. It felt impossibly heavy and she felt herself stumble both from her diminished strength and from dizziness. Her vision went black around the edges as she raised the chair, preparing to strike again. That was when the door opened.

Charley Middleton, her face glowing with perspiration, walked into the room carrying bags from a Parisian bakery. She froze, and Tesla could only imagine how shocking things must seem—this strange woman, motionless on the floor, mucusy blood oozing from her mouth, and Tesla herself, naked and bloody, wielding a chair like a club.

Tesla dropped the chair, fell to the floor and burst at once into tears and insane laughter.

By all rights Archer should have been afraid. Any sane man would be afraid. Well, he amended, any sane *normal* man, but he had never been a normal man, could not understand what it would be like to be a normal man. His brother Harris had been a normal man and Harris was dead. There was much truth to be learned from that simple fact.

He sat around a low table in a small village outside Jhelum in Pakistan, near the border of the Jammu and Kashmir. He sat with three men, all dark-skinned South Asians, and understood his own fair complexion was his greatest obstacle. He had always known it would be and he had calculated the solution. It seemed hardly possible to Archer that these men, with their suspicion of outsiders—their suspicion of everyone, really—could outmaneuver his calculations. Even so, for a moment Archer envied Sikari and the easy passage his appearance had brought him. He, a devout Hindu, had fooled these Muslims—fools, but clever fools. It could not have been easy for him and now Archer's task was that much harder.

Well, what of it? He had made it his life's work to deceive. He had deceived his brother, almost every day, greater and greater deceptions, only to see what he could get away with. *No, Harris, I don't know what happened to your books. No, Harris, I have no idea how the stolen whiskey bottle ended up in your room. No, Harris, I did not subscribe to those pornographic magazines in your name.* They were little things, of course, childish pranks, but then they had been children. But he'd taught himself how to lie, how to explain away the impossible, to make others believe him when his falsehood was so obvious.

Now he sat with the three men in the dark hovel. There was but a single light above them, a naked bulb powered by a generator that hummed outside. All three stared at him in hot suspicion and dull curiosity, but mostly only one spoke, their leader, a man named Sanam. He was very tall and painfully thin, with a long beard and very intense eyes. He wore the same white robes and taqiyah as Archer.

Sanam sipped his tea. "It is all very sudden," he said in Urdu. He had been switching all night from English to Urdu to Kashmiri to Arabic as if to keep Archer on his toes, to make him slip up, but Archer spoke all of the languages perfectly, just as Sakari had made certain he could.

"Death is often very sudden," said Archer. "My father's death is a terrible blow to me personally and of course to our cause, but it is also the will of Allah. My father has died and I will mourn him, but I will also honor him by continuing his work. It is unfortunate that he should die just as events are coming to a head, but we must not let our trials stand in the way of our goals."

"I do not love to hear this fair-haired American speak of Allah or the Prophet or the holy Koran," said Umer, one of the other men. Of the three men, he was the most uncomfortable with Sikari's disappearance from the scene. "All night you have sprinkled your conversation with such things as though you were salting your meat, but are we children to be so easily deceived? You do not look like a Muslim. You look like an American underpants model."

Archer sensed Umer would be his greatest obstacle. "I do not see how my European ancestors must keep me from following the path of Islam," he said, speaking now in Arabic. "My father raised me as a Muslim man ought to raise his son. That I am adopted is no matter."

Sanam nodded. "It would be a sin to doubt his faith because of his appearance. Nevertheless, you must understand our suspicions. These are dangerous times. We are hunted by the Pakistani government, your government, India's government. We must be cautious. We must be convinced you are who you say you are."

Archer laughed. "Who else could I be? I know my father spoke to you of his sons, so my existence cannot surprise you. Perhaps I am an agent of the CIA, an organization whose highest ranks concluded that the best way to infiltrate your organization would be to send a fair skinned, blue-eyed man. And, of course, the CIA has no higher priority than infiltrating groups that are primarily interested in the future of Kashmir." Continuing his sarcasm, he added, "And it is well known that the CIA has many agents who speak Arabic, and of course Urdu and Kashmiri."

Sanam snorted. "You raise good points. Your skill with languages ought to be enough to convince us you are not an American agent. Your knowledge of our ways and customs is impressive and seemingly natural, and the information you have offered us is not only vital, it corresponds with what we have been able to glean. My only question is, why should you care? Your father cared because he came of age in Kashmir and understood full well what it means to have our land in the hands of the infidels. You are, however much a Muslim, still an American. What does Kashmir matter to you?"

"It matters to me," said Archer, "because it mattered to my father. It was my father's jihad and so now it is mine. Is there one among you who thinks this is not reason enough?"

There were grunts of approval. Even Umer appeared satisfied and Archer was careful to keep his expression blank, to show no satisfaction. And he had every right to be satisfied. Something had shifted within the room, for Sanam now spoke much more confidently. "Let me hear how you think we should proceed and I hope you will tell me of your urgency. We have planned this attack for a long time. Why must we act within five days?"

Sanam, Archer believed, was a natural leader. His men revered him, much as Sikari's men had revered him. His was a band of some fifty or so men, an offshoot of the Harakat-ul-Mujahedeen group. It was Sikari that had convinced Sanam to leave Harakat-ul-Mujahedeen and form his own group committed to real, definitive, even final action in Kashmir. They had for years planned that event, lead by Sikari every step of the way. Sikari had used a different name, of course, convinced them that he was an Islamic extremist and so he had intended to play these men like pieces upon a chess board. He had set them up and now Archer would move them.

"The American secretary of state will be making an unannounced visit to the Baglihar dam in five days," said Archer. "I can think of no better time to attack. You will destroy not only this accursed dam which threatens to render feeble the Chenab River, but you will strike a blow against the American regime that will be felt all over the world. The secretary of state is well known—she is a household name in all nations. Her death will make certain the whole world understands the risks of taking India's side as it tries to steal Muslim land."

Sanam nodded. "There can be no better time. I agree with that."

"Even if the secretary of state were not to be there," Archer said, "the time would be upon us. Soon the Baglihar's secret heavy-water production facilities will be online. We cannot allow that to happen. We must strike soon and if we can strike *and* humiliate the American regime, I think it would be inexcusable not to take advantage of the opportunity."

Sanam nodded again. "You can get us what we need? What your father promised?"

"The explosives, yes."

"I shall consider everything you have said," Sanam announced, now rising from his table. "I will discuss it with my men and we shall let you know."

"Don't take too long," said Archer, rising himself. "We have much to do and little time to prepare."

"You shall have our answer within 12 hours."

In the car as he drove toward his border crossing, Archer listened to the men discuss their options. They had commandeered the house at random and once they were done, they would never return to it. They believed that made it safe. It certainly made it safe for Archer to bug the house. The listening device that Archer had left under the table would never be discovered because they had no reason now to sweep the room.

"We must do it," said Umer. "To finally be rid of the dam and to kill that vile woman at the same time. It will glorify Allah's name."

"So you are more trusting now?" asked Sanam.

Archer heard Umer snort. "I trust no one, you know that. But the American has arguments that are hard to refute. Who would send him to act against us? And what have we to lose? Let us agree with his plan and if the explosives appear where he says they will, we will use them. If not, we will not and we have sacrificed nothing. We cannot be any more hunted than we are right now. We cannot take more precautions than we already do. We exist to act and now is our opportunity to do so."

"I think so too," said Sanam. "And, if the truth be told, I like this American. He may be a white man with light hair, but he is one of us. I feel it."

As he drove his car, Archer laughed. One of them, indeed. He had just tricked these fools into their own destruction, into the loss of Kashmir and very possibly into the destruction of Pakistan.

Sanam's group would kill the American secretary of state. The Pakistani government, which would by then have obtained the falsified blueprints for the Baglihar dam, would naturally refuse to condemn the attack, instead accusing India of poisoning the waters of the Chenab. The Americans, outraged over the death of the secretary of state, will side with India, especially since they will regard the Pakistani claims of a heavy-water production facility as the nonsense they so clearly are. Both sides will be deceived and both sides will be utterly certain they are in the right. India, certain that Pakistan's claims are lies meant for the Muslim street, will be mad with the desire for revenge. Pakistan, believing itself wronged, will never forgive India and its Western allies. The inevitable result will be all-out war, with the Americans aiding India. Archer will goad Sanam into more attacks against American targets and soon the fight against Pakistan will be perceived as the center of the absurd War on Terror.

It was not easy to pass from Pakistan into Kashmir undetected and Archer had a difficult night yet before him, but a feeling of peace and contentment came over him. Major global events were now in his hands. Soon hundreds would be dead, then thousands, and they were like toy soldiers knocked about on a child's play table. The fight for the final disposition of Kashmir was about to begin. The only remaining problem was Middleton and his ridiculous Volunteers. Reviewing Sikari's notes, Archer was convinced his father had made a terrible mistake in targeting Middleton. Indeed, it was partially for that reason that he chose to kill Sikari rather than just killing his brother. Had his father left things alone, Middleton would never have known the value of the information he had gathered during his trip to India. Maybe he might have put it all together after the fact, but never in time to stop things. Now that he was hunted, Middleton and his team would be looking to make sense of it all and there was the danger that he would find what he did not know he had, that he would be able to piece the puzzle together in time.

That had been the danger while Sikari had lived, but that danger was past. By now, Middleton's daughter would be with Jana and the Volunteers would squander their time searching for her. Perhaps Jana would send them a finger or ear from time to time, to keep up their interest. By the time they realized that Charlotte Middleton's abduction was but a distraction, it would be too late.

At the thought of Jana, Archer felt himself growing erect. How he loved her. How he desired her. Sikari had always instructed Archer and Harris to regard her as a sister. Archer enjoyed that. It made things more interesting. He longed to have his sister with him now, but they would be together soon enough.

The journey by helicopter had not taken long, but by the time they landed much of Middleton's hearing was restored. How wonderful, he thought wryly, that the return of sound should be met by the monstrous roar of the chopper. The Russians who had pulled him in were a taciturn lot, and Middleton suspected they'd been instructed to tell him nothing, but that was fine. Answers, he knew, would be forthcoming.

Middleton glanced down at where they were landing: a beautiful mansion patrolled by "contractors" wearing the uniform of BlueWatch—the very company whose affiliate had funded Devras Sikari's education—and that he had betrayed by taking his marbles and going home.

He understood that the Scorpion had learned about him and had brought him here.

As they lowered onto the helipad atop one of the mansion's towers, Middleton had to laugh to himself over this irony. Why had BlueWatch rescued him? And what did they now want with their trophy?

The Russians on board the BlueWatch helicopter firmly, though not forcefully, escorted Middleton out of the chopper and then across the helipad and inside the tower. Only once inside, and away from the relentless noise, did Middleton realize how much his ears were still ringing. Still, he could hear the sounds of his footsteps, the rustle of clothing, the sound he made when he snorted in air through his nose.

One of the Russians, a man with a pale and pasty face and an alarmingly receding chin, and yet the shape of a body builder, led Middleton to the elevator.

"Colonel Middleton," he said in Russian-inflected English, "I understand if you would wish to clean up before greeting your host, but matters are very urgent. You may clean up afterwards, certainly."

"Well, that suggests I will still be alive," said Middleton, enjoying the sound of his own voice. "That's good news. I can't remember the last time I had a proper meal. Is there any chance my host can have his urgent conversation with me while I get something to eat?"

The Russian smiled as though indulging the whims of a child. "Mr. Chernayev can arrange anything."

"That must be gratifying," said Middleton.

The elevator brought them to a massive room that seemed to be very much like a lobby, though why a person should need a lobby in their own home was beyond him. The theme was baroque and everywhere were gilt statues and 18th century paintings in gilt frames and baroque settees along the walls. The body builder led Middleton to a hallway, with the same rococo theme, and then into a sitting room that was starkly modern, with chairs and tables with hard lines and sharp angles. On the walls were relatively contemporary portraits, but Middleton did not recognize who they were.

The body builder excused himself and Middleton found himself standing alone in the spacious room. He was not particularly cold, but he walked over to the fireplace and rubbed his hands before the fire, mostly because it was something to do and doing something distracted him from his own stench, hunger, fatigue and discomfort. Besides, his hands were filthy and bloody and he was hesitant to touch anything.

After no more than a minute, one of the doors opened and a pretty serving girl set down a tray upon one of the tables. It contained, much to Middleton's amusement, a hamburger, French fries and a glass of cola. Perhaps the body builder thought Americans were incapable of eating anything else. It would not have been Middleton's first choice, but it would do fine for now. He cleaned his hands with the warm towel to one side of the tray and then devoured the food within minutes.

Shortly after he was done, the door opened again. Middleton had been hoping for the pretty serving girl, as he'd been hoping for a refill of his soda, but it was not her.

The man standing before him was easily recognizable from the intelligence reports and press photos.

Arkady Chernayev.

And the pieces fell into place. Chernayev was the Scorpion.

The man was tall and elegantly handsome, a man who appeared in the vaguely ageless realm of men in their fifties or sixties who were in excellent physical shape and who dressed in impeccable clothes. Chernayev wore a dark suit with a perfectly knotted red tie and a high-collared white shirt. He appeared very much like a politician about to give a televised address.

"Colonel Middleton, I am pleased you are well. You have had enough to eat and drink, I hope," said Arkady Chernayev.

Middleton held up his glass. "I could use some more cola."

"Yes," said Chernayev, "being rescued from a burning complex is a thirsty business."

At once the serving girl appeared with a fresh glass. She took Middleton's old one and departed. Chernayev now gestured for Middleton to sit on one of the chairs near the fire. He did so. The Russian joined him.

"So," said Chernayev, "I understand you wish to ask me some questions."

"I do. And I have some that have just occurred to me."

Chernayev smiled very thinly. "I can imagine. You want to know why, perhaps, I attacked the compound."

"I was going to start with *if*," said Middleton, "but I am happy to move along to *why*."

"The why is simple enough. You have some very important information and I need it to get out into the world. The men who held you did not care about such things."

"Who were they?"

"They call themselves the Group. A name very preposterous in its simplicity, in my opinion, but its vagueness suits them. Their predecessors were formed in the late years of the Second World War, a gathering of scientists and academics and politicians who gathered together the leavings of the Nazi nuclear program. Mostly Germans and Russians. But they are not weapons traders, not exclusively. They do hope to exert their pressure upon world events."

The cult that his friend Ruslan was telling him about, the outfit that wanted to resurrect the copper-bracelet technology.

"You say that with such contempt," said Middleton. "You don't approve."

"I disapprove of how they do so, not that they do so at all. I would be a hypocrite to take issue with them, for I am guilty of such things myself. I take you into my confidence now, Colonel Middleton, and I hope you understand I would not do so were events not so dire. You see, I too try to shape world events, but for nobler reasons, I hope. In that capacity, I go by a code name—"

"The Scorpion."

"You know that?" he asked, surprised.

Middleton nodded.

Chernayev held up a hand as if to ward something off. "I know, I know. It is absurd. I absolutely need my anonymity, you understand that. The name 'Scorpion' was given to me against my will, but that is another story. There are so many other stories and there will be time for all of them later, but for now I know you must be tired and in need of a shower, so this meeting will be short. There is but one thing I require of you, Colonel Middleton."

"And what is that?"

"The American secretary of state will be paying an unannounced visit to the dedication of the Baglihar dam in a few days' time. It's important for you to be present on that visit."

"Where is that?" he asked.

"On the Chenab River in northern Kashmir. The nearest town is a re-settlement of people displaced when the dam was built. I don't recall the Indian name but everyone knows it as the 'Village.'"

In her Paris hotel suite, Leonora Tesla was now fully dressed, though her hotel towel turned makeshift bandage had soaked through and was stain-ing her dark blouse. Charley Middleton stood over Jana, Grover's daugh-ter. She sat on the floor, her hands tied behind her back with telephone cord, her feet tied together with an electrical cord ripped from a lamp. Her mouth was gagged with a torn shirt.

Charley Middleton held the gun, Tesla a letter opener she had found in the suite's desk.

"Nora, we really should get you to a hospital," Middleton said.

"It's mostly stopped bleeding. We'll go to the hospital soon enough, but we'll have to figure out what to do with her first."

Tesla set down the letter opener, removed the gag from the assassin's mouth and quickly stepped away. She picked up the letter opener once more.

"So," said Tesla, "perhaps you will tell us who wants Ms. Middleton and why?"

The woman looked up at both of them, her eyes dark with hatred and contempt. In French, she said, "There is no amount of pain I cannot endure."

Tesla met her gaze. "Let's find out if that is true."

12

P. J. PARRISH

A whimpering sound drew Tesla's eyes to the corner.

Charley was slumped against the wall. The Hawlen 9mm was still in her hand, but the barrel, with its long silencer, was pointed at the floor.

"Charley!" Tesla said sharply. "Keep the gun on her."

Her eyes came up, brimming with tears. When she raised the gun, she had to hold it with two trembling hands.

Tesla turned back to Jana, who was seated on the floor in front of her. Her dark skin glistened with sweat and her breath was coming so fast and shallow Tesla could actually hear the whistle of air through her lips as she struggled to keep calm.

For the third time, Tesla snapped a flame from the lighter and positioned the blackened tip of the silver letter opener over it. A slither of smoke curled from the blade—not from the char of the silver, but from the sear of the tiny bits of flesh that clung to it.

As she reached toward Jana's face, a memory flicked into her head. The beach at Cap d'Antibes. Harold questioning Balan in the same manner he questioned all suspects, no matter how vile their crimes.

Respectful, measured interrogation. There was no point in abusing prisoners, he said. It was counterproductive.

Tesla pushed Harold's face and words from her mind. That was him, not her.

Tesla held the letter opener in front of Jana's face. The woman's eyes filled with defiant tears. Her dark hair was matted with blood from the gash inflicted when Tesla hit her with the chair. And her lip was swollen from Tesla's fists. Nothing had made her even flinch. Until Tesla had brushed the red-hot metal of the letter opener against the smooth olive skin of Jana's finely sculpted cheekbone.

Vanity. That was the key to unlock this woman's tongue.

"Why are you trying to kill Charley Middleton?" Tesla demanded.

Jana shut her eyes.

"Who are you working with?"

Jana pressed back against the wall, trying to get away from the letter opener.

Tesla warmed its tip again, holding it to the flame until it glowed red. Then she pressed it against Jana's cheek.

Jana jerked to the side and screamed.

As Jana slid to the carpet, a cell phone fell from the pocket of her trench coat. Tesla saw the woman's eyes skitter to it. She snatched it up and tossed it out of reach.

"Who are you working for?" Tesla demanded.

"I never tell you," Jana whispered in English through gritted teeth. "I never betray him."

"Betray who? The Scorpion? Your father? He's dead."

"Dead," Jana whispered. "You to be dead soon." She looked to Charley. "Her too."

Tesla pressed the letter opener to Jana's cheek again. She screamed again as the smell of burning flesh filled the room.

"Stop!" Charley Middleton screamed.

Tesla's eyes spun.

"Stop it! Stop it!"

Charley had wedged herself in a corner, covering her mouth with one hand. The gun dangled from the other.

"Charley," Tesla said evenly.

But she wasn't listening. She was sobbing now. Tesla stared at her, debating whether to go to her or make her leave the room. But the bullet wound in her own shoulder was throbbing and even with Jana bound and weakened, she didn't trust herself to handle things alone right now.

And she had promised Harold she would keep Charley safe. That was the last thing he had asked of her as they parted in London. He told her of his plan to get into Russia and when she insisted on going with him, he had asked her to meet Charley in Paris instead.

Nora, I can't lose her.

Late that night, as Tesla had lain curled against his sweating chest, the sheets damp with their lovemaking, she had felt a rawness, a sadness, in Harold Middleton she had never felt before. His guilt was palpable over putting his beloved daughter in jeopardy over what he called "this quixotic crusade." In the dark, she had held him and promised to protect her.

"Poor little Charlotte."

At the sound of Jana's voice, Tesla's eyes swung back to the dark-eyed woman pressed against the wall.

"Shut up!" Tesla hissed.

Jana managed a swollen smirk. In French she said, "The daughter does not have the courage of the father."

"I said shut up!" Tesla swung and hit Jana hard with the back of her hand. The cut on Jana's lip ripped open, spraying blood on the wall.

"Stop it!" Charley cried. "No more, Nora, please!"

Tesla stared at her. What was this? Where was this coming from? For the last fifteen minutes, as Tesla had interrogated Jana, Charley had been quiet. Even as Jana's moans of pain had grown deeper, Charley had not moved, not made a sound. Now, suddenly, she was coming apart.

"No more, Nora," she whispered. "Please. Please. I can't take this. I can't do this anymore."

Suddenly, Tesla knew. For all her bravado, Charley had never witnessed anything like this—the interrogation and torture of another human being. A woman, no less. Despite Harold's willingness to let Charley play around the periphery of the Volunteers, he had never brought her into the violence of its world. Charley Middleton had hacked computers, done research. Her reality was virtual. Her hands were clean.

But her own past was clouded with violence. The brutal murder of her mother by her father's enemies. The betrayal and death of her husband. The loss of her baby.

Another thought flashed through Tesla's head. Yesterday, in a café, Charley let her guard down long enough to talk about her mother's death and what she said after. *I know you and Harry were lovers and I used to hate you for that but I don't now. I admire you, Nora.*

And second flash of memory. The threat she had made to Ian Barrett-Bone yesterday in the taxi as Charley listened: *I'll kill you for the sheer pleasure of it.*

Charley's sobs filled Tesla's ears. She glanced back at Jana, whose dark eyes glittered with hatred.

"Poor little Charlotte," Jana said, her voice almost maternal. "Death is around you. Mother, husband. Your baby cut from your—"

Tesla spun and smacked Jana hard, sending the woman into a spasm of coughing and spitting blood.

A soft thud. From the corner of her eyes, Tesla saw Charley slump to the carpet.

One second of diversion but it was enough. Jana brought her bound wrists up in a quick jerk, catching Tesla under the jaw and sending her reeling backwards. The letter opener went flying.

A second blow hit Tesla in her wounded shoulder. White knives of pain sliced through her body. For a second, the room swirled gray-going-black and she felt herself drop down to her knees.

Jana was just a blur, flailing and pulling against the electrical cord on her ankles.

Tesla fought back the waves of pain and nausea, one thought in her head. *Gun . . . get the gun.*

Tesla threw herself toward Charley's body. The dark barrel of the gun was just visible beneath the blue of Charley's running suit. Tesla grabbed the Hawlen, jerked to a kneeling position and leveled it, finger curled on the trigger.

She blinked the room back into focus.

Nothing. Just a flash of black boots and white trench coat disappearing behind the open door of the hotel room.

Jana stumbled down the stairs but when she hit the hotel lobby, she froze. A large man in a green windbreaker and ball cap was standing at the desk. His face was red and he was banging the bell on the desk.

"Hello? Hey, anybody here?"

From her vantage point, Jana could see the shoes of the dead clerk be-hind the desk but the American could not. A commotion at the door as a fat woman tried to drag a huge suitcase through. Beyond the window, Jana could see the open trunk of a taxi and the driver, letting loose a stream of crusty French as he pulled out more luggage.

The taxi was double-parked, blocking her limo. And there was no one behind the wheel.

Where the hell was her driver?

Then she spotted the Moroccan across the street buying cigarettes at a tabac. Jana cursed as she gently touched a finger to her seared cheek.

A sound behind her on the stairs. The bitch was after her. There was no time.

She bolted down the narrow hallway to the back. The tiny kitchen was a blur as she threw open the door and stumbled out into the cold morning air. A quick look told her she was in an impasse with one exit.

No choice. She would have to take her chances on the street. Jana began to run.

In the lobby, Tesla quickly assessed the situation. Body behind the desk, two bewildered and bedraggled Americans. But no Jana.

Holding the Hawlen at her side, Tesla scaled the mountain of luggage blocking the door, ignoring the American man's yelling. She slid to a stop on the street.

Tesla mentally clicked through the options with computer-speed.

Taxi? You couldn't hail one on any Paris street and there were no cabs at the nearby stands.

Metro? The nearest was George V, a good five-minute hike.

No, Jana would try to contact the person who had sent her.

Tesla gave the street a quick scan. Even at the busiest times of day, rue Pierre 1er de Serbie was a staid street of stone-facade apartment buildings. Now, at seven on this cold October morning, there was only one café owner out, the crank of his unrolling shutters breaking the quiet.

Except . . .

A lone figure in white just disappearing around the far corner. Tesla took off in pursuit.

But when she reached the corner, she came to an abrupt stop.

A swirl of motion, sound, smells and people.

Damn. Saturday. Market day.

Tesla started down the narrow aisle, eyes darting between the overflowing stands of vegetables, fruits, fish and cheeses. The crowd pressed close— young women pushing strollers, old women toting straw baskets, boys on mopeds. Tesla was careful to keep the gun down, hoping her loose slacks offered some cover. The last thing she needed was a panicked crowd.

She pushed on, her eyes raking the crowd for Jana. The woman couldn't go unnoticed for long. Her face was a pulpy mess and her white trench coat was covered in blood.

Where the hell was she?

Tesla grimaced in pain. She caught a glimpse of herself in a café window. Wild hair and a fresh stain of blood on her blouse from her seeping shoulder wound.

Her reflection was framed by orange and black crepe paper hung from the café window. Paper skeletons and black cats. Halloween. Today was Halloween, a holiday the Parisians had just recently appropriated from Americans. Tonight the Champs d' Élysées would teem with drunken kids in vampire teeth and theater blood.

Two women stumbling down the street drenched in the real thing would hardly get a glance today.

Twenty yards away, a flash of white amid the riot of color at a far stall. Tesla reached the flower stall just as Jana disappeared again. To the left was a narrow alleyway, just like the impasse back at the hotel. Tesla made a quick choice and raced to the open door about half-way down.

Kitchen. Deserted.

A brush of a heavy drape and she was in the bistro's small dining room. A thin man in a white serving coat had been folding napkins but now was just staring.

"Where did she go?" Tesla demanded.

The young man's eyes widened when he saw her gun.

"*La femme dans blanc! Où est-elle allée?*"

"*La bas.*" He pointed to a spiral staircase.

Removing the silencer, Tesla drew in a shuddering breath and started down the narrow stairs.

She quickly searched the two small toilets. Nothing. There was a third door. It opened into a small dark storage room. Tesla slapped the cold wall and her hand found a switch. The small room came to life under the single hanging bare bulb. Rough stone walls, a cracked tile floor. Piles of old tables, broken bistro chairs, boxes and crates. It was filled with junk, except for a path leading to the wine rack that stretched across the length of one stone wall.

Tesla swept the gun slowly across the shadows. She knew Jana didn't have a weapon but she wasn't taking any chances. She crept through the debris, her two-handed grip on the Hawlen tight.

She stopped and stood perfectly still, listening for any sound.

Nothing.

But then she felt it. A hard stream of cold air at the back of her neck.

She spun and leveled the gun toward the bistro chairs. She approached carefully, her eyes alert for any movement behind the ten-foot-high tangle of legs and shredded rattan seats. The stream of air grew stronger.

Tesla grabbed a leg atop the pile and gave a sharp pull. The top chairs clattered to the tile, one clipping the hanging bulb, sending it swinging wildly.

Jesus.

A small open door in the stone wall. With each sway of the bulb, Tesla could glimpse what lay beyond.

Tunnels. Not stone but some rough gray-white material. A low curved ceiling not more than six or eight feet above the dirt floor.

A dusty stench poured out.

What was this?

But then the odd smell registered. Chalk?

And with that came a flash of memory. Harold . . . that night five years ago when, in the highest heat of their affair, he had brought her here to Paris for a weekend. Dinner at Taillevent, a three-hundred-euro Haut Brion. And to impress her even more, a trip to the restaurant's wine cellar. There, the sommelier told them that the sleek vault used to be a dank cave, part of a network of tunnels below Paris that had once been the city's thriving chalk quarries. The tunnels ran for hundreds of miles below apartments, cafés and shops. All but a few had been abandoned and boarded up.

Tesla drew in a breath and stepped into the darkness.

The swinging bulb offered up moving slices of black and white. But beyond thirty feet, all light disappeared.

Tesla stood perfectly still, senses pricked for the slightest sound of movement. The drug-rush of adrenalin had dulled the pain in her shoulder.

She advanced slowly. With the dying sway of light, she could see now that the tunnel ahead branched off into two others.

A skitter. Rats.

A drip of something on her neck. Water.

A smell of something dead and close.

The blow came from the left, aimed at her bad shoulder. But she was quick enough to jerk away so the wine bottle hit her upper arm instead.

Tesla gritted her teeth against the pain and gripped the gun tighter.

A crash over her head and she was sprayed with glass and doused in something cold. Another bottle exploded and she shut her eyes against the sting of the wine in her face.

Nearby, a slap of wood against wood and Tesla saw Jana fleeing out a service door. Struggling to control the pain, struggling to breathe, the wounded woman followed her assailant as quickly as she could.

The foot pursuit, south through subdued streets of upscale townhouses and private hotels, seemed to last forever and ended only when Jana streaked across L'avenue de New York, making for Pont d'Alma. But despite her pain and exhaustion, Tesla closed in. And just as Jana made it to the bridge, she collapsed. Unable to see any further, hiding the gun, Tesla hurried through the traffic, heading directly for her assailant.

Jana managed to pull herself to her feet. She glanced up and saw that Tesla had now crossed the road and was getting closer.

Resignation and despair filled Jana's dark face.

Had Tesla not been in such pain, had she not seen in vivid memory the young NATO soldier's arm shredded by the blast Jana had ordered, had she not known what carnage this woman was capable of, she might've felt pity for her.

But Jana's face clearly explained that she knew the end had come and that she wasn't going to allow herself to be tortured any longer. She glanced over the side of the Pont d'Alma toward the Seine and noticed the approach of one of the famed *bateaux mouches*—the "fly boats" that take tourists up and down the river. Jana's eyes met Tesla's and they struggled up the railing of the bridge.

"No!" Tesla cried, thrusting out her hand.

Jana hesitated only a moment and then tumbled into the murky water, directly into the path of a boat. Tesla saw her vanish under the prow.

The ship passed, the captain unaware of the tragedy. The tour guide's voice echoed uninterrupted over the water. Tesla waited only a moment until she could see in the wake the outline of the woman's torso, floating on her belly, arms outstretched, head bent completely under the brown water.

A police car was just arriving as Tesla returned to the Queen Elizabeth hotel. She detoured to the impasse entrance and went upstairs. The door to their room wasn't locked.

"She's gone," Tesla whispered. "Dead."

Charley was curled on the sofa, hugging her knees. She looked up at Tesla, face ashen.

"It won't stop," she said.

Tesla set the gun on a table. Charley was in shock. She went and sat down next to her.

"It's OK, Charley," Tesla said.

"It won't stop."

"I know. But—"

"The phone," Charley said. "It won't stop."

Tesla's whole body ached and her head was spinning. But she realized that Charley was staring at something on the carpet. It was Jana's cell phone.

Tesla picked it up. The screen showed five calls and three messages. "Did you answer it?" she asked.

Charley just shook her head.

Tesla quickly scrolled through the calls. All from the same number but she didn't recognize it. She punched in the message retrieval. The first one was in Hindu, unreadable to her. But the second was in French: ÒU ÊTES-TU?

It was the third one that made her stop. It translated to REPORT CM MISSION STATUS.

CM? Charlotte Middleton? But what was the mission?

Tesla hesitated then punched in a text response in French: MISSION ACCOMPLISHED.

Immediately, the cell hummed then the message appeared: ALIVE OR DEAD?

So there was her answer. It was Harold's daughter they wanted. But why? Then she realized that she hadn't heard from Harold since he left—from either his regular cell or his encrypted one. Which meant he had either been apprehended—or killed. One call to Charley or her would have pinpointed their locations. Harold did not want his daughter's whereabouts discovered.

Tesla looked over at Charley, rocking slowly back and forth.

Bait, a distraction. That is what Charley was. They wanted to use her against her father somehow. She was his one weakness and if Harold thought she was in danger, they knew he would do anything to get to her.

Suddenly, Tesla knew what she had to do.

She punched in a text response. CM DEAD.

Tesla shut her eyes, waiting for the response. When it came, her blood chilled.

SEND PROOF.

Again, she looked to Charley. Could she do this? Could she get this shattered young woman to help?

Tesla went to the sofa and took Charley's hands in hers. "Charley, I need you to listen to me," she said gently.

Charley just looked up at her.

"Charley, I need to take a picture of you."

"Picture?"

Tesla scanned the wreckage of the room. She spotted the bloody blouse she had used as a gag on Jana. "Help me, quickly," she said.

Leading Charley by the hand, she picked up the blouse and took Charley over to where Jana had been sitting. "Put this on," Tesla said.

Charley recoiled. "What?"

"Please, Charley, we don't have much time."

"Why? What—"

"Charley, this will help your father. It will help Harry."

"Harry?"

"Put the blouse on."

Charley shook her head. "No, not unless you tell me why. Where's Harry? What's happened to him?"

Tesla bit back her impatience. She quickly told Charley that her father was in Russia and that he couldn't do what he needed to do unless he believed she was safe.

"Then why do you want him to think I'm dead?"

"Not your father. I want whoever sent Jana after you to think you're dead. Your father has to be able to . . . to do what he needs to do. Can you understand that?"

Charley looked away.

"Charley, do you trust me?"

She nodded slowly but wouldn't look at her.

"Then please do what I'm asking you to do. Please."

Charley took the bloody blouse and slipped it over her t-shirt. But then she stopped and went to the desk.

"Charley?"

She scribbled something with bold strokes of a felt pen and brought the paper back to Tesla. "Put this in the picture," she said.

Tesla took it. Charley had written three words: GREEN LANTERN. EVAC.

"What is this?"

"When I was little, Harry and I made up a code in case I ever got in trouble. Mom thought it was stupid but we . . . " Her eyes filled with tears. "Green Lantern is our favorite comic book hero. 'Evac' means I've gone somewhere safe to wait for him to come get me."

Tesla hesitated then wrapped Charley in a hug.

It took just minutes to position Charley for the photograph. She posed, slumped against the wall, with the backdrop of Jana's blood on the wall and carpet. Tesla positioned the note so it looked like a harmless piece of paper spilled from a waste basket.

Tesla was sending the photograph by the time Charley emerged with her suitcase. Downstairs, they hurried out the kitchen, avoiding the quickly expanding crowd around the dead clerk in the lobby.

A plan was already forming in Tesla's head. She would send Charley on the first plane to the States. Once Charley was safe, she would find a way to get to Harold.

Jana's cell buzzed. As they exited the hotel and started along rue Pierre 1er de Serbie, Tesla glanced at the cell's screen.

One word in English:

BEAUTIFUL.

13

BRETT BATTLES

"You must know what Sikari has in mind," Harold Middleton said to Chernayev. His blood had run cold when the Russian had told him the U.S. secretary of state would be visiting the Baglihar dam. He told the man about the email message from Sikari to Kavi Balan—the plan for the Village. To blow up the dam with the thermobarics explosives from Florida. Middleton now understood.

Chernayev seemed to consider Middleton for a moment. "Sikari is dead," he said.

"Dead?" The American gasped.

"By his own arrogance, from what I understand. A man he called his adopted son has assumed control of Sikari's interests. Sikari's interests were in the dam itself. It is the son, Archer, who has seen the opportunity the secretary of state's visit will create."

Middleton stared at nothing, stunned by the news. The whole point of the Volunteers' mission was to find Sikari and bring the war criminal to justice. And yet even with the man gone, it seemed more horrifying events were now in motion.

"But you're responsible, Chernayev. You sold him the explosives."

"No! My companies sell explosives, yes. And I shipped some to the site of the dam, along with a lot of other materials. I'm a partner in the construction project."

"Thermobarics are military grade."

Chernayev gave a faint smile. "That's why I had to ship them in a, let's say, circuitous route. My engineers didn't want to use TNT. The foundation work takes forever. They wanted the real thing."

"Well, that real thing is going to be used to blow the Village to smithereens."

Chernayev grimaced. "You traced me through a company of ours in Tampa, right? Sindhu Power."

"That's right."

"Before we closed it up, we were robbed. Explosives were stolen."

That explained why Sikari was interested in the place. And why the thieves had left the bomb that killed Jean-Marc Lespasse.

"Still, you funded Sikari's education."

"Ah, the past . . . the past. How I wish we could change it. Yes, I recognized him as brilliant, one of the sharpest young men I've ever known. I wanted him to work for me, creating lower cost nuclear energy for developing countries. We had a falling out. I didn't like where he was going. He wasn't interested in peaceful use of heavy metal. He was interested in weapons. But would he listen? No. Like so many young idealists, he wanted to go back to his home country and fight for independence."

"And the technology that the Group is after?"

"What Sikari developed was based on the old Nazi copper-bracelet theory. But what he created was only partially successful. It wouldn't operate as a super-generator the way he wanted . . . Look, I'm a businessman, Colonel Middleton. I make more money off the living than the dead. If something happens to the American secretary of state, it's not just war in the Indian sub-continent we will need to worry about."

Harold Middleton wasn't sure he believed everything the Russian said, but it was true that if the secretary were assassinated the whole world would reel from the repercussions.

If this Archer Sikari were truly moving forward with his father's plan, then the arrival of the secretary of state would be too irresistible to pass up. One of the goals the secretary had laid out not long after being sworn in was to ease the tensions between India and Pakistan with an emphasis on the troubled region of Kashmir. This was undoubtedly the reason she was traveling to the area.

Middleton said, "We've got to contact the State Department immediately."

"Of course they've been notified. But they're in agreement that the visit should go on. Security is going to be very high—both State Department and my company, BlueWatch. In any case, we have no knowledge that Archer even knows about the visit."

"Why do you want me to go there?"

"It's not just me." The Russian handed Middleton a decoded communiqué from the State Department. He recognized the name of one of the deputy directors. It authorized Middleton and the Volunteers to locate Archer Sikari and coordinate with local authorities to arrest him. A final paragraph added that Tesla, Carson and Chang had been notified and had acknowledged receipt. That meant they were fine.

Middleton noticed the document didn't say anything about Charley.

"I have to contact my daughter."

"Encrypted emails only," Chernayev said. "My compound is constantly scanned for cell and text signals."

He wrote out a message for Charley. Chernayev gave it to a young man in a BlueWatch uniform. He hurried off to send it.

"Now, will you go to Kashmir?"

"Of course," Middleton said.

"One of my men will take you to a room where you can get some rest. Arrangements are being worked out now and as soon as everything is ready, you will be on your way." He held out his hand to Middleton. "I wish you a safe and successful journey."

Middleton looked at the Scorpion's hand, then reluctantly reached out and shook it.

As Archer knew he would, Sanam had called him to tell him that they were ready to carry out the plan. Archer had already set in motion the delivery of the explosives through his American subcontractors. Within 36 hours, Sanam's men had begun placing the charges in the pre-determined locations within the dam.

Archer felt extremely satisfied. The only thing left to be determined was where he was going to be at the time of the big event. The dam was located in a mountainous rural area, but there were plenty of places he could choose where he would be able to see the dam as it crumbled into a useless pile of cement, carrying the secretary of state to her death.

Most of the locations were only reachable by helicopter, but that wasn't a problem for him. With his father's fortune now at his disposal, he could purchase a fleet of helicopters if need be.

He could feel the power that was rippling just below his skin. It was an electrical force he could only dream about before. On all those nights when he and Harris shared a room, and after his brother had fallen asleep, Archer had let his mind imagine this very moment—this time when he would be in charge. When he would be the power.

If there was one thing that troubled him, it was Jana. She was his sword and his lover, but he hadn't heard her voice in over two days, not since before she had forwarded him the photographic proof that Charlotte Middleton was dead.

Too bad for that. He had hoped they would have been able to take Harold Middleton's daughter alive. But better dead than running free.

Jana sent a text that said she would come to him as soon as she could, but that a member of Harold Middleton's Volunteers was trailing her, so she would have to take care of that problem first.

He so wanted to call her, but refrained. Their procedure was to avoid voice contact. This had been Archer's idea. He wanted no one to know what his voice sounded like. Even with the absolute best encryption, there was always a chance that someone somewhere would be able to break it.

Archer's power would rest in his ability to remain a ghost, feared and unknown.

So until she arrived, he would have to content himself with the anticipation of having her at his side.

Something he was already practiced at doing.

"We have a problem," Umer whispered to Sanam.

They were sitting in a small restaurant in a village 20 kilometers from the Baglihar dam. The restaurant was really the front room of a dilapidated shack. The rest of the shack served as the home for the family that ran the place.

At the moment, Sanam and Umer were the only customers. The young boy who had been serving them had gone into the back to leave them in peace while they ate.

"What is it?" Sanam asked.

"The remote controls for the detonators."

"What about them?"

"They don't work."

Sanam froze for a moment, startled by his old friend's words. "They are defective?"

"Not exactly. When we put them inside the dam, there is too much concrete. The signal must not be getting through."

"But they work otherwise?"

"I had one of the men smuggle a remote back out and I tried it. Outside, it worked fine."

The idea of eating no longer appealed to Sanam. Everything they had been working toward, the years of infiltration and manual labor, all the pressure he'd put his men under for the last two days, it was all for nothing. And the opportunity they were going to squander, undone by something as simple as a blocked radio signal. How could this have even happened?

"The American," Umer said, "we shouldn't have trusted him. He's given us equipment he should have known would not work."

Sanam could see murder in his friend's eyes. "Calm down, Umer. There's still time. I'll talk to him and get remotes that will work."

"And if they are faulty too?"

"We will deal with that if it happens."

"I don't like this," Umer said, his unhappiness still written on his face.

The sound of shuffling feet from the back of the restaurant announced the return of the serving boy. He approached their table to ask if they wanted anything else.

"Nothing more, thank you," Sanam said.

As soon as the boy had cleared the dishes and returned to the back, Umer said, "I tell you I don't like this."

"And I tell you that I understand," Sanam said. "I am not happy about this either. I will talk to the American and I will see what can be done."

Middleton's eyes flew open.

What the hell was that?

He'd been dead asleep, then something pulled him out of it so fast his heart raced. A dream? If it was, it would have been the most intense one he'd had in years. What then?

He reached over to the nightstand and checked his watch.

It was 4:09 a.m.

Middleton knew he should try to go back to sleep. Lying there awake would only drive him crazy. As he started to close his eyes he heard a muffled pop. Then another, and another.

Gunfire. It was coming from the front of the estate.

He pushed himself up instantly knowing there must have been an earlier shot, a shot that would have pulled him out of his sleep.

He threw his covers back, but before he could even push himself out of bed, he heard the rattle of a key. His door flew open.

"Quick! Get dressed. You must hurry!"

It was the guard who had brought him his dinner the evening before, but unlike last night, he was now carrying a machine gun. Behind him was another guard similarly equipped.

Middleton jumped out of bed and felt around for his clothes in the semi-darkness.

Outside the gunfire intensified. It was hard to tell how close it was, but the fact that there were two guards anxiously waiting for him to get dressed told Middleton all he needed to know.

As he pulled on his final shoe, the first guard said, "Come. Come."

He grabbed Middleton by the arm and shoved him into the hallway.

"That way!"

The guard pulled him forward and started to run. Middleton had no choice but to do the same. From elsewhere in the house, he could hear people yelling orders and feet racing down other hallways.

The guard whipped him around a corner then angled toward a wide stone stairway. Instinctively, Middleton veered for the flight leading down, but the guard yanked him to the left.

"No. Up. Up."

They took the stairs two at a time, racing upward, not stopping until they reached an open metal door. Beyond it, Middleton could see the night sky and the flat surface of the mansion's roof.

As they stepped through the door, the intensity of the gunfire increased.

"This is a dead end," Middleton said. "What are we doing—"

Suddenly another sound drowned out the sound of the bullets. It was loud, rhythmic and familiar. Middleton turned in time to see the helicopter rise up from the rear of the mansion just high enough to clear the lip of the roof. He realized it must have flown in low over the rear of Chernayev's estate, keeping out of sight of the attackers out front.

As soon as it touched down, the side door flew open.

Middleton didn't wait for instructions. He immediately began heading for the helicopter. As he climbed aboard, the pilot motioned for him to take the seat farthest from the door and strap in.

As soon as his safety harness was buckled, Middleton looked up, and gave the pilot a wave to let him know he was ready.

But the helicopter didn't move.

The runners remained firmly on the roof.

Then movement beyond the open door caught Middleton's attention. Someone else had come onto the roof. But this had barely registered on Middleton when the sky flared bright from a large explosion. The noise was deafening, even momentarily overpowering the sound of the rotors.

The moment the noise subsided, he leaned toward the pilot and yelled, "We've got to go!"

"Yes, Kiril. It's time."

Middleton turned toward the sound of the voice. Pulling himself through the doorway was Chernayev.

As soon as the Scorpion was seated, the helicopter took off. It left as it had arrived, flying low away from the firefight.

Once he felt reasonably sure they weren't going to get shot down, Middleton looked over at Chernayev. "What was that?"

"My apologies," Chernayev said. "Seems we didn't get all of them the other day."

"The Group?"

Chernayev shrugged. "Of course."

Middleton sat silently for several moments. "So where we going?"

"Same destination I told you about. India. The only difference is that I've decided to come with you."

The doctor had asked no questions. He was used to the kind of patients that appeared at his back door with any number of injuries from broken ribs to third-degree burns to knife wounds. So when Tesla showed up with a gunshot wound to one shoulder and Charley Middleton propping her up by the other, he had not even flinched. He had merely quoted a price, then did what he could to repair the damage.

Afterward, the two women took a room in a small hotel near the Latin Quarter where they hid out, venturing into the streets only when it was necessary. Most trips were for food, but once they had appropriated a laptop. The owner, probably a student, had left it unattended in a café near the Sorbonne while he went to the toilet. Charley only agreed to help if Tesla promised they would later find the student and return it when they were done. She then kept watch while Tesla slipped it into an oversized bag and casually walked out to the street.

Back at the hotel, they reestablished contact with Wiki Chang.

"Any word?" she asked.

"Nothing. The boss's phones are both out of commission."

Tesla sighed. The two of them then worked to come up with a plan to track down the person who had sent the text to Jana's phone wanting to know what had happened with Charley.

Tesla had a pretty good idea of who it might be. Ian Barrett-Bone had said that Sikari was killed by his son and that Jana was in on it. Tesla guessed the person was either the son or someone working for him.

The sender wanted to know when Jana would arrive. Where, he didn't say. But Tesla gathered from the tone of the messages that there was more than a business relationship between Jana and the sender. This made her guess that it had to be the son. And if it was, it was even more important that they get a fix on his location.

"Hey, this isn't exactly easy," Chang said. He had been at it for several hours.

His image was in a box that filled the upper right corner of the laptop.

"You say that every time, then you figure it out," Tesla said.

"Yeah, well . . . "

"You're not going to tell me the sender's phone doesn't have GPS on it, are you?" Tesla said.

"I'm sure it does, but every time I get a lock on it, it moves from Belize to Japan to Mali to Denmark to wherever. He's using software that's bouncing his location all over the place and making it impossible to get a fix on him. Locking in on his transmission signal isn't giving me any better results.

He's only sending text messages as far as I can tell. That usually shouldn't be a problem, but the origin of the messages is being immediately obscured the moment they're sent."

"So there's no way we can get a lock on his location?" Tesla asked.

"I didn't say that," Wiki said.

Tesla couldn't tell, but it almost looked like Wiki was smiling.

"What have you got?"

"Well, if we can't follow a message out, then I thought we'd just have to follow a message in. I've rigged it so I can send a text to Archer directly from my computer that he'll think is coming from the phone you have there. It'll be carrying a tracer packet to follow that'll send me back a location just as it arrives."

Tesla's eyes widened. "So why haven't you texted him already?"

"Do you really want me to write the text to him? I mean, what would I say?"

Tesla started to laugh, but stopped abruptly as her shoulder started to bark in pain. Instead she gave Chang a smile, then told him what to send.

Archer had been expecting a text from Sanam for almost 24 hours. It was almost a disappointment that it had taken the Pakistani so long to figure out there was a problem. But no matter, the contact had been made, the meeting set.

Archer chose a remote spot a kilometer and a half north of an old Hindu shrine that had fallen into neglect.

While Sanam would be traveling by car, Archer would be arriving via helicopter. This would give him the opportunity to scan the area around the meeting point for any heat signatures that might indicate a possible trap.

It wasn't that he thought Sanam would try to pull something. The Pakistani was blinded by the belief they were working toward the same goal, but it was just a good practice to be cautious. As his father had taught him, there was no such thing as paranoia in their world.

As he had expected, the only heat signature within a kilometer of the location was that of Sanam. He was standing near his car, exactly where Archer had told him to be.

Satisfied, Archer gave the pilot permission to set them down.

As soon as the runners touched the ground, the side doors flew open and out jumped four of Archer's men—men who had only recently served his father. Each was armed with a Mini Uzi obtained from a diverted shipment meant for the Sri Lankan army. They were all Hindi, but had had plenty of practice under Sikari on how to pretend to be Muslim.

Archer waited an additional 30 seconds, then he moved into the doorway and stepped down onto the grass.

Per instructions, two of his men moved over to walk just behind him, while the other two stayed near the helicopter, pretending to cover his flank.

It was a show, of course, all aimed at Sanam. Now, more than ever, Archer wanted to reinforce with the Pakistani just how powerful he was.

"*As-Sal mu `Alaykum*," Archer said, stopping two feet from Sanam.

"*wa `Alaykum As-Salaam*," Sanam said. His eyes strayed to the gunmen standing behind Archer. "You face no threat from me."

"Of course not. It is not you I am worried about. But we are in territory controlled by our enemy. And if they knew I was here, they would do everything they could to stop me."

Sanam bowed his head in concession.

"You are alone?" Archer asked.

"Those were your instructions."

"Good," Archer said, then he smiled broadly. "Shall we walk?"

They headed across the field in no particular direction. Archer could sense Sanam reluctant to start the conversation, so he took the lead.

"Your message mentioned a problem," Archer said.

"Yes," Sanam said.

"Well?"

"The remote controls for the detonators. We've tested them, but the thickness of the dam prevents them from working."

Of course they didn't work. But he now raised his voice in indignation. "Are you saying I gave you faulty equipment?"

"No, I am not saying that. The remotes under normal conditions work fine. But the radio signal is unable to penetrate the concrete."

"Perhaps you don't have them rigged properly," Archer said. He was enjoying toying with this man who thought of him as an ally.

"They are rigged exactly per the instructions."

Archer grew silent, acting as if he were in deep thought. "Somehow the security services must have added special masking material in the dam," he said. "But we cannot miss this opportunity."

"I agree. We are hoping you can get replacements that will work in time?"

"I will try. But the window is short and I fear they may not make it."

"But if they don't, we will be forced to abort."

Archer paused for effect, then leaned toward the Pakistani.

"Actually, that's not entirely true."

Sanam played Archer's words over and over in his mind on the drive back to the hut where he would be spending the night. Archer had promised to do all he could to get the new remotes, but Sanam knew the probability of this was very low.

It was Archer's suggested alternate plan that was troubling Sanam most. It would solve the problem, but Sanam wished he could come up with something better. Unfortunately by the time he arrived, nothing had come to him.

Umer and two of his other men were waiting for him inside.

"So?" Umer asked.

"He is trying to get us replacements."

"Trying?" Umer said. "If he doesn't get the replacements, all our work will mean nothing."

The other two men voiced their agreement.

"What do you expect to happen?" Sanam said, more anger in his voice than he meant. "That they appear out of the air?"

No one said anything for several moments. Then Umer asked, "Did he at least say when he would know if he could get them?"

"He told me he would contact us by the morning."

Umer nodded. "Then we will at least know if we will be able to carry out the plan. If he can't get them in time, we can use the explosives elsewhere. There are plenty of other worthy targets."

"But none as big as this," Sanam said.

The room fell silent, everyone knowing he was right.

With a deep breath, he looked at his men. "The plan will go forward with or without the remotes."

"What are you talking about?" Umer said. "How will we set the explosives off without the remotes?"

"There is a way," Sanam said.

"What way?" Umer asked.

Sanam paused, still hoping an alternative answer would come to him, but none did. "We will set them off manually. They can be rigged so only one man can do it."

Umer stared at him.

"It is the only way," Sanam said.

"It can not be just anyone," Umer said. "It would have to be someone we trust will not back out. We don't have anyone I trust that much."

"We have one," Sanam said.

Sanam locked eyes with his friend, and in that moment he knew Umer realized the only possibility.

"Me," Umer said. Not a question.

Sanam said nothing.

14

LEE CHILD

The trouble with laptop computers was battery life. The trouble with stolen laptop computers was that they rarely came with chargers. Unless you were lucky enough to target the kind of dork who carried an ugly nylon case everywhere, full of wires and accessories. But the Sorbonne student hadn't been that kind of dork. All Nora and Charley had was the guy's MacBook Air, thin, sleek, naked and eating power like it was starving. An icon shaped like a black empty battery suddenly changed to a red empty battery. Then it started flashing. It was winking away to itself, upper right margin of the screen. Directly above Wiki Chang's face.

Tesla told him, "This thing is going to shut down any minute. We'll have to find an Internet café."

Chang said, "No, don't do that. You're in Paris. For all we know the Internet cafés are hooked up to the security services."

"So what do we do?"

"Duh? Go buy a charger."

"Where?"

"Anywhere."

"It's an Apple. It's got a weird little doohickey."

Chang's eyes left Tesla's and flicked away to another screen. Then they came back. "They were planning to build an Apple store under the glass pyramid at the Louvre. Maybe it's open now."

"OK. We'll find it."

"Not yet. Stay with me. I have news. At least, I think I do. The trace on the destination cell? It's still bouncing around. I got Kashmir, Argentina, Sweden, New Zealand and Canada."

"That's not news. It means their software is still working, that's all."

"I'm not so sure. It switches every two seconds. Like clockwork. Which is how I would expect it to be written. But at the beginning it showed Kashmir for three seconds. Not two. I'm wondering if it failed to lock first time. Maybe it exposed its true location."

"That's a leap."

"Not really. Think about it from the other end. Who wrote this program? A guy like me, that's who. And what do I know about countries of the world? Not much. I can't sit here and name them all. I certainly don't know them all. To me, Kashmir is a Led Zeppelin song."

"So?"

"So I would need some kind of list."

"They're called atlases."

"A printed book? I don't think so. Not for a programmer. He'd hack a list from somewhere. The UN, maybe, but that's probably too secure. My guess is he tried an inside joke and hacked Nokia or someone for cell phone sales by country. And you know what? Turns out, Kashmir isn't a country. Not officially."

No answer from Tesla.

"And even if it was, I bet Nokia doesn't sell much there."

The red icon was still flashing.

Chang said, "OK, I know, it's only a hunch, but I think I'm right. I think the software failed, just briefly. I think Kashmir is the true location."

"We've got to tell Harold."

"Still no word on my end. You?"

"No."

"Well, there's more."

"Be quick."

"I have other programs running. Mostly for fun, but they're all linked. I got a flag from a Federal Aviation Authority database. There's a flight plan filed from D.C. airspace to Lahore, which is the nearest long runway to the Kashmir region. The tail number comes back to a crop duster in Kansas."

"Wiki, make your damn point, will you? We have no time."

"OK, a crop duster from Kansas doesn't need to file a flight plan and it certainly can't fly intercontinental. So it's bogus. It's something I've seen before. It's what they do when one of the Air Force Ones is prepping to fly."

"What do you mean, one of? There's only one Air Force One."

"No, there are three. Whichever, if the president is on board, that's called Air Force One. Otherwise it's just a government plane."

"So what are you saying?"

"Either the president or some big-shot cabinet member is going to Kashmir. Soon. And that's where the bad guy is."

The laptop screen died.

The helicopter came low over an outer Moscow suburb and banked and turned toward an airfield a mile away to the east. Not Domodedovo. A private field. Maybe once military and now civilian. Or shared. But it was a big place. Runways and taxiways were laid out in a huge triangle. There were enormous hangars and long low buildings. There were parked planes of every size. Small Gulfstreams and Lears and Grummans, big Airbuses and Boeings. Nothing less than twenty million dollars. The biggest was a wide-body Boeing 777. Two hundred feet long, two hundred feet from wingtip to wingtip, probably two hundred million to buy. Chernayev's, Middleton thought. It was a definitive Russian-rich-guy statement, and the helicopter was heading straight for it.

The transfer was fast. Chernayev and Middleton ducked low under the beating rotor and ran bent over to a set of steps set on a pick-up platform. They hustled up and entered through the Boeing's forward door and stepped into a space that reminded Middleton of the house off Pyatnitskaya Street, where he had met Korovin, which in turn had reminded him of Boodle's Club in London. There was oak paneling everywhere and dark patterned carpet and oil paintings and heavy leather furniture and the smell of Cuban cigars.

"Business must be good," he said.

Chernayev said, "I can't complain."

The door sucked shut behind them and the world went quiet, except for the hiss of air and the whir and tick of the spooling engines. The cabin PA was relaying the cockpit chatter, every statement made first in Russian and then again in English, world aviation's default language. Clearance for takeoff was immediate. Middleton guessed that no one ever kept Chernayev waiting. The engine noise got louder and the plane started to taxi. No delay. It turned onto the runway and didn't even pause. It just accelerated hard and bucked and strained and then took off, carrying two men in a space fit for three hundred.

Chernayev said, "Enjoy the flight, Harry."

Which Middleton was prepared to do, except that his musicologist's sense of harmony was disrupted by two things. First, the oil paintings were wrong. They were Renoirs. Beautiful canvases, no question, rich, glowing, intimate, and worth probably thirty million each. But inappropriate. London club decor was frozen in a time before Renoir ever picked up a brush. Gainsborough or Stubbs or Constable would have been more authentic.

The second thing on Middleton's mind was exactly the way the plane's interior recalled the club in the house off Pyatnitskaya Street. He couldn't get over the way he had pulled the SIG's trigger and nothing had happened. He had been ripped off. Which wasn't the end of the world, although it might have been. But it could be the end of the world for Chernayev and people like him.

Middleton said, "Do you own a guy called Volodya?"

"Own?" Chernayev said. "I don't own people."

"He's a gun dealer in an antiques store on the Old Arbat. Right across from where the Praga restaurant was. A guy like that in the new Moscow, someone owns him. Could be you."

"I know him. That's all I'll admit. Did he displease you in some way?"

"He sold me a SIG P229 for two grand. Plus five hundred for the ammunition. The gun didn't work."

"That's not good."

"Damn right it's not. Business requires trust. You'll suffer in the end. You'll be back in a plain old Gulfstream before you know it."

"I apologize. I'll make it up to you. When we're done I'll give you a SIG that works."

"I don't want a SIG. I prefer Berettas."

"The American military always did. But you must let me give you something."

Middleton smiled. "There was a stall selling Russian nesting dolls with foreign leaders' faces on them. My daughter would like them."

"Those things? They're just crude attempts at humor. You know how paranoid Russians are. The assumption is that behind our leaders are other leaders. And behind them, others still. Who do you suppose they paint at the very center?"

"I don't know," Middleton said.

The other trouble with stolen laptop computers was that people generally wanted them back. The student from the Sorbonne sure did. Not really because of the euro value of the hardware. But because of the value of the files it stored. His poems were on there. His play. The start of his novel. The stuff that would win him the Prix Goncourt one day. Plus some term papers. Like everyone else in the world, his back-up routine was haphazard.

He went to the cops. He took witnesses. No one had seen the actual snatch. But three friends recalled two American women. The cops weren't very interested. Paris was full of bigger stuff—Muslim unrest, terrorism, heists, dope. But then one of the three friends said that one of the two American women had been pale and moving awkwardly, like she was in pain, and she had a dark stain all over her shirt, like blood.

A possible gunshot wound, in a city where guns were still rare, and in a city where two victims had just turned up shot to death.

The cops weren't dumb. They knew the chances were that the laptop would be trashed when the battery ran out. On the other hand, the MacBook Air was an attractive thing. Very desirable. So maybe the thieves would try to buy a charger. Which gave them a limited number of destinations in Paris. Easy enough to stake them all out. No shortage of young officers willing to hang around such places. When they were bored with the shiny toys, they could look at the tourist girls.

Archer looked again at the picture of Charley Middleton, dead. He revered it, because he liked dead people, and because it came from Jana. It was like a love letter. It showed the girl down and crumpled, in a bloody shirt. The resolution wasn't great. But it was good enough to be interesting.

And good enough to be a little unsettling.

There were two things Archer wasn't quite sure about. The first was the dead girl's posture. Archer had seen plenty of dead people, some quite recently. There was nothing like the slackness and the emptiness of a corpse. And he wasn't sure those characteristics were there, in Charley Middleton's body. And the bloodstained shirt didn't look . . . organic. It didn't look like she had been wearing it at the time of death. It looked . . . thrown on, maybe afterward.

Which made no sense.

And there was a scrap of paper that had apparently spilled out of a trashcan. Scribbled green handwriting that seemed to make no sense either. A code, perhaps, or a foreign alphabet. Maybe Cyrillic. Or a combination of foreign letters and numbers. He stared at it for a long moment.

Then he turned his phone upside down.

GREEN LANTERN. EVAC.

He thought of Harris, immediately. For a moment he wished it had not been necessary to eliminate him. Harris had loved comic books. Which was a part of what had made him a useless wastrel. But he would have understood the reference, maybe.

Archer texted Jana: CALL ME NOW.

Jana's phone made a sound in Nora's pocket just as she and Charley stepped into an Apple reseller on the Boulevard Saint Germain. There had been no Apple store under the Louvre pyramid. Planned, but not yet built. Mired in bureaucracy. Old Europe. The Saint Germain place had been recommended by a clerk in an Orange cell phone store. Orange was the old France Telecom and was the exclusive carrier for the new iPhone in France. An iPhone charger was OK for an iPod, but it wouldn't fit the MacBook Air doohickey. Hence a taxi ride and a short search along a row of chic boutiques.

There were two guys loitering in the corner of the store. Tesla noticed them immediately. She thought: *cops.* Then Jana's phone made the sound and she delayed for a crucial second. She saw the cops staring at her, at her face, at her shirt, at her awkward posture.

She said, "Charley?"

"Yes?"

"Run."

"What?"

"Now."

The big Boeing flew on, straight and level, thirty-eight thousand feet. Middleton finished his soda and said, "Dams are big things."

Chernayev said, "Tell me about it. I paid for most of the concrete."

"Too big to destroy with explosives. The problem has been studied many times, both defensively and offensively."

"I know. So whatever wild card is in play here is not only wild but also quite possibly stupid."

"So why worry?"

"The dam will survive. No doubt about that. But we can't issue the same guarantee about your secretary of state."

"She dies, there'll be a world war."

Chernayev said, "I don't want that."

"Just a regional war?"

"First things first, Harry."

Tesla was hampered by the raging pain in her shoulder, so Charley got out to the street first. Nora turned at the door and flung the first thing that came to hand, which was Jana's cell phone from her pocket. It caught the leading cop hard under the eye and he spun away and crashed into a glass display case and sent small technical items skittering across the floor. The second cop stumbled and sidestepped and Tesla had a two-yard lead by the time she hit the sidewalk.

Charley had bolted straight through the traffic. Panic, probably, but smart too. Tesla plunged after her through yelping tires and blasting horns. Together they made it across.

They ran.

They had no idea where they were going. They turned randomly left and right in alleys and entrances and barged through knots of people. Every step sent bolts of agony through Nora's body and every accidental contact with passersby nearly killed her. But adrenaline kept her moving.

Moving, but not fast enough.

The cops were in their own city and they had radios. To Tesla and Charley, the streets were a maze. To the cops, the streets were a map they knew by heart. Alleys had exits and exits could be blocked. Sirens were howling everywhere, feet were pounding, whistles were blowing, radio chatter was loud in the air. Twice Tesla and Charley had to jam to a halt and spin around and take off again in the direction they had come. Twice the streets behind them were blocked, so they ducked into stores and barged through and came out through rear entrances to start all over again. Once a cop got his hand on Charley's sleeve, and she whirled and ducked and pulled loose and fled.

In the end, Tesla's pain saved them. They stopped running. Counterintuitive, but the right move in a mobile game. Fugitives run. Pursuers look for rapid movement. People sitting still pass unnoticed.

They dragged themselves through a shirt maker's door and collapsed breathless on a sofa. Two seconds later a squad of police ran past the entrance to the store without a second glance. The shirt maker approached, tape measure around his neck.

Charley said, "We're waiting for my father."

The shirt maker withdrew.

Charley whispered, "What now?"

Tesla said, "Airport."

"But our stuff is at the hotel."

"Passport?"

"Here."

"We'll leave the rest of our stuff. We have to go."

"Where?"

"Can't talk to Wiki, can't talk to Harold. It's up to us now."

"So where?"

"Kashmir."

Thirty-eight thousand feet, but Middleton saw mountains ahead on the right that looked almost exactly level with the plane. Hundreds of miles away, probably, a trick of perspective in terms of distance, but there was no doubt about their elevation. A gigantic range, white, icy, jagged, majestic, shrouded with low clouds down around their knees.

Unmistakable.

Famous.

The Himalayas.

But: on their right?

Middleton asked, "Where the hell are we going?"

Chernayev said, "Who do you think is painted on the innermost doll? Who do you think we all serve, ultimately?"

And at that moment two jet fighter planes rose alongside, one to port, one to starboard, both of them slow and respectful and gentle. Unthreatening. An escort. For safety and for courtesy. The fighter planes were painted with muted camouflage patterns and toward the rear of their slim fuselages they had bright red bars separated by red five-pointed stars.

Middleton said, "China?"

15

JON LAND

Middleton tried to use the mountains to orient himself, keep his bearings. But before long the sky stole them from him, the jet vanishing into the clouds. In the moments of silence that followed, he felt its steep descent in the pit of his stomach. The clouds cleared to reveal the mountains gone from sight and some sort of airstrip below.

"We're landing."

His words drew only a smile from Chernayev, and Middleton realized the altitude was playing tricks with his damaged hearing. His voice sounded like someone else's, and the lameness of his statement made him wish it actually had been. Middleton had landed at enough secret airfields to know this was something quite different from any of them. Far too barren to be military and much too isolated to have ever been civilian. No landing lights were anywhere in evidence until he spotted discolored patches in the ground on both sides of the strip. Those patches, his experience indicated, likely concealed high-powered halogens that could be activated with the proper signal from an aircraft approaching under cover of darkness, upon which the fake turf would recede so the lights could surface.

Someone had taken great measures to hide whatever truth lay here.

The strip boasted not a single building. Not a hangar, tower, storage or refueling facility—nothing. Well, not quite, Middleton thought, as he felt the jet's landing gear lower. Because parked at the far end of the airstrip, where the tarmac widened into a football field–sized slab, was another jet.

He heard the zooming hiss of their fighter escorts soaring away as Chernayev's jet touched down and taxied toward the second jet, a 767.

"Come," Chernayev gestured, after their plane ground to a halt.

Middleton started to rise, realizing he'd forgotten to unfasten his seatbelt. He joined Chernayev in the aisle.

"Where are we?" Middleton asked him.

"Where we need to be. Where the world needs us." Chernayev stopped and smiled almost sadly at him. "You wanted answers, comrade, and now you're going to get them. Though I suspect you may regret ever posing the questions."

The cold assaulted them as soon as they emerged from the jet. It seemed to push out from the mountains now visible again off to the west, their snow-capped peaks poking through the clouds and stretching for the sky. Middleton had known far more frigid colds than this, but the one he felt now was different, deeper somehow which he passed off to the anxiety and expectation racing through him.

As they approached a set of landing stairs set before the 767's bulkhead, the door opened to reveal a pair of armed Chinese soldiers beyond it. Chernayev led the way up the stairs into the plane. The soldiers stiffened to attention and saluted, seeming to recognize him while ignoring Middleton altogether. Chernayev return their salutes and then led the way through a curtain and into a majestic library, complete with wood paneling and leather furniture, its smell rich in the air. The sight further disoriented Middleton, casting an opaque, dream-like translucence over his vision. He tried to remind himself he was on a plane, but the thought wouldn't hold.

Then he saw the figure of a Chinese man wearing a general's uniform rise from a high-backed leather chair and stride past ornate shelves lined with a neat array of leather-bound books. He was tall and thin, his hair raven black except for a matching swatch of white over both temples. The man grinned, approaching Chernayev with arms extended. They hugged briefly, then separated and bowed to each other before the Chinese man's gaze fell on Middleton.

"And this must be the American." He extended his hand outward. "I have heard much about you, Mr. Middleton, most of it well before today."

"Who—"

"—am I? I have many names. Today I am General Zang."

"My opposite number in the Chinese government," said Chernayev.

"You mean, military."

"Same thing," said Zang. "Retired as well."

"Somewhat anyway," the Russian added.

Zang turned again toward Middleton. "We are protectors."

"Protectors of what?"

Zang shrugged. "Fill in the blank with whatever you choose. Our countries have become much less insular and mutually dependent. You know what the Butterfly Effect is, of course?"

"A butterfly flaps its wings in Boston—"

"And a monsoon sprouts in China," Zang interrupted, again completing his thought. "Especially appropriate in this case, of course. My Russian friend and I like to think of ourselves as protectors of that mutual dependence. There was a time when we looked on the Western world, rooting for the inevitable fall that would lead to a chaos capable of consuming it. Now we find ourselves dreading that chaos above all else and working to prevent it."

"Because of that mutual dependence."

Chernayev said, "Colonel, yes, I have a financial interest in the dam. But this is about far more than money." He took a pair of cigars from his jacket pocket and handed one to Zang. "Cuban," he proclaimed. "At least our Communist comrades there are still good for something."

"Mr. Middleton," Zang said, still admiring his cigar, "you have spent your career, especially with the Volunteers, fighting the same enemies and battles as we find ourselves fighting now."

"You just didn't realize it," Chernayev added.

"You have fought to preserve order; perhaps not in those words, but that has been the ultimate effect. And you have watched the world change into a much more dangerous place."

"Because of the butterfly," Middleton interjected.

"Exactly. We all grew up in an era of clarity where the enemy announced himself by the uniform he wore. Now we wear the same uniform, a business suit, which makes it all the more difficult to spot the enemies among us and all the more easy for them to disturb the delicate balance we're fighting to preserve."

"What does this have to do with—"

"—you, your quest, your daughter . . . "

"My *daughter*?"

"Our new enemies don't play by the same rules we used to. In fact, they play by no rules at all. Family members are considered fair game now. The tactics are brutal, revolting. They turn my stomach," Zang said, lighting his cigar and savoring the first puffs. "You are standing in my home, Mr. Middleton. It is too dangerous for men like myself and Comrade Chernayev to stay anywhere long enough for them to find us. There are fifty airfields like this scattered across China and I never spend more than a single night at a time in any one of them."

Middleton studied Zang closer, matching the face to a different era, a different man. Same brilliant, confident smile draped in the shadow of hair not yet touched by white. Shorter, slighter, more effusive, but with the same eyes.

"I think I know you," he started, "from the—"

"—Chinese secret po—"

"The Te-Wu," Middleton said before Zang could finish.

Zang held his cigar at arm's distance, frozen. "I'm impressed. Perhaps our paths have crossed somehow."

"Not yours, your father's. He was one of the Te-Wu charged with infiltrating the United States after the Korean War."

"Not just one of. It was his operation!"

"You sound proud."

"Of his efforts, of our heritage, yes. The Te-Wu dates back to 550 B.C."

"I've heard the group even has its own clandestine dialect that makes infiltrating it impossible."

Zang spat off some words in Chinese that made no sense to either Chernayev or Middleton. "But now," he resumed, switching back to English, "we find ourselves with a different enemy, a different mission."

"Sikari?"

"Chaos in general, of which Sikari represented only a small part, small but very dangerous because of its capacity to inflict incalculable harm on our precariously mutually dependent world."

"The butterfly . . ."

Zang nodded as he blew huge plumes of cigar smoke. "And in this case that butterfly is going to land on the Baglihar dam just hours from now. And if we do not force it to take flight again, the price will be the end of the new world stitched together by the precarious threads of euros and dollars."

"War between India and Pakistan."

"Exactly."

"No," Middleton disagreed. "We know the explosives Sikari's people have can't destroy the dam, and even if they manage to assassinate the secretary of state . . ."

Middleton let his voice trail off, something in Zang's suddenly tentative expression telling him he had it all wrong, that he was missing a crucial piece of the puzzle.

"It's not the secretary of state who's coming," the head of the Te-Wu told him.

Tesla was seated next to Charley Middleton on the last leg of a series of exhausting flights that would ultimately end in Kashmir. The coach compartment was crowded, adding ample camouflage to the clever subterfuge they'd enacted inside Orly Airport. Aware French authorities would be looking for them, as well as Archer Sikari's people alerted by the suspicious communications over Jana's salvaged cell phone, Tesla had disguised Charley as an old woman. The ruse was accomplished with a combination of make-up, hair product and clothing, all culled from shops inside the terminal, the transformation handled inside a handicapped restroom stall. Obtaining a wheelchair from the airline proved a simple matter and Tesla had booked the tickets by phone so as not to arouse suspicion spurred by a walk-up sale.

Harried authorities on the alert for two women meeting Charley and Tesla's descriptions would have no reason to pay heed to an old woman slumped in a wheelchair, chin resting near her frail chest and snoozing while her daughter eased her through the terminal. Sikari's people would be more astute and discerning, but Tesla doubted even their ability to marshal significant forces in so short a period of time. To throw them further off the track, she had tucked Jana's phone into the carry-on of a passenger bound for New York, leaving them to chase their GPS tails around the world.

Tesla met Charley's gaze in the coach seat next to her and managed a re-assuring smile. "You'll be with your father in no time."

"That doesn't mean we'll be safe."

"Perhaps you don't know your father."

"You could be right. I don't know anything anymore."

The make-up Tesla had used to age Charley had begun to cake, and she noticed tear streaks down both her cheeks, evidence she had been crying in the moments Tesla had managed to steal some sleep on this final stretch of their exhausting journey.

She didn't bother to deny the younger woman's assertion. "You're right, Charley. Once you go down the road we're on, there's no going back."

"How do you live with it, what you do?"

"Easily, because not doing it is much worse."

"At the expense of everything else," Charley muttered, shaking her head.

"If we fail, there will be no everything else. The stakes are that high. People have died and more will if we can't stop Sikari's people in Kashmir."

Charley sniffled. "I just want to go home."

"It's not safe, Charley."

"Will it ever be again?"

"Probably not."

Charley settled back in her seat, taking a deep breath. "Thank you for telling me the truth."

Tesla laid a reassuring hand atop Charley's upon the armrest. "In the end, it's all we have."

"It is the only way."

"It can not be just anyone. It would have to be someone we trust will not back out. We don't have anyone I trust that much."

"We have one."

"Me."

Standing within view of the now-completed dam, Archer replayed the conversation between Umer and Sanam in his mind. Both were fools, easily manipulated to serve his ends. And, appropriately enough, the business about the detonators and placement of the explosives was a fool's errand. But they had supplied Archer with the army he needed in the form of the offshoot of Harakat-ul-Mujahedeen, 50 loyal soldiers willing to die for the cause.

Archer and his associates had secured press credentials to accommodate all 50. It was left to Archer to complete the process of getting them their video and camera equipment, all constructed to pass the scrutiny of any security check, even one undertaken as expected by the American Secret Service.

Archer held his gaze on the dam, a bit leery over the fact that the building security apparatus was considerably higher than he had anticipated. He felt a knot tighten in the pit of his stomach, anxiety over the fact that his mission had been compromised, robbing him of his destiny and his dream.

You were a fool, father. You should have left this whole project to me.

He knew Sikari had died admiring, even revering the son who would succeed him; actually *exceed* him. But if his plan at the dam failed it would all be for naught. His dreams, and the dreams of his father, would die here, the maelstrom that would follow never to grow into the fiery inferno certain to consume the world. And when that world was remade it would be in the image chosen by Archer and others like him, an image foreseen by his father.

Starting here. In a mere matter of hours.

"Pacing will not get us there any faster, my friend," Chernayev told Middleton as their Boeing streaked through the sky en route to Kashmir, General Zang's airfield well behind them.

Middleton stopped. "We can't let this happen."

"And we won't. My men will be meeting us there. Along with U.S. security forces and Indian security. Sikari's people will be stopped."

Middleton slid closer to Chernayev's seat and glared down at him. "That isn't good enough. This is the President of the United States we're talking about. The secretary of state was one thing, but this . . . "

"I admit it's an unexpected complication."

"Unexpected complication? Is that the best you can do?"

"You didn't let me finish, comrade. It's an unexpected complication we must nonetheless not let distract us from destroying Sikari once and for all."

"Sikari's dead."

"But not his cause, his mission. We find this heir of his and we can end this forever."

"It's not worth the risk."

"You speak as if we have a choice. The president is coming here under cover. Even his most trusted advisors, believe he's sick with the flu in the White House. He is coming to the dam opening to make a statement and nothing we can do can stop him. He's been made aware of the danger and he's coming anyway."

Middleton could feel the heart racing in his chest. "In the face of a threat to his life. Those explosives . . . "

"Cannot destroy the dam. We know that now. Remember, we're not even sure Archer's there."

"Then we're missing something. We've been missing it all along." Middleton thought for a moment. "Sikari's son couldn't have anticipated his presence here either."

"Now what is your point?"

"Everything, all Sikari's plans, would've been based on the secretary of state. Less security. A different upshot to their plans."

"I don't follow, comrade."

"Zang said it for both of you: chaos. That's what this is about from Archer's standpoint. To set the world on the road to a nuclear confrontation between India and Pakistan. You know what that would mean."

"I've read the same studies you have," Chernayev said, joining Middleton on his feet. "The complete collapse of the world economy. A decade or more of deep depression. And that's just for starters."

"A possible but unlikely scenario before. Now, with the president . . . "

"Likely, if not inevitable."

"Exactly," said Middleton. "Pakistani militants will be blamed for the attack. The United States' response will be . . . God, I can't even find the word."

"The vision suffices. Pakistan's retaliation aimed at India because it's all they have. Destroy our proxy."

"Nuclear war," said Middleton. "A world of chaos."

"Not if we can stop it," Chernayev told him.

Keeping up the ruse, Tesla wheeled Charley through Srinagar Airport. The airport, and the city known as the summer capital of Jammu and Kashmir, was located in the heart of the Kashmir Valley a mile above sea level. Tesla knew the inland and low-lying waterways made it the ideal site for the Baglihar dam.

As a smaller airport, this facility offered light security, even token. But the grounds both inside the terminal and out on the tarmac itself were teeming with Indian soldiers and district police.

"What's going on?" Charley asked, still slumped in her chair to avoid detection.

"Look." Tesla pointed to a large sign that welcomed visitors to the opening ceremonies of the dam. Then she gasped, "Charley." She grabbed the younger woman's arm.

At the bottom of the sign was some information about the dam—size, electrical output and factoids, one of which was that the people displaced by the construction and flooding had been relocated to a beautiful, new town nearby. It was affectionately called "The Village."

"The warning in Balan's email! Something's going to happen here, now." She stepped to a kiosk and bought a prepaid mobile. When it was activated, she called all of Middleton's numbers—even his landlines—and sent text messages and emails.

After finishing, she slipped the phone away and wheeled Charley out the door. "If your father can get to any phone or computer, he'll find out where we are and why."

"If he's alive," Charley muttered.

"Stop it," Tesla said, though not unkindly. "He's fine. I know he is. He might even be here. If he knows about the Village."

"The two of you are fools."

"What?"

Charley cocked her gaze upward enough to briefly meet Tesla's stare. "Why bother saving the world if you can't enjoy it?"

"Charley, please . . . "

"No, whatever it is the two of you share, I want you to know I'm fine with it. I'm honestly not sure you have any better idea how to define it than I do. But you need to make sense of it, for your own sakes."

"Thank you."

The doors slid open mechanically and Tesla wheeled Charley into the steaming air. It assaulted her skin like a blast furnace, seeming to instantly melt the make-up that had already turned her face into a Halloween mask. Tesla eased the chair up to the curb and raised a hand to hail a taxi.

Almost instantly, a grime-encrusted white sedan screeched forward, cutting off another cab in the queue. A fierce exchange of explosive Hindi shot back and forth and the winning cab, the sedan, pulled up in front of the women. Tesla busied herself with helping the costumed Charley out of the chair and helping her into the backseat. Leaving the airline-issued wheelchair by the curb, she walked around and climbed in the taxi's driver side.

"What is your destination?" the ancient turbaned driver asked in awkward English. His massively wrinkled face glanced at them in the grimy rearview mirror.

"Take us to the Baglihar dam," Tesla said.

Archer still had not heard from Jana and was fearing the worst even before word reached him that she was apparently en route to the United States—at least her cell phone was. He wondered if this was some form of cosmic punishment, that taking the life of his father had sentenced him to a life in isolation without the distractions of love and romance. No matter. He was young enough to enjoy the fruits of his labors and eventual power that would come once his work at the dam was done.

Still, he found Jana's failure to contact him disturbing as he did the anomalies in the picture of the apparently dead daughter of Colonel Harold Middleton. And if Charlotte Middleton was still alive, then so was the female Volunteer Tesla, holding fast to Archer's trail. It was a good thing he'd taken precautions, another legacy bequeathed him by Sikari himself.

As if on cue, Archer's scrambled cell phone beeped and he raised it to check the incoming text message from the man he had dispatched to Kashmir.

MISSION ACCOMPLISHED

Middleton stood in the cordoned-off security area, gazing up at the sky in expectation of the president's arrival. The structure of the Baglihar dam beyond made for a magnificent spectacle. The only thing that even remotely approached it in size and scope was Nevada's massive Hoover Dam. Then, as now, construction had gone forward in essentially a wilderness; desert for the Hoover, rural unpopulated land for the Baglihar. If the concrete used here was even half what it had been there, Middleton could see no way any explosives short of the nuclear variety, including thermobaric, could possibly destroy the facility. Nor could it result in the kind of collateral damage capable of reaching the place where the president would be speaking: essentially a sprawling, natural amphitheater built to offer stunning, tourist-friendly views of the Chenab River, its vast power now harnessed between a million tons of concrete and steel.

What exactly had Devras Sikari meant in his email to Balan?

You recall what I have planned for the 'Village.' It has to happen soon— before we can move on.

As he gazed at it, he thought: No wonder Pakistan had lodged such a vigorous protest with the U.N. Irrigation to a great bulk of the nation's agriculture was now endangered, especially if the season turned any drier than normal. From one side of Pakistan to the other, people could find themselves going hungry, the perfect pretext on which to strike back. Middleton couldn't help but wonder if that had been the plan from the beginning.

"I have something you need to see, comrade," Chernayev said, suddenly at Middleton's side, holding out his BlackBerry. "The man pictured is named Umer, a known associate of both Sikari and Archer who helped them obtain the explosives. General Zang's intelligence indicates he will be the one to trigger the explosion."

"It makes no sense."

"What?"

"Why go through all this trouble to set off explosives inside a dam they can't effectively destroy?"

Chernayev shrugged. "A show of force, perhaps, of power as a precursor to something much worse."

"No, this was about assassinating the secretary of state from the beginning. Now it's the president. That's what we're facing."

"Once my men locate Archer's men, it'll be sometime before we'll have to face him again. And if we're lucky enough to find the boy himself . . . "

Middleton turned about, gazing off toward the huge throng stretching well into the thousands pulsing into the natural amphitheater from which the President of the United States would christen the opening of the dam with unprecedented pomp and circumstance.

"Any luck so far?""

Chernayev shrugged again. "It is a very large crowd, comrade. But my men are good and know what to look for."

"The BlueWatch people?"

"*Da.* And, believe me, Colonel, they've been trained for this kind of work."

"What kind of work is that?"

"Up-close termination."

"Like shooting a radioactive pellet into a defector's leg?"

Chernayev grinned, winked. "Now, comrade, where did you ever get an idea like that?"

Their eyes moved to the sky simultaneously alert by the distant *whooping* sound of a helicopter. Middleton could feel the Russian tense even as his own spine snapped erect.

The president was arriving.

"I won't be able to get you much closer than this."

"That's OK," Tesla told the driver. "We'll manage."

The driver regarded the hobbled Charley in his rearview mirror and continued, "But there *is* a VIP section, much, much closer to the official ceremony. Perhaps you have some sort of press or political credentials . . . "

"As a matter of fact I do," Tesla lied. And passed him $50.

He beamed. "Then I will do my best to get you there."

The driver swung right, drove down an isolated stretch of hastily flattened road toward a security fence manned by a trio of Indian special police. They signaled the cab to stop, one coming round to the driver's side while the other two kept to their posts ahead of the car's hood.

Tesla turned toward Charley, prepared to offer some reassuring words when a sudden flash of motion snapped her attention back to the front seat. The driver's hands were suddenly off the wheel, both grasping silenced pistols. Before she could react, he had thrust them out the window and opened fire on the approaching guard and the two standing at the front of the car.

The angle of the shots should have been impossible. Unless it was practiced. No one was around to see their murders.

Tesla gasped. Her first instinct was to protect Charley. Weaponless, there was little more that she could do.

Then, from the corner of her eye, she saw another man slip from the bushes, where, apparently he'd been waiting. Dressed in local clothing, with a long beard, he walked quickly to the driver's window. He spoke in Hindi to the driver, then turned to the women.

"You are please to come with me. Now." He said something else but his words vanished as the president's helicopter, flanked by a pair of gun ships, soared overhead.

Archer's cell phone beeped to signal an incoming text and he raised it upward, shielding it from the sun, to read Umer's message:

IN PLACE. ALL IS READY.

Archer clicked the phone's screen dark again without replying; there was no need to. He watched as the president's helicopter settled onto the secure, makeshift landing pad that had been constructed to accommodate it for the opening ceremonies. The gun ships hovered protectively overhead, their rotor wash whipping dirt and debris into a swirling cloud.

If the day had been too windy for the chopper to land, he mused, all his plans might have been for naught. Even the fates smiled upon him. He could feel his father's presence nearby, approving as well, understanding the need for his own death so that a great destiny could be achieved.

Middleton listened to the Indian cabinet minister say after his introductory remarks, "Ladies and gentlemen, it gives me great pleasure, on this joyous and momentous day, to introduce the President of the United States!"

Middleton wasn't watching when the president mounted the stage to tumultuous, ground-shaking cheers and applause from the assembled throngs. Instead he stood alongside Chernayev, sifting through the crowd with his eyes searching for Umer or any of Archer's men, for that matter. The vast sea of humanity gave up nothing. As the president began reading from his prepared remarks on the dam opening, Middleton continued his gradual progress through the crowd, angling toward the jam-packed and roped-off area reserved for the press corps. Cameras flashed and whirred, some no smaller than a palm, recording the president's every word and gesture.

How would I do it?

Middleton tried to place himself in Archer's shoes. The thermobaric explosives he'd managed to obtain had never been intended to blow up the dam itself—that much was obvious. What wasn't obvious was what did that leave? The stage and amphitheater platform itself had been dutifully checked for all varieties of explosive to no avail. Which meant . . . Which meant . . .

The explosives had never been here in the first place. And that could only mean Archer had concocted a plan to bring them in through other means, after the speeches had begun.

"On this day, I stand before you representing India's staunchest and foremost ally, prepared to welcome in a new age of energy independence that has come to your doorstep . . . "

Middleton gazed up at the helicopter gun ships that had taken positions too high in the sky to render them dangerous to the president if they exploded. So what did that leave?

Fifty men, he thought, if I had fifty men how would I utilize them? Layering the thermobaric explosives into suicide bomber vests would have been a possibility, had everyone who entered not been required to pass through portable detectors. So what did that leave?

Fifty men . . .

"Nothing," Chernayev reported, receiving another report over his nearly undetectable earpiece.

"Tens of thousands of India's people will now have light and power without damage to the environment or further waste of resources. The opening of this dam serves as an example for what the latest in wind, water and solar technology can accomplish . . . "

"We never should have let this go on," Middleton snapped to Chernayev as they were jostled suddenly when the crowd reacted to another powerful line spoken by the president.

"What choice did we have?" Chernayev challenged him. "Who would have listened to us? We will find this Umer. We will stop this."

"We'd better," said Middleton.

Umer made his way to the front of the crowd, sliding along slowly, not about to do anything that would bring notice to him. He need not get this close to trigger the blast but he had promised his men he would join them in their glorious mission and be the first to greet them when they reached heaven. It hadn't been a difficult sacrifice to make; after today, nothing he ever did could equal the service he was performing. He needed to share in that glory, be celebrated as a hero, even if that be limited to the tiny circles that knew his role.

His men shared his ambition and courage, each and every one of them knowing they had been born for this day. Each had gone into this with eyes wide open prepared to give themselves to the service of the Almighty. Umer felt strangely calm, aware in a God-like moment that he was the master of a fate controlled by the tiny detonator in his pocket. Flip the switch, press the button and the world would change forever in a nanosecond.

Umer prayed he'd be able to view the aftermath from his spot in heaven.

"Let us not let ourselves be held prisoner to the vestiges of the past. Let us embrace the future without fear of the complications that come with boldness and the bright expanse a new direction imparts. The time for fear and tentativeness is gone . . . "

"You'll never get away with this," Tesla told Archer weakly.

From the private booth in the VIP area, Archer seemed to feel quite confident that he could get away with whatever he wanted to.

"My father would have wanted Middleton to die here," he said. "But I prefer having him watch me kill his daughter. Better to have him live in misery."

"He'll hunt you to the end of the earth."

Archer's lips flirted with a smile, clearly unfamiliar with the gesture. "If he survives, which is unlikely. And if he does, let him come after me. Let his personal hatred consume his failed mission. And not long after today that earth will be a considerably different place."

Tesla thought briefly. "Is it true you killed your father?"

Archer stiffened, didn't respond.

"I'll take that as a yes. Some would call that the ultimate betrayal."

"Age betrayed him," Archer shot at her. "Weakness betrayed him. He had played the game too long."

"Is that what this is to you?"

"As it was to my father. But he no longer cared enough about winning."

"You just answered my question," Tesla said. "This was your plan all along. It was your plan and he refused to go along with it. He changed his mind, so you killed him."

Archer didn't bother denying it. "We had come to see the world a different way."

Security badge dangling from his throat, Middleton was nearing the front of the vast mass of humanity when he glimpsed a man standing off to the side. On first glance, he wouldn't have paid him any heed at all, except for the fact that his eyes were held closed, as if he were asleep. Or praying. Second glance brought a flash of recognition from the picture Chernayev had shown him:

Umer!

Middleton had barely formed that thought when one of the reporters squeezed into the press rows plowed his way into the aisle, his face a sheen of dripping sweat. Middleton watched him tear the camera strap from his neck and toss it aside, as security personnel moved toward him.

Middleton swung back toward Umer. His eyes had snapped open and his hand was digging into his pocket.

In that moment it all became clear. The fifty soldiers, thermobaric explosives, the discarded camera . . .

Archer's men were disguised as *journalists*, the explosives laden into their Nikons, Canons and video cameras.

The equipment would have been remodeled to include a lead shielding rendering the explosives mostly invisible to detection devices. Add to that the fact that thermobarics were so new that their signature may not have been identified and coded yet.

Middleton made his way toward Umer, wishing now he and Chernayev hadn't separated.

"I've got him," he said softly into a tiny handheld microphone the Russian had provided him. "Front crowd, southeast facing."

Middleton saw Umer cupping his hands around a tiny oblong detonator and raising them into a position of prayer. He closed his eyes again. He started to go for the Beretta Chernayev had supplied but didn't dare risk firing. Even a kill shot to the brain could result in a spasm more than sufficient to activate the detonator. Middleton would have to win this battle in close.

A commotion in the press corps drew Archer's gaze away from his two captives. Harold Middleton was fighting his way down the aisle.

"No," Archer rasped. And then his voice dissolved into the throaty scream of a spoiled child. *"No!"*

With that he lashed a blinding whipsaw of a blow to Tesla's throat that would have crushed her windpipe had she not turned at the last instant. The blow impacted instead against the side, still mashing cartilage and dropping her momentarily breathless to her knees.

Gasping, Tesla saw Archer jerk Charley forward and drag her downward toward the crowd.

Taking advantage of Umer's resolute focus, Middleton slammed into him from the side, hand thrust forward to jerk back all the fingers he could find. Umer whelped in pain, enraged eyes finding Middleton as if aroused suddenly from a beautiful dream. The commotion spilled those crowded closest to the front into a domino-like fall, leading Secret Service personnel to storm the stage and enclose the president in a protective, moving bubble.

Chaos.

The word locked in Middleton's mind as it raged around him. He slammed an elbow into Umer's face, crushing his nose and mashing his front teeth. He heard something clack to the concrete and knew it could only be the detonator, as Umer dropped to feel for it. Middleton joined him amid the thrashing feet moving in all directions at once. If one of them pressed down on the detonator's button . . .

On stage he glimpsed the Secret Service just now starting to rush the president to safety, still any number of long, long seconds before he was out of range of the kind of blast 50 separate thermobaric explosions would wreak. Middleton felt a knee smack his skull, a foot jab his ribs, courtesy of the fleeing throngs. He continued to grope about the ground for the lost detonator, afraid to spare the hand it would take to draw his gun on Umer. He grabbed sight of him pawing about the ground through the sea of churning legs and desperate fleeing frames.

Middleton glimpsed the detonator, its black casing now cracked, stretched a hand toward it only to have his fingers stepped on as another foot kicked the device from him. It bounced once and skittered straight toward Umer who lashed a hand toward it.

The fingers on his right hand throbbing and useless, Middleton drew his pistol with his left and fired in a single motion. The bullet took Umer in the cheek, blowing off a hefty portion of his face. He collapsed atop the detonator, shielding it from the onrushing feet long enough for Middleton to close desperately on all fours and jerk it from beneath his body.

Rising to his feet proved an arduous, almost impossible task as he clung to the detonator with both hands to protect it. His eyes fell on an impossible sight, conjured certainly by the sharp blows to his head: a vision of his daughter Charley.

But then the haze cleared, revealing Archer, holding a gun to Charley's head.

"Give it to me!" Archer bellowed, looking surprisingly young and desperate. "Give it to me or she dies!"

16

JAMES PHELAN

Archer's hand exploded and painted Charley's face with gore. A high-caliber rifle round took out his pistol.

He dragged Charley back with him to the ground and dropped out of Middleton's sight. The crowd was surging around them, thousands of people in a stampede to get out of the amphitheatre.

Middleton hunched and bent his knees to lower his center of gravity, being jostled as he went against the tide, making it over to where they'd fallen—nothing. Blood on the ground, Archer's pistol in pieces, no trail.

Middleton had made a career out of helping others. He'd never asked for anything in return. Right now, as the spooked crowd streamed around him, he wished otherwise.

Connie Carson and Wiki Chang sat in the cargo area of an MV-22B Osprey tilt-rotor aircraft, U.S. marines around them, game faces on, M4 assault rifles ready. They took off vertically as a helicopter would, the flying style converting to that of an aircraft as the two massive engines charged forward for horizontal flight and they were hammering hard and fast to the north.

Squashed between a marine three times his size and Carson, Chang hugged his backpack so tight it seemed he wanted to crawl in there to escape the incredible noise inside the cabin, as two other Ospreys flew in close formation.

He'd held on but no more—Chang threw up into the bag he'd been given by the crew chief. Carson patted him on the back.

"You're . . . smiling?"

"Been a while since I've done an infil with marines," she said, cheerleader exterior masking a former door-kicker with the U.S. military. She was not so much taking to the situation like a duck to water, but rather felt a happiness like a pig rolling in filth. She scratched at the fiberglass cast on her arm. "It's not really like a computer game, is it?"

His teeth felt like they were rattling out of their sockets. As the marine seated next to him slapped a box of rounds into his M249 SAW and cranked a round into the chamber, Chang shook his head.

Chernayev called his name over the radio.

Middleton scanned around, stood tall and tried to look over heads and was almost knocked over—there, behind the press pool, the assembly still corralled in their cordoned-off area below and out of the sightline of the president, while POTUS was being evacced and the civilians exfilled en masse. Not even all the number of security personnel present were able to control this crowd moving as one.

"Over there!"

Middleton followed Chernayev's outstretched arm and pointed finger—

Archer dragging Charley back toward the raised VIP area, the sound of a helicopter behind him.

"Two minutes!" the marine CO yelled. "Masks!"

All the marines donned gas masks.

Carson looked to Chang, his face a mixture of apprehension and pure fear. Just twenty minutes ago, they'd been stopped at the major road checkpoint ten kilometers south of the dam, and she had managed to talk the Indian military sentries into letting her speak to the U.S. marine colonel, a man who now stood looking forward through the shoulders of the pilots.

"Wiki, are we in range yet?" Carson asked.

Chang shook his head and turned a new shade of sick, swallowed some vomit that rose up his throat. She put an arm around his shoulders. Saving not only their president, but also this region from a potential nuclear war . . . Yeah, that would do it to you.

The Secret Service had the president behind a tall wall of bulletproof glass that deployed whenever the commander-in-chief was giving a public speech. The protective detail, all with service firearms drawn, were scanning the crowd, some looking up at the sound of Marine One, the big Sikorsky VH-3D Sea King coming in fast toward the landing zone.

Middleton ran hard, carving a path through anyone in his way. Weren't for the flare in his knees he could have been back 35 years, a wide receiver at West Point. A gap in the crowd, another gunshot behind him, he didn't flinch, eyes searching, sucking in air.

There. Dead ahead.

Near where the base of the dam met the stairs up to the raised VIP platform, Archer turned to face him. Arm tight around Charley's waist, bloody stump of a hand to the front of her, his other hand out of sight behind her back. Could be a gun, could be a knife.

Middleton looked to his daughter. All thoughts of the running crowd left his mind. The bombs too. It was like he was in the eye of the storm, even the sound of the helicopter was silenced in this moment. People ran screaming all around them as he stood still and faced her. Charley's eyes pleaded with him. This wasn't her fight. His work had again put her into jeopardy. No way.

A guy, one of Chernayev's BlueWatch operators, had his pistol drawn and was coming at him—his head snapped back and he fell to the ground. Secret Service or marine sharpshooter. Middleton almost wished he'd ditched the Beretta but he'd instinctively tucked it into the back of his belt as he'd stood. Hopefully it wouldn't be clocked and seen as a threat.

"The controller, Middleton, or she dies."

Charley screamed as Archer pushed something into her back.

They were ten yards away. Middleton closed the gap to five. Stopped. Held the controller loose in his right hand, visible to Archer.

"You want this?"

"This ends here, you know it."

"Maybe for me and you," Middleton replied. "It's not going to end for her."

"Maybe not—for her." Archer gave a flick of his head over his shoulder. "What about your other bitch?"

Middleton followed where Archer motioned. At the top of the stairs that led up to the VIP area, Tesla gasping for breath, a stream of bright red ran out of the corner of her mouth, her face sunken and tired. She'd been trampled by the crowd.

"Let them both go, Archer," Middleton said, turning back. "Only deal you're gonna get. You think you can draw down on me and not get taken out by a sniper, go for it."

Sixty marines in full battle dress ran flat out in double-file, carving a path through the middle of the mass exodus.

Chang had a hand on the back of Carson's belt, as instructed, and he didn't argue or question when she peeled off from the stream of marines and ran up the stairs to the VIP area to their left.

"The only way this ends, Archer. You let my daughter and my colleague go. You give them time to leave."

Archer almost smiled. Charley winced as he shifted his grip and his warm blood pumped across her neck.

"The detonator, on the ground, and I let them run for thirty seconds," Archer said. "There's a clear path behind me, into the dam's maintenance area. They'll be spared from the blast."

Middleton knew he had no choice but to go along, even though Charley's eyes said no.

"Twenty-five seconds."

He scanned right—Marine One was coming in to land. He thought of Lespasse and Wetherby, two fallen comrades. He thought of Charley's mother. He thought of all those who left too early, who were taken by greedy men. This was what he'd formed the Volunteers to prevent.

"Twenty. Leave it longer and they won't make it."

Middleton looked around again—spotted a familiar face: Chernayev was coming behind him.

"OK," Middleton said. He held his hand out and put the remote detonator on the ground, a few paces from Archer. He let Charley go, shoving her toward Tesla, who was doing her best to hurry down the stairs.

"Run!" Middleton yelled at them. "Run!"

Tesla grabbed Charley by the arm. With all her remaining strength, she dragged her away, pulled her in a run toward the safety of the dam's reinforced concrete.

The crowd had broken through the barrier and the line of security at the landing area of Marine One. Still several thousand people were jostling for a chance to escape the amphitheatre, hundreds of them taking this new route.

Secret Service were forced to keep the president behind the bullet-proof glass screen, some two hundred yards off their now-busy evac site. Marine One stayed on station, hovering directly above its LZ. They all donned gas masks, even the president and his bodyguards.

Archer squatted to the ground, revealed he had a small pistol, picked up the remote in the same hand, nursing his mangled hand across his chest the whole time. Looked at the little plastic box. Smiled. Content. Flipped the cover off the switch. He thought of that place his father had told him about, a little town of pedigree goat herders in Kashmir where Pashmina came from. Alexander's caravan was said to have passed through there almost two and a half thousand years ago and the people there still have evidence of that today, with sandy hair and ruddy cheeks and blue eyes. Since a young boy he'd longed to see it—maybe death would bring him there. Suffering has its joyous side, despair has its gentleness and death has a meaning. Every death.

Hovering above the crowd, the side door of Marine One opened, an agent leaned out, fired three CS rounds directly below onto the LZ. The 40mm grenades from the M32 launcher took less than half a second to hit the ground fifty yards below. The tear gas had an immediate effect.

"No!" Chernayev shouted through a screen of running people.

Archer pressed the detonator.

Middleton closed his eyes. He thought of Charley.

Nothing happened.

Middleton opened his eyes. Archer looked at the remote, incredulous. He tucked the pistol into his belt, pressed the button again. Nothing. Again.

Again.

"Nice try, Archer," Carson said.

She came down the stairs with Chang, who held up the POLENA handset that was wired to his backpack.

"He jammed the signal," Middleton said. He'd seen Connie Carson and Chang in the brush nearby, signaling to him that it was all right to give up the remote control. Saving him from the very difficult decision: his daughter or the president.

Chang nodded, looked worn-out and relieved, like he might faint with the passing of the adrenalin. For all his advanced computer and science degrees and language skills that had aided the Volunteers from the comfort of his desk in D.C., never was a sight so welcome in the field as this slightly built Taiwanese-American before him.

"First, I thought they might be using a garage-door opener, but then I realized that the Secret Service must be wise to that sort of thing, from all the IEDs and stuff in Iraq," he said, holding up his handset. He was taking comfort in tech-speak. "So I barrage jammed all frequencies as soon as the marines dropped us off."

Middleton smiled, looked to Archer, who was now standing up, pistol still tucked in his belt, radio detonator in his useful hand. His eyes were darting around, then he seemed to relax.

"Nice work, Wiki."

"No problem, boss," Chang replied. He looked over at the commotion of Marine One hovering to land, the bubble of security protecting the president. "Holy crap," he said, "it really is the president . . .

"And for the record," Chang added, "there was no heavy water. The copper bracelet referred to the organization."

"Yeah," Middleton said. "I figured that one out too."

He saw Chernayev approaching, a couple of his security guys with him. Looked like this was working out as a victory after all.

"Hacked into Bicchu, that search engine?" Chang said. "And you'll never guess who it's owned by—Hey!"

Middleton turned. He saw Wiki Chang on the ground, rubbing his jaw.

Chernayev had taken the backpack jammer from him. Walked over to Archer, flicking switches on the handset as he went.

"Owned by one of my corporations," Chernayev said. He dumped the jammer by Archer's feet and took the detonator from him. As a dozen heavily armed BlueWatch security men pushed onto the grounds, he glanced down at the younger man. "This should work now. *Almost* time . . ."

"And I'll see your hands please, Colonel Middleton."

POTUS was being ushered to his helicopter. A hundred and fifty yard dash. The marines were at the LZ now, a wall of 100 percent pure American muscle to keep the crowd away from the raised landing area. The gunships were close in too, their immense sound adding to the message to those below: this is *not* the way out. The press corps kept their cameras trained on the LZ, waiting for the money-shot of a gasmask-wearing president to headline the news services.

Middleton's world was spinning.

Chernayev.

He'd set this up. He built this dam to attract a U.S. official. He set it all up . . .

He lied about the communiqué from the State Department—and, of course, never sent the email to Charley. And the reference to Tampa on Balan's computer—it wasn't one of Devras Sikari's companies, but Chernayev's. Sikari was probably worried about what it meant and was going to send Balan or someone there to check it out.

And Chernayev was responsible for the death of his dear friend and colleague, Lespasse.

"Originally, I was going to choke Pakistan into being more submissive to what I could provide them," he said, his eyes drifting from Middleton to the scene of the president's detail moving through thick CS smoke. "I'm afraid I'm not that patient."

"We knew some of your Volunteers would make it here," Archer said. "In fact, we were always going to have you here, Harold, dead or alive."

"Oh?" Middleton felt Connie brush close against him. He made sure he kept his hands out front, in view of Chernayev, who had a silenced pistol pointed at them, concealed under his jacket.

"It was clear you'd come to me." Chernayev said. He motioned for Archer to see that the president was almost in the kill zone. The tear gas was dispersing, blowing to the south, chasing at the heels of the evacuating crowd.

"Even dead, which you'll be soon enough, you serve a purpose. Today's events will reshape not only this area, it will be a final nail in the coffin for your little group. Pakistan, as the world knows it, will end. Afghanistan too, Kashmir, some of India. Maps drawn up by old colonial masters will be redrawn again. This is the beginning of the end—for your Volunteers too, buying us the time we need to build up."

"The ICC and UN will be all over this."

"I don't think so," Chernayev said, a smile on his face. "We kill you Volunteers and more will come—better organized, more resourced. I get that. But we implicate you in this and your organization will be as dead as you."

Middleton looked at the president, at the hundred-yard line from Marine One, about to come into view of the assembled press, the only group here who seemed to be enjoying what was going on around them.

"My men," Archer said, "all fifty of them are pointing their cameras at your president now. Behind their lenses, copper discs."

They'd be concave, up to an inch thick. Shaped charges, designed to penetrate armored vehicles, like in Iraq and Afghanistan. Middleton knew all about them, he'd seen what they could do. It will be like fifty sabot tank rounds going off: nothing would be left. Nothing. Shaped charges kill with kinetic energy, such incredible force that converted to heat, blasting and melting through anything and everything. Game over.

Chernayev lifted his sleeve, revealing above his watch a thin copper bracelet, slightly different than the one Middleton had seen on Balan's wrist. "This bracelet? Nothing more than off-cuts from the process, made into intricate gifts, worn with pride by those involved."

"Chernayev, think about it," Middleton said. "This will start a war. . . ."

He shook his head, resolute. Took the remote detonator from Archer. Thumb over the button.

"This region will need many peacekeepers—I have a proposal with the UN right now for a hundred thousand of my BlueWatch contractors to move in to fill the security void. Where else would they come from? The U.S.? I don't think so."

A hundred thousand—that was a big army in any nation's book. Middleton couldn't imagine that the Russian had that many boots to field. But he had the money.

Then he understood. "China," Middleton said. "This is ultimately all about China, right?" His stalling tactic was tinged with genuine interest. China's secret political leadership, the Te-Wu, must have been behind the schooling of the three men. "This is so that China can move in on Kashmir?"

"They already run part of it and there's no doubt they need the living space. And water. The giant panda is dying of thirst."

China was doing the same thing here as they were with the Tibet situation in trying to choose the next Dalai Lama: back in the mid-'90s they took in the child, Gyaincain Norbu. Now a young man, he's believed by China to be the next incarnation of the Panchen Lama, a position second only to the Dalai Lama in the hierarchy of Tibetan Buddhism. He will help to choose the reincarnation of the Dalai Lama and given he's been brought up to obey the Chinese Communist Party, it will undoubtedly lead to the creation of a pro-Beijing power in Tibet. Call it insurance.

Devras Sikari, Archer's father, was part of their insurance for gaining Kashmir and maybe even more following what was set to transpire here.

"And these guys you've got out there, these bombers? And Umer? Sanam?" Middleton asked.

"They all had a purpose, as do you."

Chernayev's men from BlueWatch were hovering around. Middleton had no chance of stopping him from pressing the detonator—he'd not make it more than two paces and it was a dozen away at least.

Archer gasped, reeling from the gunshot wound, and called out in a rasp, "My father wanted your investigation cleared up. And he was right. For that, and for the future, we can't have anyone in our way. We didn't care if you came here dead or alive, so long as you were here for the crescendo."

"What?"

"The death of the president, who's nearing the kill zone now."

They looked across—Marine One was coming in to land, POTUS was in his protective bubble of Secret Service men, sixty seconds out.

Archer said, "Why not discredit the Volunteers while we achieve our objective?"

Middleton understood—he himself would get the blame.

Chernayev said, "Right now, the FBI is searching your house in Fairfax County. They're finding all kinds of IED-making material there. Including the lathe that made the concave copper discs, of which these are a by-product."

The copper bracelet on Chernayev's wrist glinted in the sunlight.

"Why the intricate carvings? A ruse, to get us here? To make us believe in something that this place was not?"

"It's more like a hobby of mine," Chernayev said. He walked over to Middleton and passed him a small Russian nesting doll that fit in the palm of his hand. It was solid, the innermost doll.

It was painted in shades of white and grey, smooth to the touch from the clear lacquer.

Marine One landed, the massive rotors of the Sea King creating a new wave of CS smoke that remained in the vicinity. The president's men hit the crest of the LZ, hundreds of camera flashes going off and illuminating the smoke. The press corps were shouting questions but the protective bubble didn't stop moving.

The doll's face was blank.

"It's whoever you want it to be," Chernayev said, standing taller, thumb on the switch. "It's your worst fears painted on there."

Middleton had heard of this exact type of doll, had even seen pictures in the ICC's files from the Russian-Afghan war investigators. They'd turned up at several sites of war crimes. A KGB OSNAZ kill team had been giving them out to high-value targets as a marker for death. The locals and even the regular Russian army started spreading rumors that it was a group of mythical female snipers, the White Tights. Unstoppable. Unscrupulous. They'd garrotte you in your sleep, they'd shoot you from two kilometers away, they'd take out your whole family with IEDs that would make modern-day Iraq's look like they belonged in the stone age. ICC files had a different name for this assassin—and they were convinced it was just one lone man assigned to OSNAZ's Alpha Group. They called him "The Doll Maker."

The name was given to me against my will, but that is another story. There are so many other stories, and there will be time for all of them later . . .

"I know who you are," Middleton said.

"Pity. We could have talked about that some more. Out of time."

Out of the corner of Middleton's eye he saw a figure running through the crowd, coming at them. Whatever, whoever, it was too late. Chernayev's hand was lifting the remote detonator.

"Arkady, why do it this way?" Middleton said to him, his voice deflated at the inevitable. Whatever name this man was known by—the Doll Maker, the Scorpion—one thing was constant: his art was death and he was about to paint his masterpiece.

"Sorry Harold. It's complicated."

17

JEFFERY DEAVER

The president was thirty yards away from the LZ, dust, leaves, branches fleeing from the turbulent wake of the helicopter. The rotors were dispersing the tear gas too.

The commander-in-chief was sprinting like a running back surrounded by a phalanx of teammates toward the goal line: the safety of the chopper.

The fake reporters, their weapons up, moved closer.

Chernayev was poised with the detonator. In thirty seconds he'd fire it.

"Get ready," gasped Archer, his face gone white. He had struggled onto a hill and had a good view of the landing zone. He was dying, but he'd see this through to the end.

Middleton strayed toward the Russian, but two BlueWatch guards painted him with their complicated black machine guns. He stopped.

"Twenty seconds."

The scene out there—the chopper, the president, the crowds, the reporters, legit and phony—was utter chaos. But this area, by the viewing stand, was nearly deserted. There were no witnesses to the horrible drama playing out.

Middleton shouted to Chernayev. "Don't, Arkady. There are a thousand reasons why you can't do this."

The Russian ignored him and glanced at Archer.

"Ten seconds," the wounded man gasped.

It was then that another voice intruded. "Actually, not a thousand, but there *are* several very good ones." A sweaty, dusty but well-dressed man broke from the brush. The accent was British. It was the man swimming through the crowd not long before. "Reasons for not pushing that button, I mean."

Chernayev stepped back, the BlueWatch shooters swinging their guns onto the Brit.

"Ah, ah, don't be too hasty there," the man said. He looked toward Chernayev. "Ian Barrett-Bone," he said, as if introducing himself at a cocktail party.

"Who the hell are you?" the Russian asked.

The man ignored the question. "First of all, my team has been recording everything for the past half hour. Pictures of you are on hard drives in several very secure locations. You push that detonator, some of the best law enforcement agencies in the world will come after you. And they will find you. That's *if* you get away, of course. Which you probably won't. Since three of my snipers are sighting on you at this moment."

The Russian looked around uneasily.

"You won't spot them. They're much better than . . . " His voice trailed off as he contemptuously regarded a swarthy BlueWatch security man nearby. The Brit continued, "Oh, the second reason you don't want to push the button and kill the president? It would be a bit of a waste of time. Owing as how he's not really the president."

"*Chto*?" The man gasped.

"Oh, please, Arkady. Think about it. American foreign policy can be counted on for some monumental blunders, but the administration is hardly foolish enough to send their chief executive into a known threat zone like this. The real president's in Washington. Monitoring everything that's going on here, by the way."

"A look-alike?" Connie Carson whispered.

"Quite so. We weren't exactly sure what would happen here but I knew it involved the Scorpion and some associate from the People's Republic. We put this charade together to flush the main ops into the open."

Archer was staring at the LZ. Dismayed, he raged, "Something's wrong. The marines and the Secret Service . . . They're not leaving. They're targeting Sanam's men."

Middleton asked the logical question. "And who's 'we'?"

Barrett-Bone said, "MI5, Foreign Operations Division. We're working with the CIA and U.S. and British military." He spoke into his collar and immediately two dozen men in serious combat gear stepped out of bushes, guns trained on Chernayev and the nearby BlueWatch security people.

Middleton recognized the uniform and the winged dagger insignia of the famed British Special Air Service, an infantry unit like the U.S.'s Delta Force or Navy Seals. The gravity of their mission was heralded by the fact that two were armed with FN Minimi machine guns and the rest had their SA80 assault rifles mounted with "Uglies"—underslung grenade launchers.

Prepared—no, eager—to light up hostiles big time, if it came to that.

"There are two hundred others here, surrounding the grounds and, to be quite honest, I doubt your BlueWatch chaps feel their paycheck is worth going up against our SAS, now don't you agree?" Barrett-Bone frowned. "Oh, and for the record, I'm obligated to inform you that we're here with the full knowledge and sanction of the lieutenant general of the Indian Army's Northern Command in Udhumpar and of Indian Special Branch . . . Which is the diplomatic way of saying, your men discharge a single bullet from a single weapon, you will all vanish and quite unpleasantly."

Chernayev hesitated. His face red with anger, he looked around. Then he bent forward, set the detonator on the ground and backed up.

In two seconds, SAS soldiers had him in cuffs and relieved of his weapon, phone and personal effects. In only a bit longer than that, Wiki Chang had deactivated the remote detonator.

The British soldiers then disarmed and cuffed the BlueWatch security men.

None too gently, Middleton was pleased to note.

Barrett-Bone spoke again into his collar. "Captain, the detonator's in our control. Move in and arrest the Mujahedeen. The thermobarics can't be detonated by them, but some may have other weapons and they're undoubtedly all fired up." He sighed. "Fundamentalists are soooo completely tedious."

A medic from Barrett-Bone's team arrived and Middleton immediately pointed out Archer. "I want him alive," he said. "Do what you can to save him."

"Yes, sir."

But before the medic got to him, Archer sat up suddenly, stared with unseeing eyes toward Middleton and then collapsed onto his back. He shivered once, then lay still.

The medic ran forward and bent down over the man. He touched his neck then looked up, grimacing. "Lost too much blood, sir. I'm afraid he's gone."

The Volunteers were sitting in a large workman's trailer, near the site of the dam. Charley was in a separate one; her father wanted to minimize the trauma she'd been through. Everyone was dabbing their eyes from the remnants of the CS tear gas.

Middleton had been on the phone with Washington, The Hague, New Delhi and London. Everything Barrett-Bone had told them checked out. The stand-in for the president, the monitoring that MI5, MI6, Langley and the Indian Special Branch had been doing.

Chernayev was being housed in an impromptu prison—another trailer, guarded by Indian Northern Command troops. And Barrett-Bone had just reported that a covert ops team had completed an extraordinary rendition of General Zang. Beijing may or may not have been allied with him and Chernayev, but they distanced themselves from him instantly and ordered two-thirds of its soldiers on the Kashmiri border as soon as feasible.

Despite the rescue, Tesla was irritated at Barrett-Bone, "You hid a tracker on us, didn't you? In Paris."

"Of course, I did. On you, actually. I wasn't sure if Ms. Middleton would go along for the ride—whatever the ride was going to be."

"But you tried to kill us!"

"Think back, luv."

"I warned you about 'luv.'"

"Sorry. But obviously I wasn't going to kill you. I was looking out for you. It would have been awkward if you'd been captured or killed."

"Awkward," she muttered.

"And I *did* need to get in touch with Harold here. We tried everything but he'd gone missing."

"You could have said something about who you were."

"How could I do that? If you were captured, I didn't know how much you'd tell. I know the Volunteers don't go in for intense interrogation, but a lot of people do, you know."

At this, for some reason, Nora Tesla fell silent, avoiding Middleton's eyes.

Middleton then said wryly to the British agent, "And you also needed to use us for information."

A knowing smile. "Obviously, Colonel. That *is* the way the game's played, right? There's a lot at stake here. I've been after the Scorpion for several years now, undercover. Posing as someone with an interest in Sikari, a businessman, a mover and shaker. But the leads dried up . . . Funny that, considering all this ado about water. We heard some chatter about that bizarre reporter, Crane, that he had some leads. We put him in play and got him to the suburbs of Paris. We tried to make him think one of us was the Scorpion—the fellow driving was our station chief in Paris. He even wore a copper bracelet I bought at Selfridge's. Crane didn't fall for it, I think. But he did follow up on our suggestion to go to your flat, Middleton."

"You used him as bait," Tesla snapped.

The British agent looked at her as if she'd exclaimed, Why, the earth is round! "It worked, didn't it? We got onto Jana that way. But she slipped us—thanks to Crane himself. He flew off someplace with her. To Dubai, it seems. A night in paradise, he must've been thinking. It turned out to be literally true, of course, since she killed him."

Tesla snapped, "That's how Jana got on to us in Paris. That wouldn't have happened, if you hadn't meddled."

"I *do* recall apologizing," the smarmy man said with irritation. "I *was* there looking after you, remember."

"But not very goddamn well, since I got shot and Charley was nearly killed."

"What's going to happen now?" Wiki Chang asked.

"We'll spirit both of them back to London—Chernayev and Zang. See what we can arrange for a trial. Zang'll ultimately go back home—and end up shot, most likely. As for your Russian friend, if the Criminal Court wants him, 'fraid you'll have to stand in line."

"They're both yours for the time being," Middleton said. "The only warrant we had was for Devras Sikari." Then he had a thought and laughed.

"What?" Connie asked.

"The Scorpion—Sikari's benefactor." Middleton shook his head. "All we knew about him was that he was 'holy, but of this world.' But I'm wondering if that was a mistake. Maybe the phrase started in English before it got translated into Hindi. The original phrase might have been 'wholly of this world.'"

The British agent said, "Can't disagree with that: It certainly describes Chernayev . . . Talk about greed. Selling out a whole country."

Middleton cocked his head. "That raises a question. Chernayev's motive was money and Zang's was annexing territory with a good source of water for China. But Sikari's motive was an independent Kashmir. So what was his real involvement in all this?" He waved his hand, indicating the dam. "It seems like he was a pawn, used by Chernayev. But he clearly had something planned for the Village—that was in his email to Kavi Balan."

There were plenty of unanswered questions, he reflected.

"I better make some arrangements for transport now," Barrett-Bone checked an extremely expensive watch. He saw Middleton regarding it. He laughed. "I didn't steal it. I come from money, my friend. Believe it or not, I'm a civil servant because I like the work. One can't be a benefactor to the world of arts and music full time and not get bored. Besides, I'm also a bit of a patriot, as out of vogue as that seems. Cheers now." He walked into the dusty heat.

Middleton pulled out his new phone and got a status update. The fifty Mujahedeen and their leaders had been taken into custody, as had the BlueWatch people. The grounds and the explosives were secure.

He now rose. "I'm going to check on Charley." His soul was heavy with the knowledge that she'd been drawn into the midst of this terrible affair—at a time when what she needed most was a chance to heal.

"I'll go with you," Tesla said.

He was nearly to the door when his phone buzzed. "Yes?"

"Colonel Middleton?" the British voice asked.

"That's right."

"Commander Ethans here. SAS."

"Go ahead."

"Stumbled on a bit of an odd situation. Thought it best to apprise you. We've got the body of that Archer Sikari. But, well, the queerest thing.

Seems he didn't die from loss of blood. He probably would have, but that's not what finished him off. He was shot. In the back of the head."

"What?"

"No question."

Middleton recalled seeing the man sit up suddenly and then collapse. But he hadn't heard any shots. He told this to the SAS officer, and asked, "What about your men?"

"No, sir. None of ours or yours were issued silencers."

"Can you clear it for me to have a chat with Chernayev?"

"I'll check with Mr. Barrett-Bone, sir, but from SAS's perspective, it's fine."

He thanked the officer and hung up. He told the other Volunteers what had happened.

"But none of the BlueWatch people would have shot him—they were working together."

Middleton said, "This one has too many questions left for me. I need some answers."

He headed out the door into the blaring sun, Nora Tesla beside him.

They approached the trailer where the prisoner was being held. Middleton identified himself to the six Indian guards, who checked IDs and then nodded them through the temporary barbed wire perimeter, after verifying that Barrett-Bone and the SAS had okayed their interview.

The trailer was big—a doublewide American model, with air-conditioning. In the front office, two guards sat in metal chairs, gripping H&K machine guns. One checked their IDs and placed another call to their superior officers and, it seemed, to Barrett-Bone. Middleton didn't mind; there couldn't be too much security with these particular prisoners.

Then he hung up and said, "You can go in, in a moment. As soon as the nurse is finished."

"Nurse?"

"British army nurse."

Middleton frowned. "Is Chernayev injured?"

"No, no. She said it was a routine check to allow him into London." He smiled. "Maybe he needs inoculation against mad cow disease."

"Allow him into London? There's no quarantine coming from India. Anyway he's not going on a commercial flight. Who approved it?"

"An officer in our command."

"Inside, now! Keep your weapons ready."

"She was just a nurse."

"I'll call Northern Command if I have to."

The guards regarded each other. They rose, readied their machine guns.

One covered the door while the other unlocked and flung it open. He peered inside, his face a mask of shock. "There is problem. No, no!"

The other Indian soldier raced into the room, Middleton and Tesla right behind.

They stopped fast, seeing Chernayev's body. It was in the middle of the small office, whose windows were covered with thick steel mesh. He'd been shot in the back of the head as he tried desperately to claw his way out.

"The nurse," a guard whispered, gesturing at the only other door in the room, leading to a third office.

"There's a back door?"

"No, just the one, the front."

The nurse was trapped. They'd keep her pinned and call in a marine tac team. "I'll get—"

"No, we will stop her."

"Wait!" Middleton whispered. "She can't—"

They flung the door open and blinked as a brilliant light, the sort used for construction site work at night, clicked on. Blinded, they staggered back as four well-placed silenced rounds found their targets—the men's foreheads.

In a blur the woman rushed out. She was dressed in a British army soldier's uniform, but the poor fit and a small red stain on the chest told Middleton how she'd come by the outfit. He didn't recognize her.

She hesitated in shock, not expecting the other two to be in the room. But before she could lift the .22 again, Middleton drew the Beretta that Chernayev had given him. When he touched the muzzle to her head she debated only a moment and dropped her own weapon.

Tesla then stepped forward, grabbed the woman and, wincing from the wound in her own shoulder, flung the attacker to the floor hard. Then she struck her furiously in the head and face.

"Nora, stop!" Middleton said, pulling her off and securing the shooter with one of the dead guard's handcuffs. "You didn't have to do that."

"Oh, yes, I did."

Middleton frowned.

Tesla said, "You don't know who she is, do you?"

"No."

"It's Jana Grover."

"In Paris, did you check on my body?" Jana snapped contemptuously at Tesla. "Did you call *les gendarmes*, did you call *Le Deuxieme Bureau*. No, of course not. What you saw floating in the Seine was my jacket. And you took that at face value. I'm sorry I escaped and deprived you of another chance to torture me."

Middleton glanced at Tesla, silent at this. He now understood the earlier reaction to what Ian Barrett-Bone had said. He let it go.

They sat in the same trailer that had been Chernayev's cell. And his coffin. The body had been removed. And a forensic team was going through the place.

In addition to Connie Carson and Wiki Chang, Ian Barrett-Bone was here. He was lip-biting mad at the Indians for letting the hit woman into the trailer. The officer who'd been bribed by Jana to okay access was in custody, but that was small consolation.

"Why?" the British agent asked.

"She treats all colleagues that way," Tesla said bitterly, "if there's any chance they might be witnesses against her. Just like she killed Kavi Balan in the South of France."

"I'm not so sure," Middleton said, again considering unanswered questions. "I think something else is going on here."

"Ah, you're as sharp as I thought, Colonel. How I wish Balan had been successful that day at the beach at Cap D'Antibes."

"I don't understand," Barrett-Bone said.

"No, you certainly do not," the beautiful Pakistani said. "You haven't understood anything—any of you, from the beginning . . . I wasn't with Chernayev or the Chinese. They were my *enemies*. I'd been struggling for months to find them and kill them."

"What on earth do you mean?"

As if speaking to school children, Jana said, "Some time ago Devras Sikari was negotiating with the Mujahedeen here in Jammu about power sharing if he could secure an independent Kashmir. But he learned that this person known as the Scorpion and a Chinese associate wanted to fabricate some terror attack as an excuse for the Chinese to invade and occupy Kashmir. They planned to blame the terrible incident on Devras. He learned about their scheme and came up with a plan to expose them: He pretended to enlist the Mujahedeen to help him blow up the dam. Yes, he arranged for some explosives to be stolen and shipped there but he knew the dam was too solid to be destroyed. He was an engineer, remember."

Tesla said, "But the email we found on Kavi Balan's computer said he planned to destroy the Village."

"Wait. No, it didn't," Middleton countered. "It just said he had something 'planned' for it."

"And he did," Jana continued. "He planned to get to the truth of the Scorpion's plot. He wasn't going to destroy the Village. He was going to *save* it—and expose the Scorpion and his associate to the world, if we couldn't stop them first."

Middleton had to laugh. He realized that he and the Volunteers were the ones who had accomplished Sikari's goal: protecting the Village and exposing the Scorpion's and Zang's plan.

Jana continued, "*My* job was to find the Scorpion and eliminate threats. That's why I needed your daughter . . . to use her to find out what you knew. After Balan failed to kill you, I learned who you were. Not some spy for the Scorpion. Or for those crazy men with the Group. But the Volunteers." Her face darkened. "I was getting close to stopping you and to learning who the Scorpion was . . . And then tragedy. Archer killed his father."

Barrett-Bone said, "Tragedy? Why, you helped him do it!"

"Are you mad?" she raged. "Devras was my mentor, a colleague of my father. He was a genius. Archer was a street thug, a fool." The woman shivered in disgust. "He never understood the politics, the culture, the depth of our region. And like most stupid men, he was easily seduced, by the Scorpion. He never realized that the last thing Devras wanted was a real incident here, especially the deaths of foreigners. It would destroy forever his hopes for a free Kashmir."

Middleton said, "So you're the one who shot Archer."

She sighed. "My only regret is that I couldn't get close enough to tell him how I despised him before I pulled the trigger."

"And Crane?" Barrett-Bone asked. "The reporter."

"I thought he would be valuable in finding Scorpion. He led me to your daughter and her." A contemptuous nod toward Tesla. "But he gave me little else."

"You wanted Chernayev and Zang stopped, right?" Connie Carson said.

"Yes, of course, I did."

"Well, they were stopped. We had them in custody. Why did you kill Chernayev?"

"Why *didn't* you?" Jana replied with contempt. "A vastly powerful man? It would only have been a matter of time until he escaped or bought his way out of prison."

"There's another reason, though, isn't there?" Tesla asked.

Jana smiled at her coldly. "Yes. Chernayev was responsible for the death of my father. He and Zang killed him and the Indian student they also sponsored. They only kept Devras alive to use him in their plot. I decided years ago that whoever the Scorpion was, whatever else he was guilty of, he'd die for the murder of my father. Poisoned by well water. He died in pain."

Middleton said, "So Chernayev using the Mujahedeen here today, that was a fallback plan, right? Originally, he and Zang were going to claim that the dam had the copper bracelet technology in it—that would be the Chinese's excuse to occupy Kashmir."

"Exactly. A weapon of mass destruction. And by the time it was learned there was none, they'd have the country all locked up. Sorry we didn't find any weapons, but we're not leaving." She offered a grim smile to the Americans. "That worked well for you not long ago, no?"

"And what *about* the copper bracelet technology?" Wiki Chang asked eagerly.

"Devras was obsessed with it. The project consumed him at university and afterward. But he never perfected a practical system. He could never recreate what the Nazis did. He patented parts of the technology, but it never could work as he dreamed. Still, he thought of the project affectionately. If anyone became dear to him, he'd give them his greatest symbol of affection and gratitude—a real copper bracelet."

Middleton glanced outside and saw a cluster of Indian troops walking past. More security, he assumed, though they no longer had the key prisoner to guard. They'd have to be satisfied with a mere hit woman.

Then he felt an itch. Something was wrong.

What was it?

He glanced at Archer's phone, which sat nearby in an evidence bag. He recalled again the last message: "Mission accomplished."

And he realized something else. Jana wasn't the least troubled by her capture. And she'd been talking quite freely. In the past ten minutes she'd admitted to several murders.

Hell, the only way she would share information like this was if . . .

Her dark, beautiful face turned to him and smiled.

Middleton understood the text message: Archer had put an extraction plan in place to get him out of the area after the explosions at the dam. One of his associates texted him that the plan was ready to go. Jana had undoubtedly been in touch and explained that Archer was dead, but she was taking over the operation and needed to be extracted from the dam site.

Middleton cried, "Everyone, get down! Get—"

Automatic gunfire erupted outside, and, with a piercing crack, a frame charge ripped a large hole in the flimsy side of the trailer. Tear gas canisters rolled inside and filled the room with unbearable fumes.

Despite the near blindness and the fire in his lungs, Middleton lunged for Jana. Her hands were cuffed but her feet weren't shackled and, though she was as impaired as the rest of them by the CS gas, she'd noted exactly where the rent in the trailer wall was before the cloud filled the room. She stumbled to it and flung herself out—into the waiting arms of the rescue party.

The band of insurgents loyal to Archer, unaware of Jana's betrayal, laid down covering fire as they retreated.

Middleton and Barrett-Bone struggled outside, crawling from cover to cover. More tear gas clouds were rising and none of the Indian or SAS troops knew what was going on.

Middleton finally spotted a group of a dozen people vanish into a clearing, where a helicopter was waiting. He didn't see Jana, but he knew this had to be the raiding party; as one man stepped through a band of sun, Middleton saw a golden flash off his wrist.

Its source, he knew, was a copper bracelet.

What was about to happen had been a long, long time coming.

This was the thought in the mind of the slim woman walking down the busy street of an overcast London. Autumn wind swirled grit and papers and crisp leaves around her.

At a street corner she paused and pulled her overcoat more tightly around her. She oriented herself and spotted her destination: the Tufnell Park mosque.

Someone jostled the briefcase she carried, but Jana Grover kept a firm grip on it. No enemy knew she was here—it was just a teenage girl obliviously on a mobile—but had a mugger tried to take the case from her, she would have killed him in an instant.

Yes, the briefcase was that important.

Indeed, its contents were the centerpiece of Devras Sikari's ultimate plan.

She glanced down at the street and saw the faded white-painted message "Look Right." A warning to pedestrians that traffic could come barreling along from an unexpected direction.

This amused her a great deal. The light changed and she started across the street, toward the mosque.

Trying to imagine the consequences of what was about to happen.

Monumental.

Dodging the stream of pedestrians. Some were Anglo: girls and boys in school uniforms or hoodies, delivery people, stiffly dressed businessmen, solid women navigating shabby perambulators. Mostly, though, Arabs, Iranians, Pakis . . . A few Sikhs and Indians, too.

London, what a melting pot.

Jana was wearing Western clothing, but pants. Also, of course, a head scarf. She had to blend in.

And she thought again: a long time coming.

Clutching her precious briefcase, she arrived at the mosque and walked around the nondescript building, which was one of the few here free from graffiti. It was one of the biggest in London. Nearly twenty-five hundred men prayed here daily; women too, though shunted ignominiously away behind dirty curtain partitions.

Jana looked for security. Nothing out of the ordinary. She needn't worry.

All was going according to the plan.

She paused near the entrance. Shivered as a gust of wind swept over her.

And she turned, walked into the Café Nero across the street, ordered a latte.

In this neighborhood, even in a Starbucks-like coffee shop chain, it was a bit unusual to see a woman alone without her husband or brother or a clutch of girlfriends. Traditional values flowed strongly here. In fact, an honor killing by a Pakistani brother of his eloped sister had taken place only two blocks away.

As Jana took her coffee, sat and shrugged off her coat, a bearded man in a turban walked in and regarded her contemptuously, despite the conservative outfit she wore and the scarf.

She decided if he made any comment to her, she would, at some point, hurt him very, very badly.

He took his tea, muttering to himself. Undoubtedly about infidels, women and respect.

Another glance at the mosque.

And she felt the exhilaration of a mission nearly completed.

The mission that was Devras Sikari's life plan.

Devras had been one of the most brilliant revolutionaries of his time. While Chernayev and Zang and Archer and the Mujahedeen believed that their goals could be achieved by explosives and gunfire, Devras knew that was short-sighted, the approach of the simple-minded. Childish.

Why, look at Palestine and Israel, look at Sri Lanka and the Tamal Tigers, England and the IRA. Look at Africa.

Oh, there was nothing wrong with violence as a surgical tool; it was necessary to eliminate risks. But as a means to achieve a political end?

It was inefficient.

Devras understood that the best way to achieve his goal of Kashmiri independence involved a different, far more potent weapon than thermobaric explosives, snipers or suicide bombers.

That weapon?

Desire, want, craving.

At Cambridge and afterward, Devras Sikari—along with her father and their Indian classmate—had indeed managed to duplicate the copper bracelet technology that had been perfected by the Germans during World War II. She'd lied to Middleton and the others about that.

In fact, the three men went far beyond the original design and created an astonishingly simple and productive system for the creation of heavy water.

But, realizing its potential and how he might exploit it, Devras insisted on patenting only a portion of the technology, leaving out key parts of the science, without which it would be impossible to bring the system online.

In the briefcase she carried now were the encrypted diagrams, formulae and specifications of these core elements omitted from the patents.

This was Devras's plan: to trade the copper bracelet technology to the major OPEC countries in exchange for their agreement to force India, China and Pakistan into partitioning Kashmir and ultimately granting independence. If the three "occupying" nations didn't do this, the petroleum producers would start to turn off the spigots of oil, and the factories and utilities and the oh-so-important cheap cars filling the subcontinent would die of thirst.

The Middle Eastern countries craved nukes; China and the Indian subcontinent craved oil.

She would spend the next few hours here meeting one at a time with representatives from these countries, men who were presently praying in the mosque. Their souls longed for spiritual ecstasy, their hearts for fissionable material.

Allah was presumably satisfying the first and Jana would fulfill the second.

She hefted the briefcase onto the table. Inside were six 8-gig thumb drives with the encrypted technology on them. She knew the men would be delighted with what she brought to the table. And what was particularly attractive was that the technology was compact and efficient and the facilities would be largely off the grid, hard to detect by even the sharpest eyes in the sky.

Glancing at her watch. The first of the representatives—from Syria—would be here in three minutes.

What an ecstatic moment this was!

If only Devras were here to experience this with her . . .

She sipped her latte and glanced again at the turbaned fellow nearby, still muttering, his face dark.

The door to the coffee shop jingled open and an Arab in Western clothes entered. She recognized him as the Syrian assistant attaché for Economic Development and Infrastructure Support.

Read: spy.

She noted his shirt, flirtatiously open two buttons, his bare head, a beard vainly trimmed. Such a hypocrite, she thought. In their countries: no alcohol, no pork, no drugs, no women other than the wife or wives. Here, in London, anything went.

Still, she smiled his way: Jana Grover was as efficient a businesswoman as she was a killer.

He glanced at her and smiled an oily flirt her way. He started forward.

At last, Devras. Kashmir will be free . . .

Then the man froze, looking out the window. Police cars were screeching to a halt, men jumping out.

No! What was going on?

He turned to flee, but was stopped by a dapper man in a business suit coming through the door. He shoved the Syrian to the ground.

Jana understood that she'd been discovered, the whole plot had been found out!

She pushed back from the table and rose, going for the High Standard .22 under her blouse.

But a strong arm grabbed her wrist and bent it painfully behind her. The gun fell to the floor.

She glanced back. It was the turbaned Arab, who had shoved a pistol into her neck. She struggled furiously.

"Bloody hell, luv. Special Branch. Give it a rest, why don't we?"

Sounding just like Ali G.

"She's all yours," Harold Middleton said to Ian Barrett-Bone, whose slacks had been badly smudged in the take-down of the Syrian. He brushed with some irritation at a stain.

They were on the sidewalk in front of the Café Nero. Jana Grover was being taken into custody for the drive to New Scotland Yard, where the Metropolitan police's Anti-Terror Unit, one of the best in the world, would interrogate her.

Middleton was the only Volunteer present at the moment, though Wiki Chang was in MI5's tech lab on Euston Road, preparing to crack the encryption on the thumb drives.

Which, according to the documents found in Jana's briefcase, included details on the copper bracelet technology—the secret elements that would make the system operative.

"You were spot on, Harry. Have to ask, how'd you figure it out?"

Middleton considered his answer. "You could say, by looking at what wasn't in front of us."

"How's that?"

"Questions. I kept coming back to unanswered questions. First of all, the email."

"Which one's that?"

"From Sikari to Balan. We found it on Balan's computer, which Sikari and Jana were pretty damn eager to destroy." He quoted it for Barrett-Bone. "It said, 'You recall what I have planned for the "Village." It has to happen soon—before we can move on. We only have a few weeks at the most.'"

"Ah, before we can move on."

"Exactly. That told me he had something planned *after* the incident at the dam."

"But how did you connect it here?"

"That was another nagging question: we had a lead to the mosque in the very beginning, but it didn't pan out. We knew it wasn't a misdirection because that was on the computer too, the one they blew up. But we couldn't find any connection when we investigated the first time. That told me it might have something to do with what Sikari had planned *after* the dam."

"And why did you think it had to do with the heavy-water system?"

"That was speculation, I admit. But I got the idea because of my kind host a few days ago: Mr. No Name—from the Group."

"Oh, those mad Nazi bastards?"

"Right. They were so adamant about finding the technology that it suggested they knew Sikari had gotten further along in developing a heavy-water system than it seemed. They'd seen the patents and known his copper bracelet wouldn't work. Then why were they so eager to kidnap me and track down the Scorpion? They suspected that Sikari had withheld some of his research."

Middleton had then contacted Barrett-Bone, who arranged for increased surveillance around the mosque, easy enough in a city that boasts one CCTV camera for every three residents.

Metropolitan police's keen-eyed team immediately recognized several cultural or economic affairs representatives from major OPEC nations arriving for prayers. There was no reason for them to be in London, let alone in this neighborhood, unless some operation was going down.

Middleton had a feeling Jana Grover would make an appearance. And, today, finally she had. Circling the mosque and then ducking into Café Nero. A Special Branch agent of Pakistani descent slipped inside for a cuppa, to verify it was she and cover her.

When the operative from the Syrian consulate stepped inside, the trap closed.

Suddenly a woman's voice raged, "You'll never beat us!"

Jana Grover was staring at him as she was being slipped into a squad car. "You'll never win!"

Seems like we just did, Middleton thought, but didn't reply.

Barrett-Bone asked, "You'll want to interrogate her, I assume. I can arrange it."

The American glanced at his watch. Barrett-Bone, the spy with Patek Philippe taste, couldn't help a faint frown of pity as he noticed the Timex.

Middleton laughed at his reaction. "Later. I have plans at the moment." Then he frowned. "But maybe there is something you can do for me, Ian."

"Whatever it might be, my friend, name it."

The houselights dimmed.

The concert hall audience slowly fell silent.

But the curtain didn't rise. And a moment later the lights rose and a voice came over the P.A. system. "Ladies and gentlemen, if I may have your attention please. The management regrets to inform you that there will be a short delay. The concert will begin in fifteen minutes."

Felicia Kaminski, standing in the wings, sighed. She hadn't fully recovered from the kidnapping, the injuries, the psychological horror. Nor from the loss of her beloved Bela Szepessy violin (she now clutched a functional but uninspiring instrument borrowed from a musician with the London Symphony).

Besides she was lonely. She hadn't seen Harold Middleton since he'd returned to London to arrest the woman who'd kidnapped Felicia. She hadn't seen Nora Tesla or Charley either.

Felicia knew she needed one hundred fifty percent concentration to give a concert of this sort. Yet, under these circumstances, she wasn't anywhere close. And now this nonsense with the delayed start, made matters worse.

The concert, she knew, would be a disaster.

What was the delay? she wondered, despairing.

The answer came in the form of a low American voice behind her.

"Hello."

Felicia turned. She gasped to see Harold Middleton. She set her instrument down and ran to hug him.

"I heard you were all right. But I was so worried."

Eyes tearing, she regarded cuts and bruises.

"I'm fine," he said, laughing. He looked her over too. "You seem all right."

She shrugged.

"You know," Middleton continued, "we have one thing more in common now."

"What is that, Harold?"

"We've both been kidnapped. And escaped."

Then she stepped away and dried her eyes. "You are, I suppose, responsible for the delayed start?"

He smiled. "You deduced that."

She nodded.

"Well, there is a security problem."

"No! What?" She looked out into the crowded hall.

"Not to them," he said. "A risk to your heart."

"What do you mean?"

"You lost your Bela Szepessy at my flat. I'm responsible."

"Harold, please . . . "

"You could play on a child's toy and make angels weep. But I thought you should have an instrument worthy of your talent. I've borrowed one for you to use until your Bela is repaired. I asked the management for a delay to let you get used to it."

He handed her a package. She opened it up. And gasped.

"It's not . . . oh, my God!" She was holding a violin made by Giuseppe Guarneri del Gesu—the same instrument she'd been listening to in Harold's flat, when she was kidnapped. Only three hundred or so still exist throughout the world, half the number of those made by the famed Stradivarius. You couldn't find a Guarneri for under a million dollars.

Playing an instrument like this just once—a dream of all violinists.

"How, Harold? They're impossible even to find."

"I made a new friend in the course of the case. A civil servant, believe it or not, but he leads a rather posh life, to use one of his words. He made a few phone calls . . . My only request is that you don't brain any kidnappers with it."

"What is 'brain'? Oh, you mean, hit anyone with it?"

"Yes."

"I'll only use cricket bats for that from now on, Harold."

"So, go tune up or do whatever you have to do. The audience is getting restless."

Felicia held the fragrant wood in her hands, light as a bird. "Oh, Harold." She took the bow from the case and tightened the horsehair strands and plucked the keys, which she found perfectly tuned and at concert pitch.

She turned to thank him again.

But he was gone.

After ten minutes of practice, she was aware of the houselights dimming again. The orchestra walked on stage and then the conductor. Finally Felicia, the soloist, entered to even louder applause.

She bowed to the audience and then to the conductor and the other players and took her place stage left.

The conductor tapped his baton, leaned forward and the concerto began. As she counted the measures, waiting for her cue, Felicia surveyed the hall.

Finally she saw them, two dozen rows back. Charley, Harold, and Nora Tesla, whose hand he was holding. She gave Harold a slight smile and, despite the spotlight in her eyes, she believed he smiled back.

Then the orchestra's part grew softer, signaling the approach of hers. She lifted the priceless instrument to her chin.

At a glance from the conductor, Felicia closed her eyes and began to play, abandoning herself completely to the music, which flowed over the audience like a gentle tide.